Three-times Goldckett
learned to pack h———————————————ed
to read. Born to a————————————e
United States, Pue———————————
addition to travelli———————————ug,
Alex, spend time w————————————on
her horse. Learn m———————— Tina from her website, or
'friend' her on Facebook.

Julie Danvers grew up in a rural community surrounded
by farmland. Although her town was small, it offered
plenty of scope for imagination, as well as an excellent
library. Books allowed Julie to have many adventures
from her own home, and her love affair with reading
has never ended. She loves to write about heroes and
heroines who are adventurous, passionate about a cause,
and looking for the best in themselves and others. Julie's
website is juliedanvers.wordpress.com.

Also by Tina Beckett

A Christmas Kiss with Her Ex-Army Doc
Miracle Baby for the Midwife

A Summer in São Paulo collection

Awakened by Her Brooding Brazilian by Ann McIntosh
Falling for the Single Dad Surgeon by Charlotte Hawkes
One Hot Night with Dr Cardoza

From Hawaii to Forever
is **Julie Danvers**'s debut title

Look out for more books from Julie Danvers
Coming soon

Discover more at millsandboon.co.uk.

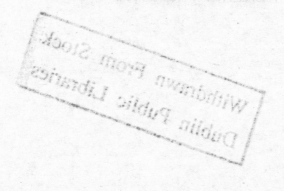

ONE HOT NIGHT WITH DR CARDOZA

TINA BECKETT

FROM HAWAII TO FOREVER

JULIE DANVERS

MILLS & BOON

First Published in Great Britain 2020
by Mills & Boon, an imprint of HarperCollins*Publishers*
1 London Bridge Street, London, SE1 9GF

One Hot Night with Dr Cardoza © 2020 by Tina Beckett

From Hawaii to Forever © 2020 by Alexis Silas

ISBN: 978-0-263-27972-6

MIX
Paper from
responsible sources
FSC® C007454

Printed and bound in Spain
by CPI, Barcelona

ONE HOT NIGHT
WITH DR CARDOZA

TINA BECKETT

MILLS & BOON

CHAPTER ONE

AMY WOODELL ADJUSTED the single strap of her teal gown one last time as she entered the swanky hotel. She'd ripped out the stitches and resewn it in an attempt to pull up the hemline just a bit. But it hadn't quite solved the problem.

In her rush to pack for her trip to Brazil, she'd brought the wrong shoes. The heels on her silver sling-backs were about an inch shorter than the black stilettos she normally would have worn. But she'd been a last-minute addition to the people who'd be attending the summer lecture program at the fabulous Hospital Universitário Paulista. And between a rushed itinerary followed by flight delays, there'd been no time to go shopping. She'd added a silver-linked belt to her waistline as an additional way to keep her dress from dragging the floor.

Glancing through the palm trees and lush tropical decor, she spotted a familiar face in the crowd. Krysta, wasn't that her name? The customs and immigration line had been long, but fortunately she'd met Krysta, who was also part of the group of visiting doctors—a specialist in otolaryngology and facial reconstruction.

They'd hit it off almost immediately, the other woman's friendly nature helping put her nerves at ease.

Amy's mom's sudden death six months ago had put her life into a tailspin, making her realize how little firsthand knowledge she'd had about her mother's heritage. Being in Brazil—her mom's home country—made her feel connected to her in a way that defied logic. And she had an uncle she'd never even met, who supposedly lived on the outskirts of São Paulo, according to an address in her mom's things.

Well, she was going to make the most of these three months! And if she could adopt a little bit of her mother's philosophy of living in the moment, even better.

Heading toward Krysta and hoping against hope that the other woman remembered her from the immigration line, she surveyed the room. Round tables were topped with silk damask tablecloths and huge flower-strewn topiaries. The colors and lush tropical theme were like something out of a pricey travel magazine. It was gorgeous.

So were the people.

And Amy had never felt more out of place.

Her eyes met those of a man across the room, his lean physique and good looks making her steps falter for a minute. He stood straight and tall, his black hair melding with his equally black clothing; everything from his suit to his tie to the tips of his polished shoes were dark.

She shivered. He could have been the angel of death or a grim reaper—albeit a gorgeous one—here to mete out swift justice. All he lacked was a scythe. He did have something in his hand, although she couldn't quite tell what it… When she realized she was rooted in place… and that she was staring—*staring!*—she forced her feet back into motion.

Oh, Lord.

Maybe he hadn't noticed. She chanced another quick peek and was thankful to see him talking to some cute blonde, his mouth curving to reveal a flash of white teeth. Her insides gave a deep shiver.

Probably his wife, Amy.

Who thankfully hadn't noticed a strange woman ogling her husband.

She made it to Krysta and forced a smile, although she was suddenly feeling even less sure of her place here. And her reaction to a complete stranger? Ridiculous.

Although if she had been her vibrant, larger than life mother, she would have marched right over and introduced herself to him. Laughed at his jokes. Fluttered her lashes at him a time or two. Cecília Rodrigo Woodell had never met a stranger. Something that used to embarrass Amy. But not anymore.

"Wow, this is quite a welcoming party. I don't know if you remember me. Amy Woodell?"

Krysta nodded. "Of course I do. You're a physical therapist, right?" She got the attention of the woman next to her. "Amy, this is Flávia Maura. She actually works in the Atlantic Forest with venomous snakes and spiders. She's here to give a lecture."

"Nice to meet you. I hate to admit it, but snakes kind of terrify me." She held up her palm, where two small scars were still visible. "Pygmy rattlers are pretty common in Florida. So are pools. And the two of them seem to find each other. A lot."

Flávia shifted her attention from something in the crowd back to Amy and Krysta, smoothing her palms down the front of her dress as if suddenly ill at ease in it.

"Yes, I'm familiar with rattlesnakes. But I'll admit the only snakes that disgust me are the ones that strut around on two legs, brag about their *avô*'s contributions to this hospital and spend much of their time insulting others."

She sent a glare back into the crowd. "But that's neither here nor there. And hopefully neither of you will have to deal with that particular *cobra*." The bits and pieces of Portuguese mixed with her English made the statement sound slightly sinister.

The image of Tall, Dark and Reaperish popped up in her head. Was Flávia talking about him? She'd kind of been looking off in that general direction. If so, Amy should be doubly glad she wouldn't have to work with him. Or flutter her lashes at him.

Although that smile hadn't made him look like a snake. Or even a jerk. But then again, looks could be deceiving. As she'd found out from her job. And her last boyfriend, who'd appeared to be totally into her. Until he wasn't. She'd learned the hard way that "ghosting" was actually a real phenomenon.

From now on she was going to keep things between her and men light and simple. Maybe somewhere in the neighborhood of "fling" territory. And the Reaper? That glance he'd given her had been anything but light or simple.

Flávia smiled. "I see movement by the podium. I think they're getting ready to give the welcomes. *Até logo.*"

"Nice to meet you, Flávia." Amy smiled back before turning to Krysta. "See you soon, too, I hope," she said with a light touch of Krysta's arm. She then began to circle the tables, waiting for further instructions. She almost tripped over the hem of her dress before yanking it up again. Ugh!

The wait was longer than she expected it to be, but just as she was trying to decide whether or not to find Krysta again, someone at the front of the room tapped the microphone. "We want to take a moment to welcome our visiting doctors and lecturers. We're very excited about this year's summer lecture program."

She shifted her weight. She wasn't a doctor. Furthering her education had been on the back burner for a long time, but recently she'd started giving it serious thought and had included that fact on her application.

The speaker's English was excellent. Since there were people here from all over the world, it made sense that they'd address the group in that language. Despite having a mother who was Brazilian, Amy unfortunately hadn't taken advantage of practicing her Portuguese. So, she'd pretty much stuck to short simple phrasings since she'd arrived, although she could understand most of what was said.

"If you haven't already done so, please consult the seating chart at the entrance to find your place. Dinner will be served shortly, so if you could take your seats as soon as possible, that would be appreciated."

Amy took a deep breath and headed over to the seating chart just as someone else was getting there. Sensing someone to her left, she turned with a smile to introduce herself. It quickly faded. It was the Reaper. And up close, those flaws she expected to see were non-existent. Also nonexistent was the blonde he'd been with moments earlier. She forced herself to speak.

"Hello. I'm Amy Woodell."

"Ah, so you are our physical therapist? I have been wondering about you."

The way he said "our" in that gruff, accented English gave the words a sense of intimacy that made her swallow. It served to reinforce her weird initial reaction to him. She forced her lashes to stay put until her eyes burned with the effort.

Stupid, Amy. Probably married. Remember?

"Yes, I guess I am. And am I the only one?" She slid a thumb under her the strap of her dress, afraid it might slide down.

"You are indeed. I'm Roque Cardoza, the head of orthopedics. We'll be working together, it seems." He glanced at the seating chart. "And sitting together. Shall we go?"

Working? And sitting? Together? Oh, no!

She blinked a couple of times in rapid succession, her composure beginning to crumble as they made their way to the table. He had a cane in his left hand. Had he injured himself? Not that she was going to ask. "It's very nice to meet you. I'm anxious to get started."

Actually, she was anxious to be anywhere but here, suddenly.

"Yes. As am I."

She shivered. It had to be the language that gave everything that smooth seductive air. She could get addicted to listening to him. And the way his eyes remained fastened to her face the whole time he'd addressed her… But not in a creepy way. Not like how she'd sized him up earlier.

Her thumb dipped out from under her strap, almost wishing it *would* slip, just so they could be on equal footing as far as staring went. Her eyes dropped to his ring finger, but it was empty. Not even a hint that one had been recently removed, although that meant nothing. Lots of people chose not to wear their wedding bands. And it didn't look like staff members had brought their significant others to the soiree, since they didn't seem to be paired up that way.

Roque indicated her seat and waited for her to take it before sliding into his own, propping his cane against the table. He hadn't used the cane to walk and there was no orthopedic boot on his foot, and he'd certainly had no problem maneuvering into his chair. In fact, he was…

Nothing. He was nothing. And he definitely wasn't light. Or simple. Her two new requirements in a man.

Time to squash those fling thoughts that kept circling her head like vultures looking for any sign of weakness.

She turned her attention to the person in the seat to her right. The woman was another visiting doctor from London who specialized in sports medicine.

"The doctor you were speaking with also specializes in sports medicine, I hear, so it'll be interesting to hear things from his perspective."

Was he listening?

"Some of my early physical therapy work was at a center specializing in sports injuries. Those are hard, since most athletes need the affected area of the body in order to perform adequately. Sometimes they never completely recover."

"Yes. Sometimes that is the case. No matter how much physical therapy they may receive." The comment came from Roque. So he *was* listening. And his words had a strange, almost angry quality to them.

Anything she might have said in response was halted as dinner plates were brought around to the tables.

She knew this dish. "This looks like shrimp in coconut milk, like my mom used to make."

"Your mother is Brazilian?"

Amy glanced at him. "Yes. I think she called this *camarão no leite de coco*."

"Very good. So you speak Portuguese as well?"

"I understand a lot. But I'm sorry to say I only have survival-skill fluency as far as speaking goes. My tongue gets tripped up."

His fingers came to rest on the table. "If you understand the mechanics, then it's only a matter of practice for the tongue. Soon it remembers exactly how to move."

She gulped as those vultures continued to circle. Everything he said carried a double-edged whammy that made her senses reel. She'd gotten all kinds of sly innuendos while working on male patients over the years. Both married and unmarried. But she wasn't getting those vibes from Roque. At all. He wasn't doing it on purpose.

And yet she found her body reacting to them—to *him!*—and that horrified her.

"I don't think I'll be here long enough to get in that kind of practice." She decided to rope those vultures and jerk them out of the sky. He was one of the first men she'd actually sat down to talk to in Brazil, so it made sense that she might notice him more than she normally would.

After her mom died, she'd realized how much life the woman had exuded. How many chances she'd taken in the living of it, and how little of herself she'd held back. When Amy was a kid, she'd struggled with having a mother who was so open, so friendly. But only now was she wishing she had a little more of her mom's joie de vivre. Fully embracing any and all opportunities. Including in the area of love.

And Roque?

Not one of those opportunities. Especially if he was involved with someone.

And if he wasn't?

She was only here for three months. If she met someone else, someone other than a man she'd be working with, why not have a little fun? And this time, she'd have no expectations. Unlike her last relationship.

Her mom had met Amy's father while he was in Brazil on business. They'd fallen in love instantly. Before they knew it, they were married, and Amy's mom had uprooted herself from everything she'd known to be with the man she loved. He'd died five years later, and her mom had stayed in Florida to be close to his grave. And now she was buried next to him.

Not something Amy could imagine herself doing. Florida was one of the last links she had with her parents. She actually worked at the hospital she'd been born in.

"If the hospital administration finds out that you

understand the language, I can guarantee they will use that to their advantage."

"And if they don't know?"

"Vão descobrir, com certeza."

She took a bite of shrimp, the rich luscious flavors rolling around in her mouth. Swallowing, she said, "They won't find out. Not unless you tell them." Too late she realized that he'd spoken to her in Portuguese.

"I think I will not have to tell them… Amy." Her name came out sounding like "Ahh-Mee," all musical and so horrifyingly attractive.

She licked her lips, trying to maintain her grip on what little composure she had left.

He was right. There was no way she could keep her knowledge of the language a secret. But the truth was, she was embarrassed to speak. She hated making mistakes of any kind. And yet Roque's English wasn't perfect, and he was still willing to try in order to be understood. And at a hospital like Paulista he was probably called on to speak English fairly often. "You're right. I'll give myself away, won't I?"

"Yes. Most assuredly."

She smiled at him, feeling silly all of a sudden. What would her mom have done in this situation? She would have tackled that language barrier and conquered it, just like she'd done when she'd married her father. While her mom had always maintained her accent, she'd spoken English very well. "Well, I won't try to hide it, then."

One side of his mouth kicked up. Not quite as big as the smile he'd lavished on the blonde, but it transformed the rugged lines of his face in ways that made warmth pool in her stomach.

She took a deep breath and dug into her food, hoping to take her attention off the man beside her. Just in time, too. Because the next speaker was at the podium giving instructions on how the scheduling would work. She forced herself to listen, since she didn't want to be lost tomorrow, when things got under way. It seemed those who were not giving lectures would shadow a staff member for the first half of their stay in order to learn the ropes. Then they would be given more latitude and allowed to have input in patient care.

That was exciting. From the information she'd seen online, Paulista would rival any hospital she'd visited in the US.

"For those of you who have just arrived, there is an envelope on the table listing who you'll be paired with. There will be two or three visiting medical professionals shadowing the same staff member. Who knows, you might even be sitting at the same table with them."

There were a few chuckles at that comment, but Amy didn't share in the mirth. Her hands suddenly turned to ice, her fork stopping halfway to her mouth.

She spotted the envelope the woman had mentioned. Cream-colored and tipped with gold, it shouldn't look ominous, but it did. Knowing she couldn't simply drop the fork and dive for the list, she forced herself to pop the shrimp into her mouth and chew as the person to Roque's left drew the sheet from the envelope and glanced at it. The man then passed the paper to Roque, while Amy struggled to swallow her food.

The orthopedist didn't even glance at the names. Instead, a muscle in his jaw flickered and one brow edged up, and he handed the sheet to her, eyes meeting hers and lingering.

Oh, God! Why? Her and...the Reaper?

That's why he'd mentioned working together. She hadn't thought he'd meant so closely together. Amy forced herself to look at the paper in her hands...to find her name. But it was all a pretense. And there it was in black and white: Roque Cardoza, Amy Woodell and two other names.

She didn't know how she'd expected this thing to work but had assumed there'd be some kind of short orientation as a group before listening to the various lecturers and participating in treatment as opportunities arose. But to work closely with someone she was already uneasy with? For half of the three-month stint? That was a whole month and a half. Of watching every move the man made.

She passed the sheet to the woman next to her. Why couldn't she be with Flávia and Krysta?

Because they were both lecturing.

The woman she'd spoken to a few minutes earlier smiled. "It looks like I'm in your group, and I've met the other man on the list as well. He's on the far side of the table."

Okay, so at least that was something. "That's great." But there was no conviction in her voice.

The speaker addressed them again. "So once you've finished dinner, find your group and set a meeting time and place for tomorrow, if you would."

Roque leaned over. "Looks like you're stuck with me for a little longer. But don't worry. I won't tell anyone your little secret."

Little secret?

The words made her heart skip a beat. Then another. Had he guessed what he did to her? Her face became a scorching inferno. "I'm not sure what you mean."

"That you understand Portuguese." He frowned. "Is there some other secret I should know about?"

Her shoulders sagged and her strap actually started to slide down her shoulder. She shrugged it back into place.

"No. No other secrets." *Liar.* "And since we both agreed it would be impossible to keep my Portuguese under wraps, I guess it doesn't matter."

Somehow she got through the rest of the meal, which was followed by a luscious crème brûlée for dessert. Then people were getting to their feet, and groups formed all over the room, the sounds of excitement building in the air.

Except the air where she was sitting.

"So here we are." Roque stood, not reaching for his cane.

She scrambled to her feet as well. "Yes, we are."

It's only six weeks, Amy. You can do this.

The sports medicine doctor introduced herself to the group as Lara Smith. And a man with light brown hair came over and shook Roque's hand and then hers. "I am Dr. Peter Gunderfeld. You must be Dr. Cardoza and Dr. Woodell?"

Everyone in her group was a doctor. Except for her.

"Just Amy, for me." Her uneasiness about her decision to come to Brazil grew. These people were all brilliantly talented in their respective fields, from what she was discovering. Maybe she should have just planned a vacation to the country and skipped the summer lecture program.

"You can call me Peter, then."

"And Lara is fine with me."

"I am Roque."

The pronouncement landed like a hammer, although she was sure he hadn't meant it to.

They went through a few moments of exchanging social pleasantries about where they were from. She already knew Lara was from England. And Peter was from Munich, Germany.

Roque was from Rio de Janeiro, originally. She had noticed a difference in his speech patterns as opposed to her mom's, who was from São Paulo. Many of his s's had the "sh" sound characteristic of the famous city.

"Did you know that the name Florida comes from the Portuguese word meaning 'flowered'?" Roque's mouth curved slightly. She forced her gaze not to dwell.

"I did." This would be a perfect time to ask what his name meant, but that might be a little too personal.

Peter had no problems sharing personal information, however. He was married with a two-year-old daughter.

"It had to have been hard to leave them at home," Lara said.

"Yes. But they're going to meet me here the last week of our stay, and then we'll vacation in Iguaçu Falls."

"Good choice. Foz do Iguaçu is worth the visit." Roque glanced at Amy. "I hope you and Lara added extra time on to your trip as well."

She hadn't really thought about that. She already had her return ticket, in fact. Maybe she should check to see how hard it would be to switch the dates.

"I've been to Brazil several times actually. And no husband or kids to bring," Lara said, smiling at Peter. "So I'm just here for the conference."

Roque hadn't commented on his relationship status, and Amy wasn't about to ask nor share hers. Not only was it not any of her business, she didn't want him thinking that she was interested in him like that.

She wasn't.

Those thoughts about flings and the flutters in her belly were strictly animal survival instincts. Nothing more. If she stuck to work topics, it should be easier to view him as a colleague and not as a person whose speech patterns did crazy things to her libido.

Maybe she did need to hook up with a good-looking man and knock some of this stuff out of her system. It had been ages since she'd had sex.

She wasn't going to number Roque in with the possible candidates for that, though. Her gaze scouted the room, and while she saw several other attractive men, there was no pull toward them.

Well, all that meant was that she wasn't shallow, right?

Hmm...and yet she'd been glued to almost every word that came out of Roque's firm, sexy mouth.

She rolled her eyes.

The man picked that moment to glance at his watch. "I have an early day tomorrow. Do you all know your way to the condominium?"

"Yes. The Fonte Cristalina, right?" Amy had already dropped her luggage off at the apartment building the hospital had put them up in. It wasn't fancy, but it was clean and had a gorgeous view of the city.

"Yes." Roque looked from one to the other. "It's within walking distance of Paulista. But it's better to do that during the day. So, let's meet in the hospital lobby at eight in the morning?" There was a slight furrow between his brows now, though.

"Very good. I must go call my wife," Peter said. "See you tomorrow."

"And I'm meeting a friend for a nightcap," Lara added a second later.

Amy said her goodbyes. Was she the only one feeling lost at sea?

Maybe Roque sensed some of her thoughts because he stayed where he was. "Would you like me to drop you off at the apartment complex?"

"Oh, no, it's okay. I can catch a cab. There are some out front, I'm sure."

"Very likely." He moved sideways to let someone through, which put him way too close to her for comfort.

Amy took a quick step back, and a sharp tug at her shoulder was followed by a distinct ripping sound. Then things began a slow slide. Straight down. Including her mind.

Oh! Oh, no!

She grabbed at the bodice of her dress just as the shoulder strap flopped uselessly over the top of her hand.

Roque turned...stared at her shoulder, before glancing down at where his foot was planted on her hem. His face turned a dull red.

"*Merde!* I am sorry, Amy. I did not realize."

Her name came rough-edged off his tongue, and she

shut her eyes as hot embarrassment rained down on her. She knew she hadn't stitched the strap enough, but hadn't given much thought to it. A huge mistake.

Just like this whole damned trip.

"It's okay, but I'd better find that cab now."

"I will take you home. It's only right."

The thought of running out of the hotel holding up her dress was mortifying, so she decided to accept his offer. "Thank you. Could you stand in front of me for a second, though?"

His head tilted sideways, but he shifted until they were face-to-face, and much, much closer than they had been last time.

Hot flames licked at her innards, and she had a hard time catching her breath. "I—I kind of meant for you to turn the other way. I want to tuck my strap into my dress so it's not as obvious."

This time, his eyes did what she'd wanted them to do earlier. Trailed over her bare shoulder and lower before coming back up to meet her gaze. That muscle in his jaw twitched the way it had when he'd handed her the list of names, but he said, "Of course," before turning away from her, shielding her from prying eyes.

She quickly shoved the strap into the front of her dress, hoping it didn't cause any awkward bulges, then she clamped her right arm across her chest and picked up her clutch purse. Where were those few lost pounds when you needed them?

"Okay, you can turn around now."

He did, his glance going back to her shoulders, now bereft of any fabric. "I will pay for the damage I caused."

No, he wouldn't. Because the real damage wasn't anything that could be seen with the naked eye.

"It's my fault. I tried to alter the length on my own, when I should have bought higher heels. I'm just glad it happened at the end of the evening rather than at the beginning."

"I know a very good seamstress. It would also be free."

Oh, God! Maybe he really was married. She could picture him trying to explain to some faceless wife how he'd practically stripped one of his charges naked in front of an entire room of doctors.

Well, not naked. But almost. She didn't have a bra on, since the dress had one built into it. "I'm sure that's not—"

"It is my mother. It would take her little time to make it right. She could even arrange for a fitting to adjust the length, if you would like. Her shop is at my parents' home."

Somehow the fact that his mom was the seamstress made her relax. "That would be an awkward conversation, wouldn't it?"

"No. She's come to expect me to be a little more... clumsy than I used to be."

Inadvertently, her glance shifted to the cane. "You're not clumsy. It was an accident."

He was the most elegant, graceful man she'd met in a long time, whatever the reasons for that cane.

"Yes, well, be that as it may, I do insist on making it right."

Amy had a feeling he wasn't going to let it go. "At

least ask your mom if she'd mind, first, before just assuming she'll say yes."

"I will. But I know she will not mind." He gave her that slow smile of his. The one that devastated her senses and made it hard to think beyond it. "Let me do this for you, Amy. This one small thing."

It wasn't a small thing. Not to her. But if she tried to keep arguing the point, he was eventually going to realize there was something more behind it. Something that made her wary of him—wary of working on his team for the next three months. Wary of shadowing him for half of those three months.

So all she could do was agree and say a fitting wasn't necessary, and hope that once the dress was returned, she could forget about this incident once and for all. Maybe then she could focus on her real reasons for coming to Brazil. Those had to do with her mom and finding her uncle. And her career, of course.

And none of those things included the man in front of her.

CHAPTER TWO

DAMN, WHAT HAD he done?

The very physical therapist he'd tried to veto having on his team seemed to be a nice person. But she carried an air of fragility that socked him in the gut and made him wish he'd stuck to his guns. But the physical therapy department was running short-staffed at the moment and couldn't spare anyone to participate in the summer lecture program.

And then he had to go and ruin her dress. And when he'd misunderstood and stood face-to-face with her, almost touching, and definitely close enough to…

Close enough to nothing!

This damned leg. Even as the thought went through his head, a phantom pain shot through his thigh. One that had nothing to do with his reaction to her. Or that dress.

He stepped on the gas as the drive to the apartment seemed to take forever, even though it was less than three blocks away. Part of it was due to navigating in heavy traffic. But also because his peripheral vision kept checking the top of her dress to make sure it hadn't crept any farther down. If that happened, he might have to do a major reboot of his sanity. Because as he'd gazed at her in that room full of people, he'd found himself wishing it would. Which was ridiculous. Not to mention unprofessional.

They finally arrived, and Roque pressed the code into the security box at the front of the building, waiting as the heavy garage door swung open to allow his Mercedes to slide past. It closed behind them with a sense of finality, trapping him in the space with her.

He forced himself to say something in hopes she wouldn't guess where his thoughts were straying. "The hospital bought several apartments in this condominium for visiting doctors or VIP patients coming in from other areas of the country. So everyone's staying at the same place."

"That makes sense." Her dress seemed to edge down a millimeter, and his mouth went completely dry.

He found a parking spot. "Would you like me to wait while you take off the dress?"

"Excuse me?"

A flare went off in his head, sending up an alarm that the rest of his body failed to heed. His thoughts about it sliding down were evidently starting to come out in his speech. "I did not mean in the car, of course. I meant in your apartment. You could bring the dress back down to me, unless you prefer to bring it to the hospital."

Yes, the sooner she was out of sight, the sooner he would be able to get that image out of his head. But he was pretty sure it would reappear—along with a few others—the second he went to sleep tonight.

"Oh, of course." She hesitated. "I'd rather not bring it to the hospital, if that's okay with you. Why don't you come up to the apartment and I can give it to you there? It's really not necessary to have your mom repair it, though."

"It is to me. And if you're okay with it, I'll come up. It will save you the trip back down."

Why the hell had he just offered to do that? Hadn't he just thought how glad he'd be to have her out of sight?

"Okay, great." Still keeping her arm across her dress, she turned sideways and tried to hit the button on her seat belt, struggling with getting her hand that far back.

Roque reached over to hit the release latch for her, his sleeve brushing her bare arm as he did and catching a light floral scent that seemed to cling to her skin. He swallowed. "Wait there."

Getting his cane from the back and climbing out of the car, he came around to her side, the tension in his jaw making itself known in his leg. He leaned a little of his weight on the cane's handle. No wonder he'd stepped on her dress. Maybe this was some elaborate joke perpetrated by karma after his response to his mom's nudging at dinner last night. She'd asked about him meeting someone special. He'd bluntly told her he wasn't interested in meeting anyone—special or not so special. Less than twenty-four hours later, he'd stepped on someone's dress and found his thoughts riveted to all kinds of "what if" scenarios.

Well, he needed to un-rivet them. *Now.*

He forced his steps to quicken, opening her door and pulling the webbing of the seat belt away from her, taking care not to touch her, this time. "Can you get out on your own?"

Deus do céu, he hoped she could.

She swung her legs out of the car and planted them on the ground, but his low-slung car wasn't helping her.

"Here. Give me your hand." He gritted his teeth and forced himself to add the obvious, "The left one."

You're a funny, funny guy, Roque. As if she's going to give you the other one.

She let him pull her up from her seat, her grip on his firm and warm and lingering maybe a second longer than necessary. Then stood in front of him, her head tilted to look at him, the overhead lights shining on cheeks that were slightly pink and far too appealing. "Thanks, I appreciate it."

"The least I can do." And it was. Especially since his thoughts were now having to run some pretty impressive evasive maneuvers, like a footballer trying to stay just out of reach of his opponent. Which in this case happened to be common sense.

She followed him to the elevator. His steps still felt a little off, but he draped his cane over his arm. And he wasn't quite sure why. He wasn't ashamed of that hitch in his stride. Was he?

And when he'd stepped on her dress. Was he being prideful by not using it? And if he had used it, could he have avoided this whole damn mess?

"Did you hurt your foot?"

Her question came out of nowhere, seeming to echo his earlier musings as the elevator doors opened. "What floor are you on?" He stalled for a few seconds, trying to collect his thoughts.

"Four." She licked her lips. "I'm sorry. I shouldn't have asked that."

"No, it's okay." He pushed the button for her floor,

and leaned against the wall to look at her. Her arm was pressed against the neckline of her dress, and he noticed two tiny scars on her hand. Very lickable scars.

Hell, where had that come from?

He forced his attention back to her question. "My injury... It seems I am not only good at tripping over dresses, but my own two feet. It's an old sports' injury."

"Which sport?" Her gaze flicked over his chest, down his abdomen...

He cleared a throat that was suddenly dry. *"Futebol."*

Her eyes were now on his thighs and it was as if she could see right through his clothes. And pretty soon, she was going to see something that was visible despite his clothing.

"Have you had physical therapy?"

The shock of her question hit him like a bucket of ice water, scalding him in a way that heat couldn't touch. If she only knew. Yes, he'd had therapy. And more therapy. All it had done was pile more grief onto an already existing wound. It seemed every female he met thought they could magically fix him and put him back to rights.

His jaw tightened until twin points of pain appeared. "Are you offering me your professional services, Amy?" He made it as clear as he could that she was overstepping her boundaries.

"No. I'm sorry. You're an orthopedist. Of course you have."

"It happened a lifetime ago. And it's permanent. What you see is what you, and everyone else, gets. All the physical therapy in the world won't change it."

Diabos. Why had he gone on the attack? She was trying to help. She wasn't like his ex-therapist or any of those women he'd gone out with who'd shown a morbid interest in his damaged leg.

He moved a step closer, so he could touch her hand. "I'm sorry. That came out badly."

They arrived on the fourth floor before he could explain further. She got out in a hurry and stuck her key into the lock of the nearest door, only to jiggle it. She took it out and tried again. "That's weird. It worked earlier. I'm not sure why it's not this—"

The door opened, and the doctor from the gala appeared.

Amy recoiled a step. "I'm so sorry. I must have the wrong..." She glanced at the key. "Heavens, I do. The key says 402. I've only been up here once."

Lara had a glass of wine in her hand, and when her eyes met his, they widened.

Perfect. She was probably wondering what he was doing coming up to Amy's apartment straight from the party.

As was he.

Should he tell her why? That he'd almost ripped Amy's dress off her at the party and had now come here so she could remove it the rest of the way? That sounded pretty damning actually.

"There were no cabs left." The lie flew off Amy's tongue with incredible speed. Evidently she wasn't any more anxious to give the real reason for his visit than he was. But anyone who'd thought about it long enough would realize, there'd been a whole fleet of taxis parked outside the venue. Even if there were no cabs, it didn't explain why he'd come up in the elevator with her. Or why the strap to her dress had suddenly disappeared. Maybe Lara hadn't noticed how she was dressed.

Amy's chest rose as she took a deep breath. "And actually, my dress strap ripped, and Roque's mother is a professional seamstress, so he offered to have her sew it back together for me."

He blinked. She'd backtracked. Why?

"Oh, that was nice of you," Lara murmured.

"Anyway, sorry for disturbing you. See you in the morning."

The other woman smiled at them and said good night, closing the door and leaving them alone in the corridor.

Roque couldn't contain a grin. "I've never known anyone who can make even the truth sound like a lie."

But when she swung around to look at him, her face was white as a ghost.

She whispered, "You don't care that she might think we've come up here to…?"

He wasn't about to admit that he'd entertained a thought or two himself.

"No. I really don't. I don't worry about what people think of me."

At least he hadn't until a minute ago when he saw the look on her face.

"My mom was like that. It must be pretty freeing."

"Freeing? I don't understand."

"Never mind." Amy moved to the next door down, double-checking the number, and inserted her key into the lock. This time it turned smoothly, opening to a white-tiled corridor and living room just beyond it. She entered, motioning him in behind her.

Roque followed her into the space, glancing around.

"Make yourself at home. I'll just go and change. There's not much in the refrigerator, since I haven't made it to the grocery yet."

"It's okay. I don't need anything."

Her suitcases were in the living room and one of them was open wide, a pair of—*diabos!*—lacy pink briefs hanging over the side of it. His gut immediately tightened and all the thoughts he'd banished came rushing back, followed by a few thousand more.

She hurried over and kicked the offending garment into the case and quickly folded it closed.

What she couldn't close was the part of his brain that had imprinted itself with that image, making him wonder what other forbidden wonders she had hidden in her luggage.

Which was none of his business.

Setting her bags upright, she wheeled one of them toward a room to her left. "I won't be a minute." With that, she shut the door with a thump.

Her panties!

She leaned against the back of the door, shutting her eyes in horror.

Oh, God, they'd been lying there right in front of him! Not minutes after being seen—and recognized— by her neighbor, someone she would have to work with day in and day out. At least for the first month and a half.

But her underwear! Why had she left that case open?

Well, she hadn't expected to have a man in her apartment on her first night.

Or the second or third nights. And now that she knew who was living next door, probably no other night, either. Any hookups would now have to happen "off campus," so to speak.

Roque might not care what people thought, but she did. Far too much. And she certainly didn't want him to hear secondhand that she was entertaining men in one of the hospital's apartments.

Entertaining men? What was this? The 1920s?

Opening her eyes, she went over to the bed and hefted her suitcase onto it, one-handed. This was ridiculous. He couldn't see her now. She let go of her dress, and sure enough, the top of her bodice slid past her waist. Quickly finding a pair of yoga pants and a loose-fitting T-shirt, she opened the side zipper on her dress and let it slither the rest of the way down.

There, are you happy now?

She glared at the garment at her feet, stepping out of it and tossing it onto the bed with a little more force than was necessary.

She then dug through her bag, aware of a little time clock ticking in her head as she tried to find her bra. She blinked. She'd worn one on the flight over, so it had to be here somewhere. Or another one. That maybe she'd packed in the other suitcase that was still in the living room. Or not?

Ack. She'd left the bra she'd traveled in in the bathroom when she'd changed for the party, since she hadn't needed it for the dress. She was not leaving this room to go grab it and waltz her way back to the bedroom with it dangling from her fingertips. That would be almost worse than him seeing her underwear. Although maybe he hadn't noticed.

Oh, he'd noticed, all right. His eyes had been right on them.

So what to do? She'd always been small up top, wishing as a teenager that she had more oomph in that department. But right now, she was glad she didn't. She pulled the T-shirt over her head. It was black and loose. Peering into the bedroom mirror, she decided you couldn't really tell as long as you weren't staring at her chest.

So hauling her yoga pants up over her hips and sliding her feet into a pair of flip-flops, she took the decorative comb out of her hair, tired of it digging into her scalp.

"I don't worry about what people think of me." Wasn't that what he'd said?

Well, maybe she could practice a little of what he— and her mom—preached. She shook her hair out, trying not to care that it was curling in all kinds of crazy directions. She then folded her dress in as small a ball as possible and shoved it into one of the plastic grocery bags she'd included in case she had any wet clothes to pack on the return flight.

There. She was ready.

Sucking down a quick breath, she opened the door and sauntered into the living room as if she hadn't a care in the world. As soon as she saw him, she wished she hadn't agreed to let him take the dress. He was lounging on her sofa, both arms stretched out over the top of it, looking as fresh in his dark suit as the moment she'd laid eyes on him. And she was...

Not caring what people thought, that's what she was.

His glance trailed over her hair, before arriving at the plastic bag in her hand. "Is that it?"

"Yes." She handed it to him. "Thanks again."

"For ripping your dress?"

Maybe. Could it be that this little mishap had provided a way to break the ice? To give her that little flaw in his perfection that she'd been searching for?

"You make a pretty intimidating figure—did you know that?"

His head cocked. "No. I didn't."

"I think even Peter and Lara felt it." Although he wasn't intimidating in a bad sort of way, like whoever Flávia had been referring to.

"Then I'll have to work on that."

He uncurled himself from the sofa and stood over her, and there it was again. That shiver of awareness. And whether it was because of the T-shirt fabric brushing over her bare skin or her reaction to him, her nipples tightened as a swirl of sensation spiraled down her belly to points below. She had to fight the urge to hook her arm back over her chest like she'd done while holding up her dress.

"You don't have to work on anything. I'm sure it's just part of being in a different country." Why on earth had she said anything to him? "Pretty much everything is intimidating to me right now."

"Don't be intimidated, Amy. You'll find Brazilians are quite *amigáveis*."

"I know they're friendly. I didn't really mean that."

"What did you mean, then?"

"I'm not sure. I just feel a little bit out of place. Everyone I've met has been either a doctor or an expert in their field."

"You are an expert in your field, or you wouldn't be here."

She hadn't thought of it like that. She'd heard the vetting process was tough and was actually surprised that she'd gotten in, even if it had been because someone else had dropped out. "Well, thank you. But not really."

"Don't sell yourself short. The team decided you were right for this position."

Something caught her attention. "The team. But not you?"

"The heads of the departments are given a list of applicants that are *préselecionados*… I think you say it as 'short-listed,' yes? And then the selections are made. You were on that list."

He was evading the question about whether or not he had wanted her. Or was he?

"But I only got on afterward, when there was a cancellation."

"There was no cancellation. The powers that be were merely trying to find where best to place you. The physical therapy department couldn't spare anyone to oversee your month-and-a-half shadow period. So you are now with me. I almost said no. Until I read one of your case files. It made me change my mind."

He almost refused to work with her? And if he had, she'd still be sitting in the States.

She did not want him to see how much that stung.

He changed his mind, Amy. That counts for something.

"Which case file?"

"The spina bifida patient who went on to practice martial arts."

Bobby Sellers. She almost hadn't included him, because he hadn't been the stellar success story she felt the hospital was looking for. But he'd touched her life. And when he told her he'd always wanted to break a board in tae kwon do, something her mom had insisted on her participating in, it had struck a chord. And she'd helped him work toward that, even going as far as attending the event where Bobby had indeed broken his board. It had brought her to tears.

"But why that case?"

"It showed that you are able to think outside the box—that you don't keep pushing where it will do no good. You tweaked the prescribing doctor's treatment plan slightly to include your patient's own personal life goals. That is exactly what I want to see at Paulista. Things don't always follow a prescribed path. As the saying goes, medicine is sometimes more art than science."

"I believe that as well. We have to look at patients as a whole, not as a conglomeration of symptoms. We have to help them adapt and change when the body won't cooperate."

He smiled and stood, leaning on his cane a little more than he had been. "And *that* is why I said yes. I should go. *I* might not care about what people think, but I have a feeling you do. And since Dr. Smith knows I'm here in your apartment…"

Yes, it was time for Roque to go. But not because of Lara Smith. Or the fact that the pink scrap of lace peek-

ing out of her suitcase was going to haunt him for days
to come. He was pretty sure she wasn't wearing a bra
under that T-shirt. But none of that was what drove him
to say goodbye. It was because of the vulnerability he'd
seen in her when they were talking about how she'd gotten into the program.

He'd sensed a bit of imposter syndrome, and he probably had fueled that even more with his honesty. But
he hadn't wanted to work with someone like the physical therapist he'd been assigned after his surgery. He
didn't want a fix-it mentality. He wanted someone with
the ability to set realistic expectations for his or her patients. In the end, Roque would not have agreed, if the
candidate absolutely didn't meet that qualification. His
patients were too important to him.

But to have stepped on her dress.

Hell. He definitely did not have the coordination he'd
had back in his days with Chutegol, his football club.
But then again, his injury had resulted in muscle and
nerve damage, and although you wouldn't know it from
the single long scar on his outer thigh, the damage to
the underlying structures had ended his football career.
Fortunately, he'd earned enough from his five years of
playing to put himself through medical school.

"Well, thank you for coming."

Amy's voice cut through the fog of his thoughts, and
he swung his gaze to her, avoiding looking at her chest.

"I will let you know when it is done." He held up the
bag containing the real reason he was here. His mother
would be happy to repair it for her. But not without a
question or two, or a mention of their earlier conversation, which made him wonder if he'd been right to offer

her services. After having women throw themselves at him during his football days, and the messy breakup of his engagement, and then the pass his physical therapist had made during treatment, he was leery of believing someone could be interested in *him*...as someone who came from simple roots, who'd worked hard for everything he had. So his relationships were short and sweet, and very, very superficial. No one who would try to "fix" whatever they thought was wrong with him.

So yes, his mother would ask some pointed questions.

But Roque took care of the mistakes that he could. And the ones he couldn't? Well, he walked away from them.

Amy wrapped her arms around her midsection. "The dress was my fault, so don't worry about it. Like I said, it's too long. I shouldn't have worn it."

The image of her with her forearm clamped across her chest to keep her bodice from falling down swam in front of his face. Were all her undergarments pink? And lacy?

Damn. Talk about mistakes. Maybe this was a bigger one than he realized.

"The dress was—*is*—quite lovely." His phone buzzed on his hip. Glancing at the readout, he frowned. Enzo Dos Santos? He hadn't heard from the owner of the football club in ages, other than a quick note saying he'd had a cancerous lesion removed from his jaw. Had things gone south? He let the call go to voice mail, making a note to call his friend back once he got back to the car. "I'll let you know when my mom has had a chance to look at it."

What he wouldn't tell her was the hoops he was sure to have to jump through before his mom actually got down to work.

"Well, thank you again."

"You're welcome. I'll see you in the morning." Roque had been dreading this three-month rotation, but there was now a weird sense of anticipation he hadn't felt in a while. One he didn't like and halfway suspected was due to the woman whose dress he'd stepped on. She was here for three months. Why risk letting things get messy, when they could stay in a neat and tidy box. And where he'd have no more mistakes to correct. So he said his goodbyes and walked out of her apartment, glancing at Lara's door and wondering if she was staring out her peephole with a stop watch. Ridiculous. Roque did not care what people thought.

Except for the owner of his former football team. When he got to his car, he tossed Amy's dress into the passenger seat and slid into the vehicle, taking out his phone and scrolling through his missed messages. Then putting all thoughts of his rotation charge out of his head, he dialed Enzo's number and waited for the man to pick up his phone.

CHAPTER THREE

HE'D GIVEN HER a choice. Take the morning off or scrub in on an emergency Achilles' tendon surgery.

It had been an easy choice. Scrub for surgery.

The surgical mask felt strange and confining, but it was also a different experience. She could now see why people said the eyes were the window to the soul.

Roque glanced at her, brows raised. "Are you sure you wish to be here?"

"Absolutely." She wondered why Lara and Peter were not in the room as well. Maybe because they both saw surgical procedures day in and day out, and a complete rupture of the tendon was probably no big deal for them. But it was to her. It would give her a glimpse into what went on before a patient arrived on her physical therapy table.

"Let me know if you have any questions, since I'll be speaking in Portuguese once we start. I'm going to do a percutaneous repair rather than opening his leg, to reduce the chance of infection."

"And if you need to graft part of the tendon?"

He looked surprised. "Good question. This case is fairly straightforward. If the ends of the tendon were say…shredded, I would then open the leg and fold down a portion of the *gastrocnêmio*… In English—?"

"Gastrocnemius?"

"Yes, that is it."

The corners of his eyes crinkled in a smile that made her swallow. Without being able to see his mouth or the rest of his face, and with his emotions being translated by his eyes, it forced her to watch carefully. That had to be why her own senses were taking in every millimeter of movement and multiplying how it affected her.

"We would use a portion of that tissue to reinforce the repair. To make it less likely to rupture a second time."

"But you don't need to this time?"

"No. This patient is still in school and young and healthy. He should be able to return to football, once he lets the injury heal completely." He glanced around the surgical room where the other personnel appeared to be waiting on a signal from him. "Let's get started. You can ask more questions as we go."

She answered with a quick nod.

His words hadn't been a dismissal. So why had it felt that way? Maybe because she knew he'd almost said no to her being in the program. And because she'd been way too caught up in their exchange of words and hadn't been quite ready to end it.

A natural reaction, Amy.

Of course she'd be interested in learning as much as she could. And she wanted to show Roque that she absolutely should be here, despite any reservations he might have had in the beginning.

The orthopedist walked over to the patient who was

already prepped for surgery and under general anesthesia. He motioned for her to join him by the table, while a nurse with a tray of surgical instruments stood on his other side. Amy watched as he made two tiny incisions on either side of the leg, using forceps to enlarge the holes slightly. He gave a running commentary in Portuguese, which she surprisingly understood, only missing a word or two here and there. "I'm going to place sutures under the skin in a figure-eight motion, catching the upper part of the tendon and using the suture material to draw it down to meet the other half."

He then ran the needle through the first of the incisions and out the second hole. When he ducked back in, he allowed the point of the needle to tell him where to make the next small cut, repeating the process down the leg until he reached the other end of the tendon. His long fingers were sure and precise, almost dancing over the surface of his patient's skin.

Not a good analogy, because her brain immediately opened up a side-by-side screen, putting her where Roque's patient was, with those fingers sliding up the back of one of her calves in a way that had nothing to do with surgery. She blinked away the image, trying to force her eyes to focus on what was happening in front of her.

"Almost done."

Amy glanced up at the clock, shocked to see that only about ten minutes had gone by. And the procedure was a lot more straightforward than she'd expected it to be. Somehow he found the tendon under the skin without any kind of imaging equipment, seeming to go by feel. But there'd been no hesitation. How many of these had he done over the course of his career? Enough to make it seem like a piece of cake.

Roque tugged on the two ends of suture line and she could almost see the ends of the tendon pulling together beneath the patient's skin, just like the ripped seams of her dress's strap would be pulled back together as his mom stitched it. An odd comparison, but it really was what had happened. Only this man's leg was alive, and a ripped tendon couldn't just be cast aside like a piece of clothing.

"These sutures are absorbable, whereas the ones I'll put on the outside will need to be removed." He tied off the inner stitches, and was handed another threaded needle, which he used to close each of the tiny holes he'd made in the skin. He glanced at her. "And that's it. Not very exciting."

Yes, it was. Too exciting actually. But not in the way he meant. Roque's eyes were brown, but without his dark clothing on, they had almost an amber hue that she hadn't caught last night. Or maybe because she'd been too busy taking in the man as a whole rather than being fixated on one small part of him.

No, not fixated. But when she scrambled around for another word, she suddenly couldn't find one.

That was a problem for later, because she couldn't exactly think straight right now.

"Thanks for letting me watch the procedure. I've done the physio for several Achilles' reattachment patients. It's a long slow process in the States."

He nodded, pulling his mask down and thanking his team, before responding. The curve of his mouth set off a line in his left cheek that had probably been a dimple when he was a child.

He wasn't a child anymore, though. He was all man.

"The process is long here as well. Andreu, our patient, won't be able to play for six months and will be in a boot for several weeks."

She sighed. "Six months can seem like forever to someone so young."

"Yes. It can seem like a lifetime. But at least *his* outcome should be a good one."

The cryptic words made her heart ache, because she knew who he was referring to.

As he moved toward the back of the room, his steps seemed a little slower, the hitch she'd noticed earlier was more pronounced. He'd left his cane outside, probably to avoid contaminating the room. It was on the tip of her tongue to offer to go ahead of him and retrieve it for him, but no one else in the room had volunteered. Maybe it was a touchy subject. And as a physical therapist, she knew that the more people could do for themselves, the better.

A thought struck her. "Was this your first surgery of the day?"

"No, my third."

"What?" She pulled off her own mask and gloves, discarding them in the trash can next to the door and glancing at the clock on the wall. "It's barely eight-thirty."

"There was an accident involving a *moto-taxi* in the early hours. The driver and his passenger both had multiple injuries."

His specialty was sports medicine, but obviously he handled regular ortho surgeries as well. "Are they okay?"

"The passenger will make it, but the driver…" He shook his head.

"Oh, no. My mom said that motorcyclists here have a dangerous life, but I'm sure that's true everywhere."

"It is very true here." He pushed through the door and took his cane, leaning on it for a minute. "Do you mind if we grab a coffee? Peter and Lara aren't due in until noon, and I have a long day ahead of me."

"You don't have to babysit me, if you need to go grab a catnap."

"Cat…nap?"

Oh! Of course he wouldn't know that phrase. "A light sleep? *Soneca?*"

"But why a cat?"

"I don't know. The cat we had when I was growing up slept a lot, and her sleep wasn't exactly light."

He smiled, and started walking, using his cane on every fourth step or so. "It's the same with mine."

He had a cat?

She blinked. Somehow she didn't picture him as a cat person, although she wasn't sure why. But the image of him baby-talking to a sulky feline made her giggle. She quickly swallowed it when he gave her a sideways look.

"Something is funny?"

"No. I was just surprised you have a cat."

"Yes. Me too. I… Let's say I inherited her from someone."

"Your parents?" Her childhood cat had died not long after her mom passed away. The second loss had hit her hard, since her mom had loved Tabby fiercely.

"No. Not my parents."

The gritted words sounded pained, although he hadn't increased his reliance on his cane. Oh. A girl-friend. Or a wife.

"I'm sorry. I shouldn't have asked."

"It's okay. My fiancée considered Rachel her cat. But when we broke up…well, let's just say there were aller-gies involved. So the cat stayed with me."

Allergies were involved in the breakup? No, that didn't make sense. Her eyes widened. The girlfriend had either cheated or found someone else soon after they broke off their relationship. Someone who was allergic to cats.

That's a whole lot of speculating, Amy.

But the curt way he spoke about it said the split hadn't been exactly amicable. "Well, I'm glad you didn't take the kitty to a shelter."

"There are very few shelters here. But I still wouldn't have. Rachel was originally a street cat, but has adapted very well to life inside my apartment."

She could imagine why. A shot of warmth pulsed through her.

And Roque had evidently adapted very well to life with a cat. Somehow the idea of Roque squatting down to pick up some terrified, emaciated cat and comfort-ing her made a wave of emotion well up inside of her. She'd always been a sucker for a man who was kind to animals. And to name his cat Rachel?

That was probably the doing of the fiancée as well. "How did she get her name?"

"There was a certain American program that my fi-ancée liked. It revolved around a café."

She'd binge-watched it with her mom. "That's a classic. Have you seen it?"

"I couldn't much avoid it." There went that tension in his jaw again. And there went her stomach.

Thankfully they arrived at the hospital's coffee shop, a trendy looking café that would rival the one in the TV show. "That looks great."

"What do you want?"

"I can get it."

"It's on the hospital."

It was? She didn't remember coffee breaks being covered. "A skinny vanilla latte, please."

She could see the wheels in his head turning as he puzzled through the words, so she tried again. "A latte with nonfat milk?"

"Ah...skinny. Nonfat milk, I see."

"What is it in Brazil?"

"*Leite desnatada*...literally de-creamed milk."

She laughed. "That makes sense."

Roque went to the counter and placed their orders, while she found a seat in the far corner. With cozy upholstered armchairs flanking a wood-topped table, the place had the feeling of a living room, where friends met to talk.

Not that she and Roque were friends, or ever would be anything more than acquaintances. He was in charge of...yes, babysitting her—until she, Lara and Peter were done with this three months. And with how slow this second day was going it might seem like forever by the end of her stay.

Dropping into her seat with a sigh, she studied her surroundings. The coffee shop overlooked the lower level of the hospital, where people were busy coming and going, including a group of medical students in white lab coats. Someone was in front of them, explaining the accoutrements of the hospital. There was another couple seated at a neighboring table. By the tiny touches and long, sultry looks, they were a pair. The sight made her heart cramp.

Amy's last relationship had left her wary of investing anything of value—like her heart. And she certainly wasn't going to start something she couldn't finish while she was in São Paulo.

Which is why she'd thought about just having a quick, casual bout of sex.

Bout? She made it sound like an illness, not something sexy and fun.

Roque came back to the table with an espresso cup, a shot glass with some kind of clear liquid and her taller latte. *"Café com leite desnatada e baunilha."* There were also two wrapped pieces of biscotti on the plate.

Wow, he could even make coffee sound sensual. She touched a finger to the shot glass. "What is this?"

"Seltzer water. It clears the palate and helps the flavor of the coffee come through."

Okay, she'd definitely heard of seltzer water, but had never actually seen anyone use it for that.

He passed her drink over, along with the wrapped biscotti, and sat in one of the other seats, leaning his cane against the wall behind him.

"Sometimes you use that and sometimes you don't," she said, mentally kicking herself for bringing it up again.

"My leg gets tired and cramps up. After the break

in my femur was repaired, the leg developed an infection, so I lost some of the muscle. It doesn't bother me all that much, but it's either use the cane or fall on my face from time to time."

"Sorry, I don't know why I keep asking about it. It's none of my business."

"You're curious. It's natural." One side of his mouth tilted at a crazy angle. "Believe me. I will not have a problem with telling you if you step over a line."

Like the question about his fiancée that kept buzzing around her head like a pesky mosquito? What kind of woman would Roque be attracted to? Oh, Lord, she was not about to ask about her. She didn't want to know anything about their relationship, or why it had failed. She was pretty sure he would pull her up short if she even mentioned it.

She took a sip of her coffee and focused on the flavor instead. It was mellow with low rich tones that blended perfectly with the milk and vanilla. "Oh, this is good."

Maybe it was the presentation—the glass showing the color to perfection…and that thick layer of foam on the top. Whatever it was, it tasted so much better than what she could buy in coffee shops back home. Or maybe it was just the fact that she was actually drinking coffee in Brazil. Brazil! It had been one of her dreams for a very long time.

"You have something…" One of his long fingers touched the left side of his upper lip. *"Espuma."*

Sponge? Oh! Foam—from the milk. She touched her tongue to the area and swept it back and forth a couple of times. "Gone?"

His gaze slowly tracked back up, and he took a visible swallow. Their eyes met. Held. They stayed that way for a long, long minute before he said, "Yes. It is gone." His voice had an odd timbre to it, sounding almost…wistful.

No. Not wistful. He didn't seem like the type of man to engage in…well, fluff.

He did have a cat, though, which she hadn't expected, either.

Roque unwrapped his biscotti and took a bite, watching her as she took another sip. This time she was a little more careful with the frothy top layer. "Do you have more surgeries today?"

"Later. I need to check in on my *moto* patient and the Achilles patient first. You're welcome to tag along if you'd like." He drank the rest of the contents of his demitasse cup.

One of his patients today had died, from what he'd implied. He had to be emotionally exhausted. Not wanting to add anything onto him, she shook her head. "I think I'll do a little exploring of the hospital, if that's okay. I can meet you at noon, when Lara and Peter arrive. Where do you want to meet?"

"How about right here." He glanced at his watch. "I'll see my patients, and then I might have that kitty-nap you talked about."

She smiled. And for the first time it felt real and unselfconscious. He was trying to use new words and not worrying about whether they were right or wrong, so maybe she should get off her high horse and be a little more adventurous. She blinked. In the language department, of course.

"I think you mean *cat*nap."

"Kitty-nap does not mean the same thing?"

"No, it doesn't mean anything, really. And I do think you should take some time to rest. You look…" Tired. That's what she'd been going to say. Not gorgeous. Not dreamy. Or any of the other crazy adjectives that were now crawling around the dark spaces of her skull.

"I look…?"

He tilted his head and regarded her as if maybe reading her mind. *Ack!* Time to think of something really unflattering.

"Kind of wrung-out."

His head stayed tilted, but now a frown appeared between his brows. He didn't understand what she meant.

"It means very tired. Exhausted."

"Ah, yes. I do feel a little tired." His glance dropped back to her lips before he suddenly climbed to his feet. "You will be okay on your own?"

Maybe she should have felt insulted that he would ask her that. But she was in a different culture and she knew it. And actually, she appreciated his concern.

And the fact that he'd just been looking at her mouth again? She wasn't going to check for foam. Not this time. Because it would just dig her in deeper. She needed to be by herself for a little while so she could regain her composure, which was being tested to the limit right now.

"I'll be fine, thank you. I have an uncle in São Paulo. I'd like to see if I can find him. I'm hoping he's still at the old address I have for him."

"Would you like help tracking him down?"

She would actually. She had no idea how to go about it, other than go to his last known address. But to just show up at the door? "Maybe. When you have time. I'm more worried about the language barrier than anything."

"I do not think it will be much of a barrier. But I will be happy to go with you, if you'd like."

She hadn't expected that. But the relief that went through her was so great that it was a struggle not to let it show. "Yes. I would like that. Thank you so much!"

He gathered their cups and saucers and started to turn toward the counter when he took a wrong step and very nearly tumbled. Her latte glass fell and shattered on the tile floor below.

"Maldito!"

Compassion poured through her, pushing aside her relief and everything else. "It's okay, hand me the other things and I'll get it." She took them out of his hands and went down on her haunches.

He made no move to kneel down to help pick up the big shards of glass, and she realized he either couldn't or he was worried that he might not be able to get up without help. And for someone like Roque, that thought was probably unbearable. He'd said he used his cane when his leg got tired. Well, if he was exhausted, that affected muscle was probably giving him fits.

The barista came over with a broom and dustpan. She murmured to let her get it and in short order had everything swept and tidy once again, taking the rest of their plates and cups and carrying everything over to the bar.

"I'm sorry."

"You don't have to be, Roque. I could have just as easily dropped them myself."

"But you didn't."

She touched his hand. "We've all been there."

"Have you?" This time there was a touch of anger in his voice. He thought she was patronizing him. But she wasn't. Yes, he had a permanent disability, but that didn't make him any less valuable than the next person. Hadn't she almost tripped over her dress at the welcoming party? More than once?

"Yes. I've dropped things for no good reason. Fallen while jogging. Slipped in the shower. All kinds of things. You're human." She forced a smile, maybe to keep the moisture that had gathered at the back of her eyeballs from moving toward the front. "Even if you don't want to believe it."

In a move that shocked her, his hand turned, capturing hers in his warm grip for several long seconds. Her heart picked up its pace until it was almost pounding in her ears.

"Of being human, I have no doubts. But thank you."

"You're very welcome. Now go get some rest. I'll see you at noon."

He let go and gave a quick nod, reaching for his cane. "I will. If you have any questions, just stop and ask someone. Our staff is always happy to help."

She'd noticed that from the time she'd arrived. But not just the hospital. Brazilians in general were a very friendly people. "I will, thank you."

With that, Roque turned and started to make his way across the coffee shop. Only this time, instead of every four or five steps, his cane hit the floor each time he bore weight on his left leg. It really was hurting him.

Damn, maybe she really should suggest he get some

PT done. Or at least a deep tissue massage to give that damaged muscle a way to recuperate some energy.

What was the worst he could say?

That she'd crossed over that invisible line.

Even if he knew she could offer him some relief?

She had a feeling it wasn't just about the pain, or whatever else he was experiencing. It was about his pride. Something that Amy was all too aware of. She could remember people wanting to help her after her mom passed away and waving them off like it was no big deal. Like people lost their moms every single day. Even as she felt like she was dying inside.

So maybe she would just have to somehow make him think it was his idea.

Really? She didn't think the man was going to come over to her and say, *Hey, could you bring those magic hands over here?*

Ha! No, he wouldn't say it in those words. At all. Because it sounded like too much of a come-on.

Besides, he'd already tried the physical therapy route, he'd said.

Yes, maybe he had. But how long ago was that? There were always new ways of doing things. Probably ways he hadn't tried, depending on how long ago the injury had occurred.

Well, that was something she could think about later. When she had a little space to breathe. Being around him was a lot more disconcerting than it should be, and Amy had no idea why.

But maybe she'd better sit down and try to figure out what it was about him that was putting her off balance, before she spent too many sleepless nights.

Because the sooner she understood why he was affecting her the way he did, the better it would be for her. And for him.

CHAPTER FOUR

ROQUE PUNCHED HIS pillow one more time, then dropped back onto it, propping his hands behind his head. He still couldn't figure out why he'd offered to go to Amy's uncle's house with her.

He'd analyzed every possible "why" over the last two days and had marked them off one by one: first explanation, she didn't know the language. Oh, yes, she did. Enough to understand almost everything that was said to her. Second possibility, he worried about her going out alone in some areas of the city. This was true to some extent, except they had the summer lecture program every year, and he had never felt the need to babysit anyone that came through the program. Third, those damned pink briefs that had been hanging out of the suitcase at her apartment. He leaped quickly over that possibility and headed straight for reason number four: there was an uncertainty about her that pulled at his gut. And this was the heart of the matter and something that had kept him up until well after midnight tonight, despite his killer of a day.

Maybe she would decide not to go and let him off the hook. Or maybe she would go without him.

He shut his eyes. Despite the awkward awareness that refused to die, and as much as he might regret offering—and even after all his tossing and turning, he wasn't sure he did—he did want to help her. At least in this one thing.

There. That was the solution. It was one outing. One good deed out of several years' worth of participating in this program. And anyway, she was nothing like the physical therapist that had made a pass at him in those early years of therapy. As long as she didn't offer to treat him, he was fine.

With that settled, Roque finally rested fully against his pillow, realizing for the first time how tense he'd been. He mentally visited each muscle group, limb by limb, and consciously forced them to relax.

He sucked in a deep breath and blew it out, allowing the darkness of the room to seep into him, doing his best to will his subconscious to do the same. Maybe then he could finally get a few hours of sleep, before the new day found him.

Three days down, eighty-seven days to go.

Oh, Lord. That was a lot of days. Amy rotated her neck and tried to work the odd kink out of it. At least things hadn't been too bad yesterday after Roque had met up with the rest of their little group.

She came in through the double doors at the front of the hospital and showed her ID to the guard stationed by the gate.

At his nod, she passed through it, heading toward the elevators and seeing several people were already there.

Oh! Krysta was waving her over. And there was

Flávia. She reached them. "I think I'm having a case of déjà vu. Only I wasn't this tired at the welcome party."

"We were just talking about how fast-paced everything is here in São Paulo."

"Did you already do your seminars?" Krysta and Flávia were scheduled to speak on their respective areas. "I haven't even looked at the lineup yet."

"No." Both women answered at once and they laughed. Krysta glanced at the elevator panel that sat out front. "Which floor are you headed to?"

"Fourth. I'm meeting Roque Cardoza."

"Is he the one you were sitting by at the party?"

"Yep. He's in charge of me for the next couple of weeks. I have to do anything he says, evidently."

Both women's heads swiveled toward her, and she realized they'd taken that the wrong way. "I mean related to the job."

"Com certeza. Só o trabalho." Flávia's voice had a touch of mirth in it. "It's not like he's hard to look at. If that's your thing."

A flame seemed to lick up Amy's face and ignite her cheeks. "You guys… I don't think of him like that at all. Besides, he's really *not* all that good-looking."

Liar.

Ping!

"Looks like that's your elevator," Flávia said. "And here's mine. See you both soon."

Seconds later Amy slid into the elevator, just as Roque showed up behind her, his cane draped over his arm today. When she glanced up, she caught a half smile on his lips. Oh, no. Surely he hadn't heard what they'd been talking about. Her face sizzled in mortification. "How are you?"

"I guess it depends on what part of me you're talking about?"

He had! He'd overheard them. "You... Were you standing behind us?"

"Only long enough to hear how not attractive you find me."

If she thought her face had been hot before, it was now an inferno. One she wished would consume her and turn her into a pile of ash.

But there was no way she would be that lucky. "Sorry. I didn't know what else to say." And thank heavens she hadn't sat there and gushed over him or worse.

"I'm glad, actually, that you don't think of me like that, because it could complicate things while you're here. It's much better to stick to the business at hand."

Something she was having a difficult time doing, although she wasn't sure why.

"Of course. I wouldn't want it any other way."

"So, the team is already upstairs waiting on us."

The rest of the ride was spent talking about cases and how her physical therapy would be used over the next several weeks. A little thrill of excitement went through her that had nothing to do with Roque, this time. At least, she hoped it didn't.

"I actually have an old friend who will be at the hospital shortly," he said. "He is going to have his mandible rebuilt after cancer surgery. He'll be looking to do physical therapy afterward, and I'd like you to handle the case."

"Me?" The elevator doors opened.

"Yes. He's had a hard go of it, and our physical therapy staff is stretched thin after a couple of therapists transferred to another hospital. His wife is English, and he has an excellent grasp of the language."

He'd mentioned kind of inheriting her because of how busy things were in the PT department.

"I'll help however I can, of course." She thought for a second. "How much of his jaw was removed?"

"Enough to make it a challenge to reconstruct it. But Krysta Simpson is more than up to the challenge, from what I understand. Our own Dr. Francisco Carvalho will be working with her on this—you'll probably meet him at some point in time. There was a bit of a glitch, but hopefully that's been ironed out."

"Glitch?"

"One of our senior oncologists wanted to take over the case, but that was pretty quickly squashed by all involved, as well as by the hospital administrator. Paulista isn't without its own share of...how do you put it? Drama?"

Flávia's comment about a snake that walked on two legs came back to her. But she wasn't sure of the man's name, so it probably wouldn't be good to ask. "Anything I should steer clear of?"

"I wouldn't think so...but if for some reason a doctor you don't know stops by once the patient starts doing physical therapy, I would appreciate a quick text or call. It's not that he'll do anything wrong, I just don't want Enzo put through anything more than he's already endured."

"Of course, I completely understand."

He nodded off toward the waiting area. "There they are, shall we?"

Today, Roque's steps were firm and sure, and her thoughts of trying to talk him into a massage or a little additional PT flew out the window. Maybe it really was only when he was tired. But watching him carefully, she thought she saw a hint of a limp, still, but it was small enough that she could have been mistaken.

He glanced back. "Coming?"

Lordy. She'd been standing staring at him as he walked. She hurried to catch up, then greeted Peter and Lara, and set out to put her mind completely on work.

She didn't think he was all that good-looking?

It shouldn't have stung, but after being up half the night thinking about her, Roque's head kept replaying the words she'd said to her friends. And hell if it didn't bother him. Maybe because he thought the woman was gorgeous with a capital G. And her smile…

Damn.

Maybe he just didn't "do it for her," or worse, maybe it was his leg. His ex had certainly changed her tune as soon as she found out he'd never play *futebol* again. She hadn't been able to get out of that hospital room quickly enough, even though she'd said it was because she needed to go and get some clean clothes, so she could stay in the room with him. Only she hadn't stayed. She'd come back for a few more visits. But once he got home, she said she wanted to give him space to recover.

She evidently needed her space as well…for something else entirely. Because not long afterward she'd broken it off, saying she was sorry but she'd fallen in love with someone else—that it had happened before he was injured. She wouldn't tell him who it was.

But then the tabloids had picked up the story and shouted the news to the world: Halee Fonseca, queen of Brazil's telenovelas, had dumped former Chutegol player Roque Cardoza. She was in love with another player. And the "who" would have been laughable if it hadn't been Roque's best friend on the team.

It had been a crushing blow. But who could blame her? She was famous and must have wanted an equally famous spouse. The pair were happily married now with two children. And Carlos had moved up to Roque's spot on the team and was still successfully playing ball.

He shook his head clear of those thoughts. He hadn't thought about Halee in years and wasn't sure what had brought her back to mind. Maybe Amy's comment. One thing he knew, even if his ex came back and wanted to get back together, he'd turn her down. He was well and truly over her.

And if Amy came calling? Would he turn her down as well?

She wouldn't. He'd heard her himself. She didn't think he was all that attractive.

But if she did?

Caramba! She doesn't. Just leave it there, Cardoza!

"Roque?"

Amy had asked a question. One that he'd totally missed. "I'm sorry. Say it again?"

"I asked if your Achilles' tendon patient will come to Paulista for his physical therapy. I'd like to at least watch and see how things differ between here and the States."

"I think you'll find it doesn't differ all that much,

which is part of the reason for the yearly lecture series. We study rehabilitation methods from all over the world, as I'm sure you have as well. We adapt the methods to work in our particular situation, but you'll find we're kind of an *amálgama* of all of the world's top hospitals."

And now he sounded defensive...or worse, arrogant, which wasn't what he meant at all. It had to have come from missing sleep last night. All he knew were that his muscles were tightening up all over again. Not a good thing for his damaged leg.

Peter hadn't said much of anything, and Lara's head was tilted as if puzzling through something, maybe sensing a little tension.

A little? Roque had been on edge ever since he stepped on that dress. Which reminded him. His mom had called this morning, saying the repairs on Amy's dress were done. She'd been determined to bring it to the hospital, even though he'd asked her just to drop it by the house. He was too hard to catch there, she'd said. Besides, she wanted to meet this woman whose dress he had.

Why was she so interested? And exactly why was he so uptight about that happening?

Was he afraid she would say something that would embarrass him? Well, his mom *had* dragged out his naked baby pictures and put them up on the big-screen television he'd bought her a year ago, thinking it was hilarious. Not so hilarious was the fact that she still wanted him married. With children. She hadn't exactly hounded him about it, but she brought it up enough to make him roll his eyes. And she'd hated Halee, so he guessed everything had worked out the way it was supposed to.

"I'm sure, which is part of the reason I wanted to come here so badly. It's one thing to read about surgical techniques. It's another thing to see them in person. Just like the beaches here in Brazil." Amy sighed. "I should have planned in some vacation time. But I didn't. So I'll have to squeeze a beach visit in during my working stay somehow."

Peter smiled. "My wife would slay me if I hadn't included her in some vacation time. Which beach are you thinking about?"

"Guarujá actually. It's only fifty miles away from the city and it sounds really beautiful."

"No." The word was out before Roque could stop himself. Everyone stared at him.

"Did I pronounce it wrong?" she asked.

Caramba. No, she hadn't pronounced it wrong. It sounded warm and husky coming out in those low tones of hers. That wasn't the problem. The problem was him…and that particular place.

"Guarujá is beautiful, but it has a reputation, especially this time of year." He suddenly knew what he was going to do. He was going to take his one good deed and make it two. Maybe then he wouldn't feel so awkward about intruding on her reunion with her uncle. He just needed to figure out how to suggest it.

Now she was frowning. "Reputation? It's a nice area, from what I read."

"It is, but…" He thought for a second. "There are quite a few wealthy individuals who live there, and that creates problems, just like it does everywhere. Guarujá can draw those who want to take from them."

Her face cleared. "Point taken. So where would you suggest?"

He glanced at Lara and Peter, deciding he didn't want either of them here for what he was about to suggest. "Would you two mind going on ahead? I left a list of patients I'd like you to look over at the nurses' desk."

Maybe he was wrong, but they both looked a bit relieved to be sent off. He hoped no one was getting the wrong idea about their relationship. Hell, *he* didn't want to get the wrong idea, so he needed to go about this carefully.

"If we can find out if your address is correct for your uncle, maybe we can combine that visit with a trip to Guarujá. How does that sound?"

Innocent enough. Even to his own ears. All he had to do was keep it that way.

"Are you sure? I hate to take any more of your time. You already had to make a trip to my apartment."

Yes, and the glimpse of those damned lacy undergarments still hadn't faded from his memory. Maybe he just needed to replace that memory with others that were less…volatile.

"I don't mind, unless you'd rather go with Lara and Peter."

She tilted her head as if thinking for a second or two. "Actually, your idea is a good one, and neither Lara nor Peter can help with translating for me. I really do appreciate your offering to help with that. Thank you."

"It's not a problem. We'll coordinate times and try to do it on my next scheduled day off."

It had been ages since he'd heard the crash of ocean waves or let the salty breeze flick along his limbs—things he'd learned to love as a child growing up in Rio's Barra da Tijuca. He'd missed making weekly treks to the beach.

That had to be why he was suddenly looking forward to the thought of spending the day with her. Maybe a little too much. But it was too late to retract the offer now. And he found he didn't want to. Besides, it wasn't like anything would happen. She wasn't even attracted to him from what he'd overheard her saying.

"Can you surf in Guarujá? I'd really love to try surfing in Brazil one day," Amy said, eyes shining in a way that made his gut shift sideways.

"Do you surf?" He tried to keep the surprise out of his voice. Of course she did. She was from Florida.

"A little. A friend taught me a few years ago, so I like to at least watch."

The image of Amy in a white bikini paddling out into the surf next to him flickered on a screen in his head. He blinked it away. He would not be paddling out with anyone, much less Amy, who was here for less than three months.

She was so different from Halee, who'd hated the ocean. The only way his ex had tolerated any bodies of water was if she was cruising down them on a yacht. They were such opposites he sometimes didn't know what they'd even seen in each other. Then again, he'd been a different person before the accident. Arrogant and far too sure of himself and his own immortality. A split-second collision on the field had taken care of that forever.

It seemed a lot of things had changed over the years. Including the type of woman he now found attractive?

His gaze collided with hers for a moment, before she smiled. "A day on the beach does sound fun."

It did actually. Roque couldn't remember the last time he took a day just to enjoy one of São Paulo's famous beaches. It had been a year or two.

"Great." It would also be nice to see his country through the eyes of a tourist. And hopefully it would help her as well. He took his phone out and scrolled through his work agenda. He didn't tend to take very many days off, so there were surgeries scattered through almost every day for the next several weeks, but he finally found an opening. "How about three weeks from Friday? I'll drive us out, rather than taking the bus."

"Should I bring a suit?" Amy asked.

"That's up to you, if you want to go in." Hell, he really hoped Amy would decide against that. He didn't need to go from imagining her wearing skimpy underthings to actually seeing her in swimwear, skimpy or not, although he had no idea why he was so leery of it. There were beautiful women everywhere in his country.

Just then the elevator doors opened. He glanced up and almost groaned aloud. It was his mom. And she was carrying a dry cleaner's bag. Inside of it, the teal color of Amy's long dress was clearly visible.

Amy also turned to look and her face quickly turned pink. Yep. Not the best scenario. And worse, his mother was striding toward them like a miniature powerhouse.

"I could have picked it up," Amy murmured to him.

"Yes, I told her that as well. But my *mamãe* does not always listen."

"*Roquinho, graças a Deus.* You are hard to locate in this place."

Roquinho? Really, Mother?

The diminutive form of his name meant Little Roque, and was one of her favorite ways to address him. It could be cute on occasion, but today wasn't one of those times.

"You could have had me paged. Or texted me."

"Oh, yes. I keep forgetting."

Her eyes zeroed in on Amy with a precision that would have made a surgeon proud. Any surgeon, except him. It brought back memories of their conversation about him meeting someone. The muscles in his gut tensed.

"This is her? The woman whose dress you almost ruined? Oh, the Fates…"

The way she said that made him close his eyes for a second or two. "Yes. Amy, this is my mother, Claudia Cardoza. Mom, this is Amy Woodell. She's here for the lecture series."

"Oh, yes, I know all about that."

Why did every word that came out of her mouth sound like she was concocting something? Something he knew he wouldn't like.

His mother handed him the dress and went up to Amy and put her hands on her shoulders, before pulling her close to deliver a resounding kiss on the cheek in true São Paulo fashion. In Rio it was customary to plant a kiss on both cheeks rather than just one, but in Brazil, people learned to adapt to where they were.

"It is very nice to kiss you, Amy."

Roque cringed at the misused English word. Especially since he'd had a thought or two about that recently himself.

"You mean nice to *meet* her, Mom."

His mom laughed and shrugged. While her English wasn't the best, her strong desire to be hospitable overrode her embarrassment over mistakes. Most people found it charming.

So did he. Usually.

Amy spoke up. "Thank you for fixing my dress, Senhora Cardoza."

She said it in slow Portuguese that was perfect, if a little formal. His mom's eyes went wide and she threw him a nod that had a world of meaning to it.

Diabos! His mom's dislike of Halee had shown in her attitude and actions. And one of the biggest problems with his mother was that her emotions flashed across her face like a strobe light in a pitch-black room. She liked Amy. And, looking back, he could see how she had probably been right about his former fiancée, but that didn't mean she was right now. It was one of the reasons he'd never introduced her to any of his dates, although none of those had been anything more than casual dinners.

He liked his life the way it was. No entanglements. No demands on his time. A night here and there he could afford, but a lifetime of commitment? Nope. Not again. He'd been ready to marry Halee, until the accident happened and she dumped him. Maybe the next woman wouldn't have dumped him, but...

Gato escaldado tem medo de água fria.

Once bitten twice shy—wasn't that how they said

it in English? In this case he liked the Portuguese version better.

"Roquinho said your, er, strap break? He step on it. Make it rip."

Amy smiled and replied in English. "It was an accident. Not a big deal. And thank you for fixing it. I would like to pay you for it."

His mom waved her hands. "No. No payment."

"But…"

"It is enough that Roque ask me for favor. He almost never ask. And now I ask favor in return. You come to dinner?"

"Dinner?"

"Yes. It would please me. Roque say your mother is from Brazil?"

"I, um…" Amy threw him a glance. "I would like that—if it is okay with Roque."

"Of course it is."

Great. His mom was suddenly making what should have been a small favor into something big and putting words in his mouth.

He fixed her with a look and responded in Portuguese, keeping his tone low. "Mamãe. Don't embarrass her."

All she did was smile and pat his cheek, making him roll his eyes, suddenly very glad that he'd sent Lara and Peter to the nurse's desk.

"Find out a time that is good for her. She needs to see something besides this hospital. She will meet your father as well."

Why the hell was that even necessary? She didn't need to meet his father. Or any other family members, for that matter. But this was one argument he wanted to have in private.

"I will ask, but no promises."

Amy's quick grin came and went. So she hadn't missed the exchange, despite it being in Portuguese. Perfect. So not only was he going to help her find her uncle and go to a beach with her. Now she would be dining at his mother's house. A house with that big-screen television and plenty of baby pictures.

But the last thing he wanted to do was talk about why that wasn't a good idea. Or have someone bring up how he'd very nearly defrocked her in front of two hundred people. Or why he'd had a vivid dream last night in which she hadn't quite caught the dress before it slid to her feet—revealing her wearing lacy pink briefs and nothing else. He'd woken up in a puddle of sweat and need that he couldn't quite shake.

So, no. The less he thought about that night at the gala or her apartment—or the consequences of them—the better for everyone involved. So he kissed his mom and thanked her and said they needed to get back to work. She took the hint, but the smile she sent Amy said that she wasn't about to forget about this meeting. Or the dinner invitation.

All he could do was give an inward groan and hope that his mom let the subject of Amy and her dress drop.

Dress drop. Damn. There it was again.

He tightened his grip on the dress's hanger and determined that this was one subject he was not going to revisit. Or at least he would set that as his current goal, and hope against hope that he could kick that ball right past the goalkeeper and into the net.

CHAPTER FIVE

"AMY WOODELL—THIS is Enzo Dos Santos and his wife, Lizbet."

Roque's dark eyes were on her as he made the introductions. More than three weeks had passed since his mom had appeared with her dress and the dinner invitation—which was scheduled to happen this evening after work.

The team had really started to sync, and Amy wasn't looking forward to being relegated to the physical therapy end of things, although she knew that was what had been planned all along.

Maybe *relegated* wasn't the right word for it, since Roque had told her about Enzo from the beginning. It seemed kind of funny to be meeting another person in his inner circle. First his mom—who'd given her a searching look that Amy hadn't quite been able to forget—and now his former coach. The man whose physical therapy she would be helping with once he had healed enough from his surgery.

"Nice to meet you both," she murmured.

Enzo's wife came forward and shook her hand, saying how grateful she was that Amy would be helping her husband recover. "Roque speaks very highly of you."

He did? Amy glowed with pride to think that perhaps Roque had enjoyed working with her as much as she had enjoyed working with him. And tonight she had dinner with his parents and tomorrow they were supposed to go on what Roque had called their field trip.

A phone call to a man named Abel Rodrigo had turned out to indeed be her uncle. Unfortunately, the visit they'd planned to make to him before going to the beach was going to have to be postponed, since her uncle was currently out of town on business. Maybe it was for the best, since she was already stressed about dining with Roque's parents and spending tomorrow at the beach with him.

Something that put her in an uneasy state of excitement, every time she thought about it. A whole day alone with him. Just her and Roque. Most of the last three weeks had been spent with the team, which she'd been glad of. At least, that's what she kept telling herself. Even though there'd been those odd moments when she sensed him looking at her. And she'd certainly glanced at him. More than once.

Lord. She needed to stop this.

Dragging her mind back to the patient, she forced herself to concentrate on what they were saying.

There was a kindness to Lizbet's manner that warmed Amy's heart. Despite that, there was something else—a spark of sadness, maybe?—in her eyes. Who could blame her? She and her husband had just gone through a terrible ordeal, one that wasn't over yet. Mr. Dos Santos owned one of the most famous football clubs in Rio. The same team Roque had once played for. He said they'd been friends for a very long time and it was obvious he cared for Enzo very much.

The man had almost lost his life to cancer. He'd certainly lost a good portion of his jaw. And now he was recovering from still more surgery. His lower mandible had been completely rebuilt. Enzo's jaws were immobilized at the moment, to allow the repairs to heal, so he had a whiteboard and marker to help him communicate. He was busy writing something and showing it to his wife.

She licked her lips, hesitating. "I, er, I don't know quite how to say this, but that doctor who tried to take over the surgery came to see Enzo again yesterday, under the guise of wanting to make sure he had everything he needed. Enzo doesn't care for him and would prefer he didn't have anything to do with his treatment."

Surely he wasn't talking about Dr. Carvalho. He was an excellent doctor from what she'd heard. "Which doctor was that?"

She handed the whiteboard back to her husband. "He introduced himself once, but he was kind of aggravating. He seems very concerned about Dr. Carvalho's involvement for no reason I can work out. After Enzo's recent difficulties…" Her voice trailed away. "I just don't want anything to set us back on a bad track. Things have been better since we've been in Brazil."

Enzo wrote something on his board and held it up.

She's worried. Felt I was depressed.

Amy could very well imagine he was. The man had been through a lot.

"I know who you're talking about," Roque said. "I'll see to it that he doesn't come see you again."

Wow. Roque could actually have another doctor banned from visiting a patient? Well, since Enzo was also his friend, it stood to reason that he would fight for him.

Was this who Roque meant when he said he wanted to be contacted if any doctor she didn't recognize tried to see Enzo? She was going to ask once they left the room.

Roque turned to her. "Amy, you've looked at Enzo's chart—do you want to give them an idea of how you'll go about physical therapy?"

"Sure." She went over the steps in her head. "First thing will be to pass your swallow test, which I don't anticipate you having any trouble doing."

Enzo nodded, writing something on his board. When he turned it toward her, the words were so unexpected they made her laugh.

If I don't cry, you're not doing your job.

"Well, I don't think I've ever had a patient that *wanted* me to make them cry before. But I assure you, you'll at least feel like crying at some point. I'll work you hard, but as long as you know my motivation is to meet our agreed-upon goals, then we'll do fine." She touched his hand. "I promise, I have the best of intentions and want us to work as a team."

The man relaxed back against his pillows, nodding and giving her a weak thumbs-up sign.

She couldn't imagine how hard it was for this strong vibrant man to be laid up unable to work. Was that how Roque had felt after his injury?

She had no idea. What she did know, though, was that she was going to do her very best to get Enzo back on his feet and working again.

Roque smiled at his friends and said they'd let Enzo get some rest. She glanced at her phone. Almost four o'clock. They were supposed to be at Roque's parents' house at six.

A shiver went through her that she tried to suppress before he noticed it.

Walking through the door, she sucked down a quick breath and asked the first question that popped to her head. "Who was the doctor you were talking about? The one they don't want involved in Enzo's treatment? Do I need to know his name?"

He looked at her, dark eyes inscrutable, a lock of hair tumbling over his forehead before he dragged it back in place with a flick of his fingers. "Let's head to my office."

Walking down a hallway, she felt her belly tighten. In the time she'd been in Brazil she'd never been back to Roque's office. There'd never been any reason to. But it wasn't like he wanted to blurt a name out in the open where someone might overhear them. He reached a door with a placard listing his name and credentials. Pushing through it and motioning her inside, he closed it behind them. "Have a seat."

His voice had suddenly gone formal and cool. Or

maybe that her imagination. Had she been wrong to ask him who the doctor was? But it wasn't blind curiosity. She wanted to be on guard if someone tried to upset her patient during physical therapy.

Her legs were suddenly a bit wobbly and she was glad to sit. Roque didn't go behind his desk; instead he leaned a hip on it. "Silvio Delgado."

"Sorry?"

"That's the doctor's name. I don't want him anywhere near Enzo. He tried to take the case from Dr. Simpson. Let's just say he was prevented from doing so."

"By you?"

"In part, but also by Dr. Carvalho and the administration. I won't go into the reasons for Delgado not being allowed near him. We'll just leave it at the fact that our patient doesn't like or trust him."

Our patient.

Had he actually said that? A feeling of warmth crashed over her, coursing through her veins and making her heart beat a little bit faster.

"I understand. Can you tell me what he looks like?"

One side of Roque's mouth went up in that devastating grin of his, making her mouth go completely dry.

"Let's just say you'll know who he is before you actually see him."

Why? Did he smell bad? Was he loud?

Ah, that was it. He was probably insufferable.

She was more and more sure that this was the snake that Flávia had been talking about during the welcome party. She'd meant to ask her who it was, but then figured it didn't really have anything to do with her, so she just forgot about it. Until now.

"Okay."

She relaxed back into the leather chair, amazed at how comfortable it was. Actually, his whole office had a welcoming feel to it, which surprised her. She hadn't thought of Roque as a welcoming kind of guy, although that image was slowly shifting the more she got to know him. He was kind of dark with an intense, mesmerizing charm that she didn't quite understand. But she also caught glimpses of warmth in those dark eyes. Like a cup of cocoa that you wanted to savor for as long as possible.

And…making comparisons like that was not very smart. Even though he looked like heaven on earth perched over her like that.

"Okay, so I'll alert you if he shows up."

"Yes. Do." He paused. "And we need to talk about tonight. I don't want you to feel pressured into going."

"I don't, but if we need to postpone it I understand."

"No, I just wanted to give you a—how do you say it?—an out."

She sat up. "I'm not looking for an out. Unless you'd rather I not come."

"My *mamãe* can be rather direct with her requests."

"Kind of like her son?" He'd been pretty direct about not wanting her to go to the beach on her own.

There went that grin again. "You think I'm direct?"

"Aren't you?"

"Maybe." He tilted his head. "But only when speaking from one doctor to another."

He'd evidently misunderstood what she was talking about. "I'm not a doctor."

"No. But I have a feeling you will be. Someday. Why did you never pursue your doctorate in physical therapy?"

That was a hard question. Her mom had been on her own for a very long time, and had helped Amy as much as she could during her years in college. Amy hadn't thought it fair that she continue her studies on her mom's dime.

"It's complicated. But I'm thinking of going back to school to get it once I get home. There are just never enough hours in a day."

"I know that feeling. Okay. So, tonight is set. And about tomorrow. Are you still wishing to go?"

Wishing? Probably more than she should.

"I am, if it's okay with you. Although I really don't mind going by myself, if you have too many things you need to take care of."

"No. I said I would take you, and I try to always keep my word."

Making it sound like he wasn't looking forward to it at all. And how did she feel about going with him without the side trip to her uncle's house?

Excited. And that scared her. Weeks were starting to fly by, and that wild, sexy fling she'd envisioned having with some man while she was here hadn't happened. There wasn't even a single prospect. By the time she finished work each day, she was too tired to feel lonely. And going to a bar by herself looking for a likely prospect seemed kind of pitiful and not very safe. Here or in the United States. There was always Krysta and Flávia, except she'd heard the venom specialist was traveling back and forth to the Atlantic Forest region of Brazil, and she'd only seen Krysta in passing, although she had suggested the pair of them meet up for a dinner or a shopping trip sometime.

"Do you want to surf or swim tomorrow?"

He'd said taking a suit was up to her, but she'd already decided against it. And there was a tension in his voice that said she'd made the right choice.

"I think I'd just like to sightsee this time, if that's okay." She was already in a state about going with him. She didn't need to throw a bathing suit and water into the mix. And although water could conceal a whole lot of what happened below its surface, if she were going to have that fling, she'd rather it be in complete privacy.

Was she actually considering Roque for the position?

No, of course not, although Roque hadn't mentioned a girlfriend, and the blonde from the soiree had never reappeared.

"That's fine. We can see more that way. We'll just walk on the sand."

She smiled. A walk on the beach with him sounded very, very nice. Too nice, in fact. "I don't want to fill your car with the stuff."

"It's seen worse." He shifted his cane, pushing it a little to the left. "How do you feel speaking in Portuguese when it's just you and me?"

Just you and me.

Her toes tingled at the sound of that, the sensation spreading up her calves and tickling her thighs. She loved hearing him speak in his native tongue. Maybe a little too much. "I—I'm not the best at it, but I can try."

Great. Now she was stammering, even in English.

"I think it would be an asset for your work. You said you live in South Florida. Isn't there a large community of Brazilians there?"

There was. She'd had a couple of patients who were Brazilians actually, and Amy had practiced tae kwon do at her local *dojang* with a Brazilian instructor. Marcos had sent a couple of people injured at tournaments to physical therapy and had offered to "hire" her if she ever needed a little extra work. She'd gotten the feeling that the interest went beyond pupil/instructor relationship, but she hadn't wanted things to get messy and ruin their professional relationship. And she'd been pretty wary of getting involved with men back then.

Maybe she should remember that decision and treat her relationship with Roque the same way. If she were smart, she'd call off the beach trip. And dinner with his folks. Except she wanted to go to both. More than she should. But she was only here in Brazil for a couple more months, so how messy could it get in that period of time?

Pretty damned messy, if she wasn't careful.

But right now it wasn't, and he wanted to start speaking in Portuguese.

She swallowed.

"You're right. There is a large population of Brazilians there. So I probably should practice."

"We can start by using the language on our beach trip, and I will correct you when you make a mistake. How's that? It will also make you look less like a tourist if we're not speaking English."

Ah, now she got the reason for it. It would make

them less of a target for thieves while at Guarujá. "That makes sense."

It would be awkward, since she "knew" Roque in English. Speaking Portuguese with him would seem intimate, even though she knew he didn't mean it that way.

And she knew her mom in two languages, so how was that any different? Maybe it wasn't, except Amy had never been required to respond in Portuguese. She'd just needed to understand what was said.

"I see worry on your face. Don't be scared. I think it will become easier with practice. And you'll find I am a very forgiving coach."

She bit her lip as the tingling spread to places far higher than her calves.

The image of him "coaching" her in hoarse tones as they practiced things other than Portuguese trickled through her subconscious, becoming a torrent as each mental picture became more explicit than the last.

Oh, God. Time to move this conversation to something else.

"Speaking of coaches. Do you miss playing football?"

Ugh! "Something else" did *not* mean reminding him of a time in his life that was probably painful.

"Or shouldn't I ask?"

"It's okay." His fingers, as if on automatic pilot, found his cane and fingered the handle. "Yes, I miss some things about it. But not others. I miss having a leg that is whole more than I miss the game."

Whole? Did he really think that?

"Your leg *is* whole. It's just a different kind of whole. It's a part of what makes you…you."

"A different kind of whole? I'm not sure I agree with that. I live in this body, I know what it feels."

From her Google search—and yes, she was ashamed to admit that she'd done more of her share of reading up on him—he'd been very good at what he did. Had been one of his team's top players, in fact.

"It's just your normal. People are not cookie cutter shapes. Everyone has their own strengths and weaknesses."

"Cookie cutter."

"It means people are not exactly alike."

He smiled, and the act warmed any chilliness that had gathered in his expression. "No. People are not just alike. And that is a good thing, I think."

"Yes, it is." Roque was like no one she'd ever met.

His hand had moved away from his cane and was now gripping the edge of his desk beside his left thigh.

A very strong-looking thigh.

She struggled to think of something to say that would stop her train of thought, which was starting to barrel into dangerous territory. "I heard Peter mention missing his wife and kids today."

"It is natural. You don't have someone at home that you miss?"

The sad thing was, she didn't. She had no serious relationship; she wasn't even dating. And although she had friends at the hospital and at the rehab center, she didn't hang out with them as much as she might expect. Many of them were married with families and, like Peter, all they wanted to do was get home to them. More and more, she'd been thinking of what Roque had said about getting her doctorate. She'd put it off as something to do later. But what if later never came and she looked back with regret. Maybe it was a time to make a promise to herself.

"No one special, but that's okay. Especially since I'm going to apply for the doctorate program as soon as I get home."

And just like that, the decision she'd been toying with for some time was made.

The hand that had been gripping his desk relaxed a little. Was he worried that she might be interested in him…in staying because of him?

The brakes on that train screeched as she applied them hard, the engine struggling to stop, the boxcars she'd added over the last couple of weeks piling up behind it.

"I'm glad you are. The Achilles' tendon patient liked what you had to say. And it would give you opportunities to teach at universities."

She'd thought the same thing. If she ever got to a place that she didn't have the strength she needed to manipulate patients the way they needed to be, it would give her options. And although she hadn't been intimately involved with that first patient's surgery she'd observed at Paulista, she had been at his appointments and observed his rehab. She was due to go again in a few days as a matter of fact.

"Yes, that's what I thought as well." She tilted her head. "When is Mr. Dos Santos going to start physical therapy?"

"In a couple of weeks. The repairs are stable and he's due for his swallow test tomorrow."

The day they'd be at the beach. "You don't want to

be here for him? I'll understand if we have to put off our trip."

"His wife will be there, and I'll check on him when we get back. I think the last thing Enzo wants are for twenty people to be gathered around to watch him. He's a pretty determined guy. I don't doubt he'll pass with flying colors, which is a good thing with where his mind has been lately. I know. I've been there."

Was he talking about what Enzo had written about his depression? Well, Roque had had a right to be depressed, if so. He'd been a brilliant young soccer player, and in the blink of an eye everything he'd worked so hard for had been taken from him.

"Sometimes things work out the way they should. You do brilliant work here at the hospital." She nodded at his left leg. "Would you be at Paulista if you hadn't been injured?"

"Probably not. I'm old enough now that my career would be pretty much over, and I'd probably be coaching or stuck at a desk job somewhere." He sighed. "That doesn't mean the road from there to here was easy. It took ten long years of school to become a doctor."

"No. I'm sure it wasn't. But where are you more needed at this point in your life?"

He laughed. "You have a way of turning things around to look at their best side."

"The dangers of being a physical therapist. We're trained to be positive and optimistic. It's a good way to motivate our patients."

"I think those characteristics come naturally to you."

Did they? She didn't always feel all that optimistic. She just needed to be "up" for her patients. Needed to be a motivator when they came in feeling life would never be the same, ever again.

The exact way Roque had probably felt when told his career as a football player was over. "Thanks, but I'm not sure that's true. It's just part of my job description. You mentioned being a coach. That never appealed to you?"

"No. I thought about it once or twice, but didn't see myself doing that. Not with my old team, anyway."

"It would have been too hard to watch them play while you felt sidelined?" The way he'd said the words gave her pause.

"That would have been hard, yes, but my reasons were more...personal."

Personal? He and the team's owner seemed to get along great; he'd even confided in Roque about that other oncologist, Dr. Delgardo. So she didn't see that "personal" reason arising there. But if he wanted her to know, he would tell her, so that was her signal to leave it alone.

Oh! Roque had been engaged to an actress, according to her search. Who was now married to a player on his former team. Of course he wouldn't want to see her day in and day out. That made perfect sense.

Her heart cramped. Surely it was better to know what a person was like before getting married to them. She could certainly thank her lucky stars now that her boyfriend had dumped her *before* marriage rather than after. Although she'd been gutted at the time.

"Things have a way of showing you a person's true colors." In case he didn't know that expression, she added, "Of seeing them for who they really are. Like your accident. When your soccer days came to an end, it revealed who you really are."

"Interesting." His smile was slow and unbearably sexy. "And who am I...really?"

The ground had suddenly gotten shaky under her feet. Why had she said that? "You're a man who cares about his patients and his friends, and who likes to keep his word."

There! That was the least personal thing she could think of to say. And they were both true.

He got to his feet. "But you could say that about almost every doctor here at Paulista."

"But we're not talking about every doctor." She was suddenly having a hard time catching her breath. "We're talking about you."

Thinking he was ready to shoo her out of his office, she climbed to her feet as well. Big mistake. Because it set her right in front of him. Close enough to catch the warm musky scent of his aftershave. To see the slight dusting of stubble across his chin. And those lips that seemed to capture her attention time and time again...

Roque made no effort to move away. "So we were. So let's talk about you. Do you want to know how I see *you*?"

She wasn't sure she did, but it was as if her mouth was controlled by forces outside of her body. "Yes."

He touched a finger to her jawline. "I see a woman in a teal dress that's an inch or two too long for her. A woman who didn't let that stop her from coming to the party." He'd switched to Portuguese, and she stood there transfixed by his touch and his voice as he continued. "I saw bits and pieces of you in that patient file you included in your application to the program. And the real you made me very glad I said yes to you being in the program."

He dropped his hand, but continued to meet her eyes. "You want what's best for your patients and those around you."

"I'm not as saintly as you make me sound."

"Aren't you?" His gaze trailed down her neck. "You're like a marble sculpture that stands in front of a church."

If he could read her thoughts right now, he might change his mind. Her pulse pounded in her head, mouth going dry as she stared back at him. "Sculptures aren't real. I assure you, I am flesh and blood. Just like you."

"Are you?" One hand slid into her hair and cupped her nape, his thumb just behind the tender skin of her ear. But that wasn't what made her take another step in his direction. That came from somewhere inside of her, from the part that wanted to know what it would be like to be kissed by him, to feel herself pressed against him. She could damn herself later, but for right now…

He looked into her eyes, maybe seeing the jumble of emotions boiling just under the surface. Then his head started a slow descent, until it was just her and him. And his lips on hers.

CHAPTER SIX

ROQUE HAD NEVER felt anything so sweet. Or so undeniably sexy. The second his mouth touched those silky soft lips of hers, Amy's arms wound around his neck.

And it was heaven.

She'd said she was no saint. But neither was he. He'd proven that time and time again when one date didn't lead to another. But right here, right now, there was nowhere else he'd rather be.

His tongue eased into her mouth and found a moist heat that set his body on fire. One arm circled her back, and he leaned his weight against his desk for stability. The last thing he wanted to do right now was fall. Or lose contact with her. And damn if she somehow didn't wind up between his splayed legs and pressed against the part of him that had dreamed of this happening ever since he stepped on her dress a month ago.

And now here he was.

Right where he shouldn't be, for so many reasons.

She was a visitor at his hospital. And she was only here for three months.

Maybe it was the latter point that kept him in place.

Amy made a sound in her throat, her hips inching

forward and back in a way she probably wasn't even aware of. But he was. He felt every little movement. A vision of his desk and her on it came to mind. That image lingered, toying with different angles and positions.

But before he could even think about turning them so that she was against the desk instead of him, the phone on his hip buzzed, the noise breaking into the silent struggle that was going on between them.

Amy froze for a second. Then she jerked back, her arms releasing their hold on him.

She kept moving until she was against the chair, and no doubt if that hadn't been there she would have kept going until she was out the door. One of her hands grabbed the armrest and the other pressed against her mouth.

Hell, what had he been thinking? He hadn't been.

When she finally spoke, she said, "I am so sorry. I don't know what… I have no idea why…"

He knew why. All too well. And it wasn't her fault, it was his. "Don't. I let things get out of hand. There's no excuse I can give."

"I was a willing participant. You would have known quickly enough if I hadn't been."

That made him laugh, despite the regret that was coursing through him at his behavior. "Really? What would you have done?"

"Put you on the ground."

"Ah, that's right. You know tae kwon do."

"I do. I have a first-degree black belt in it."

His eyes widened. "That shouldn't surprise me."

"But it does? Well, you can thank my mom. She's

the one who insisted that I go for lessons. She wanted me to be able to defend myself."

"It sounds like you can."

Roque glanced at his watch, surprised to see it was almost five. "About dinner…"

"Let me guess. You don't want me to go now."

Something passed through her eyes. Like she was expecting him to cancel on her.

"No, I was going to ask if you needed to go home to change first, because we'll be cutting it close, if so."

What looked like relief passed through her eyes. "So you still want me to come?"

"Is there a reason I shouldn't?"

She smiled. "Evidently not. You're very good at compartmentalizing, you know that?"

"At what?"

"Putting everything into separate boxes in your mind."

He was actually. Partly the result of his accident and what had happened with Halee, and partly because of his job. "This is one thing I will not hide away in a box. That way I can make sure it won't happen again."

"I can help with that. Remember that whole 'on the ground' thing?" She let go of the arm of the chair as if having regained her composure.

His smile widened, relieved that she wasn't going to blow this all out of proportion.

"You would use some of your moves on me?" And just like that, Roque was back in a different frame of mind, going over that kiss blow by blow.

"You don't want to find out."

The problem was… He did. But if he was going to get

through this dinner intact, he was going to have to keep his head. Because his mother was very, very shrewd. And the last thing he needed was for her to guess what he and Amy had been doing in this office.

Otherwise she'd be on the phone with her priest and reserving the church.

That wasn't going to happen.

If he could just remember that Amy was here for just a few months and that she had her heart set on earning her doctorate in the States, he would be fine.

He didn't want another relationship. And the last thing he wanted was to keep anyone from their dreams.

Claudia and Andre Cardoza welcomed her into the cookout area of their little getaway house with the same warmth his mom had displayed at the hospital.

"Thank you so much for inviting me."

They'd opted to host the meal outside of the crush of São Paulo, instead of at the family home. Roque said it was because his dad—a police officer—liked to get away from town on the weekends, whenever he could.

"We are glad Roque brought you." Andre was the spitting image of his son, although his dark hair was peppered with gray. With a skewer loaded with some type of meat in one hand and a brick grill behind him, he looked totally in his element.

Unlike Roque, who seemed ill at ease. Well, that made two of them. She'd actually been surprised that he wanted her to come, and maybe it would have been easier if they'd canceled their plans, but Amy had truly liked Claudia and would have hated for her to go to the trouble of fixing her a meal only to have her not show up.

His mom brought her a bottle of water. "Please help yourself to anything. Dinner won't be long. Roque, why don't you show her around."

"Okay."

He grabbed a water for himself and motioned her to follow him. The walled-in compound was alive with flowers and greenery, and there were several hammocks scattered throughout the space. A clay-tiled building was to the left, and must be where they slept when they weren't outside. It was kind of like a cabin they might have back home in Florida. Without the sand.

"What's the Portuguese word for this kind of place again?"

"It's a *chácara*. Kind of like a country home. Only not."

He could say that again. When she thought of a country home, she thought of a white stucco home with a wraparound porch. This was more like a campground. One they had all to themselves. It was charming, and under other circumstances she might have found it heavenly.

Except she was hyperaware of every move Roque made. Of his broad shoulders and narrow waist and the way he had felt against her.

He'd been attracted to her, that much was obvious. She'd felt the very real evidence of that.

And despite her talk about compartmentalizing, it was not going to be easy to lock that particular memory into a box and keep it there.

But somehow she was going to have to do just that.

A fling? With Roque?

Just hours earlier, she'd entertained that exact thought. Until she realized just how deadly his kiss was to her senses.

"How long have your parents owned this?"

"Actually, this was passed down to them by my grandparents, who built it many years ago."

A pond nestled against one corner of the property, the greenery behind it camouflaging the protective wall that kept intruders out. "Does it have electricity?"

"It does now. It didn't originally." He grinned. "They also added plumbing a few years ago."

"I bet that makes life a lot more comfortable."

He motioned to one of the chairs that flanked the body of water. "When I was a kid, I didn't seem to think about what this place lacked. I just liked being with family."

Since the only family Amy had had around had been her mom and dad—her grandparents had passed away before she was born—it was a little hard to imagine family get-togethers that involved more than just the three of them. She sank into one of the wrought-iron chairs with a sigh. "It's beautiful. Serene."

And suddenly she was glad she'd come. This place might be the perfect bridge to transport her from her heightened emotional state to a place that was more tranquil. At least she could hope. The pond boasted a small rock waterfall that had to be powered by a pump, although she couldn't see it.

"Yes. My father's job is very difficult. This helps him put things into perspective. To realize that life is more than fighting drug lords in *favelas*."

Some of the slums of Brazil were known for being controlled by different gangs, going as far as limiting who entered and left the community. "I can't imagine how hard that must be."

"I grew up knowing that my father could go to work one day and never make it home. I think that's why the Chácara do Cardoza is so important to him. He's had offers on the property, but he always turns them down."

"You'll inherit this someday, then."

"I imagine."

There was something in his voice. "You don't want it?"

"At one time, I would have said no. But that was a long time ago." He stretched his leg in front of him, propping his cane against his thigh.

"Is it bothering you?"

"No."

The answer was curt, like it was whenever she asked about his leg. He didn't like talking about it. She could understand that. No one liked to admit to having a weakness.

"Sorry."

He tipped his head back so that it leaned against the high back of the chair, then turned to look at her. "It is I who am sorry. My leg is tired from the day, but it will be fine tomorrow."

For their trip to the beach. They would have a lot of walking, from what he'd said. But it would be better for his muscles than standing in one spot doing surgeries like he probably did day in and day out. She'd been tempted to back out of their trip, but she also didn't want Roque to know how much that kiss had affected her.

"What should I bring?"

"To the beach?" He paused. "Probably the same things you would take in Florida. Sunscreen, maybe a hat. Shoes that are easy to walk in and remove sand from."

"Okay. Do you want me to meet you somewhere?"

"I think it would be better if I picked you up in front of the Fonte Cristalina. Say at nine o'clock in the morning?"

It was already past eight, but Amy was in no hurry to get back to her apartment. Maybe because she knew that once that happened, she was going to dissect every single second of her time in his office and figure out how what had started out as a completely professional conversation had gone so totally off the rails.

"That sounds like a plan."

A half hour later, Amy was sitting outside at a large farmhouse-style table laughing at stories that Andre shared about some of his most embarrassing moments as a police officer. She was pretty sure he'd also experienced some awful moments as well. A couple of times Claudia had reached across and squeezed her hand, smiling at her and asking if Amy wanted this or that and encouraging her to eat another bite of the delicious grilled meat that was so common in Brazil.

"I'm very…*satisfeita*." One of her mother's favorite words surfaced without warning, and she swallowed hard, hoping no one realized she was choked with grief—a grief she thought she'd worked through.

Roque peered at her through the growing shadows. "Are you okay?"

"Yes. Just enjoying the evening."

And she was, much to her surprise. A little too much, maybe. That's probably where that little burst of emotion had come from. Thinking about how her mom would have loved sharing this moment with her.

But they'd had plenty of other happy times. And she treasured each of them.

Roque glanced at his watch. "Well, I know you and Dad are spending the night here, but I need to get Amy back to her apartment. It's been a long day."

Claudia stood up and came around and kissed her son on the cheek and then turned to Amy and hugged her tight. *"Venha de novo, ta?"*

"I will. Thank you so much." As much as she appreciated Claudia's encouragement to return to visit, she very much doubted she would ever see Roque's parents again.

Hopefully her smile hid any sadness she might feel over that fact. But the reality was, these three months would soon be little more than a tiny moment in time. So she committed as much of this place and their faces as she could to memory.

And maybe one day she would be able to draw those memories back up and remember them with a smile that was a little more genuine than the one currently plastered to her face.

At least she hoped so.

CHAPTER SEVEN

WHY ON EARTH had she told him to meet her in front of her apartment complex? Or agreed to come with him at all? Was she crazy? She was already affected by him in ways she didn't want to think about, and now she was going to spend the day with him. Alone.

She'd gotten outside ten minutes early so he wouldn't have to wait, and in that short period of time several people had come out, commenting on her hat and the straw bag containing her sunscreen. She'd been able to repeat that she was going to the beach. One woman had asked if she wanted company! Which had gotten super awkward when she said she'd been invited by the doctor she was working with.

But it might have been more awkward if there were suddenly five people cramming into Roque's car.

Finally he arrived, and she jumped in and slammed her door, giving him the biggest brightest smile she could manage, hoping that he wouldn't guess how nervous she was. "Ready? Let's go."

He glanced at her with a frown. "What's the big rush?"

"Well, the explanations have been a little difficult."

"Why?"

The single word summed it up brilliantly. Why was it a problem? She was the one who was fumbling around and making it a bigger deal than it was. Somehow dinner with Roque's parents had been easier than this beach outing was proving to be, and she wasn't sure why. Maybe it was that whole thing of him wanting to speak Portuguese when they were alone. So far, she was not following that course, since the words pouring from her mouth were all in English.

"I don't know. I think it just feels…" She couldn't come up with the right word to save her life.

"After yesterday, do you mean?"

"Yes." As usual, he'd hit the nail on the head. If she could somehow stop overanalyzing every aspect of what had happened in his office, maybe she could put it all behind her.

"No one knows about that except us. So our outing will only appear strange to others, if we make it that way."

Which is exactly what she'd done. Maybe because she couldn't just hide her feelings the way others might. Even Roque kept his emotions tucked well out of sight. Except for yesterday.

But had that been due to an overflow of feelings? Or simply because they were a man and woman who were attracted to each other physically?

"You're right, of course. There's no reason to feel guilty. I'm just one of those people who ends up getting caught red-handed if I do something wrong."

"Well, our hands are not red, because no one saw us."

Amy laughed. "That's one way of putting it." She

loved the way he used expressions with confidence even if he didn't quite understand the meaning.

With that he started the car and pulled away from the curb. "Are you looking forward to seeing Guarujá? If you brought a towel, we can sit on the beach for a while."

"Sounds great. Have you ever been to Caraguata-tuba? Apparently there's a great surfing beach there? Do you know it?"

"Massaguaçu. The surf is not always consistent, but it can get busy at peak times of the year. If you decide to go surfing there, take a buddy."

It's not like she'd be in Brazil long enough to do that or had anyone to do it with. "I'll keep that in mind."

His fingers tightened on the wheel, and he turned to look at her. "Seriously. The riptides can be deadly."

"I won't go alone. I promise."

"Good."

An hour and a half later, they were in Guarujá, and Amy couldn't hold back a gasp. It was almost intimi-dating, with row after row of pristine condominiums. Nothing like the Chácara do Cardoza from last night.

Traffic was heavy, but not as bad as at the center of São Paulo, which many times saw bumper-to-bumper traffic and motorcycles that whizzed frantically be-tween the rows of cars.

"Are you okay?"

"Yes, just didn't expect it to look like this honestly. There must be thousands of people living here."

Roque smiled. "Hundreds of thousands. And I was right."

"Right? About what?"

"I do like seeing this place through the eyes of a tourist."

So he hadn't brought anyone here during previous years' lecture programs? If what he said was true, it appeared not.

She couldn't stop a smile as a wave of warmth poured over her. "I'll try not to disappoint you."

"You have not disappointed, Amy. Believe me."

Something about the way he said that sent a shiver over her.

He's not talking about that kiss, Amy.

More likely he was talking about how she did her job at the hospital.

Roque found a paid parking garage and slid his car into the first available spot, taking his ticket and paying the attendant.

Scooping her beach bag from the back seat, she crossed the strap of her purse over her chest and kept the wicker tote containing her beach gear in her hand.

"Do you want me to carry something?"

She glanced at his hands, noting he'd brought nothing with him. "I'm good. It's not heavy. I just have a towel and sunscreen in there." She dropped her sunglasses over her nose to help cut the glare from the sun, which was already warm.

Skirting one of the large apartment blocks, they arrived on a long sandy strip that led down to the water. On it was a sea of red striped umbrellas that stretched as far as the eye could see. "Wow, they're all dressed up for company, aren't they?"

"It's pretty impressive, I agree." He glanced at one

of the nearby buildings. "Why don't you keep going, and I'll catch up with you in a minute."

She looked over at where his attention had gone, but saw nothing, so she did as he'd asked and started across the sand. She then took off her shoes and stuffed them into her bag, enjoying the warmth beneath her bare feet.

Less than a minute later, she felt a slight tug on her bag. The hair raised on the back of her neck when she sensed someone directly behind her.

Roque had been right.

When the bump happened again, she instinctively whirled around, hooking her foot around the calf of the pickpocket and yanked as hard as she could, sending him flying to the ground.

Only at the deep "oomph" did she realize her mistake.

Roque lay sprawled across the sand, his cane about three feet to his right. "Oh, God, I'm sorry. I thought someone was trying to steal something from my bag."

He propped himself up with his hands on the sand. "I guess you really can defend yourself."

"Of course I can. I already told you I know tae kwon do." She frowned. "Wait. What do you mean, I can defend myself? Were you *trying* get a reaction from me?"

"I thought I'd see how aware you were of your surroundings." He reached for his cane. "Very, evidently."

"It was pure instinct. Are you hurt? Your leg?"

Pushing off with his cane, he shook his head and tried to get to his feet, only to have his walking aid sink into the soft sand, leaving him stranded on the ground. "My pride is the only casualty, it seems."

She reached down to help him up, and he let her,

managing to heft himself to his feet. "This feels like reversed roles. I did the same for you, when your dress was ripped and you couldn't get out of my car. Remember?"

Only too well. "Yes, well, at least you didn't step on my dress on purpose. Unlike me, who purposely tripped you."

He squeezed her hand for a minute before releasing it, leaning against her as he tried to get his cane situated. "But I did reach into your bag on purpose, just now, so you did the right thing."

He took a step, and the color suddenly drained from his face. He stopped in place.

"You *are* hurt. I am so, so sorry!"

"It's nothing." He reached down to massage his left thigh. "Just a muscle cramp. I get them sometimes when the nerves misfire."

She turned and faced him. This was her chance. "I can help with that."

"No, you can't."

There was a darkness to his voice that was at odds with the reality of the situation. She actually could help. If he'd let her.

She took a deep breath and let it out in a controlled hiss, trying to keep herself from taking his refusal personally. "I can't make your injury go away, but I can help with the pain you have right now."

"I've tried it."

She tilted her head. "And it didn't help at all? I find that hard to believe. I can do a deep tissue massage that—"

"Absolutely not."

This time, she let the anger come to the forefront. "Are you kidding me? You said you liked how I treated Bobby Sellers, said it showed I could think outside of the box, and now you're acting like I have nothing to offer."

She'd lived through this hot and cold nonsense before and wasn't about to put up with it from him.

"I did not say that."

"Not in so many words, but you implied it. Please let me try. If it doesn't help, you've lost nothing. But if it does…"

"You won't always be here, Amy, so it's better if I don't get used to any—"

"Damn it! You're the one who told me Paulista is an amalgamation of all the best hospitals in the world. There are other therapists you could go to if it turns out this works. I let your mother fix my dress. Let me try to help your leg."

"What would you do?"

He leaned on the cane with both hands. It must really hurt. She'd never seen him this vulnerable before. "I'll use essential oils in a carrier oil and massage them into your skin. The heat generated from my hands will help the oils absorb."

"And if it doesn't help? Will you then stop suggesting I seek therapy?"

She blinked. He was going to let her try? She'd somehow expected a bigger fight than that. While a part of her was relieved, another part was worried that maybe he knew something she didn't. Something that would prove her wrong. "Are you sure it's just a muscle cramp? Could you have landed wrong and damaged something else?" She'd hooked his right leg, not the injured one, but anything could have happened as he went down.

"It's not dislocated or broken, if that's what you mean. I recognize this pain. It's just muscle."

"Can you make it back to the car?"

"I can finish our tour." But when he tried to take another step, he winced and stopped again.

"No, you can't. Give me your cane."

"I don't think—"

She jerked it from beneath his hands and hooked it over her beach bag.

"What the hell, Amy?"

She moved to his affected side. "Put your arm around me."

"No."

"What's wrong, Roque? Scared? Of little ole me?"

"I am not scared."

He might not be, but she was now wondering about the wisdom of asking him to touch her, even as an offer of help.

Surprisingly, he put his arm around her waist while she jammed her shoulder under his arm, and the second he did, a sense of rightness came over her, the warm solidity of his body fitting perfectly against hers. The side of her breast nestled against his chest in a way that made her nipples tighten at the slightest hint of friction. She held perfectly still and willed it away. It didn't work.

Oh, no. Not what she wanted. At all.

She hesitated, tearing her mind apart for some other way to get him to the car and coming up blank. Maybe this was why he hadn't wanted her helping him. Because he knew how he made her feel.

Not the time to be thinking about any of this, Amy.

"Let's go. Lean on me as we walk."

Slowly they made their way back to the sidewalk and soon all thoughts of how he made her body react vanished. Roque didn't make a sound, but when she glanced up at his face, his mouth was bracketed with white lines of pain. Why had she swept his leg out from under him?

Because she'd honestly thought someone was trying to steal something from her bag, and pure instinct had taken over. He said the pain was muscular. Well, she would know as soon as she laid her hands on his skin. Either the muscles would be knotted and hard or she'd realize something else was wrong.

Lord, she hoped he was right. She didn't think he'd like having to postpone all his surgeries because of something as stupid as a case of mistaken identity.

Well, they would worry about that when the time came.

"Do you have your international driver's license?"

"Yes, do you need me to drive?"

He leaned more of his weight on her and another warning shimmy went through her stomach, bringing back all the uneasy sensations she thought she'd banished. Evidently not.

His skin was warm against her. So alive. So—

"Maybe. If you can drive a manual transmission."

He's hurt, Amy, why are you even thinking along these lines?

She responded carefully. "My car at home is actually a stick shift. We don't have quite this much traffic, though, except for when the snowbirds come to town."

"Snowbirds?"

"It's what we call people from the north when they come to Florida to get away from their winter weather."

"Country homes? Like what my parents have?"

She smiled. "Not quite, but maybe the same idea."

Fifteen minutes later, they made it to his car, and Amy helped him get inside, lifting his injured leg and sliding it onto the floor gently. The muscles of his calf were firm, no hint of atrophy from babying his leg. She drew in a deep breath. This was a man who would not baby anything. So if he was letting her do this...

He said something she didn't quite catch before muttering, "I feel like a...an...*idiota*."

That word came through in any language. "Stop it. And get ready to hang on." She then sent him a smile that she hoped was full of mischief. If she could distract him, maybe that would interfere with his body's pain receptors. She'd heard of it working.

"Maybe I should drive."

"If what I'm seeing on your face is any indication of your pain levels, then putting you behind the wheel would be even more dangerous than my mad car skills."

He leaned his head against the headrest. "I do not even want to know what 'mad car skills' means."

"Probably just as well. Okay, here we go."

She stowed her gear in the back and then climbed into the driver's seat, adjusting it to her shorter stature. Roque handed her the keys.

Getting the car started, she managed to back out of the slot and drive up the ramp that led out of the parking garage. "Anything I need to do?" Besides take note of every move the man made?

"No. I already included a tip when I paid."

"Do you have a GPS? If not, you'll have to give me some instructions on how to get to your place." One of her biggest failings was that if she wasn't driving, she didn't pay attention to the route when she was a passenger. She'd tried to correct that trait time and time again, but she either got caught up in the conversation or the scenery.

"I'll put it on my phone. You'll just basically take the Immigrantes Highway all the way back to São Paulo."

"Sorry. That means nothing to me."

"Here." He pushed a button and a voice came out of the phone. It was in Portuguese, so it took a moment or two for Amy to adjust to the computer-generated speech. "Don't worry, I'll help. My leg feels better now that it's not having to support my weight."

Now that her insistence had gotten her what she wanted, she was starting to wonder how smart she'd been in making that offer. Except she was the one who'd caused his pain. The least she could do was try to fix it.

Her heart clenched and she knew she was in trouble with this man. Not that she was going to let herself fall in love with him. She'd meant it when she said she was going back to start her doctoral studies. She couldn't do that in Brazil.

And Roque's life was here. In Brazil. Wrapped up in his work and the life he was living. Just because she liked the way his body felt against hers changed nothing.

The fact that she did meant she'd have to be even more careful. That kiss had sent her senses spiraling toward treacherous territory. If his phone hadn't buzzed...

Yes. That phone. A lifesaver for sure.

There was no room in her life for the long leather sofa she'd seen in his office. And as she'd left the office, her eyes had somehow caught and taken note of the fact that there was a lock on the door.

All they'd have to do was turn the little latch and—

Ridiculous. She needed to stop this!

The GPS said something and she forced her mind back to her driving and getting them home. "Do you live in the same part of town as I do?"

"About five miles before you get there. It's a red-tiled building."

"Tell me when we're getting close, so I can start looking."

For the next twenty minutes or so, he sat in silence, eyes closed tight. She wasn't sure if he'd fallen asleep or if he was in so much pain that he was just trying to cope.

Suddenly he straightened up, glancing at her. "Not much farther."

"On this road?"

"Yes, two blocks ahead on your right. Condomínio Apollo. Just pull into the lower level garage. The numbers are painted on the spaces. I'm 601."

She found his building, and shifting the vehicle into a lower gear, she managed the sharp curving turn that led into what looked like a maze. But the numbers were laid out in order and she found his spot down another line of spaces to the left. Fortunately, most of the tenants were at work so she could navigate fairly easily. Otherwise she might have had to make a couple of three-point turns.

She glanced at him. "Any better at all?"

"I guess we'll find out." His jaw was tight, but that

might be from anticipated pain rather than actual current pain.

"I'll come around and help." She put his keys in the pocket of her sundress, retrieved her purse and beach bag, in case she needed to catch a taxi back to her own apartment, and went around to the passenger side door. Opening it, she said, "Give me your hands."

"Let me have my cane, and I'll see if I can manage."

Without a word she got his walking stick, but instead of handing it to him she draped it over her arm. "Take. My. Hands."

"Amy…"

She got down on her haunches next to the low-slung car and looked him in the eye. "Trust me, Roque. Please. The less strain you put on those muscles right now, the more likely we'll be able to massage the knots out of them."

"Merde."

The swear word was so soft she almost missed it. Her heart ached for him in a way that it didn't for most of the cases she'd worked on. She'd learned early on that if she could harden that traitorous organ it was better for her patients, because she had to push them to help them heal. And it was often painful. She'd had strong, strapping men cry in her presence and had to promise she'd tell no one.

She stood and took his hands in hers and gave them a gentle squeeze. "I want to help. I promise. But I can't do that unless we get you into the apartment." She thought for a second. "Unless you have a wheelchair, or maybe a walker in there somewhere."

"No. No wheelchair. Let's just do it."

She helped him swing his legs around until they were both on the ground. "Okay, whenever you're ready. Grab my wrists."

She moved her hands lower until they wrapped around his forearm and waited for him to do the same. "It'll be stronger this way. I'll be less likely to drop you." She said the words with a smile only to hear him swear again. A little louder this time.

"On the count of three. *Um...dois...tres!*"

That did it. He was out of the car, although he was holding most of his weight on his right leg.

It was no better evidently.

"Okay, we're going to do like we did before. Lean your weight on me." She sensed an argument forming and cut him off. "We can work on the cane once we get into the house."

They made their way to the elevator, and she let him push the button. Sixth floor. "How many floors is this building?"

"Six."

Okay, so he was on the top floor. Once the elevator reached number six, and the doors opened, she realized there were only two doors up here. So these apartments had to be huge. The floor she lived on had six residences on it. "Are your keys on the same ring as your car keys?"

"Yes." The words came out in a short burst of air that told her his strength was flagging.

She quickly fished them out of her pocket and held one of the keys up. He nodded and reached for it, opening the door so fast that she almost lost her balance. She caught herself just in time. It would have been great to say *trust me* and then have them both collapse into the apartment.

She got him as far as the couch and lowered him onto it before saying, "Wait here. I'll be right back."

CHAPTER EIGHT

ROQUE HAD TENSED when she'd joked about him having a wheelchair in his apartment. He didn't. Not anymore. What he did still have was a walker. It was hidden inside a closet in his spare bedroom. He could barely look at his old nemesis without myriad emotions clutching at his gut and threatening to rob the strength from his legs.

He'd gone from a young man who could dance his way through a clump of football players on his way to making one goal after another, to a man who could barely put one foot in front of the other—even with the help of that walker. A man who'd aged twenty years overnight.

He'd always meant to donate it, but he didn't like looking at it, much less try to drag it down to his car.

His body had failed him once, and it looked like it was failing him again.

As much as he tried to suppress it, a hole of fear opened up inside him. What if, despite what he'd said, it wasn't just his muscle? What if the fall onto his ass had knocked something loose, or torn a muscle that he couldn't afford to lose?

His cat appeared from the kitchen and came over

and hopped into his lap. He picked her up and set her beside him. "Sorry, girl. I'll feed you as soon as I can get back up."

Amy reappeared with a trash can and he tensed. "I'm not going to vomit, if that's what you're worried about."

"Of course not. I took the liner out of it and it's clean. I'm going to put some hot towels in there, but I need to know where your dryer is because I'm going to rotate moist heat with dry." She stopped. "Aw...is that Rachel?"

"Yes."

Amy came over and tickled the cat's head, trailing her fingers over Rachel's thick fur. "Hi, there. I've heard about you. Lucky girl, I don't have allergies." Her head suddenly came up and she glanced away from him. "Dryer?"

"I don't have a dryer, but I do have a heating pad."

"Where?"

He nodded toward his bedroom door. "In the closet in my spare bedroom on the top shelf."

Moving toward where he'd indicated, she slid through the bedroom door, reappearing two minutes later. "Okay, so you do have something."

When he looked up, he saw she was holding the heating pad in one hand, and the walker in the other.

"No. Put that away. Right now."

His voice was forceful enough that Rachel hopped off the couch, giving him a baleful glance as she stalked away. But the last thing he wanted to see was a reminder of how weak he'd once been. How utterly helpless he'd felt. Especially when faced with a woman who'd had to help him walk to his own damned car.

Amy set the walker down with a frown. "It's not for forever, it's just to give your leg muscles a break tonight."

"Not tonight. Not ever."

She stared him down for several minutes before leaving the walker where it was and coming over with the heating pad. "Okay, we'll talk about it later."

No, they wouldn't. But damn, she was as stubborn as he was. An unwilling smile came to the surface, despite his best efforts to keep it down. "I wouldn't count on that."

All she did was laugh—a knowing little laugh that said she was going to get her way. Some way or another. Maybe she normally did, since she was the power person in her little physical therapy realm. But she was in his world now. And here, he was used to calling the shots.

Only he was pretty sure that Amy wasn't easily intimidated.

"Let me get set up. It'll just take a few minutes, but in the meantime, I'll plug this in and get some heat going to those muscles. Take off your pants."

Shock rolled through him. There was no way in hell. That was almost as bad as her suggestion to use a walker.

"Not happening. You can do whatever it is you want to do through them."

"No. I can't. Not only can't I, but I won't. I have a towel here." She pulled something out of her beach bag. A huge pink towel with a picture of cats.

"What is that?"

"It's an *Aristocats* towel. You know—like the movie?

You can drape it over your lap, since you seem to be so, er, modest." She said it with a twitch of her lips.

Modest. Sure. He could show her exactly how modest he was. Because despite the pain in his leg and the pain she was in his backside right now, there was a very real possibility that at some point that towel might reveal a muscle problem of an entirely different kind.

"I'll help you take them off, then." Her smile was teasing. Coaxing. And something shifted inside of him. Something he didn't want to examine. And he certainly didn't want her to catch a glimpse of it in his expression. He had to get rid of her for a minute or two, even if it meant taking his damn pants off.

"Fine. Go in the other room, and I'll get them off myself." He would do it if it killed him.

"Okey dokey." She tossed the cat towel in his lap and picked up the trash can and stack of towels and carried it into the kitchen. "Yell when you're ready. Or when you decide you need some help."

He'd just unbuttoned his jeans when she popped her head back into the room. Was she kidding him? "What?"

"I think Rachel is hungry. What does she eat?"

"There are cans in the pantry and her dish is on the floor beside the dishwasher."

This time she stayed gone, while he did his best to shimmy out of the snug garment, sweat beading his lip when he had to put too much weight on his injured leg.

Diabos. What if he had to have surgery on it? Again. Worse, what if he could no longer *perform* surgeries? Or perform at all.

After his accident, it had been two years before he'd

gotten the nerve up to actually try to have sex with someone. Some of that was because of Halee's betrayal, but some of it was also due to his *body's* betrayal.

Well, there was certainly no sign of that kind of trouble tonight. In fact…

He yanked his right foot out of the leg of the jeans and used it to push them off his other leg. He picked up the towel that sported a white cat with a big pink bow around her neck and a smaller one on top of her head.

Caramba! He draped the ridiculous thing over his legs, wondering why he hadn't asked her to leave one of his plain white towels instead. Because they weren't as big as this one was, of course.

A few minutes later, she came back in with the trash can. Curls of steam came out of the top of it.

He frowned. "Exactly how hot are those towels?"

"Pretty hot."

He glanced at her. Several strands of hair had escaped her ponytail, spiraling down her collarbone. And with her standing there in a white sundress that sported tiny little holes all over it, Roque was struck with the thought that the towels weren't the only thing in this room that were hot. Amy was, too. Even the pain in his leg couldn't erase what she did to him. And then there were her feet.

Bare feet.

"What happened to your shoes?"

"They're in my beach bag."

Thinking back, he didn't think she'd put them back on as she helped him walk back to the car. The pavement had to be blistering hot, but she'd said nothing.

And she'd driven his car barefooted. Had come up in the elevator like that and padded across his wood floors.

And that was the impetus he needed to do what she asked. If she could do what was necessary for him, he was going to cooperate with whatever she wanted him to do.

That immediately sent another flurry of thoughts spinning through his head that had no business being there.

"Will the moisture hurt your couch? If so, we'll move this operation to your floor. Or…your bed."

Um…no. Not the bed.

"It won't hurt the couch. And the back folds down to make a bed." The black leather was pretty forgiving.

"That's perfect. How does it work?"

"There's a button on the side of it." He leaned forward so the back wouldn't go sailing down with him on it.

She cranked it down. "Okay. Is the pain in front or in back?"

Even as she said it, a little twinge happened that he needed to suppress—that had to do with a pain of another kind. "It's actually on the outside of my thigh, where the scar is."

"Let's have you lie on your stomach, then, like we would if this were a massage table."

His stomach. Good choice. He relaxed slightly. "I want the towel wrapped around my waist, then."

"Your wish is my command."

And that was a phrase he didn't even want to consider. Because what he suddenly wished for, he couldn't have. Like kisses. The kind they'd shared in his office.

Between the two of them, they somehow got him covered and in position. Then there was a quick sting as she draped one of the hot towels over his left leg and then another on top of that. Then she set the timer on her phone and pulled a vial out of her purse.

He gave it a wary look. Had she gotten some kind of herbal potion from Flávia Maura? "What is that?"

"Relax. It's just a blend of essential oils that I carry around for muscle pain. It has wintergreen, peppermint, lemongrass and a few other things in it. I'm going to mix it with some olive oil I found in your pantry. It will act as a natural analgesic and will help lubricate the skin as I work it." She paused. "Unless you want to take a muscle relaxer. If you have some."

He did somewhere, but he tried to avoid taking them, having had a problem weaning himself off narcotic painkillers after the accident. It had made him leery of taking much of anything. "I'd rather not unless I have to."

"That's what I thought."

She took the towels off and traded them for another two. "Once these cool, I'm going to massage your muscles, using the oils."

Massage his muscles. Great. Well, there was one muscle that he was glad she couldn't see.

Five minutes later her hands were on him. And as soon as her touch hit his skin the pain in his leg became so much background noise. It was there, but it was not what his primary focus was. Her hands squeezed and rubbed and worked in strong capable strokes that had his eyes closing. Only to jerk back apart when she got to the seized area.

"Diabos!"

"Hurt?"

"Yes."

"Good."

His head cranked around to look at her only to have her smile. "I can feel the balled-up muscles, but needed you to tell me I was in the right spot."

"Oh, you're in the right spot, all right."

He gritted his teeth and willed the pain away, forgetting about almost everything else. But still she kept working, kneading, using the base of her palm to push against the tightness in his leg. Fifteen minutes later he realized the pain was ebbing, so slowly he wasn't aware of when it had actually started retreating, but it was fifty percent better. Then sixty. Then seventy-five. And that he could live with.

"Thank you. I think it worked."

"Just give me a few minutes longer. I think I can get the rest of it."

True to her word, when her hands finally went still, her fingers paused to trace the furrow of his scar, sending a shudder through him. She'd taken almost every bit of his pain away. And added a pain from a completely different source.

"Amy, thank you."

Her hand moved away, and he immediately wanted it back.

"You're welcome."

He cautiously rolled over and sat up, keeping the towel in place, and felt no flare in his leg. When he looked at her, though, her cheeks were flushed in a way that might have been exertion, but it also might be…

She'd traced his scar, her fingers soft and sure, and had felt totally different from what she had done moments earlier. It had hit him on an emotional level that was new to him. He normally did not like women lingering over that mark.

She was still kneeling on the rug in front of the sofa, but when she went to grab one of the towels on the floor, he stopped her with a hand to her wrist. Then, unable to resist, he stroked a finger along her cheek. "Leave all of the stuff, and I'll get it in the morning."

"How are you feeling?" She peered up at him with eyes that almost sparkled. And he found he liked it. Wanted to be the reason for that look.

"Better. I can't believe a simple massage had that much of an effect."

In reality, there'd been nothing simple about that massage. Or the effect it had had on him.

"I told you it would work. Do you believe me now?"

"I believe…*you*. I once had another physical therapist, though, who…" Not finishing his sentence, he stood, hauling her to her feet, her hands warming his and sending an answering heat straight to the area he'd been trying to ignore. He stared down at her face, watching as her teeth found her lower lip and pressed deep into the soft skin.

Damn. He should have stayed down on the couch, because now that he was standing, all he wanted to do was…

Kiss her.

He cupped her face, and she tilted it as if waiting. For him. "Hell, Amy. What was in those oils again?"

"Nothing dangerous."

That's where she was wrong. Because something powerful was coursing through his veins, taking control of his thoughts. And if he was reading her expression correctly, she was feeling its effects, too.

"Hey." His thumbs stroked along her jawline, the soft skin creating an addiction that he didn't want to fight. "If I kissed you—in this ridiculous towel—what would you do?"

A dimple played peekaboo in her cheek. "Maybe you should try it and find out."

Her smile said this was one time that she wasn't going to put him on the ground with a sweep of her leg.

So Roque lowered his head and slid his mouth against hers.

The second he touched her lips, Amy melted inside. She'd enjoyed the last fifteen minutes of that massage far too much. His muscles were firm beneath his skin, not flaccid the way she would expect them to be. He felt like an athlete. Even though he was no longer one.

His lips were firm as well, moving over hers in a way that sparked tiny fires of need all along her nerve endings. God, she couldn't believe this was happening. It was like he'd somehow read her thoughts and was thanking her for making him feel better.

Only this didn't feel like it was done out of duty. Or gratitude. It felt like he wanted her as much as she wanted him.

A fling. Wasn't that what she'd envisioned having with some stranger? Hadn't she seen it as a way to jump-start her life and send her in a new direction?

Well, who needed a stranger when she had the perfect man right here in her arms. Someone she knew... trusted. Someone who was safe. Someone whose skin she'd already touched and wanted to touch again. In a completely different way.

She didn't need commitment. Didn't want it. Not the way she'd wanted it in the past, only to be disappointed when the man she'd cared about had suddenly pulled away without so much as an excuse or a goodbye. That had hurt. Enough to not want to repeat that experience.

But she didn't need promises of a future from this particular man.

Amy settled in to enjoy, wanting nothing more than to be swept to bed and revel in his lovemaking.

Only he wasn't going to be able to sweep her up in his arms. And that was okay. She didn't need shows of strength. She just needed him, and what he could do for her.

Her hands slid up his arms, loving the way his muscles corded beneath her touch, her fingers continuing their upward journey, before tunneling into the warm hair just above the collar of his polo shirt.

Roque's head tilted, deepening the kiss, his palms skimming down the back of her dress, before pulling away slightly. He fingered the fabric. "What's the name of this?" he asked as he bunched the skirt in his hands, the cool air in his apartment caressing the backs of her thighs in a way that made her squirm against him. "I haven't been able to stop thinking about it all day."

"About what?" Her mind glazed over, having a hard time thinking beyond what she felt at the front of his towel.

He smiled against her mouth. "This material with

its tiny little holes. It looks so sweet and innocent, but there's a warm sexy side to it that makes me want to explore each and every inch of it."

Thank God that bubbling awareness hadn't been completely one-sided. She'd been more and more conscious of it as the day went by. At least until she'd kicked his feet out from under him.

"Eyelet. I don't know what it is in Portuguese."

"Mmm... I don't, either." His lips ran over her jawline and down her throat, the heat from his mouth almost unbearable. And when he reached the sweetheart neckline of the dress, he brushed along the dips and curves, making her moan. Still keeping the fabric behind her gathered up, he used the fingers of his other hand to find the zipper at the back of her dress, easing it down until he reached her waist. Then he traveled back up, finding the strap of her bra and tugging it slightly. "So you do have one on. This time."

So he had noticed that first day that she wasn't wearing one. Her senses went up in flames.

She didn't want him laying her down on the couch, since she'd worked on him there. This was one time when she really didn't want to mix business with pleasure. Plus, Rachel had come out a couple of times, trying to get their attention, and Amy would rather not have to share Roque with her right now.

Maybe he read her thoughts, because he gave her mouth a hard kiss. "I'm thinking I'd like to be somewhere else. Somewhere a little more private."

Relief swamped through her.

"I was just thinking that myself," she murmured.

Letting her dress go, he took her hand and pulled

her along with him until he reached the back of the apartment, going through a door, which he nudged shut behind them. She took a second to take in her surroundings.

A huge bed, clad in a plain brown quilted spread, sat in the center of the room, large wooden posts making it both masculine and inviting at the same time.

Or maybe that was Roque.

Reaching the bottom of her dress, he hauled it up and over her head, until she stood there wearing only her underwear and her bra, both pink. He fingered the waistline of the lacy briefs. "Are these…?"

She tilted her head. "Are they what?"

"The same underwear that were hanging out of your suitcase that first day?"

Her face flamed to life, remembering the circumstances of that visit. "Yes, they were." Had she subconsciously worn them today, thinking this was where they were going to wind up?

No, there's no way she could have planned any of this.

"They've haunted me for weeks."

She laughed. "And here I was hoping you hadn't noticed them."

He reached down as if he were going to scoop her up in his arms, but she stopped him by stepping out of reach.

"What's wrong?"

A lot of conflicting emotions chased across his face, making her realize he'd misunderstood why she'd moved away. "I don't want you lifting me. Or doing anything that might make that leg act up again. That would make me very unhappy, in more ways than one." She glanced at the bed and then went over and pulled the spread down to the halfway point. "Why don't you lie down?"

"I am not some invalid, Amy."

"Oh, believe me, I know that." To hide the quick ache in her heart his words had caused, she forced a laugh and reached for his towel, whisking it away. He stood there in boxer briefs that gave very clear evidence of what he was feeling. "There. That's more like it."

"You are impossible." But he said it with a smile that chased the ache away. "But there's something else I need. In the nightstand."

Going over to it, she opened the top drawer and found a package of condoms. He was right. They did need something. She'd almost forgotten about protection. Tossing them on the bed, she grinned at him.

"Anything else?"

He nodded. "Yes. If I promise not to do any kind of gymnastics, will you let me take an active role?"

"How active?" She needed to tread carefully.

Coming over to stand in front of her, he gripped her hips and hauled her against him. "Enough to get the job done. For both of us." His gaze turned serious. "Don't put me back in that walker, even in my head. I've been there, and I didn't much like it."

She hadn't been trying to do that, but could see how he might feel a little insecure right now, since she'd been in a place of power as she'd worked on him. Something in her wanted to press the point, but an inner voice warned her that this was one battle she didn't want to win. Because in winning, she would lose.

"An invalid is not what I think of when I look at you. But no gymnastics."

"Not this time."

He didn't try to pick her up again; instead, keeping his hands on her hips, he walked her backward until the backs of her thighs hit the mattress. Then he gave her a soft push and down she went, bouncing a time or two on the soft surface. It felt luxurious and heady, and exactly what she'd been thinking of when she'd imagined being with someone.

The bed was high enough that she could picture him doing all kinds of things to her, and that was enough to make her squirm.

Maybe he sensed it, because he stood over her for a minute and then reached for the pink lace at her hips and peeled it down her thighs. She straightened her legs so he wouldn't have to bend getting them down her calves and then they were off.

"Meu Deus. Você é a mulher mais linda do mundo."

She wasn't the most beautiful woman in the world, but it was nice to hear him say the words. And to hear that her dress had turned him on. And right now she couldn't imagine being any more turned on than she was at this moment.

When he acted like he was going to bend over to kiss her, though, she planted her bare foot on his stomach. "Stay as straight as you can."

"Bossy. So very bossy. But okay. I'll stay all the way up here and just do...this."

He used a leg to part her knees, then wrapped his hands around her thighs and dragged her to the edge of the bed. Then he was right there. Up close and personal.

"Better?" he asked.

"Yes." Her body was on fire.

"But first—" he motioned to an area beside her arm "—I'm going to need that packet."

Oh! That's right. She opened the cardboard box and retrieved one, ripping it open and tossing it to him. He caught it with ease, and set it over her navel. Then he reached down and pulled his shirt over his head and stepped out of his briefs, while Amy unhooked her bra and flung it toward the end of the bed, where it ended up getting caught on one of the bedposts.

He sheathed himself. "Sit up, *querida*."

She did what he asked and realized almost immediately why when he cupped her breasts, stroking the nipples between his fingers and squeezing.

"Ah…" Her arms went behind her to support herself, arching her back and pushing herself into his touch.

"What you do to me…"

His voice had roughened, tones lowering until they were deep-edged with need. Or at least she hoped it was.

Then he reached to cup her bottom and entered her with a quick thrust that stretched her…filled her. Her eyes might have rolled back in her head—she wasn't quite sure. All she knew was that this was like no encounter she'd ever had before. There was normally a lot of foreplay and give and take, but Roque wasn't interested in her doing anything evidently.

She'd been ready to sit and ride him to completion to save his leg from any pain. But what she saw on his face wasn't pain. It was need. Lust. A bunch of things mixed up together that she didn't understand.

What she did know was that she wanted him. Wanted this. Didn't want it to stop.

Except it would, because she was slipping closer and closer to the edge of a cliff, and once off, there would be no going back.

She didn't care, though. Only knew that as he continued to push into her body and then retreat that she was about as close to heaven as she was ever likely to get.

Tipping her face up, he kissed her as he continued to move, wrapping both arms around her back, using his tongue in ways that put every one of her nerve endings on high alert.

"I've wanted this. Almost since you arrived."

That made two of them. "Me too."

She wanted to say more, but the words wouldn't form, wouldn't come, and she was afraid if she said them she might mutter something that she couldn't take back, so she clamped her teeth together. Then she felt him there, seeking entrance, and she pried them back apart. The second his tongue entered her mouth, it was almost too much, and her hands went to the back of his head to hold him there, even as her legs circled his back and pulled him in closer.

"Amy… I'm not going to be able to…"

One of his hands slid between their bodies, seeking something. Finding it. Squeezing and sliding his thumb over that sensitized nub of flesh.

"Go, Roque. Oh, go!" The words came out in a frantic rush that he must have recognized, because he thrust into her at a speed that drove the air from her lungs, even as the edge of that cliff rushed forward and collided with her, sending her over the edge in an instant.

Her body spasmed around him as he continued to surge inside of her, giving gritted mutterings that slid past her ear and escaped into the air around them.

Still he thrust into her, taking a minute or two before he slowed, letting her sink back to the bed, where she lay nerveless and still.

He reached under her and held her tight against him as if knowing what was coming. "No. Not yet."

She echoed those words in her head, knowing once that happened, once they came apart, she was going to be left to try to pick up the shattered pieces of her composure. And she was going to be faced with the reality of what they'd done.

She'd gotten her fling.

But she was very afraid she might have gotten something more than she bargained for—something that wouldn't be easy to put behind her.

All she knew was that she was going to have to try.

CHAPTER NINE

THERE WAS AN elephant in the room that someone didn't want to talk about. And it wasn't him. Worse, his mom told him that she'd sent Amy a card inviting her to a party she was having, but that she hadn't yet RSVP'd. She wanted Roque to "ask" her to come—meaning, coax her into coming.

He was going to do nothing of the sort, although the phone call prompted him to do what he'd been putting off for the last two weeks, as he'd watched Amy frantically work alongside of the other members of the team and then drop just as quickly off the radar. As if she was avoiding being alone with him.

As if?

No, there was no question about what she was doing.

But today, he was headed down to the physical therapy department, where Amy was having her first session with Enzo. He intended to be there when it ended and have his say. Even though he wasn't entirely sure what that was.

All he knew was that he hadn't liked the way things had ended in his apartment. She'd slid out the door almost before he'd caught his breath.

The elevator doors opened and a large open room stood in front of him.

It was a beehive of activity with patients posted in different stations working on whatever task their therapist had given them.

There. He spotted Enzo.

The man gave him a quick wave. He'd passed his swallow test a couple of weeks ago with flying colors, but Roque didn't expect anything different from his old coach. He walked toward Enzo, noticing that while Amy was also there, she didn't quite meet his eyes when she looked at him.

Addressing Enzo, he asked, "How's it going?"

"She hasn't made me cry yet."

His words came out a little garbled because of the changes they'd made to his jaw, but at least he could talk. He was doing speech therapy as well and they were all hopeful that there was no nerve damage. Krysta didn't think there was. She'd been meticulous in her resection of everything. That muscle memory was just going to have to kick back in at some point.

And he was sure it would. It was just a matter of practice and reopening those neural pathways.

"Don't worry, she's still got a month and a half to work on you—there's still plenty of time."

However, Roque had decided he couldn't put off his discussion with Amy any longer.

They'd done nothing morally wrong, but her attitude told him that *she* believed they'd made a mistake. And on some level, so did he. He just couldn't put his finger on why.

This was a temporary assignment for her. And, actually, for him as well. So logically that should make it easier to resolve. But so far, it hadn't.

She really had helped his leg. The day after she'd worked on it he'd only felt a tiny twinge of discomfort that had worked itself out as the day went on. So when he'd told her physical therapy could no longer help him, he'd been wrong. It had been a knee-jerk reaction to what had happened long before she came on the scene.

"I'm feeling better," Enzo managed to get out.

Roque put his hand on his friend's shoulder. "I'm so glad. It must feel good to be at the last part of your journey." He remembered when he was almost done with medical school. The elation and fear he'd felt as he faced the future ahead of him.

Enzo was probably feeling some of that as well.

"He's worked hard today. Hard enough that I'm ready to let him off the hook. At least until next week." Amy smiled, but it was aimed at Enzo rather than him. "Make sure you do those exercises I gave you. They'll really help get your range of motion back again."

Enzo nodded and hopped off the table. They said their goodbyes, and Roque's friend headed for the double doors that connected the physical therapy area with the rest of the hospital.

Once he was gone, Roque turned back to face her. "Do you have another patient right now?"

"No, that was my last one for the day."

"Good. Do you think we can find someplace to talk?"

Her eyes closed for a second before opening. "About what?"

A muscle tightened in his jaw. "I think you know what this is about."

"Yes, I think I do." She sighed and this time looked at him. "Let's take a walk."

She started, then stopped. "How's your leg?"

"It's fine. And yes, before you ask, I am more than capable of walking."

"I didn't mean that."

He wasn't sure why he'd snapped at her. Maybe it was just that he missed some of that quick back-and-forth *jogo de palavras* they'd had before. There was no hint of that teasing manner now. Everything was stilted and formal. Professional. Just like he'd wanted. Right?

"I'm sorry. Let's go to the *pátio*."

Behind the hospital there was a small private garden area with benches where patients or relatives could get out and enjoy the sun or sit under the shade of one of the trees. It reminded him a little of his parents' *chácara* with its greenery. It was also fairly private, with little chance of anyone overhearing them.

They got out to the courtyard and slowly made their way down the bricked path. "I don't actually think I've been out here yet. It's beautiful."

"It is. I came out here a lot when I was a medical student."

She glanced at him. "I didn't realize you did your studies at Paulista."

"I did. I felt like I needed a change of scenery from Rio."

"Your parents moved here to be near you?"

"My mom's family is from São Paulo, so she had no problem relocating. To a Brazilian—as you probably know—family is everything."

He wasn't quite sure how the conversation had turned

in this direction, but it beat the chilly silence he'd tried to ignore for the last couple of weeks. And she'd seemed to relax into the conversation.

"I was always surprised my mom didn't move back to Brazil after my dad died."

"To be near your uncle, you mean?"

Maybe if he brought her thoughts back to her reasons for coming to Brazil, they could both move past the awkwardness of what had happened.

"Yes. She said she and my uncle hadn't spoken in years, though. He disagreed with her marrying so young and so quickly and moving to the States."

Amy hadn't told her uncle about her mother's death. It wasn't the kind of news she'd wanted to break to him over the phone, especially when the man was traveling on business.

Roque wanted to keep her talking, not only because it might help them regain their footing, but also because he genuinely wanted to know. She'd come here because of her mom, to learn a little more about her roots, so maybe he could help her flesh some of that out.

"Did your mom grow up where your uncle lives now?"

"I don't know. She didn't talk much about her life in Brazil. As far as I know, she only came back to Brazil once to visit. When I was a baby. My uncle evidently refused to see her."

"I bet he regrets that now."

"I think maybe he does. At least he didn't refuse to see me." She sighed. "I think the problem was that my mom didn't give him time to process what was happening between her and my dad. My dad worked for one of the major car manufacturers, which has a plant here in São Paulo. He and my mom met on one of his business trips and fell in love. Three weeks later, they were married and heading to Florida. I was born a year after that."

"That was quick."

Amy smiled. "That was my mom. She lived in the moment and gave herself fully to it, not looking back. Maybe that's part of the reason why once she left Brazil, she was loath to come back."

That thought skated through his head for a minute. So once Amy left Brazil would she do the same and never come back?

That sent a pang through him. But it also might mean that if Amy lived in the moment, she would be able to put what had happened between them in the past and not look back at it.

"Do you think you'll come back to visit?"

"I think that depends on how things with my uncle go."

Roque's leg was starting to get tired, so he found a bench and motioned her to it. Sliding onto the seat, he stretched his leg out in front of him to ease the ache.

"So it is bothering you—I thought so."

"Not much. It just gets tired."

"There are some machines back at the—"

He tensed. "I don't want to talk about the machines. I want to talk about what happened back at the apartment."

Her chin went up and she looked him in the eye. "What about it?"

Well, he could name a whole lot of things, but since

he'd brought it up, he needed to get to the crux of the issue and confront it. "Things have been awkward. And I'd like to get past that, if we can."

"I don't know if I can, Roque."

The enormity of those words was a punch to the gut. But before he could formulate a response, she went on. "I've never had sex…well, outside of a dating relationship, and certainly never with a patient. It was unprofessional and I—"

So that's what this was about.

"Let's get one thing straight. I am not your patient."

Her shoulders sagged. "I thought maybe you would wonder if I got involved with—" her hand made a little flourish in the air "—I don't know, people like Enzo or other patients."

Roque turned to look her in the eye. "After my injury, I had a physical therapist in Rio who wanted more from me. She tried to draw out my treatment even after I stopped making progress. Believe me, if I even sensed you were like that, you would be out of the program in a heartbeat." He nudged her shoulder. "You didn't take advantage of me. I wanted what happened as much as you did. We were two people who came together for one night, just like so many others before us."

She smiled. "You have no idea how much better that makes me feel. Well, since we're sharing confidences, I had toyed with the possibility of having a fling with a handsome Brazilian."

"A fling?" His brows went up. "You mean like a *caso*?"

"I don't know what that word means. Like an affair?"

He nodded. "Except neither of us is—" he tried to think of the word "—linked with someone."

"No, we're not. So you're right. I think maybe I made too much of it. Like I said, I was worried about how you might view what we did."

"I view it as completely unimportant."

Something shifted in her eyes, a quick flicker of hurt that made him pause. He'd expected relief, not this…uncertainty. He'd sensed a lack of confidence in her once or twice before. Only this time it wasn't related to her work. It was related to him. "Is that not the right word?"

Her arms wrapped around her waist. "It's exactly the right word."

Except she was no longer looking at him. "Maybe 'inconsequential' would have been a better choice?"

Nothing changed in her face. "Those are both good words to describe it."

An uneasiness gathered in his chest. He wasn't sure where it came from or why her reaction mattered. It shouldn't. He was happy with his life the way it was. No entanglements. No commitments. No one to worry about where he might wind up ten years down the road.

Seeing her holding that walker in his living room had sent acid swirling in his gut. It was like a foreshadowing of what his future might hold. Maybe it was even the reason he'd never brought himself to get rid of the thing.

He did not want to be treated like an invalid. Not by Amy. Not by anyone. It had been ridiculous to feel that way with her. And yet he had—had suddenly felt like he had something to prove, despite her words to the contrary. There was no changing it.

He pushed forward toward his original goal in bringing her out here. "So things between us are good?"

"Yes, Roque, they're good. We should just put it behind us."

And yet the stiltedness was back in her speech. He'd said something wrong, and he had no idea what it was. But he really did want to try to undo it.

So he said something crazy. So crazy he had no idea where the words had come from. "My mom told me she invited you to her party. She very much would like for you to come. And so would I."

Dammit. What the hell are you doing?

"I don't know…"

"It's nothing formal, so there'd no chance that I could step on your dress this time."

She smiled. Finally, and her expression transformed in an instant. "I stepped on it a couple of times myself that night, if you remember. I was very glad my tae kwon do instructor wasn't there to see me."

Mentioning the invitation was the right thing to do. He wasn't sure how or why, but it had clicked something in that beautiful face of hers. "I think he would have been pretty proud of the way you took me down at the beach."

She laughed. "I finally got to see how it works outside of a classroom setting."

"It was quite effective." He paused, then went back to his question. "So you'll come to the house?"

"If you're sure they don't mind. I thought maybe your mom was just being polite."

"Believe me, she wouldn't have invited you if she didn't want you there."

"When is it again?" She got to her feet.

"On the eighteenth."

"I think it depends on whether the head of the department wants me to work or not. He's a pretty intimidating guy."

He got to his feet as well, and it took him a second to realize she was talking about him. He laughed. "Not so intimidating. And no. I'm giving us that night off."

"Okay, it sounds great. Thank you."

Things might not be exactly back to where they were before this had happened. But at least they were on cordial footing again. Hopefully he could keep it that way. At least for the rest of her stay.

Amy picked up a dress off the rack, before putting it back with a sigh. She needed to hurry. Her uncle was finally back from his trip and she was planning on taking a cab to his house as soon as she finished here.

Maybe she should skip shopping and just wear the eyelet sundress she'd worn to the beach again.

No. That dress was going to be permanently retired. She couldn't look at it without remembering Roque's long fingers worrying one of the holes and trying to figure out what kind of fabric it was.

Although their work relationship was better now, there were still flashes from that conversation in the garden that came back to bite her.

Her stomach twisted.

Roque viewed their night together as "unimportant." And it was. He'd been technically right. But still, to hear those words coming from this particular man's mouth had sent shock crashing through her. Changing the term to *inconsequential* had just made it worse.

That's the damn definition of a fling, Amy. Isn't that what you said you wanted? It was one night. Not six months.

She shuffled through more dresses, getting more and more irritated with herself.

Why did you even agree to go to his parents' party?

Because of something she'd seen in his face. Something that said it wasn't as unimportant as he'd said.

And she liked his parents. She really hadn't had a chance to talk with many people outside of the hospital program. This was a chance to get to know life, as her mom had once known it. At least that was what she told herself. And, in reality, she hadn't seen Roque as much in the last week or two as she had in the first half of the program while shadowing him. And she missed it. Missed being invited to watch surgeries, being asked about her opinion on cases. She even missed seeing Peter and Lara, who were still in the orthopedics department.

Roque still technically oversaw her, but as the program was set up to do, she had been passed over to the physical therapy side of things. Enzo's PT sessions were going amazingly well, and periodically Roque had come down to watch. She now found herself watching to see if he would come through that door, which she hated, but it was like her eyes were instilled with a homing device that kept trying to track him down.

At the end of the month, they would all say their goodbyes at the sendoff party, and she would get on a plane and fly back home.

Home?

For the first time in her life Florida didn't quite feel like home anymore. But her life was there. Her career. Her future doctorate work would be done there. She couldn't just uproot herself and come live in Brazil. She barely knew anyone except for Roque, Krysta and Flávia and a few other people at the hospital. And most of those would be leaving when the summer program was over.

Amy shook off those thoughts and picked up another casual dress, although Roque said jeans would be fine. Most Brazilians loved their denim and wore it for a lot of different occasions.

Actually, maybe she would wear jeans. She had a pair that were dark and slim-fitting and showed off her figure. She hoped, anyway.

Why?

Maybe she really did have something to prove. To herself, if nothing else. She'd had her fling—she kept using that term, although could one night technically be considered a fling? She had no idea, since she'd never had one before. But there was still something in her that wasn't satisfied—that wanted more.

But never mind that. She needed to decide on an outfit, and quickly. She was supposed to be at her uncle's house in an hour. It looked like jeans it was. So giving the salesperson an apologetic smile, she headed out the door, looking for the nearest taxi stand.

CHAPTER TEN

THE DAY OF the party arrived and Amy found she was almost as nervous getting ready for this event as she'd been over the cookout at the *chácara*. So much had happened between then and now. She'd visited a beach with Roque, had had sex with him at his apartment. And had visited an uncle she'd never met.

She and Abel had laughed and cried over memories of her mom, and he'd expressed a lifetime of regret over having turned her away all those years ago when she came to visit. He'd promised he and his wife would come visit her in the States once she got back.

The calendar seemed to suddenly be tripping over itself, the dates cascading past like a waterfall. But she wasn't going to think about that. Not tonight.

She tugged on her slim-fitting dark-washed jeans, pulling out a pair of heeled boots to go with them. She then dropped a slinky green top over her head, cinching it at the waist with the same silver-linked belt she'd worn for the welcome party. That soiree seemed like a lifetime ago.

Pulling her hair back in a sleek ponytail and brushing on a coat of mascara and some gloss on her lips, she declared herself ready.

Roque had offered to come get her, but she'd opted to take a taxi instead. Maybe for the same reason she'd packed away that eyelet dress.

Forty-five minutes later, she arrived, walking up the driveway to the sound of laughter. She suddenly wondered just how big of a party this was, and the urge to turn around and run after her taxi welled up inside of her before she shoved it away.

She'd told them she would be here, and there would be questions if she didn't show. Ringing the buzzer at the gate, she leaned down expecting a voice to come over the intercom system. Instead, the door opened and Roque's mom flew down the walkway, clicking open the gate. She gave Amy a kiss on the cheek, which by now she was accustomed to.

"É bom vê-lo novamente!"

The enthusiasm in the woman's voice erased any doubts she might have had about coming. *"Obrigada pelo convite."*

Roque had been right on that front. Exchanging pleasantries in Portuguese had become a lot easier as the weeks marched by. Her tongue no longer tripped over half of the words. She still spoke to Roque in English, however. Somehow it seemed more important to get the words right when addressing him. She still hadn't quite figured out why. Only that it mattered in a way she didn't understand.

If he minded her speaking in English, he didn't let on. He just kept responding in kind, while tossing in a smattering of Portuguese words when he was unsure of something.

Like "unimportant"?

"Come in, come in. Andre is hoping to be home before dinner. He had an emergency call come in a few minutes ago."

With all these people here, it looked like it was sink or swim as far as Portuguese went.

But it was only dinner. She could last an hour or two before her mind went numb from trying to find words.

She followed Claudia into the house and found a charming array of blue and white tile and clean textiles. It was completely different from their *chácara*, but not in a bad way. The space was spotless, and the scents... Her mouth watered.

"Is there anything I can help with?"

"You can keep my son from causing trouble." Claudia said it with a mischievous smile that made her stomach flip.

What kind of trouble?

She didn't know, but as if summoned the man was suddenly walking toward her in black jeans and a white shirt, his sleeves rolled up to reveal tanned arms. Arms that she had seen and felt and...

Ack! No. No thinking about what she had seen of the man. She was pretty sure his mom would not approve of the images racing through her head.

His cane was nowhere to be seen. Wait. No, there it was. By the front door. He evidently was feeling okay.

"You came." He smiled, taking one of her hands and squeezing it.

A warm buzz of electricity traveled up her arm and

burst into pinpoints of heat throughout her body. Yep. It was still there. That awareness that had been there since the very first moment when he'd stepped on her dress. She'd learned so much about him since that time. Had seen a few of his insecurities and had witnessed his incredible, resilient strength.

"I told you I would."

"I know, but when you said you'd take a taxi I had doubts. I am glad you're here."

She didn't tell him she'd very nearly crawled back in that taxi and left. The sincerity in his voice made her glad she'd stayed. As did the fingers that were still gripping hers.

He wanted her here. Unlike when she'd first applied to come, when he admitted he'd very nearly said no.

So much had changed since their first meeting all those weeks ago.

The pinpricks grew in size, attacking her belly... her chest...

Her heart.

She swallowed.

Oh, don't, Amy. Don't. Do not!

It was too late. All the mental lectures in the world were not going to change anything. She was in love with the man.

A giggle came out before she could stop it as a realization struck her. She was a little more like her mom than she thought. But what had taken Cecília Rodrigo Woodell little more than a moment to admit—that she loved someone—had taken Amy nearly three months. And it had been accompanied by a whole lot of denial and fear.

"What's funny?"

"Nothing."

It was true. Oh, *God*, it was true. The man who'd said sex with her had been unimportant and inconsequential...

No, he'd said the words but had been unsure if he'd chosen them correctly. She was ascribing meanings to him that weren't necessarily there. And he'd said he was glad she was here. That had to count for something, right?

Realizing he was still staring at her as if she had two heads, she tried to find a subject that was straightforward—that would conceal the huge shift that had just happened inside of her. "What is your mom cooking?"

"Feijoada."

"I thought it smelled familiar. My mom used to fix that on special occasions. It was a lot of work, but it was so, so good."

"Well, my mom has three great loves in this life. My dad, sewing and cooking. Not necessarily in that order."

She grinned, not so sure why she was suddenly feeling so giddy.

It was supposed to be a fling—a one-night stand. Not true love.

Maybe it wasn't. Maybe she was mistaken. It could be the country itself that she was in love with. As in she would love to stay here.

But she couldn't. Her life was back home.

So where did that leave them? Nowhere. She had no real idea how Roque even felt about her.

Taking her hand, he towed her into the living room. He was at ease in this environment. And as he introduced her to aunts and uncles and three or four cousins, she spotted something on a tall shelving unit in the corner. As Roque continued talking to his relatives, she tugged her hand free, making her way over to the case, where trophies and ribbons and newspaper articles were encased in ornate frames.

She read the name on a couple of the awards and realized these were Roque's. All of them. From his football days. In one framed photograph, a very young-looking Roque stood with Enzo Dos Santos, who introduced him as Chutegol's newest player.

She glanced at Roque to find him watching her. He didn't look quite so carefree anymore as he made his way toward her. And that hitch in his step was a constant reminder of what had changed in his life.

He grimaced. "She treats it like a shrine. Refuses to throw it out. Any of it."

Amy's eyes widened. "You don't seriously want her to, do you? This is part of your life history. Your journey to where you are now."

"It's not relevant anymore. I'm not a fan of hanging on to things that are in the past. Or of saying long goodbyes to things I can't retrieve. I'd rather the cut be swift and final."

The almost brutal words jogged something inside of her. She tried to connect them with something, but couldn't find where to put them.

Just then Roque's mom called them to the dinner table.

She sat next to the orthopedist while seven other people gathered around the meal. In front of them were long wooden trays loaded with different types of meat and sausages. Rice and beans were in deep, black cauldron-like bowls. There were orange slices and shredded sautéed greens. And it looked like home. Like her mom. She blinked moisture from her eyes.

"Andre isn't back, but that's the life of a *polícia*. He'll understand if we start without him."

Claudia stood and served everyone, rather than passing bowls around the table like they might do in the States. When she got to Amy, she said, "Can I put a little of each on your plate, or is there something you don't like?"

"I think I will love all of it."

Including your son.

Soon they were all served and dug into their food. As she suspected, it was luscious and succulent and she was pretty sure she would have to waddle her way out of the house by the time it was all over. Claudia was a wonderful hostess, engaging everyone and making each person feel special.

Including Amy.

She'd half suspected the woman to try to matchmake or make a sideways comment, but she never did. She just smiled and kept everyone's plates and glasses filled.

Maybe it was the wine, but as she looked around the table, she was suddenly glad she'd gone to see her uncle, hoped someday she could meet her cousins as well and have a little of what Roque's family seemed to have. They were full of happiness and hope and just plain love of life.

When Claudia tried to fill her glass again, she shook her head. "Thank you, but I am very, very full. It was all so delicious."

"Mamãe, would you excuse us? I want to give Amy a tour of the house."

"Of course." His mom lifted her glass and smiled over the top of it. "I'll make sure to call you if your father comes home."

He showed her the grounds and the various rooms of the house, taking her up the stairs, showing her the guest bedrooms before walking into his childhood room. Once she was inside, he closed the door and leaned back against it while she looked around. Only in here there were no trophies or pictures of his various accomplishments in football. Instead, there were clippings of various medical cases he had helped with. Pictures of him graduating from medical school.

"*This* is my life. Not the football stuff. I want to live in the present, not cling to the past."

Amy turned to face him. He was speaking in riddles today, and she wasn't quite sure what any of it meant. But when he pushed away from the door and walked toward her, Amy's mouth went dry. He had the same look in his eye that he'd had the day they made love.

"Did I tell you how beautiful you look tonight?"

"No. But then I didn't tell you how handsome you look, either. But you do."

"I thought you didn't find me all that attractive."

"I lied."

He laughed, then reached for her hand and slowly reeled her in. "I've had a hard time taking my eyes off you all night."

Splaying her hands against his chest, she tipped her head back to look at that firm jaw, the slightest dusting of stubble across his chin making her want to slide her fingers across the scruff, let it tickle her cheek, her neck... Her lips parted as the thoughts continued.

"I didn't really want to give you a tour of the house, you know. I wanted to get you alone."

"You did?" She smiled. "I never would have guessed."

"I think that is yet another lie."

"Maybe." Happiness shimmered in her belly, making its rounds as it captured more and more of her doubts and locked them away. "Why did you want to get me alone?"

"So I could do this." His kiss took her by surprise. It wasn't the hard, desperate kisses from their night together. No, this was the slow brushing of lips. The touch and release that repeated over and over until she was breathless for more. He whispered her name, drawing it out in a low murmur that set her heart on fire, made her hope he actually felt something for her, despite what he'd told her in the courtyard at the hospital.

"I want to come to your house, after this. Say yes. Please." His hand came up and cupped her breast, thumb finding her nipple with a precision that made her breath catch. "Afterward I want to talk."

Talk. If his behavior right now was any indication of what he wanted to say to her, it couldn't be bad. Right? Because right now the man was burning red hot and setting her on fire right along with him.

"Yes. And I have something I want to tell you, too. I think I—"

A long pained scream from below shattered the intimacy in an instant.

"It's Mom."

He let her go and opened the door, hurrying down

the stairs and leaving her to follow. When she got to the bottom Claudia was in Roque's arms sobbing uncontrollably, her choppy speech too broken up for her to follow.

And then Roque's eyes came up, and in them was a kind of pain she'd never seen before.

"My father has been shot."

CHAPTER ELEVEN

ROQUE DIDN'T CALL her like he'd said he would when he'd dropped her off at her house on his way to the hospital. And as the hours grew longer she became more and more concerned. She'd offered to go with him, but he thanked her and said he needed to be with his family right now, effectively shutting her out.

She didn't think he meant to; he was just in a hurry. Completely understandable. He was worried.

Well, so was she. She cared about his parents, too. Maybe more than she should.

And she'd been almost convinced he cared about her, too, after the way he talked to her in the bedroom.

She finally gave up waiting and tried to call his cell phone, but it went straight to voice mail after one ring. She didn't leave a message. There was no need. He would know what she wanted. She decided to just go up there instead. She could at least show him support, even if he had to stay by his father's bedside.

Or was it too late? Had he died, and they were all trying to come to terms with it? Seeing Claudia broken and weeping in her son's arms had torn her heart in two. She'd felt helpless, unsure what to do.

She still did.

And that look in Roque's eyes…

She saw it every time she blinked. The despair. The horror.

Calling a taxi, she went to the elevator, glancing at Lara's door and remembering the day of the party and how her eyes had widened when she saw Roque standing in the corridor with her. How embarrassed she'd been.

It seemed like forever ago. And now it was almost over. The goodbye party was rushing toward them at breakneck speed, and once that happened she would have one more day before she boarded a flight taking her back to the States.

And she hadn't told Roque how she felt. She'd started to in the bedroom just before he got the news about his father. And she certainly couldn't do it now.

The taxi ride took a mere ten minutes, but it seemed like hours. The closer they got, the more uneasy she became. If he'd wanted her there, he wouldn't have taken the time to drop her off at the house; he would have just gone straight to the hospital.

Unimportant. Inconsequential.

He'd never taken those words back.

Roque had been a star footballer. He was probably used to adulation and women throwing themselves at him.

Do you really think he could fall for someone like you?

The insecurities she'd felt when she first came to Brazil surfaced all over again: What did she think she was doing here?

But the taxi had pulled up outside of the hospital, so it was too late to turn around. So swallowing, she got out of the vehicle and paid the driver before slowly walking toward the entrance of the hospital.

She spotted Roque immediately; he was sitting in one of the chairs facing the glassed-in entrance to the emergency room, his head between his hands. No one else was around him.

Oh, God. Had his father died? He was a police officer, one of the most dangerous jobs in all of Brazil. She hesitated by the door, trying to decide whether or not she should intrude. Then his head came up and he speared her with a look. He looked neither angry nor glad. He just looked...empty.

She slowly made her way over, clasping her hands together. She sat, leaving one chair in between them, just in case he really didn't want her there.

He sucked in a deep breath and blew it out. "I saw that you called."

Amy had assumed he was busy with his father or trying to comfort his mother. But maybe he just hadn't wanted to talk to her. "I didn't leave a message. I figured you had other things to think about." She hesitated. "How is he?"

"He's in surgery. They don't know if he's going to make it or not." He swore softly. "He went into one of the *favelas* to make an arrest and there was a shootout. A bullet nicked his femoral artery. He almost bled out at the scene. His heart stopped on the ride over."

"I'm so sorry. Your mom...?"

He looked away. "She's in the chapel, praying."

And Roque was not. He was out here. Alone.

The people who were at the house were nowhere to be seen. Maybe they were in the chapel with his mom.

She wanted to touch his hand, but the space between them seemed too great, and not just in terms of physical space. There was something distant in his attitude. Maybe it was just fear and worry.

"What can I do?"

"Nothing. If he lives, he'll have a long recovery ahead of him. That has to take priority for me." He turned to look at her. "I've asked to be replaced for the rest of the lecture series, so you'll be working with someone else for the remainder of your stay. I probably won't be at the sendoff party. Or see you before you leave. I'm sorry about that."

He was sorry that he wouldn't be there to see her leave? But not about the fact that she *was* leaving? That he might never see her again?

She was being selfish. The man's father might die, for God's sake. She could always talk to him on the phone before she left.

And maybe it would go straight to voice mail like it had tonight.

What had he said back at the house?

His voice ran through her head as if he were reciting the words all over again: *"I'm not a fan of hanging on to things that are in the past. Or of saying long goodbyes to things I can't retrieve. I'd rather the cut be swift and final."*

He hadn't offered to keep her updated on how his dad was doing, while she was here or once she left Brazil.

Her stomach cramped with grief.

She wasn't going to sit by the phone and wait, though.

Not this time. Evidently ghosting could occur while the person was sitting right beside you.

She stood. "I understand. You need to be here with your dad. Please tell your mom that I'm thinking about her and hope Andre will be okay."

"Thank you."

Amy looked at him for a long time, committing the lines and planes of his face to memory. Then in a soft voice she said, "Goodbye, Roque."

And with that, she turned and walked away.

She was right. He didn't contact her—although she had heard that his father pulled through his surgery. Nor had he come to see the final days of Enzo's physical therapy treatments. And he was nowhere to be seen at the party, which was now in full swing.

These festivities didn't seem as new or full of hope as the welcome party had. Amy could see Francisco Carvalho chatting quietly to Krysta, his face full of sadness. And her friend told her that Flávia had been bitten by a venomous snake not long ago and had almost died. Thankfully she'd made an almost miraculous recovery. Amy hoped there were enough miracles floating around to touch Roque's dad in his long rehabilitation. She still wished Roque well. Despite a heart that was swollen and heavy. Of all the people to fall in love with.

All she could do was go home and do her best to forget him. Pack him away like that white eyelet dress of hers.

She could throw herself into her doctoral studies where she had no time to think about anything except school. Roque was right about one thing: letting go of the past. She'd held on to her parents' home for far too long, treating it almost like a shrine, the way Roque's mom did with his football memorabilia. She loved her mom and dad and they would always be with her, but she needed to make a fresh start. Maybe even in another part of the country.

This time she could do things right and not hold on to what she couldn't have. So, taking one last look around the swanky decor with its loud music and sad goodbyes, she looked for the nearest exit and showed herself out.

Roque's dad was finally out of the woods after three grueling weeks of advances and setbacks. He was going to have to go through cardiac rehab to strengthen the damaged muscle in his heart, and it would take months before he could go back to work, and that might not even happen if he couldn't recover enough of his strength. But he was nearing retirement age and was thinking about just handing in his badge and drawing his pension. It was certainly what his mom wanted.

And what did Roque want?

He knew he hadn't been exactly welcoming when Amy came to the hospital, but his thoughts had been so chaotic he hadn't had time to think. His dad's surgery had made him realize how uncertain life was. How painful endings could be. As he'd sat in the waiting room his thoughts had turned to Amy right about the time her call came through.

When Roque's own injury had sidelined him, he'd tried his damnedest to hold on to his old life, convincing himself that he was going to play football again. It had taken the reality of using a walker for months, and a visit from Enzo Dos Santos, to make him realize he needed to let go.

Which is what he'd needed to do with Amy. She had her whole life ahead of her. Her whole career. He told her he knew she was going to get her doctorate one day, and she said she was planning to start working on it when she got home. She couldn't do that if he was sitting there clinging to her, like he'd clung to his football dreams.

He'd had no business sleeping with her. Or anything else. It had been rash and irresponsible, and if he'd followed through with what he'd been about to tell her in his childhood bedroom, he could have derailed her life. It had been on the tip of his tongue to ask her to stay in Brazil. With him.

He realized as he was sitting at his mother's dinner table that he loved the woman. In a way that he couldn't say of any other woman. Not even Halee.

And as his mom sat in the chapel of the hospital, begging her husband to stay with her, begging God to keep him there by any means necessary, he knew he couldn't do the same with Amy. He wasn't going to ask some deity to make her stay, wasn't going to make promises he couldn't keep.

He was going to let her go. *Because* he loved her. Because he wanted her life to be as rich and full as it could be. His life before his accident had been selfish and self-serving. He thought he'd grown past all of that. Until he realized he'd be going back to his old ways if he asked her to stay.

There was a knock at his office door. He grunted

at whoever it was to come in, only to meet his mom's chiding face.

"Roquinho, is this how you greet your mother?"

"I'm sorry. Is Papai okay?"

"He is in rehab and doesn't want me there. He can't stand for me to see him weak. What he doesn't know is that he's the strongest man I've ever met." She leaned over his desk, her hands planted on its surface. "And I thought you were just like him. But now I am not so sure."

He barely kept himself from rolling his eyes. He knew exactly where she was headed with this. "She's going to continue her education, Mamãe. I'm not going to keep her from her dreams."

"Did you *ask* her what her dreams were?"

"I already know what they are."

"So you didn't. And when you were hiding in your bedroom with her? Why did you not ask her then?"

He couldn't hold back a laugh. "How did you know where we were?"

"I know where all young men want to go with a pretty woman. One they're in love with." She dropped into the chair in front of his desk. "Don't try to deny it."

He gritted his teeth and forced his way through. He did not want to talk right now. Not about Amy. Not about anything. He wanted to work.

"It changes nothing."

She leaned forward. "Why not ask her?"

"I already told you. I know what she wants." He picked up a pencil and twirled it between his fingers. "Asking her to give that up would be selfish."

"Why would you ask her to give it up? A…what did you say? Doctorate? It takes how long to get?"

"I don't know. Three years. Why?"

She blinked. "Oh, Roquinho. Don't you see? Three years is not such a long time."

"I don't see how any of this—"

She held up her hand. "She left Brazil to pursue her dream, yes? So why can you not leave Brazil…to pursue *her*?"

He sat back in his chair, the creaky wheels in his head starting to turn again. For someone who was not even a surgeon, his mom had cut clean through to the heart of the matter. Why couldn't he go to the States to be with her, while she worked on her degree? With his credentials, he could probably do something while he was there, maybe even research how to get his certification in the States. But that wasn't what was important; it was something that could be decided afterward. Once they both got what they wanted: Amy her degree and a fulfilling career. And maybe Roque…could somehow, in some weird twist of the universe, get Amy.

If she would even have him after the way he'd brushed her off.

All he could do was try. The question was, was he willing to?

Yes.

He came around the desk and took his mom's wise face in his hands, giving her a hard kiss on the cheek. "Have I ever told you how glad I am that you're my mother?"

"I think you just did."

She stood up and hugged him tightly. When she let him go, he saw tears in her eyes.

"Now, go. And tell her I would like to work on another of her dresses. This time it will be white with layers and layers of lace."

"I'll tell her. I promise."

CHAPTER TWELVE

AMY SAT IN her first day of classes, trying to concentrate on what the professor was saying. But even two months post-Roque, her thoughts still returned toward him. And it made her furious.

He doesn't love you, Amy. Get over it.

He would have made some effort to contact her if he felt anything at all. She'd been so, so sure that he cared when he kissed her that last time in his bedroom. But she'd given him every opportunity to say something. And instead there was only silence. A silence which continued even now.

Class was dismissed, and she headed out to the parking lot, slinging her book bag over her shoulder. Getting her degree seemed so worthless right now. *Right now* being the operative words. Once she stopped daydreaming about a certain Brazilian orthopedic surgeon and stopped seeing him at every turn, like at that lamppost over there.

She rolled her eyes, until she realized she'd never actually seen him teleported from her head to a physical location. Looking again, thinking she'd just mistaken someone else for him, she stopped dead in her tracks when she realized she wasn't mistaken. And he hadn't teleported.

He was here. In Florida, looking just as outrageously gorgeous as he had in Brazil.

Then he smiled. And, just like always, something inside of her somersaulted.

What was he doing here? Was he at a conference?

Maybe—but that didn't answer the question. Why was he *here*? At the university where she just happened to be studying.

He pushed away from the post and walked toward her, his cane nowhere to be seen.

"Is…is your dad okay?"

"He's still in rehab. And retiring from the force, which makes my mother very happy."

"I'm so glad." And she was. She knew Andre had survived his surgery, but the last news she'd heard after that was that it was still touch and go.

She had been in contact with Krysta and Flávia, and it seemed she wasn't the only one who'd had man trouble while in Brazil. She'd been too busy with her own love life to realize that her two friends were also sliding down the same slippery slope she'd been stuck on.

She hoped they both got their happy endings, but as for her, she'd been so sure she wouldn't be one of them…

Except Roque was here.

"Let's try that again, shall we?" The smile was still in place. "Hello, Amy."

"Hi."

Good going—you couldn't think of anything more profound than that?

"You look good. You've started on your studies obviously." He nodded at her bag.

"I have." Why wasn't he telling her why he was here? Was he trying to torture her? Had she left something behind in Brazil?

Ha! She had. But it wasn't something you could pack in a bag and carry through customs.

"Can we walk?" The last word stuck in her throat. She remembered the last time she'd suggested they do that. It had been to say that sleeping together had been a mistake. And it evidently had been. But try as she might, she couldn't make herself regret the short amount of time they'd spent together. She'd hold it with her for the rest of her life, just like that shrine Roque's mom had made out of his football artifacts. Because he was wrong. Some things shouldn't be tossed away as if they never existed.

He fell into step beside her, that little hitch of his still in evidence. But she loved it. Still loved everything about him.

"I don't know where to start. Other than to say I was wrong."

"Wrong?"

"Wrong to not call you. Wrong to not try to work out some kind of alternate solution for a very real problem."

She stopped, her heart flipping around in her chest. "What problem is that?"

"The fact that I live in Brazil, and you live in Florida." He smiled. "It took my mom to make me realize that it's not such a big problem at all."

Was he kidding? This wasn't just a matter of physical distance. He'd been like a water spigot. On one second and off the next.

"But you were hot, then cold, and now… I'm very confused." Her mind was still stuck somewhere behind her and was pedaling as fast as it could to catch up. "I thought you weren't a fan of long goodbyes."

"I'm not. But I was mistaken in thinking this had to be goodbye at all."

And just like that, the spigot was on again. She wasn't sure she'd be able to survive if he suddenly turned it back off. She needed to be sure. Very sure.

"Are you saying you don't want it to be?"

His fingers bracketed her face, and her eyes shut at the exquisiteness of feeling his skin on hers once again. "No. I don't want it to be."

"But how can you be sure? You were so distant at the hospital."

He gave a pained laugh. "Part of it was the shock of the shooting, but part of it was the realization that your future was half a world away from mine. I was trying to do the right thing and let you walk out of my life."

"Try? You were very good at it, from what I remember."

"I know. And you don't know how many times I've regretted it. Am I too late?"

No, he wasn't. And hearing his explanation made all the missing pieces fall into place. She finally understood why he'd seemed so distant. So completely unmoved by her presence. She'd done quite a bit of pretending herself over the course of her time in Brazil. Suddenly she knew what she was going to do. He'd sacrificed something. Maybe it was time for her to do the same.

"I can drop out of the program. I only just started and—"

"No. You're not going to do that. I want you to finish."

She reveled in his words, his touch…his very presence. In those talented hands that were bringing hope back to life. "I don't want you to feel you have to wait for me, though."

"My grasp of English is not always good, but I think if we change out one little word, it will make more sense. I'm not going to wait *for* you, Amy. I'm going to wait *with* you. Here in Florida." He stopped for a second. "I love you. I was wrong not to say the words earlier, to let you go the way I did. Once I realized the truth, there was still my visa to get and flights to be arranged. What I had to say couldn't be said over the phone, which is why I didn't call you."

He kissed her cheek. "I'm hoping maybe you feel a little something for me, too."

There were a couple more things she needed to understand, although she was pretty sure she already knew the answers.

"You called our time together unimportant."

"Yes. I knew that I'd chosen the wrong word. Because it wasn't unimportant. It turned out to be the most important thing I'd ever done in my life. More important than my football days. More important than my medical career. I found love, when I thought I never would again."

She shut her eyes, and when she reopened them, he

was still there, the imprint of his lips still fresh on her face. "You crazy, gorgeous surgeon, I do love you. You had to realize."

"I thought I had. But when my dad was shot, I realized I didn't want you giving everything up for me. But you don't have to."

She thought for a moment. But that still left… "I don't want you giving everything up for me, either."

"That is a bridge we can cross in three years. When you walk down the aisle of the university and hold your degree in your hands."

He was really going to do it. He was moving here. For her. Because of her. With her. There were all kinds of prepositions she could substitute that would each end with her being with the man she loved.

"Paulista let you leave?"

"They did not have a choice. I was coming, whether they liked it or not. But the administrator assured me that I would have a job waiting if I ever decided to come back."

If he ever. "You mean you might stay here? For good?"

"It's a possibility. I actually contacted a nearby hospital and asked what the process would be to have my medical license transferred over. They want me to come in for talks. But I didn't want to commit unless I know where your heart is."

"That's the easiest question of all, Roque. My heart is wherever you are. I love you."

He leaned over and kissed her, this time on the lips, right there in the parking lot of the university. The world around them was still turning, but she felt like this moment was suspended in time. When he finally raised his head, he said, "Before I forget. My mom has a message for you."

"She does?"

"She wants you to know that she has dreams of her own. Of working on another of your dresses. Only this one would be all white and would see me waiting for you at the end of another kind of aisle."

He reached in his pocket and fished out a little velvet container. But when he started to go down on one knee, she stopped him. "Your leg."

"My leg will survive. Let me do this." He knelt in front of her and snapped open the lid of the box. Inside was a gorgeous ring, a center diamond flanked by two glowing emeralds. "Amy Woodell, will you marry me? Both here and in Brazil?"

"Yes. Oh, yes! I'll marry you wherever you want."

"We can have the ring resized, but I wanted to bring it." He plucked it from its velvet bed and slid it onto her finger. It fit almost perfectly. "I love it." She couldn't stop looking at it, almost too afraid to believe this was happening.

"Amy?"

"Yes?" She shifted her attention back where he was still kneeling in front of her.

"When you're done admiring that, I may have overestimated the abilities of my leg."

She stared at him, then realized what he meant and burst out laughing. Laughter she tried her best to suppress. It was no good. In between chuckles, she managed to get out, "Here. Let me help."

She hauled him to his feet, and soon all thoughts of laughter were swept away by the power of Roque's kiss. And by the very strength of his love.

EPILOGUE

AMY WAS NOT the bride. Not this time, anyway.

That had happened six months earlier, and Claudia had indeed made her dress.

But she *was* one of the bridesmaids at this particular ceremony, as was Flávia. Her two lecture series friends had also gotten their happy endings, and she was thrilled for them both.

Krysta and Francisco stood in an intimate circle of their family and closest friends and repeated the vows they'd written to each other, their voices ringing with happiness and conviction.

Roque gripped her hand tightly, leaning slightly on his cane today. But it was okay. They'd each learned to provide support to the other when it was needed the most.

Krysta's wedding was much different from her own, but it was still beautiful, their love for each other permeating the air around them.

She glanced to her right and caught sight of Flávia holding her baby against her chest, her husband's arm around her shoulders. No one had realized the venom specialist was pregnant during the last part of their stay in Brazil, not even the man standing next to her.

Those days spent together at Paulista seemed like an eternity ago. But the hospital's pull on them was still strong, the bonds forged during their time together proving to be unbreakable. Unlike Roque's words, she didn't want to say goodbye to that past, since it had played a role in the future they were carving out together.

And whether they decided to come back to Brazil after she earned her degree or stay in the States, she knew it wouldn't matter one way or the other as long as they were together.

Evidently the other two couples felt the same way, because standing in a simple garden in a small Brazilian town near where Francisco's family lived, the friends were bearing witness to a love they'd all found.

The officiating minister lifted his right hand and pronounced Krysta and Francisco husband and wife. And when he invited the bride and groom to kiss, it wasn't the only kiss that was had in that tiny garden.

And it wouldn't be the only kiss in the days to come. For Brazil had woven a tapestry of love and friendship in their lives that would endure long after they said their goodbyes and left for different parts of the world.

Because that was what love did.

It endured. For always.

* * * * *

FROM HAWAII
TO FOREVER

JULIE DANVERS

MILLS & BOON

CHAPTER ONE

As SHE STEPPED off the plane in Honolulu, Dr. Katherine Murphy shook the last few drops of water from her snow boots. When she'd boarded the plane in Chicago, snow had caked her boots and dusted her winter coat. A few droplets of water were all that had managed to survive the flight, and now she shook them off with relish. Back home, temperatures were below freezing and the snow was several inches deep. But here in Hawaii a steady, gentle breeze rustled through the palm trees.

Goodbye, ice and cold, Kat thought, stepping into the early-morning sun.

Although she was still wearing the winter clothes she'd had on when she left, her carry-on luggage contained sixteen bathing suits, a floppy hat and sunglasses, and numerous pairs of flip-flops. At the last minute she'd remembered to throw in her white coat and a stethoscope before zipping the small suitcase shut. The rest of her belongings had already been shipped separately to her new home on the island of Oahu.

Kat couldn't believe that just three weeks ago, she had been one of the most respected physicians in Chicago. Three weeks ago she'd expected to be promoted to head of the internal medicine department at Chicago Grace Memorial, the prestigious hospital where she'd completed her residency and spent most of her career. Three weeks ago her future had seemed stable, secure and predictable.

Three weeks ago she and Christopher had been days away from getting married.

Kat glanced at the faint line on her finger where her engagement ring used to be. She still felt a hard lump rise in her throat every time she thought about the breakup.

Tears blurred her eyes, but she fought them back and tried to smile as an airport attendant greeted her warmly and placed a beautiful *lei* of purple orchids over her head. Kat shook the tears away and raised her chin. Her new job as an internist and infectious disease specialist at Oahu General Hospital was a chance for a fresh start, and there was no point in dwelling on the past.

Goodbye, old life, she thought. *And goodbye, Christopher.*

Leaving her steady, predictable life in Chicago and moving to Hawaii ranked very high on the list of things Kat had thought she would never do. But then, she'd also never thought she would lose her promotion, her job and her fiancé on the same day.

In her mind, she thought of it as the Day of Doom.

Three weeks ago she'd huddled under a thick down blanket inside her apartment, the outside world covered with an even thicker layer of February snow, trying to figure out how she could ever face the world again. Everything she'd ever worked for—her medical career, her wedding, her family's hopes and dreams for her—had disappeared in an instant.

She'd just begun thinking about how long she could reasonably hide in her apartment before she would need to forage for food when her best friend from medical school had called with an intriguing proposal. Selena was the clinical director at a small hospital in Hawaii, and she'd called to ask if Kat knew anyone who would be interested in working in Honolulu for one year, to assist with research into and treatment of a rare strain of flu.

Kat had shocked herself by volunteering for the position.

Her mother and her friends in Chicago had been equally shocked. Kat couldn't blame them. Making spontaneous, impulsive decisions wasn't exactly her strongest personality trait. From the time she was sixteen and had decided she wanted to be a doctor, every important decision she'd made had been the result of careful planning and research. Everything in her life from her career to her closest relationships had been built on a foundation of logical, practical choices.

Kat's friends told her she was "certifiably Type A," and Kat had to admit that they were right. She was never one to leap without looking first.

But that had been the old Kat. The Kat who had been blissfully unaware of how much life could change in a single day.

Kat had always thought that her cautious, well-planned approach to life would protect her from unexpected surprises. She'd believed that if she was prepared for anything then she would be able to handle whatever life threw at her. But now, as she felt the empty space on her ring finger, she realized that what people said about best-laid plans was true: you could plan and plan, but you never really knew what would happen next.

Kat had spent her life planning, but she still hadn't been prepared for the breakup. And she definitely hadn't been prepared to lose her job—a job she'd loved and had spent her entire career working toward.

Yes, m'dear, you have definitely hit a low point, Kat thought to herself as she stepped out of the airport.

And caught her breath.

She had never seen such lush natural beauty in her life. Pink and yellow plumeria flowers lined the sidewalk, their scent wafting toward her and mixing with the perfume arising from the *lei* of orchids she wore around her neck. In the distance, mountains rose to meet a cloudless blue sky. Each path was framed by tall palm trees with large fronds that waved gently in the cool breeze.

Kat stopped and took in a slow, deep breath. The air itself smelled of flowers, and she wanted to savor the scent.

As she inhaled, she suddenly wondered when she had last stopped to breathe so deeply. She couldn't remember. Her life after medical school had been all about the fast pace of the ER. Someone had always needed her time or her attention, and needed it right away. But now, for the first time in years, there was no emergency to attend to. In this moment no one was expecting anything from her. No life-or-death decisions awaited her attention.

In this moment, all she had to do was breathe.

She blinked in amazement at herself. Thirty seconds in Hawaii and she was already stopping to smell the roses—or, in this case, the hibiscus. It was a decidedly un-Kat-like thing to do, and yet she felt more like herself than she had in weeks.

After everything that had happened she'd begun to feel as though she didn't even know who she was anymore. But now, as she gazed at the fairyland-like landscape before her, she started to feel something she hadn't felt in several weeks—something she hadn't even realized she'd lost after the Day of Doom.

It was hope.

Hope and something more than that—excitement.

There was something about the mountains in the distance that suggested endless possibilities, and Kat closed her eyes and noticed that the gentle rushing sound in the background wasn't just the wind; the ocean was adding its voice to the air as well. She was well on her way to falling in love at first sight—with Hawaii.

Maybe I'm not at such a low point after all, she thought. *Maybe this is the start of something.*

As she gazed at the natural beauty around her Kat realized that she didn't want to go straight to her new apartment. Going directly to her new home and getting things settled was something the old Kat would do. The old Kat would want to carefully organize her things and research her new neighborhood for essentials like the grocery store and the post office. But the new Kat, she decided, was going to have different priorities. And the new Kat's first order of business was to relax.

But how?

It had been so long since she'd had a moment to

herself that she had absolutely no idea what relaxing even meant to her. In all her years of study, after all her classes on chemistry and human anatomy and physiology, she had overlooked one important thing. She had forgotten to learn how to relax.

She resisted the urge to look up a dictionary definition of the word *"relax"* on her phone.

I guess this is what comes of all work and no play, she thought.

She hoped she hadn't completely lost her ability to live in the moment. She had dreamed of becoming a doctor at an early age, and it had been a dream that required an incredible amount of study and discipline. She'd been so focused on her medical career that she'd never had the chance to have a wild, carefree adolescence.

Well, maybe it was time. Could someone in their late twenties still have a wild adolescence? Kat decided she would damn well try.

This year in Hawaii would be her chance to learn how to let loose and be spontaneous. She'd spent her entire life being responsible, and where had it gotten her? Jobless. Jilted—practically at the altar. If all her careful planning, her endless pro-con lists and her thoughtful decision-making had led to so much heartbreak, then maybe it was time to try a different approach to life.

She only had one year. One year away from the expectations and preconceptions of everyone who knew her. Surely there was no better place to learn how to relax and live in the moment than a gorgeous setting such as this?

She heard the faint sound of the ocean again and it

deepened her resolve. This year wasn't just going to be about putting Christopher behind her, she decided. It would be about putting the old Kat behind her.

But how did one *learn* to relax?

It can't be that hard, she thought. *If I can master organic chemistry, I can master this.*

In fact, Kat decided, she might be able to approach learning how to relax and getting over Christopher in much the same way she had gotten through organic chemistry and her other difficult classes. She would make a detailed list of her goals and then follow through with each step.

A small voice in the back of her head suggested that this might be the most Type A way that she could possibly approach relaxation, but she chose to ignore it.

How to relax in an island paradise while getting over a devastating breakup. Step one: find a beach, she thought.

Kat looked down at her snow boots in dismay. Considering the cold in Chicago, and on the flight, the boots had been a sensible choice. But now that she was here they looked ridiculous. Her feet were stifled; she couldn't wait to feel sand beneath her toes.

She had her favorite blue-and-yellow-striped bikini on underneath her heavy winter clothes. She'd fantasized about going for a swim on her first day here in Hawaii, but she'd thought she'd see her new home first. Now that she was actually here, it seemed impossible to wait.

A few moments of research on her phone informed her that the nearest beach was "a pleasant twenty-min-

ute walk from the airport." Surely there would be somewhere she could change out of her clothes?

Kat hitched her carry-on bag over her shoulder and
headed toward the water, her face set with determination. She was going to learn how to relax or die trying.

Jack Harper wasn't usually an early riser, but he'd been
wandering the beach since dawn. He held his father's
letter crumpled in his fist. Choice lines were burned
into his brain.

> *Many medical schools have a rolling admis-*
> *sions policy.*
> *I could make a few phone calls and you could*
> *easily start in the winter semester.*

Jack ran his hand through his dark hair in frustration. He *liked* being a paramedic, dammit. But it didn't
matter how many times he'd told his father he was never
going back to medical school. There was no other path
that his parents could understand.

> *It's time to apply yourself.*
> *You've had your fun in Hawaii. But now it's*
> *time to come back to real life.*

To his father, real life meant Lincoln, Nebraska.
Jack couldn't imagine a place more different from
Hawaii.

Lincoln was as fine a hometown as any, but he'd been
glad when he was able to exchange the cornfields, cows

and cold winters of his childhood for the lush mountain landscape surrounding Honolulu.

His parents, grandfather, and two brothers still lived in Lincoln, where they were all physicians. Both of his parents were highly respected, world-renowned medical researchers, his younger brother Todd had joined their grandfather's small family practice, and his older brother Matt was a surgeon.

Five doctors in the family. Five Type A personalities who were convinced that they were always right. Five people with egos larger than the Hawaiian mountains that loomed over the ocean.

In Jack's opinion, five doctors in the family was plenty. Three years of medical school had been enough to convince him that a doctor's life wasn't for him. He was much happier as a paramedic—especially here on the island of Oahu.

After dropping out of medical school to join the Navy SEALS—another life decision his parents had disapproved of—he'd completed his basic training in Hawaii and never lived anywhere that felt more like home. He'd rescue a burn victim one day and deliver a baby the next—all while surrounded by an island paradise that meant more to him than anywhere else on earth.

He loved his job—both for the adrenaline rush and for the opportunities it gave him to save lives. But his parents wouldn't take his career choices or his desire to live in Hawaii seriously, and they continued to act as though he were on some sort of extended vacation.

He and his parents were very different people.

Nowhere was this more evident than in the last paragraph of his father's letter.

> *You're thirty-one years old. You have to start thinking about your future.*
> *Plenty of women in Nebraska would like to start a family, and your mother's getting older and would like more grandchildren—*

At that point Jack had stopped reading. He couldn't believe either of his parents would bring up marriage after his older brother Matt's betrayal. Matt—the golden boy of the family.

Jack snorted. It had been four years since he'd spoken with Matt or Sophie, but Jack's heart still twinged every time he thought about his older brother and his former fiancée. After being betrayed by the two most important people in his life, the last thing he wanted was to get emotionally involved in a relationship again.

As far as Jack was concerned, getting emotionally attached meant getting hurt, and that wasn't something he was willing to put himself through again. Oh, he'd had his share of dates, and there were many women willing to enjoy his company for an evening, or even a few evenings. There were certainly plenty of tourists who seemed to want Jack to fulfill their fantasies of an exotic island fling while on vacation, and Jack was happy to oblige.

But he was careful never to get too involved with anyone. If protecting his heart meant that he had to keep his guard up and keep his distance, then so be it.

Jack smoothed out the letter one last time, then crumpled it into his fist again. He resisted the urge to throw it into the ocean. The sky was clear, the water was calm and perfect, and there was no point in brooding on the beach about a past he couldn't change. He and Sophie were done, and had been for a long time. Everything that had passed between him and Matt and Sophie was long in the past.

So why did all of it still bother him so much?

Sometimes Jack wondered if keeping himself emotionally distant from everyone had actually made it harder to recover from his disastrous engagement to Sophie. But when he thought about the memories it was too painful. He hadn't just lost Sophie—he'd lost his brother, too. The one person he'd thought he could count on, no matter what.

Growing up in a family full of doctors had had its own unique pressures. Sometimes it felt to Jack as though he'd begun to feel the weight of his family's expectations the moment he was born. But, as much as Jack had felt pressured to succeed at school and in his career, it was nothing compared to what Matt had gone through.

Matt, two years older than Jack, had experienced all the pressure Jack had as well as the added expectations that had gone along with being the oldest Harper sibling. Their parents had always expected Matt to be responsible for Jack, and as a child Matt had taken that responsibility seriously. Whenever Jack had been hurt, whenever he'd had trouble with friends or begun struggling in school, he'd been able to talk to Matt about it.

In return, Jack had hero-worshipped Matt throughout their childhood. If Jack was honest with himself, he'd hero-worshipped Matt for a good part of his adult-hood, too.

He'd always thought that he and Matt would stand by each other, no matter what. But after Matt had confessed what had happened with Sophie, Jack hadn't been able to stand being in the same room with him. They hadn't spoken in four years.

A faint cry for help broke through his thoughts and he scanned the water with the trained eyes of a first responder. There—a woman swimming, far out from the shore. Too far. And going farther. She was caught in a rip current that was carrying her out into the ocean, and she was going to exhaust herself trying to swim against it.

Jack snapped into action. This was one of the quieter beaches; there were no lifeguards on duty. He dialed the emergency number on his phone and let the dispatch unit know what he was about to do. Then he dropped his phone and stripped off his shirt, revealing a smooth, well-muscled chest and the powerful arms of a former Navy SEAL.

A crowd of children who had been playing in the surf began to gather on the beach, having spotted the danger the woman was in.

"Let me borrow that," he said to one of the children, grabbing the boy's body board without waiting for a response.

He ran out into the ocean, letting the rip current do the work of carrying him out to the swimmer. When he finally reached her, he could see he'd been right. She'd been trying to fight the current instead of swimming parallel to the shore. And she was clearly terrified. He knew he could get them both back to safety, but first he'd need to calm her down.

Despite the woman's terror, he couldn't help but notice her fiery red hair. He'd always liked redheads…

Focus, he thought. *She has to stay calm. Help her relax.*

"Looks like you swam out a little further than you planned," Jack teased, attempting to lighten her fear. "You do realize it's not possible to swim all the way back to the mainland, right? You'll need to book a flight for that."

The woman coughed and choked. She looked frightened, but Jack could tell she was doing the best she could to keep her fear from overwhelming her. He admired that. Most of the time during water rescues the bulk of his work involved keeping the victim from making things worse by panicking. But this woman was doing her best to follow his instructions.

"The current…" she gasped. "It's too strong. We'll never get back to shore."

Jack forced himself to stay calm, even as the rip current continued to pull both of them further from the shore.

"Of course we'll get back," he said. "But first, I need you to relax."

He put as much warmth and confidence into his voice as he could, but for some reason, at the word *"relax"* the woman's eyes seemed to widen in terror—as though Jack had told her she'd need to survive by learning how to fly, or something equally impossible.

He decided to see if he could get his arms around her— the sooner she stopped fighting the current, the better.

"I'm going to put my arm under your shoulders, okay?" he said.

He swam behind her and slipped a firm arm under her shoulders. The support he lent her had the desired effect: once her body was directly against his she stopped struggling against the water and allowed his strength to keep her afloat.

"Can you hold on to this?"

He put the body board he'd borrowed in front of her, and she clutched at it.

"Good," he said approvingly. Her panic seemed to be receding by the minute. He had to admire how quickly she was gaining control of herself; most people would still be struggling and swallowing seawater at this point.

"What's your name?" he asked her.

"Kat," she said, with a strangled gasp.

Good, Jack thought. If she could speak, then her airways were still clear.

"Kat, I need you to listen to me," he said. "We're going to survive this, but you have to trust me. If you do everything I say I promise you that we're going to get to shore. But the first thing I need you to do is stay calm."

"I'll try," she said.

He chuckled. "I can feel you trembling." She scowled at him, and he quickly added, "It's all right to be scared, but you don't need to be—because we're going to get out of this. First time getting caught in a rip current?"

She nodded. "It's my first time swimming in the ocean. First day in Hawaii, actually."

He could see that she was trying to talk herself into a calmer state, and was doing her best to keep a cool head. She had nerves of steel. He also couldn't help but notice the lithe shape of her body as she clung to him.

First things first, he told himself sternly. Maybe they should get back on dry land before he started trying to find out anything more about her. Most likely she was one of the thousands of tourists who came each month, eager for adventure and completely unprepared for the dangers of the ocean.

"Well, *aloha* and welcome to Oahu, Kat. Can you lean forward onto this body board? If you rest on your arms, I can paddle us in. Don't worry, I won't let you go."

Somehow Kat knew that he was telling her the truth.

At first, amidst her terror and the waves going over her head, it had been hard for her to get a good look at this man who had swum out to help her. All she'd been able to sense was a well-muscled, masculine presence and a steady, reassuring voice. A voice that was warm and soothing, like a spoonful of honey.

But he'd reached her with surprising speed, and she tried to trust that he knew what he was doing.

Pressing her between himself and the flotation device he had with him, he used his body to help her gain leverage as she shifted herself onto the board. As soon as she was resting entirely on it, he let go of her waist to swim beside her, and she felt a twinge of regret as the supportive arms released her.

"Great job," he said. "Hard part's over. Now just keep holding on while I tow you in. We'll be back to shore before you know it."

He continued swimming by her side, guiding the

board as he pulled them both parallel to the shore. A
rough wave knocked them unexpectedly, and Kat felt
a sharp pain in her leg. She must have let out a yelp because the man instantly grabbed her around the waist
again.

"What is it?" he said, his face concerned.

"My leg," she said. "I must have scraped it against
something. I don't think it's bad."

"Just hang in there," he said. "We're almost back to
the beach."

To Kat's relief, the shore was becoming closer and
closer, until finally she felt the ocean waves pushing
them both toward the beach instead of pulling them
away.

She collapsed in a heap on the sand and he fell beside
her, one arm draped protectively over her body. They
both lay there for a moment, exhausted. He was close
enough that Kat could feel the heat radiating from his
body next to her on the shore.

She turned to thank her rescuer.

She'd been grateful for his strength during the rescue, but now that she was back on dry land she was
able to appreciate quite a bit more than just his strength.

His eyes were the exact same shade as the Hawaiian
ocean—a blue-green-turquoise. He was muscular, but
his physique was track-star-slim. A shock of dark hair
fell over his forehead, and Kat had to resist a sudden
urge to run her fingers through it. Their eyes locked,
and for a moment Kat felt an electric charge between
them.

His arm still rested over her. Sheltering her. He was
gazing down at her, making sure she was all right. She

tried to speak, but it came out as a cough, and it was several moments before she was able to recover.

"That's it," he said. "You've had a nasty shock. Take some time to let yourself breathe."

She sat up. He pulled his arm away and leaned back from her. Was it wishful thinking, or did he seem to move his arm slowly, as though he wasn't ready to let go of her?

As Kat lay on the beach, slowly regaining her breath, she gradually became aware of her bedraggled appearance. She was covered in muddy sand and the water that she'd coughed up, and her hair hung in strings around her face. But she was alive—thanks to the man next to her, whoever he was. His eyes radiated concern, and he patted her back gently as they both waited for her airway to clear fully.

"I'm all right," she told him, as soon as she was breathing steadily. "All this attention is unnecessary, really. But I do have to thank you for saving my life, Mr.—?"

"Jack Harper," he said.

"Well, Mr. Harper, thank you," she said.

"Don't mention it," he said. "Just give your body the time it needs to recover."

Kat sat with her knees bent and her feet flat against the sand. She held her head down, trying to slow her breathing. Keeping her head down also had the added effect of distracting her from the fact that Jack Harper was still sitting quite close to her, his powerfully built body radiating heat, his eyes examining her face with concern.

"I don't know how you can be so casual," she said. "I was certain we were both going to die."

"It was dangerous, but you kept calm and that was half the battle," he said.

She shuddered, thinking of how close she'd come to being swept out into the ocean. "Maybe I looked calm, but I definitely didn't feel it. I always thought I was a strong swimmer, but I wasn't prepared for those currents. I was trying to swim parallel to the shore, but it seemed like no matter what direction I went in the current wanted to pull me somewhere else."

"You aren't the first person to be surprised by the strength of a Hawaiian rip current. It's a shame that your first swim here nearly killed you—especially on your first day. That's no way to welcome you to the islands."

"Really? And here I was hoping that almost drowning on my first day here would turn out to be some sort of tradition." She laughed. And then, before she could stop herself, she said, "Maybe a better way to celebrate arriving in Hawaii and surviving a near-death experience would be to take my rescuer out for dinner sometime."

She couldn't believe she'd said that. She wasn't anywhere near ready to date again. But she wouldn't mind hearing that rich, deep voice more often. Or feeling those arms around her again. Preferably in a situation where she wasn't about to drown.

Learning to relax. Step two, her brain piped up. *Find an island hottie to help you move on from your devastating breakup.*

Stop it, she told herself.

She'd just been jilted at the altar—well, technically there had still been three days until the wedding, but it had been close enough that she felt jilted. The last thing she needed was to get involved with anyone right now. She needed to get her mind off Jack's voice and arms right away. What was she *thinking*, offering to buy him dinner?

Kat forced herself to shift her attention away from Jack's beach-tanned body. This was no time for distractions, she told herself firmly. She'd just come close to getting swept out to sea, and she was still shaken by the thought of what might have happened if Jack hadn't been there to help her back to shore. She needed to clear her head and get her bearings. She also needed to find a way to turn her attention from Jack Harper's taut skin and chiseled chest muscles so she could focus on what he was saying.

"I appreciate the offer, but there's no need to thank me," said Jack. "It's part of the job." He motioned to where an ambulance had arrived, further down the beach.

"Are you a doctor?" she asked.

"Paramedic," he replied. "And I'm sorry to say that any dinner plans will have to wait—because before you do anything else we need to get you to a hospital to get checked out. We're not far from Oahu General Hospital—I'll go with you."

"Oahu General? Oh, no. I can't go there."

Now that Kat no longer feared for her life, she was becoming deeply embarrassed about the commotion her rescue had caused. More than anything, she wanted to avoid being taken to a hospital—especially Oahu General.

She could think of few things more humiliating than showing up to her new hospital as a patient, wearing nothing but a bikini. And she definitely didn't think it would be a good idea to spend more time in close quarters with Jack. If she wasn't careful that voice and those eyes would start to have an effect on her. And she had no intention of diving headlong into a fling with the first man she met in Hawaii—no matter how closely his eyes matched the color of the ocean.

"Really, I'm fine," she said.

"You're bleeding," he told her.

"What?" Kat looked down at her leg, surprised. The place where she'd felt that pain in her leg while Jack was towing her to shore had a gash of about an inch that was trickling blood. "Oh, crap. That must have happened when I hurt my leg, back in the water. It doesn't look serious to me, though."

Privately, she thought that she might need a few stitches, but she wasn't about to let Jack know that.

As he leaned in closer she caught his scent: a masculine blend of sunblock, salt water and sand. He smelled like the ocean, like the hint of salt in the air that had filled her with such excitement and called her to the beach the moment she'd stepped off the plane. She definitely needed to stay as far away from him as possible if she wanted to avoid making a fool of herself.

"It doesn't even hurt that much," she said, though she was gritting her teeth through the stinging pain that was now beginning to make itself felt.

"I'm sure it doesn't, but that's the point," said Jack. "You've just had a near-death experience, and adrenaline is coursing through your system. Right now you probably feel like you can do anything—but that's just the adrenaline. It can mask a lot of problems, includ-

ing pain. You might think you're fine, but humor me—
it's best for you to get to the hospital so we can get you
stitched up."

"There's really no need," said Kat briskly.

But she could see that Jack wasn't going to give up
easily, so she decided to try appealing to him as a medical professional.

"Look, to tell you the truth I'm a doctor, and I can
take care of this myself. I'm starting my first day working at Oahu General on Monday, and I really don't want
their first impression of me to be...*this*." Kat motioned
to her string bikini.

Was it her imagination, or had his expression seemed
to change when she'd revealed she was a doctor? For
a split second it had seemed as though a shadow had
passed over his face. Most people seemed to be *more*
at ease with her when she revealed her profession, but
if anything Jack almost seemed...disappointed?

But then he sighed and said, "Doctors always make
the worst patients."

Oh. He had a valid point. As a doctor, she'd always
had a difficult time allowing herself to be in the patient
role, and she knew many colleagues who felt the same
way. It was hard to sit back and let someone else follow
procedure when she could feel her own natural tendency
to take charge of the situation rising within her. Also,
she hated being the center of attention.

As she took in Jack's piercing blue eyes she knew
she shouldn't want to be the center of *his* attention. Her
knees were still shaking, and she had a feeling that it
wasn't just the onset of hypothermia.

She hoped he wouldn't notice. But of course he did.

He was clearly a skilled paramedic, and Kat suspected that he didn't miss much.

"Your knees are shaking," he said. "You should know better than anyone that the biggest risk after a near-drowning in water of any temperature is hypothermia. You shouldn't be going anywhere until we can make sure your core body temperature hasn't dropped too low."

Kat groaned inwardly. Her irritation was all the worse because she knew that Jack was right. She shouldn't take care of the cut on her leg by herself—especially with the risk of hypothermia. His stubbornness was a wall she wouldn't get past, and he clearly wasn't going to be intimidated by her medical credentials.

She couldn't decide whether his determination to take care of her was incredibly annoying or attractive. A little of both, she thought.

And it didn't help that the small, rebellious voice in the back of her mind was wholly in agreement with Jack, and was shouting that spending some time in the close quarters of an ambulance with him wouldn't be an entirely unwelcome experience.

Just get in! the voice screamed. *He can be your next impulsive decision!*

Enough of that, she told herself.

Jack Harper was certainly attractive; there was no question of that. Those blue-green eyes of his seemed to change shade every minute, as though their color changed with his mood.

But Kat had felt herself getting swept away by the ocean, just moments ago. That had been scary enough.

The last thing she needed now was to let herself get swept away by someone she'd just met.

Although she had to admit that Jack's air of authority was rather refreshing. She could see that no matter how much she argued he was taking her to the hospital—even if she went kicking and screaming.

As a respected internal medicine physician, Kat wasn't used to having anyone disagree with her. Her decisions were almost never questioned by her team. To have someone insist on taking care of *her* for once, in spite of all her protestations, was an utterly new experience.

It was almost a little bit sexy.

But sexy was the last thing Kat was looking for.

Not now.

Not three weeks after Christopher. Not after the disaster of their almost-wedding.

"Is it really necessary?" she asked, knowing her appeal was doomed.

"You know it is," he said.

His voice was that of a determined man who would not be denied.

Definitely a little bit sexy, the rebellious voice in her head noted.

She didn't want this kind of complication right now. She didn't want to be attracted to anyone. Three weeks ago she hadn't thought she was even capable of feeling interested in anyone else, because she'd been about to marry the love of her life. She should be returning from her honeymoon now—not standing on a tropical beach arguing with a frustratingly attractive paramedic who didn't understand when to quit.

Kat saw the stubborn set of Jack's jaw and realized that she really was going to arrive at her new place of work borderline hypothermic, muddy, and wearing a string bikini—in the company of one of the most attractive men she'd ever seen.

This, she thought, was the opposite of learning how to relax.

CHAPTER TWO

KAT DECIDED THAT if there was no chance of changing Jack's mind, she would try bargaining with him instead.

"I'll go if you insist, but at least let me find something different to wear," she said.

Riding in an ambulance with Jack while wearing nothing but a bikini would be bad enough, but she would do anything to prevent her new co-workers from forming their first impression of her while she was nearly naked and dripping wet.

"Do you have anything else with you that you could put on?" Jack asked.

"Oh!" Kat remembered. "My luggage. It's right over there, down the beach."

She started to rise, but Jack pushed her down firmly. He wrapped a blanket around her and tucked in the ends as though she were a child. Kat's cheeks burned.

She started to protest, but Jack stopped her. "I'm not taking any risks just because you're a doctor who thinks she knows better than a paramedic. Sit still and I'll bring your luggage to you."

He headed down the beach while Kat fumed. As much as she didn't want to admit it, she was secretly

glad that Jack had pushed her back into a sitting position. Her legs felt like jelly, and it would have been
difficult to stand. And it was nice to have the blanket.
But she needed him to understand that, as a doctor, she
was perfectly capable of deciding what she did or did
not need for herself.

When he returned with her things she said, "Look,
this is very kind of you, but all this attention just isn't
necessary. I happen to be an excellent doctor. I was the
youngest chief resident of internal medicine that Chicago Grace Memorial Hospital ever had."

He rolled his eyes. "I'm sure you were."

"And I graduated from Northwestern University in
just three years. I was in the top five of my class at
medical school."

"Sounds like you're very smart."

Now her cheeks were burning with a different kind
of embarrassment. Would he think she was the kind of
person who bragged about her achievements? She realized that she was doing exactly that. Why was she
acting this way? It was more than just wanting to appear competent in front of a potential new colleague.
For some reason she couldn't explain, she wanted Jack
to think well of her.

"I'm just trying to say that you don't need to fuss
over me. You don't need to treat me like a patient,"
she said.

"Because doctors always know best, right?" he replied.

She was flustered. "Well…yes. Frankly, I have the
most medical expertise between the two of us. I think
I'm qualified to decide whether or not I'm all right."

He looked directly into her eyes and she felt a jolt go through her. His gaze was really quite arresting.

"As far as I'm concerned you are *my* patient," he said. "No matter what your medical background is, I'm the one responsible for taking care of you right now, and I intend to see that responsibility through."

His voice was firm, but warm and resonant, and she felt all her resistance melt into a puddle under his gaze. She could listen to that voice all day... She made another feeble attempt to protest, but her breath caught in her throat as he continued.

"You may think you're all right but, as I said before, that's the adrenaline pushing you through. You swallowed a lot of water out there, and I'm not leaving you alone until I'm sure you're stable."

The point apparently settled, he lifted her luggage onto the back of the ambulance and began to rummage through it.

"Hey!" she cried. "That's my stuff! How about a little privacy?" What did he think he was doing, rummaging through her personal things?

"Here we go," he said, pulling her white coat out from beneath a tangle of bathing suits and flip-flops. "Looks like your sweater's all sandy—you don't want to put that back on. But you can wear this."

She pulled the white coat over her swimsuit and wrapped it around herself. "Are you always this stubborn and bossy?" she said.

"Afraid so," he replied. "Especially where my patients are concerned—no matter where they ranked in their class at medical school."

As irritating as he was, Kat had to admire his persistence. Jack Harper might have his flaws, but being lax about patient care obviously wasn't one of them. His stubbornness both annoyed and intrigued her. Who *was* this commandeering man with the arms that had fit so perfectly around her waist?

At least she had one clue: the tattoo in flowing script along his arm. "'The only easy day was yesterday,'" she read. "You were a Navy SEAL?"

He nodded, clearly surprised. "Most people don't recognize the motto," he said.

"My grandfather was a SEAL," she said. "He always said Navy guys make the best boyfriends."

She flushed even more deeply. Why had she said a thing like that? She sounded like some sort of man-hungry flirt. It was all *his* fault—he had some sort of effect on her that made her want to punch him and jump into his arms all at once.

Her resolve to get away from him before she embarrassed herself further returned. She removed the blanket and tucked her white coat around herself. "Look, it's very kind of you to offer me an ambulance ride, but I'll be fine on my own," she said.

"Be my guest," he said, clearly deciding on a different tack. "But, just so you know, it's a long walk, and I'm going to be driving alongside you the whole way."

"That's your prerogative," she said.

She stood up, prepared to march away from the beach—and immediately began to sink into the sand as her legs shook under her. Her entire body was shaking.

Just before she fell onto the sand Jack caught her and lifted her into his arms. She was surprised at the surge of relief that flooded through her as she felt his strong arms scoop her up. As much as she hated to admit that he'd been right, she could tell that shock was hitting her, and she knew that the time for trying to prove she was strong was over—realized that the adrenaline rush had indeed been carrying her through the moment.

And now Jack was carrying her through *this* moment.

"Maybe it wouldn't be such a bad idea to head to the hospital," Kat said, her voice shaking. "But no sirens, okay? I really don't want to make a big entrance. This is already embarrassing enough."

"No sirens," he agreed.

He lifted her into the back of the ambulance and nodded to the driver before hopping in himself and closing the doors behind them.

Jack berated himself for agreeing not to use the sirens as he climbed into the back of the ambulance. Kat was probably fine, but she was still a patient in his care and he didn't want any harm to come to her. She was such a typical doctor—assuming she knew best, even when she was the one who needed help.

Of course the first woman he'd been genuinely attracted to in ages would *have* to be a co-worker. And not just any co-worker, but apparently an ambitious and career-driven doctor.

Jack had one hard and fast rule when it came to dating: no doctors. After everything that had happened with Sophie and Matt, he didn't need yet another doctor involved in his personal life. But he couldn't help but notice that the white coat Kat wore over her bikini made her legs look even longer.

None of that kind of thinking, he told himself sternly.

Kat might be attractive, but it would be best for the two of them to put some distance between each another after today.

Although if they were going to be co-workers, distance might not be an option.

He wondered how long she would be at the hospital—what department she would be in. Maybe he wouldn't have to see her that much. He decided to do some casual reconnaissance, hoping she wouldn't pick up on just how curious he really was.

"So you're the new doctor at Oahu General?" he said, as he settled himself across from Kat and pulled out his suturing kit.

But instead of responding, Kat angled her leg away from him. "Oh, no, you don't," she said, as he opened the kit. "The cut's not that bad. It just needs a stitch or two. I could probably do the suturing myself."

Jack glared at her. He had to admire her persistence, but there was such a thing as taking it too far. The fact that Kat would even *suggest* doing stitches on herself told him that she was probably still experiencing some mild shock.

Besides, it would be a crime to allow a scar to form on one of those legs.

"How about you let me be the one to take care of the patient right now?" he said, glowering at her to make sure he'd got his point across.

"It's not as though I can't do a simple stitch," Kat muttered rebelliously.

Jack gently shifted Kat's leg toward his body, so he could reach the cut. He leaned forward and locked her gaze with his. "Listen, I know you were in the top five percent of your class at Northwestern, but I promise you'll be better off if you let *me* handle this," he said. "If you'd stop being so stubborn and let me be in charge for one minute, I'd actually be able to help you."

Kat fell silent, and for a moment Jack regretted his harsh tone. She was probably mortified at the thought of meeting her new co-workers in a few moments, dressed like this. But no, he thought, it was better to be harsh. For her own safety as well as his. *She* needed to accept that she was in the patient's role—a hard thing for a doctor—and *he* needed to make sure that he didn't get carried away by the effect she was having on him. Being clear about maintaining firm professional boundaries from the start would be the best thing for both of them.

Then, in a small voice, Kat muttered, "Top five."

"What?" said Jack.

"I was in the top five of my class at Northwestern. That's much more impressive than being in the top five percent."

He was about to make a sarcastic response, but then, to his surprise, she winked at him.

"I just wanted you to know that I'm a total big shot, okay?" she said.

He couldn't help but laugh. "Noted," he said.

Great, he thought. *Smart and funny.*

Just what he didn't need. He should keep up a detached, professional demeanor—he really should. But he couldn't help teasing her back.

"With all due respect, Dr. Big Shot, do you think you can relax and let me give this cut the attention it needs?" he asked.

She groaned, startling him.

"What's wrong?" he asked, immediately concerned. "Does it hurt?"

"Oh, no," she said. "It's just…there's that word again. *Relax.* You keep telling me to do the one thing I have no idea how to do."

"What…relax?"

He started to apply lidocaine to the wound on Kat's leg. He wanted to stay detached, but he couldn't help being curious about her. Besides, if he could keep her talking it would take her mind off the stitches.

"I've never been very good at relaxing," she said. "I've gotten so used to having a busy life that I think I've forgotten how to live in the moment…or maybe I never really knew how. Just before I went down to that beach I thought to myself that I'd learn to relax or die trying. And I guess I almost did."

"*Almost* being the operative word," said Jack. "Not only did you not die, you actually handled yourself really well out there."

"Really?" she said. "Because when you came out there and told me to *'just relax'* that's when I thought we were both doomed for sure."

Jack shook his head. "No, you stayed calm in a terrifying situation. Most people make a rescue more difficult by panicking, but you kept a cool head."

He saw her let out a slow breath that she probably hadn't even realized she was holding.

"I was so scared," she said. "I didn't feel calm at all. I was lucky that you were there."

She had been lucky—that was true enough. Rip currents were incredibly dangerous. But her survival had been more than just luck. Jack had been impressed by how well Kat had stayed focused on his instructions during the rescue, despite her terror.

He started on the first stitch, trying not to notice the thin line of bare skin down her front where her white coat had fallen open.

"You're having an eventful first day in Hawaii," he said. "Do you plan on staying long?"

"Just a year," said Kat. "I used to be an internal medicine doctor at Chicago Grace Memorial, but… I was offered a job here, and…and the timing was good, so I took it."

For a moment Kat seemed sad. Jack wondered what she'd meant about good timing, but he didn't want to pry. If she was only staying for a year, then that meant her appointment at Oahu General was temporary. Maybe he wouldn't even see her that much.

He caught himself noticing how her red hair fell in delicate tendrils around her slender neck and decided that it would probably be for the best if they didn't see each other much.

He said, in what he hoped was a light tone, "You're a visiting doctor? We get a lot of those. What department will you be in?"

"Apparently the infectious diseases department is short-staffed," she said. "They need an internal medicine doctor with a specialty in infectious diseases to head up research and treatment on a new strain of flu."

So she was a doctor of internal medicine? That meant they'd have plenty of opportunities to work together— and he'd have plenty of opportunities to notice the way her hair offset her translucent skin.

He finished the stitches he'd given the cut on Kat's leg. "Infectious Diseases is always short-staffed," he said. "We get new strains of flu every year, and we're always hit by large outbreaks in the spring. It'll be good to have more hands on deck at the hospital." He gave Kat's leg a pat, trying not to think about how her skin felt underneath his fingers. "There," he said brusquely. "Good as new."

With the stitches complete, Jack realized he had no way to distract himself from Kat. There seemed to be nothing to do but sit across from her, trying not to notice that the outline of her body was clear underneath her white coat, which had become damp from the water on her skin.

He cleared his throat. *Stay professional,* he thought to himself. *Right now she's a patient, and even if she wasn't, she's a doctor. You never date doctors.*

Jack decided to keep her talking—both to break the silence, and to distract himself from the way Kat's coat was slipping off one shoulder.

"There aren't too many top med school grads taking jobs at little hospitals in Hawaii," he said.

"It seemed like a good opportunity," she replied.

"Really?" he said. "People usually don't come to the islands to practice medicine unless they've got a personal reason—maybe family lives here, or maybe they grew up in Hawaii and want to move back."

For a moment that expression of sadness crossed her face once again. But then it disappeared just as quickly, to be replaced with cool professionalism. "It was a good opportunity," she repeated. "And I won't just be seeing patients—I've also been offered the chance to lead the internal medicine unit in an administrative role. I'll be able to make some major changes to Oahu General's hospital policy in a way that I've never been able to do at any other hospital before. I wouldn't be able to do that at a larger or more prestigious hospital, so this could be an excellent stepping stone for me."

A stepping stone. This was exactly what irritated Jack about the doctors who came to Hawaii for temporary positions. They were never invested in the islands or the community. They were interested in their careers, and they loved trying out their grand new ideas at a tiny, insignificant hospital where the stakes were low. A tiny, insignificant hospital that happened to be his professional home, with colleagues and patients he cared about.

"Oahu General may not have much prestige, but it's a great hospital, with great doctors," he said.

"Oh, I know," she said quickly. "I didn't mean to imply otherwise. But there's a lot I've learned from working at Chicago Grace Memorial about how to increase efficiency and improve patient outcomes. I'm so excited to start putting some of my ideas in place—I'm sure there's so much that can be improved."

So much that can be improved? thought Jack. She hadn't even seen the hospital yet. How could she know what needed improvement?

It was obvious to him that Kat was a typical big-city doctor, assuming she would be able to change everything. As though the hospital didn't already have good systems in place, built by people who lived in and cared about Hawaii.

His ex-fiancée Sophie had been the same way.

Career-driven, independent, and unabashedly pursuing what she wanted from life. They had all been qualities Jack had wholeheartedly admired…until he'd realized that when it came to choosing between her career and the important people in her life Sophie would do whatever it took to advance her career. Even if it meant that people would get hurt.

He'd only known Kat for a few moments, but that was long enough to see that she was smart, funny, beautiful…and completely certain that she knew what was best for everyone.

At least she's only here for a year, he thought. *There's no need for things to get complicated.*

He tried very hard not to notice that Kat's medical coat had fallen open just a little further, revealing another inch of bare, creamy skin. Instead, he focused on packing up the items from his suturing kit, in a manner that he thought was very detached and professional indeed.

Despite Kat's frustration at being treated like a patient, she couldn't help but notice that Jack had handled her stitches swiftly and competently. He clearly knew what he was doing. And as she'd watched Jack complete the stitches she'd felt the soothing effect that observing a simple medical procedure had always had on her.

No matter the emergency, she took comfort in knowing that there was an established process to handle things. Simple injuries like this were almost comforting to face, because it was such a relief to have a plan, to know exactly what to do.

Watching Jack work gave her another chance to appreciate just how muscular his arms were. He'd put his shirt back on when they'd gotten into the ambulance and she wondered if she'd ever be able to get another look at what lay underneath it. But then she sternly guided her thoughts back to the present.

You're still getting over a relationship, she told herself. *You're heartbroken, remember? The last thing you need is to get involved with another guy. Besides, you've already made a fool of yourself in front of this one.*

Her cheeks burned when she recalled how she'd bragged about her accomplishments. She'd only meant to reassure him that she knew what she was doing, but she'd come off sounding so stuck-up. He probably thought she was completely full of herself.

Her body, however, was pushing her in a very different direction than her cool, logical mind.

Do you see how wavy his hair is? her body screamed. *Just run your fingers through it! Do it!*

In the three weeks that had passed since the Day of Doom, Kat had felt an anesthetizing layer of numbness settle over her heartbreak. But the moment she'd taken a good look at Jack something had pierced that and gotten through to the aching heart underneath.

She wasn't ready for it. Feeling attraction to someone wasn't part of this year's plan.

This year's plan was to recover from losing Christopher and losing her job, while learning to embrace life against the serene backdrop of a tropical island setting. Eventually—*much* later—she might start dating again, if the right person came along. But for now it would be completely illogical and inconvenient to feel attracted to anyone. Especially a bossy, overconfident paramedic.

Kat liked her plan. It was a good plan. The thought of deviating from the plan made her nervous. And her attraction to Jack was definitely a deviation, so it would have to stop.

It almost came as a relief when Jack seemed to become increasingly irritated as she discussed her plans for changes at Oahu General Hospital. Dealing with his irritation was much easier than dealing with her feelings of attraction.

Although she couldn't understand what he could possibly be irritated about in the first place.

"Am I missing something?" she said. "Is there some issue with me wanting to make changes at the hospital?"

"Why would there be an issue?" he said.

She didn't buy his innocent act. "I'm not saying there is. But I can't help noticing that you've gotten awfully quiet since I started talking about my job."

"It's just…" He seemed to be choosing his words carefully. "I think you might want to actually get to know the people and the hospital you'll be working at before you start thinking about making any sweeping changes. People can get very set in their way of doing things, and you don't want to push too fast for too much change."

Kat pressed her lips together, trying not to let her emotions show on her face. Jack's words reminded her of what the administrative director at Chicago Grace Memorial Hospital had said, about thirty minutes before she'd been fired.

Kat had spent nearly a year doing research before she'd made her presentation to the hospital board. In it, she had proposed that the hospital open a nonprofit clinic to help provide free and very low-cost care to patients who struggled to afford treatment. She had the financial information to prove the hospital could support it.

All her data indicated that the poorest patients struggled to get well because of their limited resources. They came in to the hospital far too late, after their illnesses had progressed significantly—sometimes too late for help. A nonprofit clinic would be life-changing for some of the hospital's patients.

All the board of directors had to do was approve her proposal.

But, to her shock, the administrative director had told her that the hospital was there to make a profit, and that if she wanted to make such sweeping changes she should have gone into politics instead of medicine. She was pushing for too much change, too fast, he'd said. And she'd been stunned to see the other board members nodding in agreement.

And the director had been so condescending and sanctimonious. At one point he had even referred to her as "little lady." His attitude had infuriated her and, unable to stop herself, she'd shared a few choice words with him. The director had fired back, tempers had flared, and before Kat had known it, she'd been out of a job.

When her friend Selena had offered her the job at Oahu General, Kat had been honest about her firing—and the events leading up to it. But no one else knew except for Christopher. And after Christopher's reaction... Well, *that* conversation hadn't gone well at all.

If she could help it no one else would ever know

how she'd lost her job. She couldn't reveal to Jack just how much his words had activated her worst fear: that her new plans for the hospital wouldn't work and that her time at Oahu General would lead to a repeat of the Day of Doom.

But that was unlikely to happen again, she reminded herself. This time things were different. She had the full support of the hospital director. And her plans for changes in policy and procedure were good ones... She just needed a chance to prove it. Her year at Oahu General would give her that chance. And if Jack or anyone else had a problem—well, they'd just have to get used to it.

At least she didn't have to worry about losing her job *and* her fiancé on the same day again. After all, she no longer had a fiancé to lose...

She realized her thoughts were hitting too close to emotions she wasn't ready to face. Especially not while she was sitting partially dressed across from a certain dark-haired, half-shaven, irritatingly self-assured paramedic.

"You did that pretty well," she said, indicating her stitches. "You've clearly got some skills." She'd barely felt a thing, and she could already tell she was unlikely to have a trace of a scar.

He looked up at her, seeming surprised by the unexpected compliment.

"You must have gotten lots of practice in the SEALs," she said.

"Actually, I had three years at medical school. So it wasn't exactly a challenge. But it's nice to have my abilities appreciated." He cleared his throat. "You've…um… you've got good skin. So this should heal up very nicely."

His hand was very warm where it rested against her leg. He'd applied the stitches so deftly she tried not to think about anything else his hands might be able to do.

"Three years of medical school would have put you past the worst of it," she said, trying to keep her head clear. "Why didn't you keep going?"

"I happen to love being a paramedic," he said. "I knew medical school wasn't for me, so I left."

Kat was surprised by the defensive tone in Jack's voice. She'd only known him for a few moments, but he struck her as a supremely confident sort of person. Surely he couldn't be sensitive about being a paramedic?

During her career she had met a very small number of physicians with extremely arrogant personalities—her old hospital's administrative director came to mind—who seemed to believe that doctors were somehow superior to other medical professionals. It wasn't a view she agreed with at all. Paramedics and nurses simply provided a different kind of care than doctors. Different and vitally important.

Perhaps Jack had run into a few doctors who held such antiquated views. She hoped he didn't think that she was one of them. But in her pre-hypothermic state, and in her desperation to avoid arriving at Oahu General in an ambulance, she'd probably given him every reason to think that she was as arrogant, stubborn and overconfident as…as *he* was.

"Well, in my opinion you left medical school not a moment too soon," she said lightly.

He looked up at her in surprise.

"If you'd become a doctor you wouldn't have been there on the beach today," she explained. "You wouldn't have been able to save my life. So I'm extremely grateful you decided to become a paramedic instead, no matter what the reason was."

He gave a low, dark laugh. "You're probably the first person who's ever been happy that I left medical school. Well, maybe the second, after me."

There was something more he might have said, Kat could tell. But he didn't speak any further.

Her thoughts turned again to his tattoo. "Are others in your family in the military?" she asked.

"Not exactly," he replied. "My grandfather's a doctor...as are my parents and both of my brothers."

Ah... Suddenly Jack's defensiveness was a bit more clear. With five doctors in the family, there had probably been many expectations about Jack's career options.

"I knew a few people in medical school whose parents were physicians," she said. "But lots of people don't want to do the same thing as their parents. And I can imagine that being a paramedic in Hawaii would be the best of both worlds to someone who's a former SEAL and a former medical student. You're still able to help people, but you get the rush of adrenaline and excitement that comes with the job."

"Exactly," he said, but again, he didn't elaborate.

I get it, you don't like to talk about the past, she thought. *Duly noted.*

That was fine with her.

She felt the ambulance pull into the hospital docking bay and saw the driver step out. As Jack started to open the back door Kat put her hand on his arm to stop him.

"Wait," she said. "I haven't thanked you properly. If you hadn't been there today I probably would have drowned."

She could tell that he was as surprised as she was by the softness in her voice. What was she *doing*? She had only meant to say thank you, but the emotion behind her voice had been more than just gratitude. And now that she was looking directly at him…now that he was holding her gaze with those ocean-blue eyes…that same electric charge that she'd felt on the beach was there again, keeping her eyes locked with his.

"You mostly saved yourself, by staying calm and trusting my instructions," he said, his voice soft and low. "I was just there to help."

They were by themselves in the back of the ambulance and there was silence. His gaze met hers and Kat couldn't look away. His eyes were pools of cerulean blue. His nose was inches away from hers.

For one insane moment she thought he was going to kiss her—which was a ridiculous idea. Why would Jack want to kiss her? She was a bedraggled mess. And he probably thought she was completely full of herself after she'd bragged about her medical background.

But she'd only bragged because he'd been so bossy at first. So, really, that part was his fault.

And Kat couldn't think why *she* would want a man as irritating as Jack Harper to kiss her.

She only knew that she did.

They were so close. She could smell his sea-salt scent. She felt an undeniable pull toward him, as strong as the current that had pulled her out to sea earlier. But this time, instead of panic, she only felt safety. Calm. A sense of certainty about what would happen next.

But just as his face began moving toward hers, close enough for her to feel the warmth of his breath on her face, two EMTs pulled open the back door of the ambulance.

Kat gave a jump and a start, and she and Jack quickly pulled away from one another. She instantly regretted her sudden move away from Jack, realizing that her re-action would probably make the situation appear even more suspicious to any gossip-prone EMTs. She needed to make it clear to everyone that she and Jack were just co-workers, and she needed to do it quickly.

She pulled the white coat tightly over herself and stepped out of the ambulance. Despite her protests, the EMTs insisted she sit in the wheelchair they'd brought out to meet her.

As they left, she turned back to Jack and said, in her coolest, most professional voice, "It was nice to meet you, Jack. It's good to find out firsthand that I can trust my co-workers to do such a competent job. I think it's great that we'll be working together profes-sionally. Just great."

As Kat was wheeled away Jack let out the long, slow breath that he'd been holding since the driver had stepped out and left the two of them alone together in the ambulance. He had no idea what he'd been think-ing in the moment before that almost-kiss with Kat. In fact, he hadn't been thinking at all.

If he had been, he would have been able to tell him-self that he and Kat made no sense. That the reasons not to get involved with her far outweighed any attraction he might feel. He ticked them off in his mind. Kat had deliberately emphasized their status as colleagues as she'd left the ambulance. They'd be working together, and workplace relationships were always a mistake. And then there was his most steadfast rule of dating: no doctors.

Not since Sophie. They'd been in medical school together, and then she'd gone on to one prestigious medical research fellowship after another. He'd been fully supportive of her, but when he'd left medical school, she'd let him know in no uncertain terms that she was interested in being the wife of a *doctor*—not a military man or a lowly paramedic.

As hard as it had been to accept, he'd thought he understood. After all, he was the one who had changed, deciding that a doctor's life wasn't for him. He couldn't fault her for wanting something different than what *he* wanted.

But wanting something different was one thing. Finding out that she'd been with his brother for six months before breaking up with Jack was quite another.

Sophie had always been extremely ambitious. And Jack's parents were well-known in the medical field, and the Harper doctors were a valuable connection.

It was one reason he disliked talking about his family with others—especially those in the medical field: he never knew if people were just trying to get close to him in order to claim a connection to his family. Had Kat made the connection? Harper was a common enough last name, but there weren't many people who had five doctors in the family. If she did suspect that his family was essentially medical royalty, she hadn't said anything.

He'd always wondered if the reason Sophie had cheated on him with Matt, of all people, was so that she could still marry into the Harper family—simply swapping one Harper brother for another.

Matt, for his part, either hadn't seen it that way or hadn't cared. Matt had always liked Sophie, Jack knew…but he'd never realized just how far that attraction went until it was too late. He'd trusted Sophie. He'd trusted both of them.

Jack didn't want to go through that kind of heartbreak again. Ever. And as far as he was concerned he wouldn't have to. There was no shortage of short-term dating prospects on the islands. Hawaii was full of tourists with romantic ideas about a whirlwind affair before they returned to the mainland. They expected nothing more, and neither did he.

As far as he was concerned love was an illusion, and the best way to protect yourself from heartbreak was to keep from getting close to anyone in the first place.

The more he thought about it, the more he realized that his attraction to Kat wasn't going to be a problem. Kat would only be here for one year. Lots of doctors came to Hawaii for brief appointments—Hawaii's shortage of doctors was well known in the medical community, and visiting doctors weren't rare—but the vast majority of physicians returned to the mainland eventually. Kat seemed like someone who would put her career first, probably over just about anything. She'd leave once she'd gotten over whatever island fantasies she harbored and realized that practicing in Hawaii meant focusing on patient care rather than professional advancement.

He would simply wait out his attraction until she left, and hope that she would forget all about that awkward moment in the ambulance. Which hadn't even been a moment, really. At the time it had felt like an almost-kiss, but now that the moment had passed he realized that she'd probably just meant to express her gratitude. In fact, he might have just completely embarrassed himself by assuming even for an instant that she'd been leaning forward for a kiss.

Yes, she'd been leaning in and turning her face toward him, so close he'd almost been able to count her individual eyelashes…so close he had noticed the tiny freckles dotting her nose, felt her breath on his cheek. But it didn't mean anything. Hell, she might have just been reaching for something.

But he had no intention of asking her about it. That moment in the ambulance was best left forgotten. He'd simply be careful to avoid Kat while they were at work, and then he should have no problem putting her out of his mind. He wouldn't spend any time thinking about that red hair of hers, hanging in dripping ringlets around her neck.

Or the tiny freckles that dotted her nose.

Or her soft, kissable lips.

No, he wouldn't be thinking about any of those things at all.

CHAPTER THREE

"YOU CERTAINLY KNOW how to make an entrance," said Selena.

It was several days after Kat's dramatic first arrival at Oahu General Hospital, and Kat and Selena were sharing coffee in her friend's office. Although they hadn't seen each other in several years, Dr. Selena Kahale had been one of Kat's closest friends when they'd attended medical school together. After Selena had returned to her home in Honolulu, her hard work and natural warmth had helped her to climb the ranks quickly to become clinical director of Oahu General Hospital.

But apparently her esteemed professional position didn't get in the way of teasing an old friend.

Kat blushed, remembering the amount of good-natured ribbing she'd endured as soon as the EMTs had learned who she was. Despite her protestations that she was fine, they had insisted on wheeling her into an exam room, still wet, with her medical coat wrapped around her concealing her bikini.

"I wasn't planning on showing up on my first day dressed like that," said Kat, completely embarrassed.

Selena might be an old friend, but she was now

Kat's boss, and Kat wasn't sure how she'd view the whole incident.

She let out a breath of relief when Selena said, "Relax. It's Hawaii. No one stands on ceremony here. You'll find things are much more informal than what you're probably used to back in Chicago. Tommy Bahama shirts are basically considered formalwear. My only worry is whether you'll be able to get used to how casual things are around here."

"It's certainly a big change," said Kat.

That was an understatement. The environment at Oahu General Hospital was sometimes so casual that she was taken aback. After her first day she'd scrapped any thoughts of showing up in a power suit—she would have felt ridiculous wearing a formal blazer here.

Back at Chicago Grace there had been a clear hierarchy among the staff, and everyone had known where they stood. Kat had often wondered if the culture of strict adherence to authority there had interfered with patient care, since some of the doctors were too afraid to question a senior physician's diagnosis, or to make changes to treatment plans that their supervisors might disagree with.

But at Oahu General Hospital the atmosphere felt completely different. Everyone seemed to genuinely respect one another, regardless of hierarchy. Doctors routinely took advice from nurses and paramedics, everyone's input seemed to be valued, and there was an easy banter among the staff.

This relaxed atmosphere presented her with a new challenge. In Chicago, whenever she'd acted as the attending physician, her team had listened to her and carried out her instructions because she was in charge. Simply being in a position of authority had been enough for her team to respect her. But here in Hawaii she saw she would have to earn the respect of her colleagues, as well as their trust.

Selena seemed to sense her thoughts. "Every hospital's culture is a little different," she said. "Even I was a little taken aback by the informality here at first, and I grew up on the islands. But I've come to realize that Oahu General is a special place. We're like family here. You'll grow to love it, I'm sure. And I know that everyone will love you too. Just give them time to get to know you."

Selena paused to sip her coffee, and then continued.

"You might be surprised at how well you fit in here if you can just give yourself time to adjust. The Kat Murphy I remember from medical school was so idealistic, so committed to making a difference in her patients' lives. Maybe getting sacked from Chicago Grace was a blessing in disguise."

Kat blinked. "What kind of blessing involves spending a year doing research for a proposal that ultimately fails?"

"Think about it," said Selena. "Chicago Grace Memorial may be one of the most prestigious hospitals in the country, but ultimately it's a for-profit hospital. The Kat I know could never be completely happy working at a hospital where patients are seen based on their ability to pay. That's not you. It's not where you come from."

Kat mulled this over. She and Selena had been close friends at medical school, and Selena knew how important it was to Kat to use medicine to make a difference.

But when Kat had first begun working at Chicago Grace she'd been so excited about the hospital's reputation and the research opportunities it provided that she hadn't thought much about how the hospital's values might differ from her own.

As she'd continued working there it had become impossible not to see the truth in front of her: there were too many patients who couldn't afford the care they needed.

She knew how that felt.

When she was growing up her parents had always waited until the last possible minute to seek medical care. Even as a child Kat had understood that money was tight in her family. Although her parents had always taken her to see a doctor promptly when she was ill, she knew that they'd often put off their own medical care in order to save money.

Then, when she was ten, her father had come down with an illness. "Just a cold," he had said, reassuring Kat and her mother.

When the cold had persisted he'd said it must just be the flu, and that he would see a doctor when he had time to take a break from his job. He'd kept telling them that he would see a doctor in just a few days. A few weeks later, the flu had turned into pneumonia, and by then her father's condition had been severe. He'd passed away just one day after being admitted to a hospital.

So it wasn't enough for Kat simply to be a good doctor. It hadn't been enough simply to work at Chicago Grace, with all its glamour and prestige. She wanted to make a real difference in the medical community. And more than anything she wanted to make sure that no child, no family, had to go through what she'd gone through as a little girl.

Which was why she had wanted the director of Chicago Grace Memorial to accept her proposal to open a nonprofit clinic at the hospital. It would have been her chance to finally make a true difference—a contribution to medicine that came directly from her personal experience and her professional values.

She had thought that ultimately the board of directors—many of them physicians themselves—would agree that any impact on the hospital's profits would be a small price to pay for a vast increase in quality of patient care.

How naïve she'd been.

Instead of simply rejecting Kat's proposal, the board members had expressed deep indignation at her research findings, which had shown that wealthier patients recovered faster than poorer patients. They'd complained that her findings were terrible for the public's view of the hospital, and they'd told her to bury all her data.

Kat had refused, and it had been that refusal, as well as the choice words she had exchanged with the hospital director, that had resulted in her being fired.

She'd finally had her chance to make a difference and she'd failed. She hadn't been able to convince the hospital board to open a nonprofit clinic. She hadn't been able to control her temper when the hospital director had been condescending and rude. And she hadn't been able to make Christopher understand why all of it was so important to her.

She'd expected his support, but instead he'd seemed just as shocked as the hospital board members. Instead of sharing her anger he'd been angry with Kat, for exchanging insults with the hospital director.

"How could you?" he'd said. *"You might as well have thrown away your career."*

She'd been furious with him. Devastated and furious.

Tears pricked as she remembered their conversation and how cold he'd been. She stared into her coffee mug, hoping Selena wouldn't see those tears that still sprang to her eyes whenever Christopher came to mind.

"You know, as glad as I am to have you here, I was a little surprised when you took the job," Selena said. "Hawaii's so far from Chicago. I would have thought you'd try to look for something a little closer to your family."

"I needed a change," Kat said. "A big change."

The last thing she wanted to admit to her old friend was that she'd moved to Hawaii because of the breakup. It was such a cliché. And Selena would expect her to be professional.

She took a deep breath and tried to think of how she could explain in a way that Selena would understand. But before she could start Selena said, "It was the breakup with Christopher, wasn't it?"

Kat choked on her coffee in surprise. "How did you know?"

"Come on, Kat! *Three days* before the wedding you post online that it's over? And then there's complete radio silence from you—none of your friends can get in touch with you. That's not just a breakup—that's a broken heart."

"I don't want you to think I moved here just because of what happened with…with him," Kat said. It was still too hard to say Christopher's name. "I'm serious about this job—I'm not here just to get over a guy."

"You think I don't understand that? I'm a single mom—I know exactly how it feels to have your life change completely and unexpectedly. You don't have to go through this alone."

Didn't she? Kat was glad to have Selena's support, but now that she was nearing the end of her first week in Hawaii she was beginning to realize that she felt more alone than she ever had in her life.

Now that the excitement of moving to the island was wearing off, Kat felt as though she wasn't sure who she was. She wasn't a top internal medicine doctor at one of the most prestigious hospitals in the country. She wasn't Christopher's fiancée—she definitely wasn't his wife. And she wasn't living in Chicago, the city where her family and friends lived, where she'd planned to spend the rest of her life.

For as long as she could remember she'd tried to be the best doctor on the staff, the best fiancée to Christopher. But if she wasn't trying to prove herself to anyone then how did she know who she was supposed to be?

Kat blinked back tears, willing her eyes to dry. "The point is, it's in the past," she said. "I came here to try to let go of him…of everything that was holding me back. But I just don't know what I'm supposed to do next."

"Oh, Kat." Selena set her coffee aside and patted Kat's shoulder tenderly. "I think you really have come to the right place." Then she gave Kat a wicked smile. "And it looks like you're already making friends. Didn't one of Oahu's most eligible bachelors fish you out of the Pacific recently?"

"Eligible bachelors? Are you talking about Jack Harper?"

"Who else? If you wanted to meet him you didn't have to nearly drown yourself—I could have set you up on a date."

"Selena! I am *so* not ready to date yet. One of the reasons I came here was to try to learn how to slow down and relax."

Selena raised an eyebrow. "Forgive me for being skeptical, but I don't think 'slow down and relax' is a phrase I've *ever* heard you use."

"Maybe I don't have the strongest reputation in that respect, but I'm trying to change that," said Kat. "I'm trying to let go of the past and do something new. Which means I'm definitely not looking to get romantically involved with anyone right now. And even if I was, Jack and I aren't right for one another."

"Okay, first of all, you *are* ready to date—you just don't know it. You've already completed the first essential step to getting over a breakup."

"Which is?"

"Getting out of the continental U.S. as quickly as possible. Now you need to move on to step two: the rebound. And for that purpose Jack is *perfect* for you."

Kat swallowed. How much did Selena know of the kiss that had almost happened between her and Jack? Had the EMTs decided that their brief glimpse of Jack and a half-clothed Kat in close quarters was gossipworthy after all?

She responded carefully. "I'm not so sure I'd say he's

perfect for me. He seems pretty bossy. And even if I were interested—which I'm not—he probably doesn't want anything to do with me."

"Why on earth would you say that?" said Selena. "From what I heard, you two were getting pretty cozy just around the time the ambulance pulled up to the hospital."

Damn, thought Kat. So there *had* been gossip. She needed to set the record straight with Selena as soon as possible. What had happened with Jack—or what had almost happened—had just been a misunderstanding, nothing more.

"I don't know what people have been saying, but Jack was simply taking care of the cut on my leg. Both of us were completely professional. We did get to know each other a little…"

"And?" said Selena, rapt with anticipation.

"And I don't think I'm his type. We kind of got off on the wrong foot. I hate to admit it, but I don't think I made the best first impression—I may have sounded a little full of myself. I blame the hypothermia. And I think—no, I'm *sure*—Jack would agree that since we're to be co-workers it's best not to let emotions get in the way of our working together."

Selena waved her hand dismissively. "Honey, that's all *relationship* stuff. What you need is a *fling.*"

"I'm not really sure I'm a fling kind of girl."

Selena narrowed her eyes. "Kat. Sweetheart. Did you not hear me say that I'm a single mother? When I'm not working, my days involve making lunches and spending way too much time discussing purple crayons with a toddler whom I love to pieces but who has barely mastered words of two syllables. I need some excitement. I need to live vicariously through someone else's love-life. And I need you to be that person because I don't have time for that kind of drama myself!"

Kat laughed. "Sorry, but my love-life's never been all that exciting. If you're looking for vicarious thrills you'll have to look somewhere else."

"Oh, come *on*!" said Selena. "I thought you came here to let go of the past and try new things?"

"Well, yes, but… I'm not sure I want Jack Harper to be one of those 'new things.'"

"Why not? Jack is great. And he's ideal for you right now because he's not a relationship kind of guy. Don't get me wrong—he's a good person. And I love working with him. He's great at his job, really funny, and a good friend. But he's tailor-made fling material; he never dates *anyone* for long."

"I'll just bet he doesn't," said Kat through gritted teeth. Selena was simply confirming her first impression of him.

Selena continued to gush about Jack's virtues.

"He's a lot like you, actually," she said. "He could have worked anywhere on the mainland, but he chose to come here instead. And he's not just *any* paramedic. His parents are *the* Harpers—from the University of Nebraska in Lincoln—"

"Wait a minute," said Kat.

Jack *Harper?* It was quite a common last name and she hadn't given it a second thought till now.

"You mean his parents are Michael and Janet Harper? The famous research scientists? I still have some of their books from medical school on my shelf."

She remembered Jack had touched on the subject of his family in the ambulance, and now knew her feeling that he'd been holding something back had been spot-on. She couldn't understand how he could have talked about his family without ever mentioning that his parents were famous in the medical world.

"What the hell is the son of two of the most well-known medical researchers in the country doing working as a paramedic at a small hospital in Hawaii?" she asked.

"Shouldn't you be asking yourself a similar question?" Selena's eyes twinkled. "What's one of the most respected internists in the U.S. doing at my little hospital? I'm sure he has his reasons, just as you do. You see? You two *are* a lot alike."

"Sure, if oil and water are alike…" Kat muttered.

"I don't know why he wants to work here, but I'm glad he does," Selena continued. "He's a gifted paramedic. Most of the patients he brings in are already stable by the time they get to the hospital, no matter what the emergency."

"Yes, I could tell he was very competent. But I made it clear to him that I was a doctor and he still flat-out ignored me and did everything his own way."

"You're too used to medical hierarchy," Selena told her. "Here we're more egalitarian. We make our decisions with everyone's input rather than automatically deciding that whoever's in charge knows best. It's a team approach. It takes some getting used to, but it's one of the things I love most about practicing here. And I think you'll learn to love it, too."

Selena's eyes grew mischievous.

"And maybe you'll fall in love with something else as well. Some*one* else…with blue eyes and dark hair and—"

"Oh, my God, Selena, let it go!" Kat held up one of the sofa pillows, threatening to throw it at her friend. "Jack and I are *not* going to happen. Maybe if he were the last man on this island I'd consider it. But only then."

Selena's eyes twinkled. "We'll see," she said. "It's a pretty small island."

Kat cleared her throat. "Is there perhaps something we can discuss *besides* my love-life? Something involving medicine?"

"Right!" said Selena. "The whole reason you're here. The virus outbreaks."

Selena sat behind her desk and pulled out several files for Kat to examine.

"Because of its location, Hawaii is vulnerable to all the strains of virus that sweep through Asia, so we try to keep an eye on what's happening there in order to be prepared for what could happen here."

She drew Kat's attention to one of the files.

"We're calling this one H5N7. There have been a few isolated cases on Oahu. Catching the signs early and keeping people quarantined to prevent the spread of infection has been key. But our hospital is too small to handle a major infectious disease event. My biggest worry is that a larger outbreak would strain our resources to such an extent that we wouldn't be able to provide effective care to patients who would otherwise be cured."

Kat nodded. "On the mainland you can rely on the resources of other hospitals, but here you can't simply call in for reinforcements or send your overflow of patients to another hospital nearby."

"Exactly. Sending patients to hospitals on the other islands can be a huge hassle. And even if we could, the only Level One trauma center for all the islands is located right here in *our* hospital—there's two thousand miles of ocean between us and the next nearest one. So we're observing very strict contamination procedures with any patient who comes in."

Kat passed the files back to Selena. "As far as I can tell you're doing the best you can to stay ahead of this thing," she said. "What's the status of any potential vaccine?"

"We're working with a team at the University of Hawaii at Manoa to see what can be done. So far their results are promising. In the meantime we're following the strictest quarantine procedures for any patients brought into the hospital with signs of flu, or any health workers who have been exposed. That means full haz-mat gear when we're working with affected patients. I've put a policy in place stating that any hospital staff members who come into contact with potentially infected patients will be housed here at the hospital, in a secure holding area, until we can confirm whether or not they've been exposed to the illness. If blood tests do confirm exposure, then it's a mandatory 10-day quarantine so that we have time to observe whether symptoms manifest, and so we can start treatment immediately if necessary. Bottom line, make sure you're taking the standard universal precautions with every patient, but be on the lookout for the rash and other symptoms so that you can be extra-careful with affected patients. So far, none of our staff have been exposed yet, and I intend to keep it that way."

Kat nodded. "Like I say, sounds like you're doing everything you can."

"We are," said Selena, "but I feel better now that you're here." Selena squirmed uncomfortably. "Actually…you may have to communicate quite a bit with Jack on this."

"Why? He's a paramedic."

"Exactly. If the outbreaks do increase, paramedics and EMTs will be at the greatest risk. They're the ones who will be exposed to the victims first. So it's essential that they keep us abreast of any risk of the flu spreading because they'll be the first to know."

Kat sighed. It seemed that avoiding Jack Harper would be harder than she'd thought.

After several weeks Kat began to settle into a rhythm at the hospital. She worked with the researchers from the University of Hawaii on the flu virus and shared ER shifts with the other doctors. They were a relaxed, easygoing bunch. And as Kat got used to the hospital's informality she began to appreciate the casual atmosphere.

She made friends with Kimo, the shift coordinator, who would bring in extra *kalua* pork sandwiches his mother had made. She got to know Marceline, a cardiologist, who would regale Kat with lurid stories of her former life as a webcam girl. "Modeling" skimpy outfits in front of her computer had helped Marceline pay for most of medical school. And one of the surgeons, Omar, was rumored to be royalty in his home country, but he was very clandestine about it. Kat had the feeling that he allowed the rumor to continue because it added to his air of mystery and seemed to improve his dating prospects quite a bit.

It was a colorful cast of characters, and nothing at all like the strait-laced, buttoned-up doctors she'd worked with back home.

The patients were different, too. Kat was used to seeing patients who were seeking second or third opinions on the prognosis of serious or rare illnesses. People came to Chicago Grace Memorial Hospital when other physicians had reached the end of their knowledge and were unable to provide more guidance, and Kat had typically used her expertise there to make hard-to-call diagnoses of illnesses that were extremely rare or difficult to treat.

Oahu General Hospital ran itself more like a small general practice. She saw children who had stuck innumerable crayons up their noses, and tourists with sprains or fractures because they'd taken risks while hiking.

She also saw entirely too much of Jack.

Somehow she always seemed to be on shift when he was bringing in patients. As if that wasn't bad enough he seemed to be constantly flirting—with everyone except Kat. Every time Kat saw him he was flashing his hundred-watt smile at the receptionists, or sharing private jokes with the nurses, or twinkling his eyes at patients.

She wasn't sure why Jack's behavior should bother her so much. She didn't care who he flirted with. After all, she wasn't interested in him, and he wasn't interested in her. She simply felt that one should maintain a professional attitude at work. A casual atmosphere was all well and good, but people could take these things too far. There was no need for Jack to go winking his ocean-blue eyes at everyone in sight, or giving his bright white smile to every woman who crossed his path.

Good God, she thought one day, when Jack smiled at a nurse who'd helped him lift a heavy patient off a gurney. *Even his teeth are perfect.*

It was all very distracting. And that was the problem, thought Kat. Jack's flirting with other people didn't bother her the least little bit. It was simply annoying to be constantly distracted by his tanned skin or his muscular arms. Why did he have to wear such tight shirts?

She'd tried to avoid him, but working at such a small hospital made it difficult to avoid anyone. He brought her just as many cases as he brought the other doctors—if not more. But he seemed to delight in bringing her the most ridiculous cases he could find. And then he wouldn't simply leave, the way most paramedics did. Every time he brought in a case, he would linger, as though he wanted to see how she would handle things.

When she'd challenged him on it he'd claimed that he was merely staying nearby in case she needed additional assistance. She didn't believe him for a minute. She was certain that he was sticking around so he could watch her reaction—which, in her opinion, proved that he was bringing her preposterous cases on purpose.

She dealt with it the only way she knew how—by maintaining a distant, cool, professional demeanor. And for his part Jack seemed to have no trouble keeping his face completely deadpan. Even today, as he pulled back one of the ER privacy curtains to reveal a young couple on a gurney. The woman sat upright, and her boyfriend was lying on his side.

Kat listened to their story.

"So where are you saying the zucchini is now?" she asked patiently.

After the couple had left, with a treatment plan and some stern words of warning about the inadvisability of placing vegetables in bodily orifices, Kat grabbed Jack and pulled him behind the curtain.

"I know what you're doing and it needs to stop," she hissed.

He blinked at her innocently. "I'm just doing my job. It's not my fault if I'm bringing patients to the ER while you happen to be on shift."

"There are other doctors on shift! Find one of them! The other day you had an acute appendicitis case and you brought it to Omar. But what kinds of cases do you bring *me*? College students who stick vegetables God knows where! A toddler who's pushed thirteen marbles up his nose! An elderly woman with dementia who ate all the little cakes her granddaughter made from Play-Doh because she thought they were real!"

"Hey, I thought she was sweet."

"She *was* sweet! That's not the point. You're doing this on purpose!"

"Doing what on purpose?" he asked innocently.

"Giving all the weird cases to me."

He shook his head. "Why on earth would I do that?" he said.

"I have no idea. Don't ask me what the motives of a sociopath are. But I've got news for you, pal. I've seen just about every crazy ER case in the book. Marbles are nothing—you wouldn't believe some of the things I've seen kids stick up their noses. You're not going to shock me with anything."

He held his hands up. "I believe you—I'm sure that you're unshockable. But I swear I'm not doing this on purpose. You've had a run of strange cases lately, I'll admit, but I promise I'm just bringing the patients as they come in."

As he spoke Kat realized just how close she and Jack were in physical proximity to one another. What had she been thinking when she pulled him behind a curtain? They could have had this conversation in public. Once again she'd ended up getting herself caught in close quarters with Jack. How did that keep happening?

She yanked open the curtain, deciding that it would be best to get out of the enclosure as quickly as possible—but she was stopped short by the small crowd of hospital staff that had gathered just outside.

There were several orderlies, as well as Marceline, Kimo and Omar. They tried to act casual, but they'd clearly been listening to her argument with Jack. *Great*, thought Kat. If their moment in the ambulance hadn't been enough, then rumors would definitely be flying about the two of them after this.

Jack really wasn't trying to hand off the most bizarre patients to Kat—it was simply a matter of bad timing. He knew they'd gotten off on the wrong foot. But he wasn't used to having his decisions questioned or challenged while he was trying to save lives. And yet, as argumentative and challenging as Kat had been, there was a strong air of feistiness about her that he admired.

She didn't seem like someone who gave up easily, whatever the circumstances.

He might have come off as bossy, but hadn't Kat acted the same way? He had been trying to provide her with medical care, while she'd been trying to convince him that she knew best by waving her credentials in front of his face—as though she couldn't possibly trust his expertise over her own.

Did she think he should be impressed by her credentials rather than her competence? It was the same kind of thinking he'd often noticed among his family members, who seemed to value the achievements and connections of medical professionals more than the skill they demonstrated.

Now that he'd spent a few weeks working with Kat he could tell that she was one of the most competent doctors he'd ever worked with. But he'd had no way of knowing that before.

And, just as he'd thought, Kat had started trying to implement changes at the hospital right away. Some changes had gone down better than others. First she'd required the EMTs and paramedics to switch from a three-point to a five-point triage system, and even he had to admit that it had been a *good* change. But her most controversial decision had been to ask all hospital staff to spend eight hours a month working at the hospital's nonprofit walk-in clinic.

Granted, she'd adjusted everyone's schedules so that this didn't impact too much on anyone's working hours.

But, while he might be able to acknowledge that Kat's changes so far were an improvement on an intellectual level, he still felt frustrated. Kat's ideas might be good, but that wasn't the point. The point was that she was a big-city doctor who thought she could just walk into a little hospital—*his* little hospital—and turn his job and his emotions upside down.

At first he'd tried to keep his distance, to give his feelings a chance to subside. But, if anything, avoiding Kat had seemed to intensify his attraction toward her, and he'd constantly found himself wondering how she was adjusting to her new job, whether she was talking to the other staff members, or if she was wearing that green blouse that offset her eyes so well.

To make matters worse, as he continued to work with Kat he became increasingly certain that he wasn't just attracted to her—he *liked* her as well. She had a wry sense of humor, and she seemed to possess wells of infinite patience and compassion with even the most difficult patients. She had a warm and ready smile, and she smiled often—just not at him.

So he'd decided to change tactics. Instead of avoiding Kat, he'd started to make a point of being sure to acknowledge her each time their paths crossed. He'd been trying to keep their encounters polite and casual. But that strategy had become more complicated when the hospital had suddenly been hit with a run of cases that bordered on the absurd.

Jack wasn't surprised that Kat thought he was bringing her weird cases on purpose, but he wished there was a way to convince her that it was just a coincidence that her caseload of late had been a bit unusual.

At least she'd never brought up their almost-kiss in the ambulance. His hunch was that she was just as eager to put that incident behind them as he was. He wondered if it would be possible for them to have a fresh start. The sooner he could convince her that he wasn't bringing her strange cases on purpose—that he did not, in fact, have any special interest in her, in any way— the sooner he could start trying to convince himself of the same thing.

He wasn't quite sure how, but he'd find a way.

A few days later, the doors of the elevator in the hospital's parking garage were just closing in front of Kat when a hand reached out to stop them. They automatically shifted open again, and Kat was surprised to see Jack standing in front of her.

"May I?" he said, motioning inside the elevator.

Kat shrugged. "Plenty of room," she said.

He got onto the elevator with her, and they began their ascent from the basement to the trauma unit. But Jack surprised Kat again by pushing the emergency stop button.

Before she could speak, he said, "Look, I know we got off on the wrong foot, and I just wanted to clear the air. Back in the ambulance, I...um..."

Oh, no, thought Kat. Was Jack was about to bring up their almost-kiss? She needed to take control of this conversation, and fast.

"I was a jerk," she said quickly. "You were just trying to help, and I argued and fought you every step of the way. I blame the hypothermia. You were just doing your job."

"That's true," he said. "But I have to admit that I'm not used to treating patients who have medical experience…just like you probably weren't used to being in the patient's role."

He was trying to offer her an olive branch. Maybe she should take it. They did have to work together, after all. She'd tried desperately to deal with her attraction by avoiding him, but that strategy didn't seem to be working. If anything, she thought about him more than ever.

Maybe the problem was that she wasn't seeing Jack as a real person. The distance between them was causing her to focus too much on his physical attractiveness. Maybe if she spent more time with him, got to know him as a normal person whom she had to see every day, whom she had to work with, then he'd lose some of his luster. This man with his dark, wavy hair and perfect teeth was sure to have some flaws—she simply hadn't been around him enough to notice any of them. Maybe once she discovered a few of them her heart and stomach would stop doing flip-flops every time she saw him.

And it would be nice to stop being so distracted by his scent, as well. How did he always manage to smell like the beach? It filled the elevator now—the scent of sunblock, saltwater, and pure masculinity. Maybe she'd get desensitized if she were around him enough…

"I really haven't been bringing you the weird cases on purpose," he was saying. "I don't know why all of the odd ones have been coming in during your ER shifts, but I promise I haven't been giving them to you intentionally."

"Hmm…" she said. "Not even that toddler who swallowed the voice box from his teddy bear, and we could all hear Teddy's disembodied voice coming out of the kid's lower abdomen every time he pressed on his stomach?"

"*Especially* not that one." Jack shuddered. "That was creepy."

Suddenly Kat found herself laughing. The case really had been ridiculous. And anyway, even if he *had* been bringing her odd cases on purpose, dealing with the unexpected was part of the job.

His relief at her laughter seemed sincere, so Kat thought that his apology probably was as well. "All right, Jack," she said. "How about a truce?"

And finally—*finally*—after all this time, she found herself the recipient of his smile. The full force of it was just as dazzling as she had known it would be. Her knees felt a little weak, but she managed to casually grip the bar on one side of the elevator, as though she were just shifting her stance.

"A truce sounds good," he said. "I have a feeling that if we're not bickering we might actually find out we like working together."

Kat wasn't sure what to say.

Certainly not, *I'd like that, but I'm very attracted to you, and that's really interfering with my ability to recover from a fiancé who practically left me at the altar just a few weeks ago.*

No, that response was probably off the table.

She settled for giving him a small smile instead.

He released the emergency stop button and the elevator began moving upward again. This would be good, thought Kat. They would get to know each other a little better, and soon enough she'd get used to him. He'd never need to know how badly she wanted to run her fingers through his dark hair.

When the elevator doors opened on the trauma unit all was in chaos. Even Selena was sweeping around the ER floor, conducting triage.

She nodded at Jack and Kat as they stepped out of the elevator. "Major car crash on the expressway," she said, by way of explanation. "We've got multiple trauma cases coming in at once. Grab one and get to work."

Jack and Kat nodded at one another. At the end of the hallway a team of EMTs were wheeling a gurney with an incoming patient on it toward the ER; Kat rushed toward them, with Jack close behind her.

"What've we got?" Kat asked Marco, the head EMT on duty.

"Man who looks to be in his late fifties with multiple fractures. His breathing was shallow when we first picked him up, but now he's not breathing at all. He got smashed up pretty bad in the expressway crash. We had to use the jaws of life to get him out from under his car."

"How long has he been unresponsive?"

"Less than a few seconds."

"His pulse is thready," said Jack. "Could be something obstructing the airway."

Kat placed her stethoscope on the man's chest. She could hear a heartbeat, but there were no sounds of respiration. "We'll need to intubate," she said. "Let's get him to an operating room."

She was about to ask Jack if he'd be able to come with her, but he'd already moved to the other side of the gurney and was helping her push it down the hallway.

"Thanks," she said breathlessly as she tried to keep pace with him. "I know they need you out there."

"You need me in here," he responded as they pushed the patient's gurney into the OR.

He immediately began attending to the pulse oximeter, and Kat was relieved to see there was no need to talk him through the procedure; he'd clearly done this before.

Before she could ask, he handed her a laryngoscope. Kat tilted the patient's head back and inserted the scope into his mouth, taking care to avoid the man's teeth. As she pushed the endotracheal tube into the patient's airway Jack began to inflate the balloon that would deliver air into his lungs. He continued inflations as Kat positioned her stethoscope first above one lung and then the other, to listen for sounds of respiration.

There.

Kat relaxed her shoulders as she identified the ragged but unmistakable sound of breathing in both lungs. They'd need an X-ray to ensure correct placement of the tube, but hearing respiration from both lungs meant that the patient should stabilize quickly.

She straightened up from where she was bent over the patient and looked at Jack in astonishment. "I don't think I've ever gotten a line into a patient so fast," she said.

He flashed a smile at her and Kat felt another pang. Just a few minutes ago she'd been hoping that spending more time with Jack would help desensitize her to his charm. But now, finding that they were able to work together so seamlessly… Kat thought she might actually *want* to work with Jack more often if it meant that her medical procedures would go this smoothly.

If she could just get her heart to stop going into overdrive every time he smiled they'd be a great team.

"One of the easiest intubations I've ever done," he agreed, looking at the patient's pulse-ox levels on the monitor. "I'd say we should take him down to X-Ray to ensure correct placement of the line, but…"

"What is it?" said Kat.

"Come look."

Kat came around to Jack's side of the gurney and was suddenly filled with dread.

The distinctive rash of the super-flu was spread over the man's legs and abdomen: small red bumps. And she and Jack had been working on him without hazmat suits, and with only standard levels of protection between the two of them.

Kat realized that her plan to take the edge off her attraction to Jack by getting to know him better was about to blow up in her face.

She was going to get to know Jack better, all right. Kat remembered what Selena had told her about the hospital's policy regarding virus exposure.

Kat looked at Jack's face, and knew what he was thinking, too.

They might be about to spend a long time together.

CHAPTER FOUR

KAT AND JACK had only been in the secure holding room for a few hours before Kat was certain of one thing: no matter how much time they spent together, she was never going to become desensitized to Jack Harper.

She'd wondered if being quarantined with Jack would let the two of them get to know each other better. But she quickly realized he was as guarded as ever when she mentioned that the research team working on the virus had been using studies conducted by his parents for reference. She'd only meant to reassure him that she thought the team was close to developing a vaccine, but his reaction surprised her.

"Look," he said, "I deal with this every time we get a new doctor at the hospital, so I'm just going to tell you this now: I haven't spoken with any of my family members for more than four years. So if you're trying to wangle an introduction to any of the great Dr. Harpers, you're barking up the wrong tree."

"What?" said Kat, surprised. "Jack, you've totally got the wrong idea. I just meant that your parents' research has been extremely useful."

When he still looked skeptical, Kat went on.

"Selena mentioned your family during my first few days here. What I don't understand is why it should be any sort of secret. If I came from a family like yours I'd be telling everyone. With those kinds of connections in the medical field—"

"Connections with the Harpers are only useful if you're doing what they want you to do," he said. "If you're trying to forge your own path, then being a member of the Harper family is more of a liability than an advantage."

Kat nodded slowly. "I'm guessing they didn't love it that you dropped out of medical school."

"That about sums it up," he said.

She wanted to ask him more, but she could see that the subject was closed.

Why did he have to smell so good? Her plan—the plan that had sounded so good in her mind earlier that morning—was not going to work.

She'd had high hopes that if she could simply spend more time with Jack she might start to think of him as a normal person, instead of someone she felt unaccountably attracted to. But the more time she spent with Jack, the more tantalizing he became. The question of whether his eyes were blue, or more of a deep sea-green, was becoming a matter of some urgency to her, as she found her mind wandering back to his eyes anytime she tried to concentrate.

She and Jack had been housed together in a small room at the far end of the hospital's rarely used west wing. Selena had apologized for the small size of the designated isolation area and had made a halfhearted offer to try to find a way to provide separate rooms for them, but Kat could tell her friend was concerned about the hospital's limited capacity due to the influx of patients from the highway crash. Kat and Jack had both reassured Selena that they would be fine sharing a single room with privacy curtains, although secretly Kat wasn't thrilled at the idea, and from the expression on his face, she could tell that Jack felt the same way. But if sharing a room with Jack would help to make room for more patients, then Kat would cope with the situation the best she could.

Selena had arranged for the infectious disease team to run blood tests on the affected patient. It would take anywhere from a few hours to a few days to be sure. If the team confirmed that the patient did have the super-flu, then Kat and Jack would be spending at least the next ten days together, to ensure that neither of them showed any sign of having contracted the virus.

Kat hoped with all her heart that the patient didn't have the virus—both for the patient's sake and because she wasn't sure how she was going to be able to sleep knowing Jack was a mere two feet away from her.

The room was sparse: it contained two gurneys with privacy curtains, a shared bathroom, and an old television set that could access about three network channels. With their limited entertainment options Kat could tell that it was going to be a long ten days, if it came to that.

It didn't help that their close quarters only served to highlight how different they were from one another. She could tell by the way that Jack had haphazardly thrown his belongings about the room that he was the kind of person who didn't seem to mind clutter. She, on the

other hand, preferred things to be neat and orderly—
even if they would only be staying there for a few days.

"We should decide which parts of the room are yours
and which are mine," she said. Maybe keeping their
things to separate areas would help her to ignore the
mess.

He blinked, looking around the tiny, five-hundred-
square-foot room. "Isn't that kind of irrelevant in a room
this small?" he said. "I don't think there's much we can
do to avoid each other's space."

Kat gritted her teeth. She had a feeling that she
wanted to tolerate his clutter about as much as he
wanted to talk about his family.

"Some people might say that in a tiny space it's even
more important to be clear about what goes where,"
she said.

"Fine," he replied. "How about I stay on my gurney
and you stay on yours, and the rest can work itself out?"

She took a deep breath.

You're learning how to relax, she reminded herself.
*You're learning how to let go and live in the moment.
Maybe this is your chance to practice that.*

The Old Kat would have insisted on trying to win
the argument. The New Kat was going to disengage.

She unpacked a small mountain of meditation workbooks and arranged them at the foot of her gurney in a
neat stack, making sure they were organized by subject
and author's last name. If she had to be in quarantine
she might as well use her time productively.

When Selena had heard about Kat's mission to spend
the year learning how to relax she'd provided Kat with
an extensive collection of self-help workbooks, medi-

tation recordings, and podcasts on mindfulness. Selena had termed the project "Operation Rebound," while Kat preferred to think of it as "Operation Inner Peace." She'd gotten through about a third of the workbooks, but inner peace was still proving elusive.

Learning to relax was a much more daunting task than she'd originally thought.

The key to achieving a relaxed state, according to all of her meditation recordings and workbooks, was to practice putting aside distracting thoughts in order to turn her mind to the present moment. So she sat on her gurney with her legs crossed and her eyes closed as a soothing voice through her headphones instructed her. And she tried to follow the instructions—she really did.

First she turned aside all thoughts about Jack's eyes.

Then she turned aside all thoughts about his hair, and what it might feel like to run her fingers through it.

Then she turned aside her thoughts about whether that tantalizing scent of his might have a bit of sandalwood in it. Was the smell just *him*, she wondered, or did he put on some sort of cologne?

It was strange, she thought, that she didn't have to try very hard to keep her mind off Christopher. It was Christopher who'd broken her heart, after all. Just three days before their wedding. Her heart still ached to think about it. But, even though she was sad about the wedding, and the end of all the things she'd envisioned for their lives together, she didn't find Christopher crossing her mind very often.

Sometimes she found herself feeling sad about the breakup, or angry about the way he had gone about it, but oddly she didn't find herself thinking about Christopher *himself*. She certainly didn't find herself constantly distracted by thoughts of him. Not the way she was by thoughts of Jack.

Jack's main goal, in most relationships, was always to avoid getting too close. As someone who had been overshadowed by his family and their prestigious medical careers for much of his life, it was important to Jack to be his own person. But avoiding closeness was difficult in the tiny quarantined room. It had only been a few hours, and he already wasn't sure he would be able to make it for that much longer.

At first their sharing a room had seemed practical. But now that Jack was faced with the fact that he would be sleeping just a few feet from Kat that very night... He tried to make certain his behavior was as gentlemanlike as possible at all times. If he couldn't hide his attraction from himself, then he at least wanted to hide it from her.

Kat sat meditating on her gurney. She seemed so serene. She was ambitious, just as Sophie had been, but then, he could never picture Sophie practicing at a hospital like Oahu General, focusing on patient care rather than prestigious research projects.

Kat certainly wasn't like Sophie. Usually when people in the medical world learned who Jack's family was they couldn't wait to talk to him about how his father's books had changed their lives, or how his mother had inspired them to go into medicine. But in six weeks Kat hadn't said a thing to him, despite knowing.

Except for just a moment ago, when she'd simply

mentioned his parents' books and he'd assumed the worst. He wondered now if he'd acted prematurely.

Kat was obviously at the top of her field. She should be at a prestigious hospital on the mainland. Somewhere far away from him. Then he wouldn't have to think about the red curls cascading down her back. What was she doing here, on his island, at *his* hospital?

With all those books she looked as if she should be going on some sort of meditation retreat.

When he stepped over to the carefully organized set of workbooks that were piled in a neat stack at the edge of Kat's gurney she yanked her headphones out.

"Sorry if I interrupted," he said.

"I wasn't having much success anyway," she said. "It's kind of hard to focus on the present moment when you're stuck in a small room with bad lighting, waiting to find out if you've contracted a life-threatening illness."

He nodded in agreement and picked up one of the books. "'*Zen and the Art of You,*'" he read aloud. "'*Finding the Inner Child Within Your Inner Self.*' What *is* all this stuff?"

"It's part of my project to learn how to relax," said Kat. "I thought I'd use this time to get into my Zen."

"Into your... Zen?"

She tried to explain. "It's like...trying to live in the moment. To take life one step at a time. Not to plan, but to accept what comes in each moment."

"To go with the flow?"

"Exactly," said Kat. "Only, it's harder than it sounds.

Especially since I've never been a very go-with-the-flow type of person."

He raised his eyebrows in mock surprise. "You're kidding?"

She glared at him, and he briefly considered whether he might need to duck and run for cover.

But then she groaned and said, "Look, this stuff doesn't come naturally to me. I've never been very good at letting go of all the things I have to worry about. When I lived in Chicago, sometimes I tried going to the beach on Lake Michigan to de-stress—but you know what happened every time? I couldn't shut my brain off. I'd think about the patients who needed me, or the things I'd left unfinished, or other doctors and nurses I needed to communicate with. Or the hundred other things I had to do the next day. It was so hard to figure out how to let it all go that eventually I stopped trying."

"But you're trying again now? What changed?"

Her face grew sad. "The Day of Doom," she said.

That sounded pretty intense. Was that the reason Kat had wanted to move to Hawaii? He'd simply assumed that she wanted a break from her regular life, or had romantic illusions about working in a tropical setting. It had never occurred to him that she might be running away from something.

"I suppose it does sound dramatic," she continued.

For a moment he thought she might be blinking back tears, but it must simply be the way the light hit her eyes.

"It was just a bad breakup, really. That and some other things all happened at once. Just bad timing."

Ah. So she wasn't running from something so much as some*one*. "Breakups are hard," he said. "If it makes you feel any better you're not the only one who's ever run off to Hawaii after a bad breakup."

She lifted her eyebrows. "You?"

"Me. After my own exceptionally hard breakup."

She gave a soft chuckle. "So we're both unlucky in love? And I thought you and I had nothing in common."

He snorted. "I'd have to believe in love first, in order for us to have that in common."

"Oh, no, you don't," she said.

"Don't what?"

"Don't try to beat me at cynicism. My breakup was way worse than yours—I guarantee it. No one believes in love less than I do. Trust me, pal, I have given up on love."

He raised his eyebrows. "Have you?"

"What—you don't believe me?"

"You just don't seem to be the type to give up on love."

"Oh, but I have. I've given up on love way harder than you ever could."

"Wait a minute," he said. "Has this become a contest, Kat? Are we having a contest to see which of us believes in love the least?"

She laughed. "Yes. We're having a contest to see who is the saddest and unluckiest in love, because that might be the only way to cheer ourselves up. So tell me if you can top this: my fiancé left me just three days before our wedding."

"Hmm…" he mused. "That *is* going to be hard to beat. But I think I can."

"I don't know... I think when it comes to sad love stories, getting jilted three days before your wedding is going to win every time."

"How about this? My fiancée left me for my brother."

Jack didn't know why he was telling her this. He never talked about Sophie with anyone. But talking to Kat felt so easy.

She stopped laughing and grew quiet.

"It's all right," he said. "It was a long time ago."

"What happened to her?"

"She lives in Nebraska now. She's a doctor too."

He wasn't sure he was ready for this after all. He flipped the pages of one of Kat's workbooks, which seemed to contain very specific instructions on how to achieve a relaxed state.

"You know, I'm not sure you're doing this right," he said.

"Excuse me?" she said. "Is there a *wrong* way to relax?"

"I'm just not sure relaxing is something you can learn from a book," he said. "I mean, doesn't it seem like what you're doing is the exact opposite of what you're trying to learn?"

She bristled. "What are you talking about?"

He picked up the color-coded document that Kat had printed out, which outlined each major school of thought on meditation and Kat's views on their various pros and cons.

"You're meant to be trying to learn how to live in the moment, but you're doing it exactly the way you've always done things: by planning, organizing, and obsessively studying everything there is to know about relaxing. You're practically getting yourself another doctorate in relaxation."

She snatched the document from him. "That may be the case, but this is the only way I've ever been able to learn anything. I got though medical school by throwing myself at my books and studying longer and harder than anyone else."

"Yeah, but you're not in medical school anymore. You're trying to enjoy life—not study it."

"Then what do *you* think I should do, if you're so certain all my workbooks aren't going to help?"

He considered for a moment. "So much of your life is about taking care of other people," he said. "You need some excitement that's focused on *you*, not someone else. You need something that gives you a thrill."

"A thrill?" She looked doubtful. "That goes against everything I'm reading here. All the exercises in these books are about slowing down and focusing on the present moment."

"Nothing gets you focused on the present like an adrenaline rush."

He warmed to his theme. Every time he jumped out of a helicopter to reach a patient in a remote or inaccessible area, every time he resuscitated a patient from cardiac arrest, or delivered a baby on the way to the hospital, he was completely caught up in the present moment.

"Think about it," he said. "When do you feel the most calm, the most confident?"

"Hmm…" she said slowly. "Probably those moments in the ER when we're slammed with trauma cases."

"Exactly," said Jack. "It's the same for me. You get

totally lost in the moment. You forget about any of your own worries and problems and just focus on what's in front of you."

"Okay," she said thoughtfully. "You might be on to something. But I can't just spend my entire life in the ER. That kind of defeats the purpose of learning how to relax when I'm not at work."

He shook his head. "You don't have to spend your life in the ER."

"Then what?"

"It could be anything," he said. "Something that feeds your sense of adventure. Something new… something exciting. Something crazy and out of the box. Hiking, surfing, cliff jumping…"

"Cliff jumping?"

"Hurtling yourself off a cliff into the ocean is a great way to gain mental clarity. You're never as certain of what you want in your life as you are when you're falling through the air."

"Um…because you're facing death?"

"Facing death? Absolutely not." Then, before he could stop himself, "I'll take you. We'll only jump in places where I know exactly how deep the water is and what the rocks are like underneath. Safety first. Safety is what makes it exciting instead of terrifying."

Wait a minute. You're supposed to be trying to spend less time with her—not more. The second this quarantine is lifted you're out of here, remember? Whether that's ten hours or ten days from now.

But she was already smiling back at him. "Spoken like a true paramedic," she said.

At the sight of her smile he could feel his resolve to keep his distance slipping away. He needed to regroup.

"Well," he said, "when we get out of here maybe a group of us can go. The two of us and Marceline, Kimo…"

He saw something change in her eyes. Was it disappointment? Or relief?

"Sure," she said. "What better way to bond than over dangerous, death-defying stunts?"

"Not dangerous—*exciting*," he said. "I wouldn't let anything happen to you."

She gave him another small smile, making her face glow. "I'm starting to believe that's true. But, since the two of us are stuck in here for now, would you happen to have any ideas about what kind of exciting thrills we could enjoy in a five-hundred-square-foot, poorly lit, windowless room?"

Jack didn't dare voice the first suggestion that came to mind. Or the second. Or the third.

Instead, he simply said, "I play a mean Gin Rummy, if that's the kind of thrill you have in mind?"

A few hour later Kat lay on her gurney, trying unsuccessfully to sleep.

She kept replaying that conversation with Jack in her head. For one moment she'd almost thought he was suggesting they go on a date. But that was stupid. What had he ever done that would even remotely have given her that impression?

He'd simply meant to help her as a friend. He'd been watching her try to relax and he'd actually come up with a pretty good idea. How had she never thought of it before? Jack had been absolutely right to notice that she felt the most like herself when she was caught up in life-or-death situations. It was one reason she loved her ER shifts so much. The intensity of getting a patient's heart going again, or rushing to alleviate a trauma survivor's pain, was thrilling for her.

Cliff jumping.

As crazy as it sounded, Kat couldn't stop thinking about it. Hadn't her entire decision to come to Hawaii been one giant, impulsive leap into the unknown? After making such a huge change to her life, jumping off a cliff might almost feel easy in comparison.

It had been kind of Jack to offer to take her. Although he'd been eager to clarify that he was only suggesting they go as friends. And he'd been so adamant in asserting that she wouldn't come to any harm. He'd seemed almost fierce in his protectiveness of her.

But that was probably because he was a responsible person. He'd be protective of any friend he was with.

So why couldn't she sleep? Why was she just lying here, feeling disappointment settle into her stomach over and over again?

She thought about when he'd told her he didn't believe in love. She'd said the same to him. But did he really mean that? And what if he did? Why should it matter to her?

Suddenly Kat couldn't stand it for a moment longer. She was done with being in quarantine.

She sat straight up on her gurney and threw off her blankets.

This ends now, she thought. *I'm not staying here another minute longer than I absolutely have to.*

She had a plan, and she had no doubt that Jack would agree with it. After all, it was what a good friend would do.

Several feet away, Jack was failing to get any sleep as well. He glared at the privacy curtain that surrounded his gurney. Why the hell did it have to be so thin?

To his surprise, he saw it was rustling. And then Kat appeared in front of him.

"Hey…" Her voice was low, husky. "Can we talk for a sec?"

"What is it?" he asked as she stood in front of him in a pair of pink silk pajamas.

He didn't want to admit just how much he'd allowed this very scene to creep into his wildest fantasies—fantasies he'd been trying to push out of his mind since the moment they'd been put into quarantine together. The ridiculous idea that she'd slip into his enclosure, gaze into his eyes, and say something like…

"We need to take our clothes off."

Jack looked at her in disbelief, uncertain of how to take in what he'd just heard. "We need to *what?*" he said.

"Strip," she replied matter-of-factly. "I don't know about you, but I can't take it in here for another minute—and I'm sure as hell not spending the next ten days here. All my research with the experts from the university has indicated that patients with the super-flu virus become symptomatic within the first twelve hours of exposure. Neither of us has shown even the slightest sign of having contracted the virus. So here's what we're going to do. You'll examine me, I'll examine you, and once we've confirmed that there's absolutely no sign of the illness in either of us we'll call Selena. After all, I'm the one who's been studying this illness more than anyone on staff. I think I should be qualified to tell whether the two of us have been infected or not."

Jack noticed that Kat was shaking. Was she really so desperate to get out of here? He wondered if she was starting to get claustrophobic in the cramped space. Or maybe she just wanted to get away from him.

"If this is about needing to get some space, I'm sure we can tell Selena that we've changed our minds and want separate rooms," Jack said.

"That won't work. The hospital's at capacity. But that actually works in our favor. If we can convince her that we're showing no signs of the virus right now, it means one more free room in the hospital."

Jack considered this. Compared to the prospects of limited entertainment, uncomfortable sleeping arrangements, and hospital food, the thought of getting out of here was tempting.

The problem was, the idea of a naked Kat in front of him was pretty tempting, too.

The pajamas that Kat wore were pretty thin. He could see the curve of her hip underneath her pajama top. The silk shorts revealed long, slender legs.

He decided to try reasoning with her on a professional level.

"If this is about you being afraid of having contracted the flu, I wouldn't worry too much," he said. "The chances are extremely low. They've just got us quarantined in here out of an abundance of precaution.

I know it's a hassle, but it's the appropriate procedure to follow."

"It's not that," said Kat. "I doubt either one of us actually has the flu. I just have to get out of here."

Jack was trying to muster his better self. In all the ways he had pictured the two of them together—and despite himself, despite every rational thought, he *had* been picturing it—he had never imagined it like this: him and Kat quarantined together in an isolated hospital room, surrounded by medical supplies.

To make matters worse, her request meant that she clearly thought of him as nothing more than a friend. She'd never ask such a thing of him if she had the slightest inkling of his feelings for her—or if she had any feelings for him.

He made a last weak attempt to do the right thing. "Wouldn't you rather wait until morning?" he said. "The blood test results might not take much longer—maybe the infectious disease team will have some good news for us by then."

"I can't wait until morning," said Kat. "I can't wait another minute."

She hastily began to unbutton her pajama top.

It was too much for Jack.

"Hold on," he said, putting his hands over hers. He could feel her trembling, just as she had been in the water when they'd first met. "Are you sure this is what you want?"

She gritted her teeth and grabbed his T-shirt. "Jack. We are getting out of here. *Tonight*."

There was no arguing with the determination in

her voice. Or her eyes. Jack had a feeling that no one crossed Kat when she was in this kind of mood.

The authority in her voice was intimidating.

Her eyes burned into him.

He took a deep breath. His only hope was to remain as professional as possible. He didn't know how he was going to handle seeing Kat naked. He had been trying so hard to avoid thinking about her body…and now it was going to appear right in front of him. Only not in the way he'd fantasized about. The only way he was going to get through this was by putting as much professional distance between himself and Kat as possible.

"All right," he said. "If we're going to do this, we're going to be professional about it."

"Agreed," she replied. "Let's get the lights on."

Jack flipped a switch and harsh fluorescent lighting flooded the room.

Perfect. The least romantic lighting possible in one of the most sterile rooms imaginable. This is about as unsexy as it gets, and that's exactly how it needs to be right now.

He pulled a coin from the nightstand next to his gurney. "Flip to see who gets examined first?" he said.

"Don't bother. I'll go first," she said.

I hope you know what you're doing, Kat thought to herself.

She was certain that if she could prove that neither she nor Jack were showing any sign of the virus then she'd be able to convince Selena to let them leave this room. Then she wouldn't have to deal with this tantalizing closeness any more.

It had seemed like a great idea just a few minutes ago.

Now, in the harsh reality of the fluorescent overhead lighting, she was having second thoughts.

But she and Jack were both medical professionals. Surely they could be professional about this? They'd do a thorough examination of one another and then they'd be able to go home. As a doctor, Kat had long ago set aside any sense of squeamishness about undergoing or conducting examinations. This was simply what needed to be done—for the sake of her well-being and Jack's.

She couldn't stand waiting for the blood test results for another minute. She was at her absolute limit. She needed to get away from Jack as soon as possible. Seeing him naked might be a bit overwhelming, but only for a few moments. She could withstand a few moments of being close to him if it meant that she would be on her way home after it was over.

Her fingers shook so much that she kept fumbling the buttons of her pajama top.

"Here," he said. "Let me help."

He briskly undid the remaining silk buttons of her top, one by one. The top fell open, revealing the inner curves of her breasts. She kept her eyes locked with Jack's as he slipped the top from her shoulders and it fell to the floor with the quiet rustle of crumpling silk.

He cleared his throat and then, in a clipped, professional voice, said, "Let's start from the top."

Jack cupped her face, palpating her jawline.

"I'll need you to come a little closer so I can see your scalp," he said.

She stepped forward, only inches away from him. She couldn't stop herself from breathing in deeply. This close, his scent was intoxicating. She could barely stand. But Jack was pulling her inward, looking through her hair for any sign of the flu rash on the skin of her scalp and the back of her neck.

She tried to remain perfectly still. She didn't want to make the situation any more uncomfortable than it had to be. She was the one who'd asked for this, she reminded herself. And she was probably the last person that Jack was interested in seeing naked. He was doing her a favor. The least she could do was be professional about it.

After a few moments Jack stepped away from her. "Everything up top looks good," he said. "Let's take a look at the rest of you."

Was it just her imagination or had his voice seemed to break just a little at the end? Was he nervous? Kat couldn't think why he would be. He'd made it clear that at the very most he was only interested in her friendship. Examining her naked body was probably, for him, just the same as it would be when he examined any other patient.

He placed both his hands on her shoulders and ran them down her arms, feeling for any inconsistencies in her skin. Then he turned her around and ran his hands lightly over her back. His hands felt rough— rough enough to have a texture, but not too much. She could tell he used them often, both for hard work and as sensitive instruments. They were hands that could rescue a drowning swimmer or pound a heart back to life.

Her own heart was pounding pretty hard. She couldn't help but give a small shiver.

"Sorry," he said, instantly attentive. "Are you cold?"

"N-no. I'm fine," she managed to stammer.

His hands moved faster now. Over her back and arms, rubbing her skin as though he were trying to warm her up. He turned Kat's body so that she was facing him again, and brought one of his hands up to touch her breast.

But before going on he stopped, his hand in midair. Their eyes locked.

Suddenly Kat knew that what she wanted had nothing to do with a professional examination. And it had nothing to do with any remote worry that she might have contracted the virus.

She stood in front of Jack, vulnerable, exposed, and she didn't know what to do next. She reached for him, ready to tell him that this whole idea was a mistake and that he didn't have to continue with the examination. She stepped an inch closer to him, reaching for the hand that still hovered over her breast.

Before she knew what had happened she found herself enveloped in Jack's arms. His mouth was covering hers, and she was kissing him back just as passionately. The scent of sun and salt water overtook her senses. His strong arms held her close to him, and then she was fumbling to reach under the soft gray T-shirt he slept in, which chafed enticingly against her bare breasts.

They broke for a moment as she lifted the shirt over his head, and then he kissed her again, and she lost herself in the feeling of her skin against his, his arms circling her.

He hoisted her onto the gurney and then climbed in himself. She lifted her hips so he could slide her pajama bottoms down and then off. A voice in her head cried out that *this* was what she had wanted—had, in fact, been looking for since he'd rescued her. There was no logic to it. There was only feeling: a solid, steady feeling that *this* was what she needed, *this* was the feeling she had been craving. *This* was living in the moment.

There had been no planning, no agonizing over the right decision, no making a pro versus con list and calculating her next step. She was completely caught up in the sensation of *Jack*—the roughness of his palms against her shoulders, her breasts; the strength of his chest and arms, the sweet-salt taste of his mouth crushed against her own.

Suddenly, they both froze. Someone was knocking on the door of the quarantine room.

"Kat?" Selena's voice rang out. "Jack? Is it okay if I come in?"

They leapt away from one another.

"Just give us a second!" Kat called out.

Kat stuffed her legs into her pajama bottoms at a furious pace. She tried to fasten the buttons on her top, but kept matching the buttons with the wrong hole. Finally she gave up and settled for wrapping the top around herself and folding her arms tightly in front of her, hoping Selena wouldn't see anything amiss.

Jack threw his shirt over his head and nodded at Kat. "C'mon in," he called to Selena, once he and Kat had perched themselves casually on a gurney, looking for all the world as though they'd been enjoying a casual midnight game of cards.

Selena entered the room and took in the scene: rumpled sheets, and a breathless Kat and Jack sitting next to each other on the same gurney.

"Sorry to visit you two so late at night, but I thought you'd want to hear right away," she said. "We've had a false alarm. The patient did not have the virus. It was just an ordinary case of shingles, which both of you will have been vaccinated against. So there's no need for either of you to be in here any longer."

"That's great!" said Kat and Jack, both at once.

"I had a feeling you'd be glad to hear it," Selena said. "I'm sure you're both eager to get out of here."

"Can't wait," said Kat.

"Neither can I," said Jack. "I'm not sure either of us could have handled one more minute stuck in here."

"Glad to be the bearer of good news," said Selena, turning to leave. "Oh, by the way, Jack, your shirt is on inside out."

CHAPTER FIVE

KAT FLOPPED HERSELF onto the sofa in Selena's office and let out a groan of frustration. A week had passed since the night she and Jack had been quarantined together. They hadn't seen much of each other since then, but when their paths had crossed they'd been friendly, polite, and professional with one another. There had been absolutely no discussion of their heated moment in the quarantine room.

As far as Kat could tell Jack seemed to want to pretend it had never happened. And if that was what he wanted, then she was happy to oblige.

Or so she told herself.

She might be able to stop herself from talking about that moment, but she couldn't stop herself from thinking about it. The way his hands had felt on her back, her shoulders, her thighs. The way his scent had completely enveloped her...the way his arms had enfolded her so completely.

The way he'd slipped off her pajama bottoms seconds before Selena had knocked on the door.

She was mortified by her behavior. Jack had been completely cool and clinical while he examined her—

until she'd thrown herself at him like some sort of sex-crazed maniac. Her cheeks burned at the memory. He'd been trying to maintain a professional atmosphere. *She* had been the one to completely misinterpret the situation.

It was true that as their kiss had continued he'd seemed just as caught up in the moment as she had been. He hadn't objected when she'd removed his shirt, hadn't hesitated to assist her in the removal of the rest of her own clothing. But that only meant that he'd been swept away by the moment—a moment *she'd* instigated. His actions didn't mean that he'd shared the same feelings she'd had.

Kat agonized over what might have happened if Selena hadn't made her appearance.

In that moment her whole body had been crying out for Jack.

How far would they have gone?

Would having sex with Jack have cleared away all that tension, or added to it?

Kat realized that all those questions simply left her head spinning. Once again she was overanalyzing everything—trying to solve her situation with Jack like a puzzle, rather than focusing on what was right in front of her.

And what *was* in front of her?

A pile of evidence indicating that, at best, she and Jack were friends and nothing more. Two people shut up with one another for any period of time with nothing to do were bound to get confused into thinking they were developing feelings for one another.

But Jack didn't have any feelings for her that Kat

could discern. She'd been practically naked in his hands and he'd been calm and collected, focusing on his examination of her skin. *She* was the one who had thrown herself at him. She hadn't been able to help herself. The sensation of his hands on her skin, of her bare breasts against his chest, still left her feeling a little dizzy.

Fortunately she was already slumped on Selena's couch, so dizziness wouldn't be a problem.

She'd wanted to keep the details of her time in quarantine with Jack a secret, but it ached to come bursting out of her. She was desperate for someone to understand, and Selena was one of her oldest friends.

Still, unburdening herself would probably be a lot easier if Selena's eyes weren't glowing with so much excitement over the rim of her coffee cup.

"I knew I should have found you separate rooms."

Despite her words, Kat caught Selena's wry smile as she sipped her coffee.

"This is serious, Selena," said Kat. "I don't know what to do."

"Why do you have to *do* anything?" asked Selena sensibly. "It sounds to me as though you like him. And, from what you describe, it sounds like he's into you as well. Didn't you say he asked you out on a date?"

"Not a *date* date. Not at all. Just a group thing… with friends."

Selena made a face of disgust. "'Group thing?' What a cop-out. If he likes you, why doesn't he just ask you out?"

"I'm not so sure he *does* like me," said Kat. "That kiss could have meant anything. For all I know it was completely one-sided. He was a perfect gentleman when

I asked him to examine me. He was completely professional about it. I was the one who made it awkward by practically throwing myself into his arms."

Selena rolled her eyes. "Even if you *were* the one who started things, it sounds as though he was pretty willing to go along with it. Maybe…and I know this is a crazy idea, but hear me out…just maybe, the two of you might try *talking to each other* about how you feel."

"Oh, God," said Kat. "That's what I was afraid you were going to say. Selena, I can't bring this up with him. I just can't. What if he doesn't feel the same way?"

"Now, there's a good place to start. You say you're worried he may not feel the same way…but, Kat, do you even know how you feel about Jack?"

Kat paused and thought for a moment. How *did* she feel about Jack?

"I guess…after Christopher… I thought I was ready to swear off relationships… Not forever, but for a long time. I don't even know if I believe there's such a thing as love anymore."

Selena's eyes bored into Kat's skull. "Kat, I don't believe that you don't believe in love. I've known you for years, and that's just not you. But I *do* believe that you've been hurt, and that you're afraid of what could happen if you let yourself get involved with someone again."

Kat sighed. "I wish there was some way to test the waters without the chance that either of us could get hurt."

"Well, I guess you could just renounce love, cover your heart in armor, and never feel anything for anyone again. But that's just not you."

No, it wasn't. Selena knew her well. She was lucky to have such a wise friend who could offer her sage, sensible advice in times of need.

"Then again," Selena continued, with a gleam in her eye, "maybe there *is* a way you can find what you're looking for without either of you getting hurt."

Kat looked at Selena warily. "What are you suggesting?"

"I'm suggesting that if your feelings for Jack are purely on a physical level—if you truly don't think either of you are ready for a relationship of any kind—then why don't you just deal with those feelings?"

"Oh, come on, Selena!" said Kat. "Are you suggesting I just walk up to him and suggest that we… we just…?"

Selena raised her eyebrows. "Start doing the dirty deed? The hibbety-dibbety?"

Kat choked on her coffee. "Those are quite the colorful terms," she sputtered. "And even if I were going to act on it, I wouldn't know where to start. I don't even know if he's interested in me. Not in *that* way. If he was, wouldn't he be seeking me out? We barely talk to one another."

"You haven't been seeking *him* out, either," said Selena.

What if it was that simple?

What if Jack was just as eager as she was to finish what they'd started in quarantine, but didn't know how to approach her?

He couldn't possibly have any *romantic* feelings for her, but what if he was at least physically attracted to her?

They'd both said that neither of them believed in love…but what if there was a way to take emotion out of the equation?

She thought again of Jack's suggestion that she needed a thrill. Well, there was more than one way to seek excitement…

An idea began to form in her mind. It was risky, of course. But the only potential negative consequence was that she might feel embarrassed. And since she'd already embarrassed herself as much as she possibly could in front of Jack, one more moment of humiliation wasn't going to make much of a difference.

All she had to do was find him and pop the question.

Jack was having a hard time staying focused.

He was in one of the hospital supply closets, gathering up various medical supplies to restock the ambulance's med kit, but he was finding it impossible to keep his mind on his work.

He kept taking the wrong items, or looking down and finding that he'd put too much of something in his box. Jack scowled at himself. He'd completely lost count of what he'd taken. Inventory was going to be pissed.

It had been like this for the past few days. He was able to focus just fine during emergency jobs. Just like always, when he was in the middle of an emergency he was at his peak performance. There was something about getting caught up completely in the moment and focusing on a medical emergency that allowed him to re-center himself, no matter what kind of emotional turmoil he might be going through.

But during the quieter times…when his mind had time to wander…it wandered straight back to Kat.

And specifically to that kiss.

He was completely mortified by his lack of professionalism. He'd been struggling to maintain a detached, clinical demeanor, and he'd utterly failed. Kat had been vulnerable and afraid and he'd taken advantage of her vulnerability. He couldn't have felt worse.

But he also couldn't keep his mind from returning to the way his hand had fit perfectly around her hip. To the softness of her skin. The way her hair had tickled his face when he'd buried his nose in it and inhaled the faintly tropical scent that wafted from her.

To make matters even worse, not only had he failed to hold himself to his professional standards…he'd *liked* kissing Kat. He'd felt…*desire.*

The plain fact was, he wanted more of Kat. And, try as he might to deny it, he knew deep down that he wasn't going to stop thinking about her. His body burned to finish what they'd started.

But would Kat even want to talk to him after he'd let himself get so carried away? They'd known each other for a little over a month, and this was already the second time he'd been unprofessional with her in a medical setting.

And yet during their kiss he'd felt her hands clutching at him, sensed her body pressing against his. In the heat of that moment she had wanted him, too.

But did she still want him? Or had her reaction to him simply been a response to a tense, pressured moment? In either case, he didn't know what to do.

More than anything, he wished he could call Matt.

Even if his brother couldn't solve the problem, he would at least listen and understand.

But for the past four years that he and Matt hadn't been speaking Jack had had to work through his emotional problems on his own. He had lost his wingman and his confidant—the person he'd relied on most when it had come to figuring out his feelings.

His solution had been simply to avoid deep relationships, even non-romantic ones, and all the troublesome emotions that went along with them. But now that Kat was in the picture he wasn't sure how well that strategy would work.

He had tried to give Kat plenty of space since their time in quarantine had ended. He didn't want her to feel that he expected any more of her than she wanted to give. If she was interested in him, then she could make the next move. But he wouldn't blame Kat if she never wanted to see him again.

Which was why he was completely surprised when he turned around with his supply box and saw her standing in front of him.

"Sorry," she said. "Didn't mean to startle you."

She walked up to Jack and took the box from him, setting it on the floor.

"Well, this takes me back," she said. "It's been a couple weeks since we were in such close quarters together."

Was she angry at him?

Her face bore the same resolute look, the same determined set of her lips, that he'd noticed while they'd been in quarantine. Whatever she wanted to talk to him about, he realized there was no avoiding it. Not when she looked like that.

"I've been thinking," she said. "We're both adults. And we've gotten to know each other quickly, in a pretty short amount of time, due to circumstances beyond our control. But, no matter how unusual those circumstances may have been, they don't change the fact that we're in this situation now."

"And…what exactly *is* our situation?"

She took a deep breath. "I've been thinking a lot about that moment in quarantine."

He waited without breathing. He thought his heart might have stopped.

She went on. "You know the moment I mean. When we…kissed."

Her eyes flickered straight to his and he knew his heart hadn't stopped after all. It was pounding jackhammer-hard.

"I don't know about you," she said, "but I've had a hard time *not* thinking about it. The kiss, I mean. And I know you said that you don't believe in relationships. Neither do I. But in a way that makes us kind of ideal for one another right now."

He wondered where this was going. "How so?" he said.

"Well," she continued, looking nervous, but clearly determined to carry her point through, "anything involving emotions would probably be a terrible idea— for both of us. But then I started thinking that not every relationship has to involve emotions. Some relationships have a more…physical basis."

He was suddenly very aware that without the supply

box in his arms there was nothing between the two of them. He would barely have to reach out to slip an arm around her waist. Her nose was inches from his. It was very hard to think clearly with her standing so close.

"Emotions are complicated," he agreed, his voice growing husky. "Are you suggesting that we try letting things get more…physical between us?"

She nodded, gazing up into his eyes. He noticed that the top of her head would fit perfectly underneath his chin if she were just a few inches closer.

"I was thinking that, since we seem to have some physical feelings for each other, we could deal with those feelings on a physical level. But no deeper emotions. No romance."

It was exactly what he wanted—so why did he feel a surge of disappointment? Hadn't he been trying to avoid his physical attraction to Kat precisely because he didn't want to toy with her emotions or awaken any of his own?

He needed to be clear with her about who he was, to make sure she didn't get hurt. "I don't do hearts and flowers," he said.

"Who the hell said anything about hearts and flowers?" she replied.

"I just want to be clear about who I am. And what you're looking for."

"I know exactly what I'm looking for. Look, I was engaged to someone I thought I loved. He did the whole hearts and flowers thing. I've had enough of them. I've had enough of thinking about the future, the long term, the happily-ever-after. I want something different. You said when we were in quarantine that you don't believe in love. Well, neither do I. Love's not what I'm looking for right now. If I were, I'd be looking somewhere else."

"Are you sure this is what you want?" he said.

Despite the dim light in the supply closet he thought he could see a wicked gleam in Kat's eye.

"You were the one who said I needed a thrill," she said. "I'm trying to learn to live in the moment. And you did say you would help…"

"As long as we're clear about our expectations from the beginning."

"Crystal-clear," she said.

Kat pressed close against him. Any fleeting resistance, any reasons not to get involved that he might have briefly entertained were fading away.

And then his lips were brushing hers before he even knew what had happened. She was kissing him back, more deeply, and his tongue explored her mouth, desiring every inch of her that she could give. Her lips crushed against his, and he felt himself become swept away with the taste of her.

He wasn't sure how much time passed before she broke their kiss, pulling her head away from his. She still leaned against him, and his arms remained around her waist. As she looked up into his eyes he thought he saw flecks of gold within the green.

"So," she said, "I take it that we're in agreement? A purely physical relationship, to address an attraction that's on a purely physical level?"

"If you're in, I'm in," he said. "Purely physical. No emotions, no strings attached."

She let out a breath, as though she'd been holding it. "We should probably set up some ground rules," she said, suddenly seeming nervous. "Maybe we should make a list of what we expect from one another, to make sure things don't get too emotional…"

He pulled her closer to him again. "Here's the only ground rule I want to work out right now," he said, his voice husky. "My place or yours?"

The next night found Kat laying out three different outfits on her bed, repeatedly accepting and rejecting each one.

It didn't matter what she wore, she tried to tell herself. She and Jack weren't supposed to be trying to impress each other. She didn't need to care if he liked what she wore. And yet somehow tonight it was unusually difficult to make an outfit choice.

The more she thought about her arrangement with Jack, the more confident she became that it was a brilliant idea. She'd only had a few boyfriends in her life, and all the way up until Christopher she'd been a serial monogamist, going through one long-term relationship at a time. Part of her was still a bit shocked at her proposal to Jack—but mostly she was excited about her first foray into spontaneous thrill-seeking. She was nervous, but excited, and she intended to enjoy every minute of it.

Even though it would be her first time having sex since before the breakup…

It's just a meaningless fling, she reminded herself. *Don't put too much pressure on it.*

Over the two years she'd dated Christopher she'd tried to meet his expectations in every way possible. He was a career-driven perfectionist, and she'd thought she'd admired those qualities in him. She'd even thought that she and Christopher were a little bit similar in that way.

But Christopher's perfectionism had always seemed to involve making her feel *less*, somehow. Every time he'd told her that she'd look great if she worked out a little more, or that her hair would look nice if she'd only wear it in a certain way, she'd believed him, and tried to do what would make him happy. But it had never seemed to be enough. And in the end it hadn't been.

Her arrangement with Jack meant that neither of them had to worry about expectations. The thought of that was wonderfully freeing. Tonight would be her first serious attempt to let loose and let go.

Kat's heart pounded in her chest as she pulled into the driveway of Jack's house on the beach. She wrapped her black leather trench coat more tightly around herself as she stepped out of the car. Her outfit was a risk; she was wearing the trench coat, heels, and not much else. She'd been a little worried about what might happen if she got pulled over, but she'd been very careful to drive at exactly the speed limit for the entire drive to Jack's house.

The nice thing about keeping their relationship on a physical level, she thought, was that now she could freely admit her attraction to Jack without worrying about where it might lead. It would lead to sex with Jack and no further. Nice and simple. No other complications to worry about. No reason to be nervous.

Two hours is an awfully long time to spend deciding what to wear when you're supposedly just interested in a purely physical relationship, a small, disloyal corner of her mind piped up as she stepped out of the car.

She considered leaving her purse inside the car, underneath the passenger seat, but then she remembered the pack of condoms she'd brought with her, color-coded by type. Would Jack have thought about protection? Probably, but you never knew... Better to be on the safe side.

She grabbed her bag and walked up the sand-covered sidewalk.

He opened the door and stood in front of her, in dark jeans and a very tight white T-shirt. The T-shirt left very little to the imagination. Even in the dim porchlight she could see the firmness of his torso underneath the shirt.

And as she looked at the well-defined muscles all traces of the worry she'd had about the wisdom of her decision melted away. Whatever happened after tonight, it was going to be worth it if it gave her a chance to feel those arms pressing her against that chest one more time. This was going to be *good*.

He stood in the doorway, leaning on one arm, and she could see him taking her in. He was looking at how tightly she had her black trench coat wrapped around herself. He raised an eyebrow rakishly, taking in her bare legs, and she had a feeling that he was drawing the obvious conclusion about what else she might be wearing under the coat.

She saw him swallow, and suddenly she felt much more confident. Whatever false bravado he might display, she could tell that Jack wanted this every bit as much as she did.

She might have thrown herself at him at the hospital, but that had been then. Right now he was looking at her as though she were a package he couldn't wait to unwrap. Or a meal he'd like to devour.

She gave a shiver that had nothing to do with the cool breeze coming from the beach.

He smiled and reached down to grab one end of the belt of her trench coat, using it to pull her forward until she was pressed against him. He slipped an arm around her and pressed her closer, nuzzling his nose into her hair.

"You really came dressed for the occasion," he said, reaching down and putting his palm against her bare thigh. He murmured the words into her hair, his lips brushing against her neck as he spoke.

Her cheek was pressed against his chest, and her nose came just to the small hollow in his neck. Kat inhaled deeply. Ah, there it was... Eau de Jack Harper. She could finally allow herself to revel in it.

It was nice to be enveloped by Jack's scent without having to try to force her mind off it. But they were still outside. There was only so much that could be accomplished.

Kat marshaled her thoughts enough to say, "You have no idea. But if you want to see the rest of this outfit you're going to have to invite me in."

As she lifted her face from his chest he bent to kiss her. He still held her in his arms, though, and as he turned back into the house, he took her with him, so that they were just inside the entrance when he shut the door. He continued to kiss her, pressing her against the wall. His kisses were soft at first, then deeper and more deliberate.

Kat was grateful for the support of the wall behind her—it kept her from melting into Jack's arms right away. Her senses were full of nothing but him. But then she heard a faint ringing sound from further within the house.

Jack stopped kissing her and said, "Oh, right...the bouillabaisse. I set the timer."

"Bouley-*what*?"

"Bouillabaisse. It's French; it's a kind of stew with seafood and herbs. It's very good."

He headed further back into the house, presumably toward the kitchen, and Kat followed. Her mind was swirling. *Jack had cooked for her?* Why? She'd thought they were just going to have sex. Having a meal together...a meal he'd *cooked* for her...didn't quite fit with her idea of an emotionless night of physical passion. But then, maybe it wasn't a big deal. Plenty of people liked to cook. It didn't mean anything special.

Jack was shutting off the timer as she entered the kitchen and he grabbed a spoon. "Here, have a taste," he said, turning the heat on the stove to a low simmer and holding the spoon to Kat's lips.

Her eyes widened as she tasted the broth. "Wow, that's really good!" she said. "I don't know what I'm more excited about: eating that delicious stew, or...or..." She blushed. "Or some of our other plans for this evening."

He set down the spoon and put his hands against her hips. "Speaking of which," he said, "we were in the middle of something before that timer so rudely interrupted us..."

He leaned in and brushed her lips against his.

"Should we have dinner first?" she whispered. "I didn't know you were going to go to all this trouble."

"Actually, I'm more of a dessert-first kind of guy," he said, flicking off the stove and giving her his full attention.

Kat felt her thoughts slowly melting away as his body pressed against hers and their lips came together. And as they kissed her need for him began to intensify. The pent-up frustration of their interrupted moments had been building for days, and finally—finally—there was nothing between the two of them.

Well, not much, anyway...

Jack's hands moved to the belt of her trench coat. It was tied tight, but with a good wrench in the right direction the coat fell open, revealing her black lace underwear and nothing else.

"Wow," Jack said. "That is *not* what I expected to see under there."

"Hmm... Well, I have a few button-up blouses in my closet at home. Maybe I should wear one of those next time?" she said.

"Don't you dare," he replied, pulling her roughly to him.

He slipped the coat from her shoulders, then began kissing her neck and breasts. He lifted one breast from the cup of her bra and she gasped as his tongue circled her nipple. An arc of pleasure shot through her as he attended to one breast with his mouth while he teased and stroked the other. Then he slipped his hands under her buttocks, and she instinctively wrapped her legs around his waist as he lifted her and took them both to his bed.

She could feel the tantalizing hardness forming under his jeans…could feel that her own body was eager for him.

He tossed her onto the bed and Kat sighed with pleasure as he slid her underwear from her. She waited for him to get onto the bed with her, but instead he simply looked at her, drinking her in with his eyes. Then he knelt down by the side of the bed and pulled her forward by her hips, dragging her to the edge. He kissed the inside of one thigh, and then the other, and suddenly she realized what he was about to do.

"You—you don't have to do that," she stammered. "I mean, I've never asked anyone to…and no one's ever wanted to…"

"Then don't you think it's about time someone did?" he said.

And after that Kat couldn't speak any more, because he was placing his mouth on the hot, warm space between her legs where she felt the most ready for him to be. His tongue attended to the small nub he found there until Kat thought she would burst with the heat and the wanting. She began to cry out, but he was relentless— he was going to make her explode. And explode she did, unable to control herself against the onslaught of his mouth against her.

Kat let herself sink into the mattress, shaking. She'd wanted him, and she'd known he was ready for her, but she hadn't expected this welcome detour.

She worried that after the intensity of the pleasure she'd just felt she wouldn't have the energy to move from where she lay, rendered immobile by the sensations that washed over her, lasting and lasting. But then she saw Jack taking off his shirt, and the sight of his washboard torso gave her renewed energy.

The faint line of hair that trailed from his chest to his stomach and disappeared into his navel suggested tantalizing possibilities. She reached out for his waistband and pulled herself to a sitting position. Fumbling with the button at his waist, she pulled his jeans and boxers off in one smooth motion, revealing his firm, erect manhood.

Something clamored for attention in a small, forgotten corner of her mind. *Oh, right—protection.* But her purse was all the way out in the living room. For the briefest of seconds she despaired at the thought of having to interrupt this moment by running out to rummage through her purse. But before she could mention it Jack reached down for his jeans, where they lay on the floor, and took a condom from one of the pockets.

Kat felt gratified that she hadn't been the only one planning for their safety—and she was especially glad that having a condom close at hand meant they wouldn't have to leave the bed right now.

He eased onto the bed with her, his body firm and warm between her legs. The length of him was hard, but velvety to her touch. He locked his gaze with hers and she nodded to let him know that she was ready. He entered her in one long thrust. She lifted her hips, pressing them against his so she could let him into her as completely as possible. Their bodies joined in a timeless dance, responding to the heat and desire each felt in the other.

It felt as if it had been ages since she had made love. And lovemaking had never felt like *this*. His rhythm matched hers perfectly, his long, slow strokes mirroring the rise and fall of her body as if they were meant to fit together.

She lost all awareness of herself as sensation overtook her. She was lost in the smell of him, in the feeling of his hands on her hips and the backs of her thighs as he pushed himself into her. She ran her hands through his dark hair, as she'd wanted to since the moment she'd first laid eyes on him, arching her back. His chest was hard and warm against her breasts.

There was no sound but that of their ragged breaths melding together. Nothing existed outside of the sublime feelings that promised bliss was only moments away. She rocked her hips against his more quickly, unable to withstand the craving any longer, and his strokes came faster, pushing her toward euphoria.

She cried out in ecstasy as she felt herself shatter. And as she did, she felt him tremble within her, heard him say her name. As she raised her lips to meet his once more, she felt a tightness somewhere deep within her loosen.

They lay entangled in one another's arms, her head resting against his chest. She felt wonderfully free. There were no pressures, no tasks to accomplish. *This* moment was the moment she wanted to live in, and nothing could take her out of it.

CHAPTER SIX

JACK WOKE FIRST, to an unfamiliar whirring noise. Kat's cell phone was buzzing on the nightstand next to her side of the bed.

He gazed at Kat, who still slept peacefully, her back curved against his chest. It had been a long time since any woman had spent the night with him, but she had dropped off soon after their second round of lovemaking and he soon after.

He caressed the soft red waves of her hair, which spilled over the white pillow. The early-morning sunlight dappled her face, filtered by the tall palm trees just outside the window. She looked so peaceful.

When Kat was awake he could always read the worry in her face. She was so preoccupied with caring. No one could speak to Kat for five minutes without realizing that she was constantly thinking about everyone else: her patients, her co-workers, her friends…

Jack wondered if now he might have made it onto the list of people in Kat's life that she worried about. Cared about. And he wondered how Kat felt about the night before.

She'd seemed satisfied, but they hadn't really had the

opportunity to discuss it. He was grateful that they'd put their arrangement to keep things purely physical in place. Kat might deserve more, but he knew he wasn't the one who could offer it to her.

But, if nothing else, he could offer her a good breakfast.

He'd been thrilled to find that she liked his cooking. After they'd made love the first time they'd eaten the bouillabaisse with crusty French bread. He'd loved watching her eyes widen as she'd tasted her first sip of broth, and her exclamation later, when she'd tried his homemade rosemary and strawberry ice cream.

Then, after the ice cream, they'd gotten back to the reason they'd agreed to meet in the first place. He'd loved watching her other reactions as well: her eyes drinking in his body, resting on his manhood, her breath catching as he eased his length into her.

Yes, that had been nice. More than nice.

Now, he resisted the urge to kiss the nape of her neck. He leaned over to silence Kat's cell phone and then slipped out of bed, pushing back the thick white down comforter. The heavy blanket was probably overkill in the Hawaiian heat, but he liked to be warm in bed— and it seemed she did, too.

He wondered if it was a Midwestern thing. Both he and Kat were originally from places with cold, severe winters. There'd been some winters in Nebraska when he'd feel the cold in his bones. Maybe after coming from a place like that you could never get warm enough.

He went into the kitchen and surveyed the items in his refrigerator. He wanted to make something that would let him show off a little bit, but that would also look as though he hadn't gone to too much trouble. He pulled the ingredients for crepes from the refrigerator and the pantry, setting out blackberries, strawberries, and blueberries for toppings.

He'd loved to cook ever since he was young. His parents had thought it a waste of time—why learn to cook when you could hire someone to do it for you?—but Matt had always been supportive of his hobby.

For just a moment he thought again that it would be nice to be able to call Matt, to tell him about Kat. He shrugged off the wave of sadness that always came over him whenever his brother came to mind, and tried to focus on the pleasant view of the palm trees just outside his kitchen. It was a beautiful day, as so many Hawaiian days were. They could have breakfast out on the lanai.

He wondered if Kat would want to talk about last night when she woke up. Try as he might to turn his mind to the crepes he was preparing, he couldn't get his mind off what she might be thinking...how she might be thinking of him.

As a paramedic, Jack required a certain amount of daring. He was used to running toward dangerous situations—not away from them He had to take risks every day. But for some reason those risks seemed a hell of a lot easier than talking to Kat about her feelings.

Kat woke up in Jack's bed, blinking against the morning sun. At first she was dismayed to find herself alone, but then she noticed the noises and smells from the kitchen.

Surely Jack wasn't making breakfast?

She snuggled deeper under the covers, savoring the delicious memory of the night before. Then she frowned. The plan had been for her to arrive at Jack's place, have some brisk, efficient sex, and then return home.

But nothing had gone according to plan.

Instead, everything about last night had been a sensory feast: the taste of the food he'd made for her, the feeling of their bodies intertwined, the tenderness of his gaze matching the softness of his bed.

She'd never imagined that he would cook her dinner. She'd been expecting a purely physical interaction, as they'd agreed: just sex and nothing more. But Jack had made it feel like a date. And the food had been so delicious it had almost felt as though he was trying to impress her. But why would he care about doing that?

She shivered underneath the warm comforter, remembering the feeling of Jack's skin next to hers and his hands exploring the curves of her body. Remembering his attention to her, the sensations he'd created, teasing her until her body sang with pleasure. A girl could get used to that kind of thing.

She'd meant to leave immediately afterward, but she hadn't been prepared to feel so utterly replete. She and Jack had lain in bed for some time after that first time, each of them basking in the pleasant glow that had radiated from the other's body.

She could have stayed like that forever, but then Jack had heard her stomach rumble. He'd wanted her to stay for dinner, and she hadn't felt she could leave without eating when he'd gone to so much trouble. And then they'd had ice cream afterward…and he'd kissed some of the ice cream off of her nose…and she'd returned his kiss more ardently than either of them had expected…

And then they'd returned to his big bed. And if the first time had been an expression of fierce need, the second time had been a slow and tender discovery of each other. Afterward, she'd fallen asleep without a second thought. But she'd never expected that she would wake up in his bed the next morning, listening to the clamor of pots and pans clashing together in the kitchen while he made breakfast for the two of them.

At least, she assumed it was for the two of them. Jack probably wasn't going to make something for himself and wave her out of his home.

Mission accomplished, Kat thought.

Her goal had been to let loose, and she had accomplished exactly that. All according to plan. Their "no emotions" agreement was working out just fine. Barely two months in Hawaii, and she was starting to get the hang of spontaneous thrills.

She shivered again, remembering the feeling of Jack's strong arms enveloping her, his hot skin next to hers. She could hear him humming in the kitchen. Whatever he was cooking in there, it smelled amazing. That clinched it. She was getting up.

She slipped out of bed, grabbed her phone and stumbled into the kitchen.

"Crepes okay?" Jack asked when he noticed her standing in the doorway.

She felt a surge of excitement upon learning that breakfast was indeed for both of them, although she tried to quash it down.

No emotions, remember? He's just being polite.

"I'm getting seriously spoiled with all this French food," she said.

For a moment he looked worried. "Do you like French food?" he asked. "I can always make something different if this isn't what you're in the mood for."

Kat lifted an eyebrow. She hoped it made her look like Marlene Dietrich, but she worried it made her look like a librarian giving a scolding.

She hurriedly let the eyebrow down, and said, "I'd hoped last night was enough of an indication of exactly what I like."

He seemed pleased.

Her phone whirred and she resisted the urge to check it, pushing it far away from her on the kitchen counter so that she wouldn't be tempted to look at it again.

"Do you need to get that?" said Jack.

"It's work. But we've both got the day off," she replied. "Whatever it is can wait until later, because I've decided that this morning is all about living in the moment. And *this* moment is all about crepes."

She popped a berry into her mouth, enjoying the sensation of sweetness as it burst over her tongue.

"Well, look at you, all relaxed and devil-may-care," said Jack, flipping the crepes in the pan. "Who *is* this woman who's so carefree all of a sudden?"

She shrugged and smiled. "I guess I finally found my Zen."

He spun more batter into the pan. "How does your Zen feel about crepes?"

"My Zen is very much in favor of delicious breakfast foods. And I'm so glad I get a chance to try more of your cooking. I wanted to last night, but I...we...kind of got caught up in some other things."

He smirked. "'Other things,' huh?"

She smiled and said, "You know…like the hibbety-dibbety."

"The hibbety-*what*? I don't think it's been called that since the Roaring Twenties. I think my great-grandparents might have used that one."

She blushed. "It's a private joke. A colorful euphemism Selena came up with a few days ago."

"You two seem pretty close?"

"Oh, yes, she's one of my best friends," said Kat. "We talk about everything with each other."

"Everything, huh?"

"Oh—well, now that you mention it… Maybe we should talk about how you and I are going to talk about the…"

"The hibbety-dibbety?"

She laughed. "Yes, that. What if people at work find out about us?"

"Well, we should probably take care to make sure that they don't."

For a moment she felt hurt, but then she reminded herself that Jack was just being practical. Their relationship wasn't really a relationship.

"Yes, broadcasting this around work would probably complicate things," she said.

"Exactly what I was thinking," he said. "Besides, since we've agreed to keep feelings out of it…well, it's not as though there's really anything to tell."

She lifted the coffee cup he'd given her. "Here's to not believing in love."

"Cheers," he said, clinking his own coffee cup against hers.

They were sticking to the plan. *Good.* Absolutely nothing had changed from the moment she had smelled the crepes from his bedroom to the moment they'd sat down to have breakfast together.

The Hawaiian sun beamed onto Jack's lanai just as brightly as ever, but if nothing had changed, why did she suddenly feel so…

Her thoughts were interrupted by her phone, which was whirring again.

"I've got a ton of messages from work," she said. "They want me to come in right away."

Jack looked at his own phone. "Looks like they want me as well. The hospital's facing a huge surge in patients, and they want the paramedics helping out in the ER with triage and first-line care."

"So much for our day off," Kat said. "It must be a major emergency if they want us both to come in. Are you ready to see how well we can keep our secret?"

Jack left first and arrived at the hospital several minutes before Kat. The ER was inundated with patients, all of whom were presenting with symptoms of the super-flu.

He joined a group of doctors and nurses at the reception desk, where Selena was briefing the staff on the situation.

"This is my worst fear," she said. "There's been an outbreak of the super-flu on the westward side of the island, and now people are coming here with flu symptoms." She paused and nodded at Kat, who had just arrived. "The good news is that thanks to Kat's great work with the infectious disease team, we were able to develop a vaccine ahead of the outbreak. All hospital staff have been vaccinated by now, which should increase the safety for everyone tremendously."

"We'll need to triage," said Kat. "Patients with no symptoms go to one wing of the hospital, where we can administer vaccines. Everyone showing symptoms goes to another wing, and from there we can determine level of care."

Selena nodded. "I want some of our more experienced paramedics staying in the ER today. Let's leave the ambulance callouts to the Emergency Medical Technicians. The patients who are going to need the highest levels of care are most likely already here at the hospital."

"It's all hands on deck," Selena finished. "Grab a patient, grab a chart, and get going."

Jack spent the rest of the morning caught up in the flow of ER triage. He administered vaccines to patients without flu symptoms, and sent those with more severe medical needs to the appropriate department.

He'd been working so hard that he wasn't even sure how long he'd been at the hospital when a woman pulled at his arm and begged him to take a look at her teenage son.

It was the first case Jack had seen that morning that caused him serious concern. The boy's mother said his name was Michael, and reported that he'd had a high fever and vomiting since the day before. Jack leaned in to examine Michael's cheeks, which were ashen. His face was contorted in pain, and he was holding his hand to his lower abdomen on the right side.

With a sinking feeling, Jack realized the boy probably had appendicitis. He'd need a doctor to confirm it,
but based on the boy's pallor and the pain that seemed
to be coming from the vicinity of his belly button, his
guess was that if the appendix hadn't burst already, it
would soon. Even as Jack examined the boy, he could
see that his breathing was labored, and he seemed to
be moving in and out of consciousness.

Michael would need surgery, fast... And Jack knew
for a fact that it would be at least an hour before any of
the hospital's surgeons would be free.

Jack waved at Christine, one of the nurses who was
also helping with triage. "We need a gurney over here,"
he said. To the boy's mother, he added, "Don't be afraid.
I'm going to come back with one of our doctors, and
we'll do the best we can for him."

Jack straightened up. He looked out over the sea of
patients that filled the ER and spotted Kat at the far
end of the hall.

"Kat!" he yelled, waving to flag her down. "We've
got a problem."

"What is it?" she said.

"There's a kid in the ER with what's probably appendicitis. Looks like he could be close to peritonitis."

"So call for a surgical consult."

"I will—but I already know that Ernest is out sick,
and Jacquelyn's already working on a patient with a
coronary artery bypass. Omar's on call, but he's at a
continuing education conference across the island. Bottom line: it'll be at least an hour before a surgeon can
get to this kid, and I'm not sure he can wait that long."

They'd already begun walking back toward the boy.

Two nurses had already wheeled a gurney toward Michael and were easing him onto it while his mother stood by, looking worried.

"He's fading fast," said Christine quietly. "We should bag him now, because we'll need to intubate the second we get him into the OR."

Jack could see that Christine was right—Michael's breathing was so shallow as to be almost nonexistent. She had already positioned a bag-valve mask over the boy's nose and mouth. The self-inflating bag attached to the mask could be compressed to deliver oxygen to Michael's lungs until he was put on a ventilator and prepped for surgery, which needed to happen soon. Jack nodded and used both hands to apply slow, steady compressions to the bag.

"I already put in the surgical call, but it's going to be a while," Christine said. "We're going to need to make some quick decisions."

Kat's lips were a thin line. "I did a year on surgical service before I switched to internal medicine," she said.

"So you've done appendectomies before?" said Jack.

"I have, but it's been years," Kat replied.

"You might be the kid's best shot," added Jack. "Think you can do this?"

Kat paused.

She looked at Jack and Christine.

It was her call.

A year ago she might have refused. Not because she couldn't do the procedure, but because regardless of her training it wasn't her place, as an internal medicine doctor, to do surgery. But now she looked at her team and realized she had their full support.

Christine was awaiting her decision; Jack seemed confident in her.

If they could be confident, then so could she. She'd worked long enough at Oahu General by now to know that its team could handle anything.

"Okay," she said. "Let's get him into the OR. Worst-case scenario: we keep him alive until a surgeon gets here." She yelled across the ER floor to the reception desk: "Kimo! Call Tom from Anesthesiology and tell him we're prepping a patient in OR Two. And stick your head into OR One and make sure Jacquelyn knows what we're doing, in case she closes early."

They wheeled the gurney down the hall to the OR, with Jack continuing to apply compressions to the bag-valve mask, keeping pace with the team. Michael's mother ran after. "Can I come in during the surgery?" she asked.

"Not during the surgery, but you can wait right outside," Jack said. "And I'll be out right away to let you know how things are going."

"Please," she said, "stay with him. I'll feel better if I know someone's in there looking out for him."

"Don't worry," Jack said. "Your son's in good hands."

Kat knew how Michael's mother felt, though. Jack had a way with patients that made his presence inherently reassuring. She'd felt it herself. In a crisis situation, he emanated a steady calm. She'd seen patients draw from it, no matter how much distress they were in, and she'd felt herself draw from it, too. As Kat and her team scrubbed in, while the patient was prepped for surgery, Tom, the anesthesiologist, poked his head into the scrub room.

"Just wanted to let you know that his fever spiked even higher just before we put him under," he said. "My guess is the appendix ruptured."

"Then it's a good thing we're almost ready to go in," she said.

With the patient intubated, there was no longer any reason for Jack to stay, but Kat stopped him before he left to return to the ER.

"Wait," she said. "His mother asked you to stay with him."

"Don't worry," he said, nodding toward the surgical nurses. "You're in good hands, too." But Kat thought he must have seen the fear in her eyes above her surgical mask, because after a moment's hesitation, he said, "But I'll stay to observe, if you think it's a good idea."

Kat hadn't had much chance to see the surgical nurses at Oahu General in action, but it was clear that they were experienced and knew each other well. They bantered with an ease Kat didn't feel as she began her first incision.

Her hand didn't shake, but she felt nervous. It had been several years since she'd done this procedure. Still, there was no question that the boy would die without immediate intervention. As Kat continued with the procedure her confidence grew. It took less than a minute for her to locate the appendix. As soon as she had it isolated from the other organs, she asked the nurse to place the Babcock clamps at its base.

Kat eased her scalpel along the appendix, removing it from tip to base. A cheer went up among Jack and the nurses as the appendix was removed, and Kat smiled. This atmosphere was so informal compared to what she was used to—and yet a cheer and a moment to enjoy a successful surgery seemed so appropriate to her now.

She began to close, making careful stitches on the patient's abdomen.

"Nice work," said a voice behind her. She looked over in surprise, to see Omar watching her with an appraising eye.

"Omar?" she said. "When did you get here?"

He must have driven at breakneck speed to get to the hospital from his conference.

"You were about halfway through the procedure when I got in. But you were doing so well I thought I'd just let you continue. No reason to interrupt a great job. Maybe we should get you on the surgical rotation?"

"No, thanks," she said. "Consider me a one-time pinch-hitter."

"Well, you did a great job," Omar said. "That patient is lucky you were here today. We all are."

Kat looked across the patient at Jack. She didn't know if she would have been able to do the appendectomy without him, but she was certain the procedure had been made much easier thanks to his quiet confidence pulling her through it.

Jack leaned over to look at the stitches she was finishing. "Nicely done," he said.

"See?" she replied. "I told you I was good at stitches."

It had been an exhausting day. After hours of conducting triage, administering medication and vaccines, and performing a surgery she hadn't undertaken for several years, Kat was spending the last moments of the day on the hospital's roof. She'd learned it was an excellent place to take in the Hawaiian sunrise.

She was usually alone up there, but today Jack had followed her. "You did great today," he said.

"Great?" She snorted. "You must have seen how clumsily I made that McBurney incision. You must have seen how nervous I was. It's been years since I did any surgery."

"You saved a boy's life," he replied. "Try to focus on the big picture."

She gave a dark laugh. "I've never been very good at that," she said. "Why focus on the big picture when there are a thousand small details I can obsess over?"

"I know it's not always easy for you to stay in the moment, but this is a good one," he said. "I'm not saying the little things don't matter—I'm just saying enjoy the good you did."

"I'm trying to," she said, watching the sky change from gold to rose as the sun went down. "But it's never come easily to me. My family aren't all doctors, like yours. It was my father's dream for me to become a doctor, and after he died my mom had to work two jobs to help me get through medical school. It's important for me to be the best doctor I can be. Not just for myself, but for them, too."

He nodded. "But maybe sometimes you forget that you don't have to try to be the best anymore. You got there. You fulfilled your dreams and theirs. Now you can just be who you are."

"Be who you are?" she repeated. "It sounds so simple. But it's not." She turned toward him. "Do you know why I really came to Hawaii? I got fired, Jack. From my job at Chicago Grace."

"Why?"

"I had this whole plan I wanted to implement. This huge, sweeping plan. And I still believe in it. But I didn't bother to see if it was a good fit for that hospital. I just tried to push it through. The result was a complete disaster. And the worst part was that I felt as though I'd completely let my father down by losing my job. I didn't just want to be a good doctor there, I wanted to make a real difference in medicine… Only, once I got fired I wasn't on the superstar track anymore. And he'd always seen me as a superstar. So it wasn't just the firing that hurt…it was the feeling that I wasn't good enough."

"Maybe they weren't good enough for you?"

"The best research hospital in the country?"

"Yes. Maybe they weren't good enough for you." He put his hands on her shoulders, turned her to face him. "Kat, I know something about walking away from a path that everyone else *thinks* you should want so you can pursue what you *actually* want. It never makes sense to other people. But if it makes sense to you, then that's all that matters."

"It must have been hard for you to grow up in such a famous family with such high expectations," Kat said.

"You have no idea," Jack replied. "The only person I was ever really close to was my brother Matt. As far as our parents were concerned, our hobbies were going to school and doing our homework. Anything non-academic was out of the question. And then, when I did try medical school, I could never trust any of the

students or professors to be real with me. No one wanted
to get to know *me*. They just wanted to know what it
was like to be one of *the* Harpers."

"For me it was different," she said. "My family is
poor, and I'm the only one who's ever gone to medical school. I felt like I had to prove to everyone that I
was good enough. And then I met Christopher, who I
thought was perfect. But the more I think about what
happened between us, the more I think that he may have
thought he was perfect too. So I had to prove to Christopher that I could keep up, that I was good enough."

"Like I said before—maybe he wasn't good enough
for you."

Kat gave this some thought. It felt different to think
about other people living up to *her* expectations for a
change.

"Whatever happened back in Chicago, I'm sure your
father would have understood," Jack said. "I know you
well enough by now to know that if you believed in
something enough to get fired over it, then it must have
been important. Being fired doesn't matter. Being the
version of yourself that you want to be is what matters."

The version of herself that she wanted to be.

The question came at her again. Who *was* she? Not
anyone's fiancée, not a superstar... But today, as she sat
on the hospital rooftop watching the sun go down, she
felt as if she was exactly what she had always wanted
to be: a doctor.

She slipped her arm through Jack's and wondered
if, amidst all the chaos and crises of the day, she might
have found a little bit of inner peace.

* * *

As Kat's first few weeks began to turn into her first few months at Oahu General Hospital, she thought that she and Jack were maintaining the guise of being in a purely professional relationship fairly well. No one seemed to suspect anything.

Selena had given Kat a few knowing looks, but had stopped after Kat had assured her with a deadpan expression that there was nothing worth discussing between herself and Jack.

It wasn't even a lie, Kat thought. She'd said there was nothing worth discussing—not that there was nothing happening. And, since she didn't want to discuss her trysts with Jack at all, her statement was technically true. Besides, Selena herself had suggested that Kat needed a "fling." If this—whatever it was she was having with Jack—was just a fling, then there was no need to discuss it with anyone.

She didn't think that she and Jack were acting any differently at work. He handed off cases to her as they came in, giving her brief, professional summaries of the patients. They nodded to each other whenever they passed in the hall, and included each other in collegial conversations.

They also slipped into the supply closet in the hospital's rarely used west wing at every opportunity.

As far as Kat could tell, no one seemed to notice how frequently Jack needed to stock up on painkillers just moments after she happened to slip in to the closet to check on the availability of gauze.

The supply closet was the perfect place for their meetings, because it was the furthest from the ER and therefore the most rarely used. This meant that not only were they unlikely to be interrupted, but that there was plenty of empty shelf space for Kat to lean against as Jack kissed her. He was a few inches taller than her, and it helped to have a clear space where she could let her shoulders lean as she lifted her head to reach his, and where he could wrap his arms around her without fear of knocking anything over.

His nose nuzzled into her collar now, as he peppered her neck with tiny kisses. "Don't…you have…a meeting…to get to?" he queried, between each kiss.

"Not until later," she said, arching her back to press herself into him, pressing her mouth to his so she could explore every nook.

He twined his arms around her waist, holding her close to him, breathing in deeply as though he could inhale her very essence.

Usually, they were able to make the most of the little time they had together. But Jack's mention of the meeting brought Kat back to earth with a crash. She'd been trying not to think about it, but now that he'd mentioned it she couldn't get it out of her mind.

She'd hoped he wouldn't notice her distraction, but as usual he noticed everything. "What's wrong?" he said.

"It's nothing. It's just…" They'd said no emotions, but she needed someone she could talk to. "I could really use some advice," she said. "Selena's great, but she's such a close friend that I worry she wouldn't be honest with me, because she'd be so afraid of hurting my feelings. I need some advice from someone whose opinion I respect but who doesn't…*care* about me."

She couldn't be certain in the darkness, but she almost thought she saw him frown.

"I know we said no emotions or personal stuff," she said, quickly.

"No, it's okay," he said. "How can I help?"

"Do you think I fit in here?" she asked.

He pulled away from her, looking surprised. "Of course," he said. "Look at how well you're doing. You've helped develop a vaccine for a serious illness threatening the island. You did an appendectomy when you hadn't done one in years. How could you think you aren't fitting in?"

She sighed. "I had a meeting with the other doctors yesterday morning. We were talking about some of the policy changes I've put in place since coming here. Specifically, the one that's had the most impact on their work: the requirement that everyone spends eight hours a month working at the hospital's walk-in clinic."

There had been lots of grumbling about that—not without justification. The doctors felt it was an unfair increase to their workload, even though Kat had tried to adjust the schedules to prevent their hours from increasing.

"That's really important to you, isn't it?" Jack said. "But you're worried about a repeat of what happened at your last hospital?"

She nodded. "At Chicago Grace I tried to get them to open up a free, nonprofit clinic. We could have subsidized the extra cost with research and grant proposals. There would have been a *very* slight impact on the hospital's profits over the first three years, but that would have evened out over time."

He winced. "I bet they didn't like hearing that."

"No, they really didn't. In fact…" her face looked more worried than ever "…that's what they fired me over."

"What? *How?*"

"They wanted me to bury all my data showing that only wealthy patients improved after leaving the hospital. Those who couldn't afford follow-up care just stayed the same or got sicker. I refused."

"I can't believe they fired you for something like that."

"Maybe I should mention that when I refused I was shouting at the top of my lungs. And I may also have told the entire board of directors that they should lose their medical licenses because of their lack of compassion for poorer patients."

"Wow! Good for you."

"And I also told the hospital's administrative director that he was a money-hungry prick."

He let out a low whistle.

Kat nodded. "I know," she said. "It doesn't really sound like me, does it?"

"Actually, it sounds *exactly* like you," he said. "I've never seen anyone more passionate about providing good patient care. I know it sucks, getting fired, but I'm glad you don't have to work with those people anymore, and I'd have thought you would be too."

"That's the thing," she said. "I thought the problem was that I was working in the wrong environment, with the wrong people. Everyone here's been wonderful—except they seem to hate my changes, too. I *know* my idea for a nonprofit clinic can work…but only if all the doctors agree to work full shifts there. And no one seems to want to do it."

"It sounds like a great idea," he said. "But did you *ask* the doctors here what they thought about it? Or did you just rush to put your ideas into place? Did you even think about asking Marceline what she wants? Or working with Omar to figure out what he thinks would help boost patient outcomes?"

"I guess I just rushed in with my own ideas," she said. "It's not that I don't care about what they want—I *do*...so much—but it's not how I'm used to doing things. Back in Chicago, the doctors and the hospital administrators held all the authority. I can't remember the last time a hospital administrator asked me what I might need instead of telling me about some new system they wanted to implement. That kind of thinking is exactly what I wanted to get away from, and instead I've just ended up recreating it here." She looked up at him. "Do you think there's any way I can fix this?"

"I *know* you can fix this," he said. "I have a feeling you can do anything. But I'll give you a tip: here in Hawaii, informality will get you further than formality. Spend some time talking to the staff about what they need. Take things slower. They'll come around once they have a chance to see how passionate you are about this and that you want what's best for them as well."

She was smiling again. "You're really good at this, Jack."

"At what?"

"Helping me figure things out. I really appreciate

it. And now I *do* need to get going, so I can get ready
for my meeting."

"Hold on—let's get you presentable," he said, gently
smoothing her hair and tucking a few loose strands
behind her ears. Then he stopped, as though a sudden
thought had occurred to him. "You know, supply closets are nice…" he said.

"Yes," she agreed. "I'm developing a certain affin-
ity for them."

"But they can be a little claustrophobic. I was wondering if you might be interested in meeting up in a
non-closet, non-quarantine, non-enclosed-space-of-any-
kind type of setting."

She fixed him with a steady gaze. "Jack Harper, are
you asking me out on a date?"

"Yes," he said firmly. "I do believe I am."

When Kat got off work that day she was still thinking about it.

A date. A date with Jack Harper.

It wasn't consistent with their agreement for a purely
physical arrangement, but maybe it wouldn't hurt to see
what happened when they took their relationship outside of the bedroom. She was surprised, though, that of
all the possible moments when Jack could have asked
her to go on a date he'd done so after she'd explained
how she'd been fired.

Christopher's reaction to the news had been quite
different.

Christopher was one of the best surgeons at Chicago
Grace Memorial, and Kat had always believed their re-

lationship was storybook-perfect. While they'd been dating she'd been proud to be with someone so disciplined. Christopher had always been the one to get up for a five a.m. run. He lived off kale smoothies…ate nothing but protein and vegetables…

Kat had always felt that she fell short of living up to his regimented lifestyle. But Christopher was handsome, he was disciplined, and she had thought he loved her.

She had never thought he wouldn't support her when she was fired from Chicago Grace.

"I thought we were people who were serious about our careers," he'd said. "I thought I was about to marry the head of internal medicine at one of the best hospitals in the country. Not an idealistic fool who would throw her career away because she can't hold back from insulting the hospital's board of directors. Well, I won't be foolish with you. You can do what you like with your own reputation, but I won't let you damage mine."

He'd had more to say, but by then she'd slammed her engagement ring on the table and left.

At the time, she'd thought she was heartbroken. But now she wondered if her heartbreak was really about Christopher at all. Her sadness had more to do with having had to let go of the expectations and the life she'd thought she'd wanted. Christopher hadn't been the love of her life after all—he'd simply been a symptom of a larger problem. He'd simply fitted in perfectly with her own high expectations and perfectionism, her misguided idea that she somehow had to earn the right to be accepted.

But since setting foot in Hawaii she'd begun to feel accepted just as she was. And the more time she spent with the people she cared about—Selena, her co-workers and, yes, Jack—the more she felt she didn't need to change herself. She only needed to *be* herself.

CHAPTER SEVEN

KAT WAS SKEPTICAL about Jack's plans for their date, but he assured her that shave ice was a beloved Hawaiian delicacy.

"You can't truly say you've been to Hawaii without trying shave ice," he said. "Personally, I think it's an absolute travesty that you've been here this long without having any."

Kat was reluctant to crush Jack's enthusiasm, but based on his description she wasn't sure she could see the appeal.

"It sounds like it's basically a snow cone," she said.

"Blasphemy," he said. "Shave ice is *nothing* like a snow cone."

"But it's essentially shaved ice covered with syrup?"

"Okay, first of all, it's *shave* ice—not *shaved*. Please try not to embarrass me when you order."

"So they shave the ice…?"

"Into a very fine, snowy powder—yes. And then you pick the flavor of syrup you want to go over it."

"So, like I said, it's basically a snow cone."

"Not one bit," he said. "Don't let anyone hear you say that. You'll get voted off the island immediately."

She rolled her eyes and elbowed him in the ribs.

But the shave ice did turn out to be different from a snow cone. In fact, it was different from anything she'd ever eaten before. Snowy, powder-soft ice shavings were packed on top of coconut ice cream, then covered with tropical fruit syrup and a topping of condensed milk. The result was an incredibly soft, fluffy confection that made Kat think of ice-cold pudding.

"What do you think?" asked Jack.

She took another bite and closed her eyes. "It's like eating a cloud," she said, "or a fluffy milkshake."

He snorted, but she could see that he was pleased that she was enjoying the icy treat.

"A fluffy milkshake, huh?" he said. "That's one I haven't heard before."

They sat down at a colorful picnic table to eat. The shave ice stand was crowded, and Kat could see that Jack was right: shave ice was extremely popular. The lawn in front of the stand was densely packed with people.

But they had barely taken their first few bites before they heard a commotion at the far end of the lawn. Kat stared, wondering what was going on, and then she heard faint cries of, "Oh, my God! Somebody call 911!" and "Is there a doctor anywhere?"

Jack leapt into action, with Kat close behind him.

A man was slumped over his bowl of shave ice and now he slid from the picnic table. He didn't seem to have fainted, but Kat could see he was in danger of losing consciousness. He was slightly overweight, aged about forty. A woman who seemed to be his wife stood next to him and two children, a boy and a girl, stood nearby.

The boy appeared to be trying not to cry; he had his arm around the girl, who looked to be about five and was crying profusely.

"He was fine just a minute ago…" The woman was distraught.

"It's okay—I'm a doctor and he's a paramedic," Kat said, and motioned toward Jack, who was checking the man's vitals as best he could without any equipment. "I need to know what happened."

"He…he said he was tired. We'd been hiking, and we missed lunch because of the hike," the woman said.

"Okay, deep breaths," said Kat. "Does he have any medical conditions that we should know about?"

Given the suddenness of the man's fall, and the fact that he'd missed a meal, her money was on some form of hypoglycemic shock—possibly due to diabetes.

Just as she was forming that thought, Jack said, "Kat, he's on an insulin pump." He pulled at the lower half of the man's shirt to reveal the device.

The pump was common for people with Type One diabetes. Small and portable, it could be worn discreetly under most clothing. It was meant to deliver small, continuous doses of insulin to the body throughout the day, rather like a portable pancreas. But insulin pumps weren't always reliable, and the danger could be significant if a pump malfunctioned.

"Check to see it's functioning properly," Kat said.

"Doesn't look like it," Jack responded. "I can't even read the screen."

"Did he complain of any dizziness earlier today?" Kat asked the man's wife. "Any shakiness, sweating, rapid heart rate?"

"It's hard to say," the woman responded. "We've just been up Diamond Head. He was a little shaky, and sweating quite a bit, but so were the children and I. We assumed it was just the result of a long hike in the heat."

"Could just be heatstroke," said Jack. "Although the broken pump makes insulin shock more likely. Does he have a glucagon rescue kit?"

The man's wife buried her face in her hands. "He was prescribed one six months ago but we never thought we'd need it. We left it in the hotel…an hour from here."

"Call it in," said Kat, but Jack was already on his phone, talking to ambulance dispatch. "What are his vitals?" she asked him.

"Pulse is fast. He's conscious, but just barely."

"Can he swallow?"

Jack looked up to see an employee of the shave ice stand among the gathered crowd. "Can you bring us a bottle of syrup?" he said. "Any flavor. We need to get his blood sugar up *now*."

A moment later someone handed Jack a bottle of strawberry syrup and a paper cup. He poured a small amount of syrup into the cup while Kat knelt by the man's head and tried to keep him conscious.

If the man could stay conscious long enough to swallow the syrup, they'd be able to raise his blood sugar enough to revive him, so that he would simply need to be stabilized at the hospital. But if he fell unconscious there would be no way to raise his blood sugar until the ambulance arrived.

Kat knew the nearest ambulance was at least twenty minutes away, and every minute counted. Every second their patient continued to suffer from insulin shock was crucial, and she desperately wanted to prevent the man from slipping into a coma and suffering all the complications that would arise from that.

"Raise his head a little," said Jack, and Kat supported the man by his shoulders.

His wife knelt down to help her support the man's weight.

"Here, let him lean back on you while he drinks," Kat said to her.

Jack held the cup to the man's lips and tipped it back slightly. The man managed one swallow, then two.

"Easy does it," said Jack. "We just want to give the insulin something to work with, so that your blood sugar can stabilize. Right now it's way too low. The good news is that you're still awake, so you can keep swallowing this syrup."

Kat was impressed with Jack's calm tone. She'd heard him use the same one while bringing patients into the ER, and she knew firsthand how reassuring his confident tone could be. She knew that he wanted to try to normalize things for the family, to reassure the children that help was here for them and for their father. Sometimes talking helped everyone to stay calm.

Jack kept on tipping the syrup into the man's mouth, one swallow at a time, until the man was able to hold the cup himself. Kat was relieved. He was probably out of danger.

After a few more minutes the ambulance pulled up. Kat recognized two EMTs from Oahu General, who nodded at her and Jack as they took over.

"You're in good hands now," Jack said, patting the man's shoulder and giving a reassuring glance to his wife.

As Jack and Kat moved back from the patient to give the EMTs a chance to safely assist him into the ambulance, the manager of the shave ice stand appeared behind them. He was holding large-sized bowls of the same ices they'd ordered.

"On the house," he said. "I noticed you didn't get to eat yours before they melted because you were busy saving that man's life."

As they were eating, Kat said, "Jack, you really are an amazing paramedic. With skills like yours...with a family like yours...why didn't you become a doctor?"

He put down his spoon and gave her a grim look. "That question answers itself."

"I'm not sure I understand..."

He sighed. "You have no idea what it's like to be constantly noticed as one of *those* Harpers. With a family like mine you always have to wonder if people really care about *you*, or if it's just about your connections and the career advancement those connections can provide. When I was in medical school I was always wondering... Does this person want to be my friend, or do they want my dad to offer them a summer internship? Does that professor really think I did a good job on that procedure, or does he want me to mention his name to my mother?"

She thought about that. Jack was right; she didn't have any idea what that would be like. She'd been the first in her family to graduate from college, let alone go to medical school. She'd known plenty of other students who'd come to medical school already having family and other connections in the field, and she'd often been envious of those connections, but for Jack it sounded like having a family that was so well-known in the medical community was more of a liability than anything else.

"I bet there were times when it really sucked," she said. "Not only would you be constantly wondering whether people liked you for *you*, but you'd also be dealing with some pretty high expectations."

"You have no idea," he said again. "Most kids get to dream about what they want to be when they grow up. For my brothers and me it was a foregone conclusion: we were going to be doctors, whether we wanted to or not. And everyone assumed we wanted to. My brother Matt was the only person I could really talk to about it."

"Do you get to see him much?"

"Not really. Have you always known you wanted to be a doctor?" he asked quickly.

She had a feeling he wanted to change the subject, and she was happy to oblige. She was curious about him, but she didn't want to push for more than he was ready to give.

"It's been a dream of mine ever since I was very young," Kat said. "My dad passed away when I was ten. Pneumonia. Maybe things would have been different if he'd been able to see a doctor sooner, but he was always working, and sometimes he'd put off going to the doctor to save money."

Jack nodded. "That's why the idea of opening a nonprofit clinic at Chicago Grace was so important to you? That's why you got so mad when they told you no?"

Kat gave a terse nod. "If there's any way I can make it so that fewer families have to go through what mine did, I'll do it."

"I can't imagine losing a parent at such a young age," Jack said. "It must have changed everything?"

"Pretty much everything," she agreed. "I think that was the beginning of my Type A tendencies. I turned into a little adult. If I wasn't the one worrying about the bills our electricity would go out. I can't fault my mom, though. She might not have been the most organized person in the world, but she worked hard to put me through school."

"It doesn't sound like you had the chance to have much of a childhood."

"Yes and no. My family was poor, but I never felt poor because I felt loved. And even though I had to work pretty hard—I started working part-time jobs when I was sixteen to save up to pay for school—I still feel it was all worth it in the end." She brightened. "And it's not as though I can't make up for lost time. Maybe I didn't get the chance to do anything wild or reckless when I was younger, but opportunities continue to present themselves." She gave him a wicked smile.

"Oh? And what kind of opportunities might those be?"

"Well, I believe I recall one of us suggesting cliff jumping as a fun recreational pastime."

He laughed. "You can't be serious."

Her eyes widened innocently. "Why not?"

Truth be told, she'd been wildly curious about the idea of cliff jumping ever since he'd suggested it. And she didn't want to wait around to see if any of their friends wanted to go. She wanted to go now—with him—before she lost her nerve.

"I think you were right when you said that I needed

some excitement, some kind of thrill. This is my chance. Besides, you said it was great for mental clarity."

"That's true," he said, his face growing thoughtful. "You're never more certain of what you really want than when you're hurtling through the air at top speed. Into appropriately deep water, of course." He glared down at her. "Safety first," he said sternly.

"Of course," she said. "So—are we doing this?"

"Let's go."

Jack had been driving for about an hour. They were almost to the spot of coastline that was his destination—the perfect spot for cliff jumping. Something was still bothering him, but he wasn't sure how to bring it up.

Just say it, he thought. *You're about to literally jump off a cliff with this woman. If you're not afraid of that you shouldn't be afraid of an emotional conversation.*

He summoned his courage. "Earlier…when you were telling me about how hard you had to work to get through medical school… I couldn't help but feel guilty," he said.

"Guilty? Why on earth should you feel guilty?" she asked.

"Because I walked away from something you worked so hard for," he said. "I left medical school at the end of my third year but I could have sailed through—because of who my parents are, and because my family have money. You had to scrimp and save and plan your whole life to get something that I gave up."

"It wasn't what you wanted," she said. "Becoming a doctor has always been my dream. But it doesn't sound as though it was ever yours. Why feel guilty just because you decided to walk away from the path that I chose?"

He was relieved to hear that she wasn't appalled by his decision. But Kat wasn't finished.

"There is something I wonder about, though," she said. "You said earlier that you were closest to your brother Matt, but that you don't see him much now. Why not?"

"My older brother and I haven't spoken in four years," he said.

He wasn't sure why he was opening up to her. Maybe because she'd been so sympathetic. His struggle was nothing, compared to hers, but she seemed to understand exactly what he was saying.

"Oh," said Kat. "This wouldn't happen to be the same brother you told me about while we were in quarantine? The one who cheated with your fiancée?"

"That's the one," said Jack.

He'd always refused to talk about Matt and Sophie. He'd simply decided to leave that part of his life behind. He wasn't sure why he felt he could talk about it now, except that there was something about Kat's ability to understand him that seemed to make his words come tumbling out.

"Matt was the only person in my family who I could really be myself with," said Jack. "I looked up to him."

"Sounds like you were pretty close," said Kat.

"We were. Matt was a great older brother while we were growing up. He always stood up for me, listened to me, and he helped me out whenever I needed it."

"So what happened?"

"It's complicated," he said. "When I left medical

school to join the SEALs Sophie felt that I'd let her down. She was in medical school too, and she'd always planned for a certain kind of life. She wanted to be married to someone who was a doctor, like she was, and she wanted a big house in the same suburb my parents lived in. And then I didn't want those things anymore."

Kat placed a hand on his arm. "It's hard when people grow apart," she said. "But if you wanted such different things maybe it's for the best that you didn't end up together."

"I can see that now," Jack said. "But at the time I was heartbroken. It wasn't just that she didn't want to be with me. I could have understood that. She'd thought all along that I wanted one kind of life, and then I started trying to explain that I wanted something different… Even though I'd hoped she would understand, I would never have faulted her for still wanting a different life than the one I'd started looking for. If it had just been that I would have gotten over it in time."

He took a deep breath. "But then I found out that she'd been cheating on me with Matt. She left me for him the next day. I confronted Matt and told him that I couldn't believe he would do that to me."

"How could he?" said Kat. "How could your family accept that from either of them?"

He sighed, and then he said, "Sophie was pregnant."

Kat paused for a moment, and Jack's heart went cold at the shocked expression on her face.

"You have a child?" she said. But then understanding broke through. Her hand went to her mouth. "Oh, no. It wasn't yours, was it?"

He winced. "See? I told you I was naïve. *You* put it

together right away." He gave a dry laugh. "Matt knew the baby was his. He and Sophie had been cheating on me for six months. I've always wondered if she viewed Matt and I as somehow interchangeable. As long as she married into the Harper family she'd have the connections she needed to work at any hospital she liked for the rest of her life."

"But that's not all, is it?" asked Kat.

"What do you mean?"

"Jack, it sounds to me like you and your brother were incredibly close. To lose that relationship, especially when you didn't have many other people you felt you could count on…it must have been devastating."

He shrugged, reluctant to let her know how right she was.

"Have you ever thought about calling him?" she asked.

"No way," he said. "I don't need the complication."

"Jack, family isn't a complication. It's *family*. You have a niece or nephew to get to know."

"No," he said. "I *thought* I had a family. Instead I have a group of people back in Nebraska who are interested in prestige and not much else, and who all happen to share the same last name."

He was taken aback by the bitterness in his own voice, and surprised when Kat said softly, "I can understand why you'd feel that way. It sounds like Sophie confirmed your worst fear: that people were only interested in you for your family's prestige and connections."

"Exactly. And then when you came, with your incredible reputation and your plans to change all the policies at the hospital…"

"You thought I was some bigwig who'd put my career over the people in my life."

He had the grace to blush. "I can see how wrong I was about that now. People come here all the time, thinking they're going to escape their problems, or they're going to jumpstart their careers by being a big fish in a small pond. But it's *my* small pond, and I'm very protective of it."

She thought for a moment, and then she said, "It might surprise you to hear this, but I know how it feels to be used for your connections."

"Oh?"

"When I got fired from Chicago Grace, Christopher called off the wedding right away. We'd both thought I was going to be promoted to director of the internal medicine department, and when I didn't get the promotion, and then got fired, he broke up with me."

Jack shook his head. This Christopher guy was a complete idiot.

"Anyway, this whole year I've been trying to figure out why I'm not grieving Christopher more. I was going to marry him. I thought he was the love of my life. But I feel like I've been more upset over losing my job than losing my fiancé. *Ex*-fiancé."

"Well, your job was something you worked hard for most of your life. Your career was about you and about your connection with your dad. Who never even met Christopher. So it makes sense that losing your job would have affected you much more deeply."

"Yes, but it's more than that. I don't think Christopher and I were really meant to be. I thought he loved me… But now I think he just loved the idea of being married to a department head at a top Chicago hospital. He liked the prestige. But when it came to really making a difference in the way I wanted to he didn't care."

Jack pulled off the highway and parked underneath a tree just beside the road. They'd reached their destination.

As they both got out of the car, he said, "It sounds like we've both broken away from our old lives. And now we can figure out what to do with our new lives— what the next steps are."

They approached the edge of the cliff at the golden hour—the hour before the sun set and cast everything with a luminous glow. It was one of Jack's favorite spots in all Hawaii: a stretch of coastline on the island's north shore. This part of the shoreline was made of high cliffs, with deep water below. It was an ideal spot for cliff jumping, if Kat decided she wanted to go through with it.

Being so close to the shoreline awed Jack, as it always did. And as he looked at Kat he could tell that she was just as taken by the island's beauty as he was.

"It's incredible," she said. "I've never seen water this shade of blue before. It's like looking at liquid lapis lazuli."

Jack realized he'd never really taken in the islands through someone else's eyes. Kat's response to the wild beauty of Oahu made him feel as though he were seeing it all again for the first time.

"You love this place," he said.

"I think I do," she replied. "Even though I haven't spent much time here. From the moment I got off the plane I felt like I was home. Chicago is a great city, but it's very…flat. I've never seen a place that radiates so much natural beauty as Hawaii."

Speaking of radiating beauty, Jack thought, *she should see how her face softens and her eyes shine when she looks out over the cliffs.*

Somewhere along their hike to the cliffs she'd plucked a plumeria flower and placed it in her hair. The effect was breathtaking now, as Kat looked out over the coast, framed by the sea and sky, her tangled red hair waving in the wind. She turned toward him and somehow, before he knew what had taken hold of him, he'd reached out and she was in his arms, her face tilted up toward his.

He felt as though she'd always belonged there—as though he'd reached out for some lost piece of himself that he hadn't known was missing. But to have her so close was confusing. He couldn't think clearly with her pulled into his arms, pressed against his chest, her hair smelling of flowers.

He found himself saying, "There's no reason to be scared," and he couldn't be sure if he was saying it to her, or to himself.

"Scared?" she said. She looked up at him, confused. "Why would I be scared?"

A fair enough question. She rested securely in his arms and he would damn well *never* let any harm come to her if he could help it. She was in the safest place she could possibly be, even if she didn't know it. So why should either of them be scared?

He searched his mind for an explanation of what he'd said—something that would make sense. "I was talking about the cliff-jumping, if you decide you want to try it," he said. "It's always scary the first time, but there's nothing to be afraid of here. The water's deep, but we're close enough to shore that we can swim back safely, and the current isn't overpowering."

She looked up at him, still folded in his arms, her eyes filled with emotion. "Jumping off a cliff doesn't scare me," she said. "I know that might sound strange. But you were right, Jack! I was never going to learn to relax from a book. I need to try new things, and I need a thrill. I'm the kind of person who relaxes by finding excitement—not by sitting in a quiet room meditating. But before coming to Hawaii I never realized that about myself because my whole life has been about studying. I never even had a chance to experience an adrenaline rush until I started working in the ER. I don't think I ever realized that *that's* what I love about medicine: the excitement, the unpredictability, having to think quickly. At least, I didn't realize it until I met you."

Jack wondered if Kat could feel his heart beating underneath his shirt. He'd pulled her to him and she hadn't pulled away. She was still resting in his arms, her head against his chest, as though she belonged there. As though she *wanted* to be there. As though whatever was between the two of them wasn't about being friends, or having a physical relationship with no emotions.

She held him as though she wanted him.

She held him the same way he was holding her.

"I'm not scared of jumping off a cliff, Jack," she continued. "Why would I be? I trust you. But I'll tell you what I really *am* scared of." She locked her eyes with his. "I'm scared of the two of us hiding from how we really feel about each other."

And then she was kissing him, her lips seeking his with ardent desire, and he found himself kissing her back just as passionately, his tongue desperate to explore every last corner of her mouth and his arms pressing her against his body, right where she belonged.

Some time later their kisses became shorter and softer, until they simply held each other close, their foreheads pressed together.

"What do you think?" he said. "Should we take the leap?"

She looked over the cliff. "The relationship leap or the actual leap?"

"Both," he said.

"I want to, but I'm not sure I know how," she said.

He held her close. "I think there's only one way to do it," he said. "Take a running start, hold hands, and jump together."

Kat's head broke the surface of the water. She felt exhilarated. She looked around and for a moment was worried not to see Jack, but then there he was, swimming toward her.

The leaping off—pushing her legs up and out, away from the cliff—had been the most frightening part, but it had helped to have that running start. And it had also helped to know that Jack was holding her hand. They'd run for the edge together, holding hands for as long as they could before they leapt into the air and broke apart.

For an endless moment that had seemed to exist outside of time she'd hung in the air. It had been the closest thing to flying she'd ever experienced. With her feet springing away from land, the sea rushing toward her and the salt air surrounding her, her senses had been completely enveloped. There had been no room for her to fret about the past or worry about the future. The only moment she'd been able to completely exist in had been the present.

Then the water had rushed up to greet her and surrounded her body. She'd let herself sink, and then relaxed her body until it had naturally begun to rise toward the surface. She'd kicked her way up to the air, breaking the water's surface with a gasp.

And now Jack was swimming toward her with sure and steady strokes.

He'd been right. About so many things. About her need for excitement. About the two of them taking a chance on one another.

He swam toward her, wrapped his arm around her waist, and kissed her.

Jumping off the cliff had felt like a microcosm of her life, she thought. You could plan and plan, she thought, but nothing could prevent you from hitting the water in the end. The question was, did you want to fall off or jump off freely, feeling the sensation of flying?

She looked over at Jack. The future would come, and life would have its twists and turns, its bumps and bruises, no matter what she did. She'd never be able to completely avoid life's setbacks or challenges.

But she could choose who she'd be holding hands with when they came.

CHAPTER EIGHT

IN CHICAGO, IT had often been hard for Kat to face the cold gray mornings. If the sun made an appearance at all, it usually didn't show up until nine a.m., and then it was often obscured by clouds, unless the weather was exceptionally nice that day.

But mornings in Hawaii felt as though they were taking place in another world. The sun was up early, and as a result so was Kat. Her apartment wasn't far from the beach, and she enjoyed taking early-morning walks by the ocean as she sipped from a mug of coffee.

She couldn't believe how much she'd already changed during the time she'd spent in Hawaii. No one back home would ever have thought of her as a morning person. But the early hours before her shifts at the hospital were now her favorite part of the day. It was so relaxing to hear the rush of the ocean mixed with the wind and birdsong in her ears.

She smiled to herself. Just a few short months ago she hadn't known how to relax, let alone how to relax at the beach. She'd been worried she might have permanently lost her ability to live in the moment. She'd

164   FROM HAWAII TO FOREVER

spent so long trying to build her career that she'd forgotten to focus on herself as a person.

But whatever it was she might have lost after the breakup, and everything that had happened on the Day of Doom, she'd managed to get it back. Apparently she had no trouble being spontaneous anymore. Hadn't she signed up for surfing lessons just that morning?

She couldn't wait to tell Jack. He'd mentioned that surfing was something he'd never gotten around to learning. She wondered if they might be able to learn together. Or maybe she could take the lessons on her own and then teach him. Her mind hummed with possibilities as she made her way back to her apartment.

She'd left her phone on the kitchen counter so that it wouldn't distract her from her walk—something the Old Kat never would have done. In the past she'd had to obsessively check her emails and other messages before she even got out of bed, but now she liked to savor those early moments before she started her day.

She picked up the phone. It was early, but she saw that someone had already tried to call her several times that morning. The number had a Chicago area code, though she didn't recognize it as belonging to her mother or to any of her friends.

The voicemail was fuzzy and crackly, but the important parts came through. Chicago Grace Memorial had had a major overturn in staff. There was a new hospital director, and the voicemail was from the director herself.

She said she understood that Kat's recent firing had been the result of some differences in vision between Kat and the former hospital director. But now he had been let go, along with several members of the hospital's board, so would Kat be interested in having her old job back? With an increase in pay and a promotion to Head of Internal Medicine? Chicago Grace wanted her to return very much. Could she call back as soon as possible, to let them know if she was interested?

Kat gasped. Of *course* she was interested. This was everything she'd ever wanted.

And yet somehow, she felt...flat.

She thought of all the things she'd need to do, but it was as if she were going over a laundry list. She needed to pack, to talk to Selena, to transition all her patients at Oahu General to other doctors...

Her mind went through the list mechanically. Four months ago she would have been thrilled to get a job offer like this. But now she wasn't sure how she felt.

Without thinking, she pulled a suitcase from underneath her bed and began throwing items of clothing into it.

Wait, she thought. *You haven't even called this woman back yet. You need a timeline...you need to prepare...you need to make a checklist of all the things you have to do to get ready to go back...*

She froze. She had to go, didn't she? People didn't just turn down opportunities like this. Who knew when another chance would come along?

But if this was such a clear choice why did she feel so flat? She'd only intended to stay for a year in the first place. Selena probably wouldn't mind if she needed to negotiate a few months off her contract. Or maybe the hospital in Chicago could be convinced to let her stay the whole year in Hawaii and resume her work there after her contract was up.

There was so much to do. Should she call the hospital director back first or talk to Selena first? When should she tell Selena she was leaving?

Then her heart flipped over.

When would she tell Jack she was leaving?

And *was* she leaving?

She realized she was treating it as a foregone conclusion. But was it really what she wanted?

She paused for a moment and searched her feelings. She wanted to stay here in Hawaii. But she also missed Chicago.

She'd done the thing she'd been trying so hard *not* to do the moment she'd first laid eyes on Jack. She'd fallen for him. Leaving him was going to break her heart all over again. But it was her chance to get her career back on track.

Or was it?

Somehow, the idea of returning to Chicago Grace Memorial didn't thrill her the way she'd thought it would. She was just reacting automatically, without asking herself what she really wanted.

But what *did* she want?

She stood in her apartment, listening to the silence. Just a moment ago she had felt so happy. Now she had no idea what she wanted at all.

"So that's the situation," Kat told Selena later that morning. "They've had a change in the hospital administration and they've decided they want me back."

"I knew it was too good to be true," Selena muttered.

"I get one of the top infectious disease researchers in the country to work at my hospital and of *course* she's going to leave after only four months."

"That's just it," said Kat. "I'm not so sure I want to leave."

Selena's eyebrows shot up. "How could you *not* want to leave? I mean, I love this hospital, but even *I* have to admit that it's no Chicago Grace. We're a good hospital, but Chicago has the researchers and the prestige and the funding—"

Kat cut her off. "I know it has all of those things. And I feel like I'm *supposed* to want those things… But I'm not sure that I still actually *do* want them."

"Well, if that's how you feel then it sounds like you have a lot of thinking to do— Wait a minute," Selena said abruptly. "Is there something you haven't told me?"

"Like what?" said Kat innocently.

"Like maybe the situation has deepened between you and a certain dark-haired, blue-eyed paramedic?"

For a moment Kat felt a sense of shock that Selena had clearly guessed that something was going on between herself and Jack.

Oh, what the hell? More than anything right now, you need to talk this over with a friend.

She felt a little guilty, because it was Jack's secret as well as hers. But she needed her friend's advice.

"Jack and I have been seeing each other—" she began.

Selena squealed and said, "I *knew* it!"

"It started out as a purely physical thing. We promised not to get our emotions involved. But then, somehow… I think our emotions *did* get involved."

"And do you regret that?" asked Selena.

"The only thing I'm certain of right now is that I don't know how I feel," Kat said.

"Have you told Jack that you've been offered this new job back at your old hospital?"

"No," said Kat. "And I'm not going to. Not yet, anyway. It's a big decision, and I feel like I have to make it myself."

"Why don't you take the next few days off while you think it over?" said Selena.

"A few days off? I don't need that. And the last thing I want to do right now is take time off when I might be about to leave anyway. You asked me to come down here to help you out. I don't want to leave you in the lurch."

"Kat, we're fine. This is actually a really good time for you to take some time off. We're not facing any upcoming outbreaks right now. Thanks to the vaccine, and your initiative with the outpatient clinic, there's been a noticeable reduction in cases coming through the ER. With better access to follow-up care patients are less likely to need emergency response, because we're catching things early instead of at the last possible minute, when things are in crisis. So, largely thanks to you, we do have a moment for a breather right now."

"Time off, huh...?" said Kat. "It was bad enough when I spent just a few hours stuck in quarantine. I don't know what I'm going to do with myself if I'm not at the hospital."

Selena put her hand on Kat's shoulder. "You don't need to connect with your doctor self right now," she said. "You need to figure out what you want for *you*."

* * *

Jack stood outside, stunned by what he was hearing. Selena's office door was open just a crack. He hadn't meant to eavesdrop; he'd been coming to Selena's office to follow up on a request for some of the EMTs' time off to be approved. But he'd stopped when he'd noticed that she and Kat seemed to be having a private conversation.

Just as he'd turned away, he'd heard Selena.

"Have you told Jack that you've been offered this new job back at your old hospital?"

He'd frozen. When had that happened? How long had Kat known? And why had she decided not to tell him?

Now, as the initial shock wore off, he realized he was still hovering outside the door. He quietly eased himself away from the entrance to Selena's office and headed into a stairwell down the hall so he could think.

It shouldn't bother him that Kat might be leaving. She'd only ever planned to stay for one year.

But she'd been on the island for…he mentally calculated the days since they'd met…a little over four months. He hadn't expected that she would leave so soon.

And if she did leave what did it matter to him? She had a life back in Chicago, and they'd both always known that she'd planned to return to it. So what if that happened much sooner than either of them had expected? They'd both agreed to have a fling. A no-strings-attached, no-expectations, no-commitment island fling.

For the rest of the afternoon he tried to avoid her as he went about his duties at the hospital. He knew

he'd want to confront her if they spoke, but he didn't
know why. For some reason the thought of Kat leaving seemed to have awakened something ugly in his
chest—something angry and hurt and furious at the
unfairness of it all. And whatever that ugly beast was
he needed to hide it from Kat—because, rationally, he
knew it made no sense.

He had no right to be angry. No right to confront her,
to demand an explanation of what he'd overheard between her and Selena. Getting attached to one another
had never been part of the plan. They'd agreed to that
from the start.

But he wanted to confront her, to ask her exactly
what that conversation with Selena had meant, and what
she planned to do. Even though he wasn't sure if he
could maintain control over his emotions.

Oahu General was a small hospital, and despite his
best efforts to avoid Kat he filed a patient's chart behind the reception desk and turned to find her right in
front of him.

"Supply closet. Five minutes," she whispered into his
ear, and before he could respond she'd scooted away.

For a minute he considered not meeting her there.
But he knew he had to. He couldn't stand not knowing
if she was leaving for a moment longer.

His face stoic, he headed down to the supply closet.

Kat stood waiting for him in the darkness. She knew she
should tell Jack about the job offer—she really should.
But not yet. She wasn't ready. She wanted to enjoy her
time with him for just a little longer before anything
else got in the way.

But when he arrived, instead of slipping quietly inside the closet as he usually did, he switched the lights on. Her stomach dropped when she saw his face. His expression was cold, even angry, she thought. And his next words confirmed her worst fear: he already knew.

"So when were you planning to tell me that you're going back to Chicago?" he said.

His voice was dull and wooden. And his eyes weren't angry, she realized. They were pained.

"How did you find out?" she asked.

"Does it matter?"

She flinched at the coldness in his voice. "For your information, I haven't decided yet whether I'll go back early or not. I did receive the offer of a job at my old hospital, with a promotion. But I made a one-year commitment to stay here, and it's important to me to honor that."

"And what happens to your job offer while you're honoring your commitment here? Are they going to wait around for you for another eight months in Chicago? I doubt it. You're going to take their offer, and you're going to take it now—because this is the kind of opportunity that a doctor like you can't stand to pass up."

"A doctor like me? What is *that* supposed to mean?"

"You know exactly what I mean. You talk a good game about healing people, but it's really all about the prestige and the glory."

She was absolutely disgusted. "I'm not your ex, Jack, and I'm not your family. Don't start confusing me with people from your past. Yes, I'm successful and ambitious, but you have no right to tell me what my priorities are."

"Is that so? You're not exactly difficult to figure out. You come to this island a big-city doc, thinking that you know better than everyone else, and then the minute something better comes along you leave. It's all about the next step—it's never about caring about where you actually *are*!"

She glared at him. "Maybe if you'd quit living in the past you wouldn't have such a hard time planning for your future!"

"*I'm* living in the past?" he said. "You've been living in the past since the moment you arrived. You just wanted a break from your normal life—you never wanted to think about how the people who live here are actual *people*. You say you want to learn to slow down and live in the moment, but the truth is you just wanted a place to recover from the *one time* someone didn't recognize your brilliance. And now that the world is ready to shower you with applause again you're going to kick the dust of Hawaii off your heels and head back to the city as soon as possible. You talk about wanting to change your life, but you haven't changed at all. You're just going right back to the life you left behind."

Kat was ready to throttle him. He was partly right— just a little bit—and that little bit was enough to set her blood boiling. But she certainly wasn't going to give him the satisfaction of letting him know that some of his words had hit home.

"At least I was able to leave it behind—even if it was only for a little while!" she said. "*You* haven't left the past behind at all. You're living in it every day."

"I am not!"

"Are you kidding me? You let your past control every

single thing you do. Because you won't face any of it. You say you don't date doctors, but that's complete nonsense. You *like* doctors. You work with them every single day. You don't have a problem with doctors. You have a problem with the one you're related to. Matt. *Your brother.*"

"What happened between me and my brother is none of your business."

"Then I'll tell you something that *is* my business. Your whole no-strings-attached thing with relationships is ridiculous. It's not the real you—it's just you trying to avoid pain."

He inhaled sharply, as though she had cut him to the quick. And maybe she had gone too far. But she felt the truth of what she'd said deep within her. Jack's whole defense system—his guardedness, his pretense of being unemotional and uninterested in relationships—none of it was the *real* him, the Jack she'd gotten to know after four and a half months on the island. Even if he couldn't see it, she could—and she had to tell him, even if it hurt.

He had grown quiet, his face dark. Then he said, "If no-strings-attached is ridiculous, then where does that leave us?"

She didn't know what to say. She wished more than anything that she could have had this conversation with Jack when she was more prepared for it. After she had made her decision and had planned everything she wanted to tell him.

The silence grew. Finally, she said, "Look, Jack, this is just terrible timing. We've been having... *I've* been having a wonderful time. I thought we'd have more of it..."

His lips were a thin line. "I don't think it's terrible timing," he said. "In fact, I think it's *great* timing. Not a moment too soon."

"Please believe me when I say that I haven't made a decision yet. I'm not sure what I'm going to do. Chicago Grace is one of the best research hospitals in the country, and I can't turn that down lightly. But when I think about my time here... I don't know what to do."

"Stay, go—it doesn't matter to me," he said. "We agreed no emotions, remember? This was never supposed to be anything more than physical. So it makes no difference to me what you decide."

"It doesn't?"

"No. In fact, I think you should go."

She felt something in her chest shift and crack. She tried to look into his eyes, those blue eyes that had so captivated her the day they met, but his face was turned away from her and his eyes appeared to be fixated on a random spot on the supply closet wall.

He cleared his throat and said, "You can't turn it down. It wouldn't make any sense. You belong at a big research hospital where you can shine—not in a remote little hospital in the middle of the ocean."

"I just..." Her voice quavered and she blinked back tears.

"Congratulations on your new job," he said.

Hours later Jack was brooding on the beach—much as he had been the day he'd met Kat. He couldn't stop thinking about their argument.

"You let your past control every single thing you do," she'd said. *"Because you won't face any of it."*

What did she know about it, anyway? What business of hers was it whether he let his past control him or not? They'd agreed to keep things on a purely physical level, so why should she care about his past or how it affected him? *She* was the one who'd proposed their fling in the first place. They'd both always known that she was only here for a short time, and she knew that he didn't like getting his emotions involved in relationships.

"Your whole no-strings-attached thing with relationships is ridiculous. It's not the real you—it's just you trying to avoid pain."

It was true. In the heat of their argument he hadn't been able to bring himself to be honest with Kat, but he could be honest with himself now. She was right. He kept himself distant and guarded from women because of the pain he'd felt over Sophie. More specifically, over Sophie and Matt.

If it had been an ordinary breakup he would have gotten over it long ago, but the fact that Sophie had betrayed him with Matt meant that he'd lost the one person in the world he'd thought would always be there for him.

Strange, he thought, how he'd tried so hard to avoid repeating the pain of heartbreak and yet here it was, as fresh as ever. Even though he'd tried to convince himself that his relationship with Kat was purely physical and emotionless, it wasn't true. It really had been just his attempt to keep himself from getting hurt.

Despite his best efforts to stay distant they'd gotten close, and before he knew it he had allowed himself to hope. When they'd tried to keep their relationship purely physical their lovemaking hadn't quenched his thirst. It had only brought about a desire for more. He thought perhaps she might feel the same way, although he couldn't be sure. And now he could never ask her. As much as he was hurting right now, the last thing he wanted to do was make it harder for Kat to leave him.

You always knew she was here for just the one year, he told himself. *What were you expecting? Don't blame her just because you got your hopes up for something you knew perfectly well was never going to be long-term in the first place.*

But even though he knew it was the right thing to do, the mature thing to do, it was hard to accept the end of their relationship so soon after it had begun. He couldn't say what their time together had meant to Kat. But for him it had felt like the beginning of something. Something he wanted to explore to its fullest extent to see where it would lead.

He knew that it wasn't realistic or fair of him to hope that Kat would change her career plans for him. After all, they'd only known each other for a few months. And when he stepped back from the hurt of it all and really thought about it he knew that he would never dream of asking her. As much as he, personally, didn't believe in putting a career over personal happiness, that was *his* choice. Kat's career was the thing in her life that made her happy.

He'd never get in the way of her happiness—not for one second.

Even if that meant that they couldn't be together.

The thought of it tore at his heart.

For almost Jack's entire life there'd only been one person he'd felt cared enough about him to help him figure out situations like this. More than anything he wanted to talk to that person now. He wanted his advice, he wanted his reassurance that things would be okay, or that even if things weren't okay they'd stick together and figure it out.

He just wasn't sure he had the guts to make the call.

"You don't have a problem with doctors," Kat had said. *"You have a problem with the one you're related to. Matt. Your brother."*

His anger flared again. Was this what she'd meant when she'd said he let the past control him? As though he was too much of a coward to face his feelings?

But now his anger was more with himself than with Kat. Because right now he needed help from someone he could trust. Even if that person had made a mistake. His inability to forgive was holding him back from getting what he really needed.

Jack picked up his phone. He dialed a number that he'd deleted from his contacts but that had burned itself into his memory long ago.

He wasn't sure if he was ready for this conversation. But, ready or not, it was time for him and his brother to talk.

The phone rang once, and then Jack heard a familiar voice answer.

"Hi, Matt," he said.

CHAPTER NINE

EVER SINCE SELENA had advised her to take a few days off, Kat had been moving nonstop. She'd been packing, calling Selena, calling her mother, and logging in to Oahu General's system to update her files. She'd been researching flights to Chicago and looking up the number of the real estate agent who'd found her apartment to see about getting out of her lease early.

She had a million things to do, and she knew, all of a sudden, why it felt as though she had to complete every single one of those tasks *right now*: it was because preparing to leave helped her to keep her mind off Jack.

As long as she kept herself busy she wouldn't have to think about the pain in his eyes. And she wouldn't have to dwell on that sensation of something cracking, deep within her chest. It was a feeling that had started as soon as she'd looked into Jack's eyes and told him about the job offer. She was trying, and failing, to ignore it.

She believed in love. She knew that with great certainty now. When she'd told Selena months ago that she didn't think she could believe in love or in relationships she'd been lying to herself. She'd been trying to figure out who she was and what she believed at the same time she'd been trying to mask the pain that she'd felt about Christopher. The result had been a ridiculous cynical statement that she knew now wasn't true.

There was no denying her feelings for Jack. It was true that she hadn't known him for long. She'd only been in Hawaii for a little over four months, and even less time had passed since she'd given herself permission to acknowledge her true feelings for Jack. It was too soon to know where things would go if they stayed together. And yet she felt deeply enough to know the relationship deserved a chance.

She might not know how to describe her feelings for Jack, but she knew that the only thing that held her back from using the word *love* was time. If she left now she'd spend her life wondering what might have happened if she'd stayed. Wondering if he might feel the same way.

But she had to leave, didn't she? Jack had practically insisted she go. Chicago Grace Memorial was one of the most prestigious hospitals in the country. How could she possibly turn it down?

The answer was that she couldn't. Of course she had to go. People didn't simply turn down positions like this. Did they?

But if she wanted the job so badly why was her heart sinking? What was wrong with her? Normal people didn't react with disappointment when they were offered everything they'd ever wanted.

Taking the job would make her one of the leading infectious disease researchers in the country. She'd be able to do good, important work, and she'd be recognized as a valuable contributor to the field of medicine.

When she thought about that, she recognized herself. It felt like who she was. But she wasn't so sure she was as excited at the prospect of what daily life in Chicago had to offer. She knew that life well. Long, cold winters. Late nights spent at work. She knew she could handle that life, because she'd already done it for years. But handling day-to-day life and relishing it were two different things.

In Chicago, she knew she would earn respect from her colleagues, but would she be able to count on their friendship? Before working at Oahu General she'd never dreamed there could be a hospital with such warm collegiality among its staff. She'd come to depend on her regular chats in Selena's office, on the casual banter among the paramedics, nurses, and physicians. These past four months had been among the happiest of her professional life.

When she thought about returning to her old life in Chicago, she had the strangest sense of dread. But surely no one in their right mind would pass up a prestigious job opportunity just because…just because they were *happier* where they were?

Before moving to Hawaii she would have known the answer to that question. Happiness could wait. She was busy building her career. She would worry about enjoying her life after she'd retired from twenty or thirty years as a respected physician. Maybe then there would be room in her life for her to make decisions based on what she wanted for herself rather than the next logical step in her career.

But since she'd moved to Hawaii she'd been able to get a taste of what it would be like to have balance in her life right *now*. She still worked hard—that was certain.

But when she came to work she wasn't just passionate about her career: she had fun, too. She would genuinely miss the staff and the environment they'd created.

Leaving the hospital would be hard.

Leaving Hawaii would break her heart.

She paused in her packing to savor the cool breeze coming through the window. There truly was nowhere else on earth that was like this place. Where else would she be able to walk to the beach from her apartment and see dolphins frolicking off the coast? And she'd gotten used to the riot of color among the flowers that lined Honolulu's sidewalks. The thought of exchanging those tropical flowers for gray ice-covered walkways was disheartening.

It wasn't just that Hawaii was pretty. If it were only that her decision would be so much easier. There were plenty of pretty places in the world and she couldn't live in all of them—it wasn't physically possible. If her reluctance to leave was simply a matter of craving natural beauty, that was a problem easily solved. She could take a vacation somewhere beautiful any time she started to feel burnt out.

No, the islands were beautiful, but it wasn't their beauty that called to her. It was something deeper than that—more primal. Something she'd known in her bones the second she'd arrived. The moment she'd stepped off the plane she'd felt a sense of coming home. She couldn't remember having had such a feeling of belonging somewhere since before her father's death.

Her father had had such heady hopes and dreams for her, and by great good fortune she had shared those same hopes and dreams for herself. It had meant so much to her to live up to his expectations—especially after he'd gone. And then, as she'd grown up, it had become important to her to live up to the expectations of her teachers, her professors at medical school, her supervisors as a student and her superiors at work.

And because many of those expectations that others had had of her were also those she'd had for herself, she hadn't noticed that her own happiness was no longer a priority. Her desire for her happiness had slipped away as she'd focused on the needs and expectations of others.

So it had felt natural to live up to Christopher's expectations of her, as well. No wonder none of her friends had liked him. She hadn't been able to understand it at the time, because it had felt so natural for her to agree with Christopher and to try to please him. But she wondered now why it had never seemed as important to please herself.

But the minute she'd stepped off the plane in Hawaii she'd felt something new. That same breeze that had brought her the scent of the plumeria flowers had also brought her a sense of glorious possibility. The possibility of being herself. The mountains and the ocean had promised her adventure; the birds, the flowers and the meandering paths had hinted at peace. And the people had offered an acceptance that she'd never thought was possible.

She'd been so nervous about earning her place at Oahu General Hospital that she'd never realized she didn't *have* to earn it because her place was already there. She didn't have to work hard to belong. Instead she simply belonged.

Jack had once told her that he did his best thinking at

the beach. He'd said he'd been out on the beach to think on the day they'd met, when he'd rescued her from the rip current. Kat had decided that the beach might not be a bad idea. And, thanks to Jack, she was now an expert at using the beach as a place to think, too.

Those days when she'd felt as though she couldn't turn her brain off, couldn't stop worrying about all the people who mattered to her and all the work stresses were over. The worries were still there, occasionally, but now she could set them aside and focus on the sand and the waves.

Jack had been right about her need for excitement, too. But as she strolled barefoot on the beach, feeling the sand underneath her toes, she knew that she needed the serenity that these islands could offer her as well. She wondered if she would have been able to appreciate the stillness and the calm of the ocean if Jack hadn't shown her how much she needed excitement first.

However she'd gotten to this point, she was glad that she was finally able to relax enough to enjoy something as simple as a walk on the beach. She wanted to soak up as much of Hawaii as possible. She gazed out over the ocean, marveling at its endlessness. She took in the sun, shimmering on the water's surface, and far in the distance she could see the other Hawaiian islands, where a cloudy haze formed around the green mountains of each one.

The sand was cool under her toes and for a moment Kat felt completely at peace. She was completely absorbed in the way each part of the beach touched her senses: she could feel the grains of sand that had collected on her feet, the warmth of the sun on her skin, and she could hear the sound of ocean waves in her ears, punctuated by a few birds flying overhead and calling.

She'd never felt this way about any place she'd ever been to or any choice she'd made. The closest comparison she could think of was the day she'd learned that she had gotten into medical school. In that moment she'd felt the strongest feeling of peace and security wash over her—the knowledge that she was going to do exactly what she was meant to be doing with her life.

She had that same feeling about Hawaii—that this was where she was meant to be and that she should spend the rest of her life here and continue feeling it was meant to be.

You could almost call it a kind of love, she thought. And it had been Jack who'd shown her how to fall in love with the islands, how to take advantage of all they had to offer.

I could visit, she told herself. *I could take trips to Hawaii every so often—maybe every other year or so. I could come here for holidays and long weekends.*

You don't visit the love of your life "every other year or so," her heart responded. *Not if you have any choice in the matter.*

But did she have a choice? At first, it had seemed as though she hadn't. She'd just reacted without thinking. She hadn't thought about how Jack would feel at all.

She felt a stab of pain in her chest as she remembered the hurt in his eyes. She hoped she hadn't sounded callous.

Jack had a hard time trusting anyone with his feelings. He'd grown up in a family that had put career above everything—even personal happiness.

When she'd gone through her breakup with Christopher her family and friends had rallied around her. True, she'd holed up in her apartment for several days, hiding from everyone, but once she'd been ready to face the world again she'd been inundated with supportive texts and voicemails from all the people who cared about her.

But when Jack had suffered the worst betrayal of his life he hadn't been able to go to the people he needed the most for support. That was the kind of family Jack had grown up in.

She'd gotten the impression that there hadn't been much importance placed on emotion when he was a child, and that that emotionless existence was one of the very things he'd come to Hawaii to get away from. Lonely, emotionally deprived Jack had known exactly what he needed, and he'd come here because he'd known that the islands could provide it.

And he'd known what she needed, too. He was the first person to have spoken to that wild part of her—the part that needed adventure and excitement. The part of herself that she'd gotten a glimpse of on rollercoasters and waterslides as a child…the part that she'd had to bury so deep underneath her cool, professional exterior.

A light breeze had picked up over the beach. It felt like a caress over her sun-warmed skin. She picked up a handful of sand and watched it run through her fingers. She wondered if she was doing the same thing to herself: holding happiness in her hand and letting it run through her fingers.

Jack had been able to decide that his life was about living up to his own expectations of himself. And his expectations of himself were good because he was a good person. She knew that to her core. She could see that Jack felt the same way she did about caring for the people around him—not just his patients, but everyone in his life. She and Jack might have taken different paths, but they'd gotten to the same place in the end.

Maybe her life could be about not living up to anyone's expectations but her own? Not Christopher's, not those of her family, her friends or her employers. Her father had wanted her to be a doctor, but Kat was sure that he'd wanted her to be happy, too.

But what did she want for herself?

It had been so long since she'd thought about what she wanted, rather than what everyone around her needed, that her brain felt rusty as it mulled over the question.

Jack had told her that cliff jumping was great for mental clarity. She smiled, recalling that moment. He had certainly been right in saying that you were never more certain about what you wanted than when you were hurtling through the air. But right now she felt she needed something different.

She stood up from the warm sand. She could have stayed there all day, but it was time to move on. The sun was heating the sand to the point that it was almost too uncomfortable to sit on. Soon it would be too hot to touch.

She smiled to herself. It was as though Hawaii was telling her to get a move on. Hadn't the island always known what she needed? Even from the start, when she'd thought the island was trying to drown her, it had just been bringing her and Jack together.

It was just as Jack had said: she was never going to

solve the problem of what she wanted by thinking about it. She could analyze and analyze, obsess and worry and make dozens of pro-con lists without ever figuring out the answer.

In order to work out what she wanted, she need to understand how she *felt*. And in order to know how she felt, she needed to be at peace.

Fortunately, while taking these past few days off, she'd learned a new skill that was great at offering her peace.

She'd started her surfing lessons just a few days ago. At first it had been difficult, but she'd gotten the hang of it quickly. She'd anticipated having to learn with a bunch of tourists, but to her very great surprise, in addition to teens and adults, her introductory surfing class had included very young children—children who seemed young enough that they'd barely mastered walking, let alone surfing.

Her instructor had told her not to worry, that she'd pick it up in time, with enough practice. And then, to Kat's great surprise, the instructor's *dog* had hopped onto a surfboard of its own and paddled out with them.

No one else in the class had seemed the least bit surprised, and as Kat's lessons had progressed she started to understand why: they saw at least five other surfing dogs every morning. Apparently the dog lovers of Hawaii hated to leave their furry friends on the beach.

Determined not to be outshone by surfing dogs and babies, Kat had thrown herself into learning to surf. After all, if she was indeed leaving the islands, she'd only have so much time to learn.

She was getting better, too.

Now, she paddled her board out to the waves and sat up on it, letting the waves rock her gently. It was a pleasant way to sit and think. She listened to the sound of the waves lapping and inhaled the salt scent of the seawater.

It was astounding, she thought, how the island seemed to have a way of knowing just what she needed. It had pushed her into Jack's arms that first day, even though she'd been so certain she didn't want a relationship. And it had pushed her toward excitement, toward new ways of challenging herself. Did the island know her better than she knew herself?

She was still thinking about that when a rogue wave knocked her from her surfboard and pushed her under the water's surface.

CHAPTER TEN

THE PHONE CONVERSATION hadn't been as difficult as Jack had expected. In some ways it had felt like old times. And by talking to his brother Jack felt as though an entire piece of his identity had come back.

But after several years without speaking things were also different. Jack wasn't just Matt's little brother anymore, forever living in his shadow. And Jack felt that Matt respected him in a way that he never had when the two of them had been growing up together. He got the distinct impression that Matt admired him for making the phone call that he had been too afraid to make.

"I'm not sorry that Sophie and I ended up together, but I am sorry for how it happened," Matt had said. "It was unforgivable. We should have told you as soon as it started. For my part I kept the secret because I wanted to protect you... I didn't want to hurt you. But I was a coward. I should have realized that the lie would hurt you more than honesty ever would."

Jack had felt tears prick his eyes. "All that was a long time ago," he'd said.

He'd told Matt all about Kat, explaining that she was really the person who had given him the courage to make the call. If he'd never met Kat he'd probably never have tried to reconnect with Matt in the first place. And then he explained that Kat was leaving, and that he was about to lose the first person he'd been able to open his heart to in years.

At which point his brother had said something that had surprised him.

"It sounds like when she got the job offer you told her to go, to follow her career," he said. "It even sounds as though you tried to push her away."

"I didn't want her to feel as though I was trying to hold her back," Jack said. "I would never ask her to make such a major life decision based on her feelings about me. I want her to do what's best for her."

"Yeah, but who are you to decide what's best for her? Doesn't that get to be *her* decision? And wouldn't she make the best decision if she had all the information?"

"What do you mean, all the information?"

"You told her to go. But is that what you really want? I thought you said the *aloha* culture was all about being real with people? But you haven't been real with her. Why don't you tell her how you really feel about her leaving? You say you don't want to get in her way, but from everything you've said she sounds like a pretty independent woman. Don't you trust her to make the right decision for herself?"

Jack had been silent as he'd thought about this and Matt had continued.

"She can't make an informed decision if she doesn't have all the data. Maybe you think you're trying to protect her by hiding your feelings and keeping them to yourself. But if there's one thing I've learned, it's that secrets only hurt."

Jack could see the truth in that, but he was still unsure…afraid.

"What if I tell her how I feel and it doesn't matter?" he'd said. "What if she still goes back to the mainland?"

"I don't know what will happen," Matt had told him. "There's no way to know for sure. But if you tell her how you feel, with no expectations of her and no strings attached, then at least you'll know that you were honest with her and with yourself."

Honesty, Jack thought now, as he worked through his shift at the hospital. Now, there was a deceptively simple concept. Hadn't he and Kat been struggling with honesty since the moment they'd met? It had been a Herculean struggle for the two of them to be honest about their feelings with one another. And then, when they'd almost gotten there, it had all been snatched away.

Matt was right, though, Jack thought. Kat was a strong woman. She could handle the truth. And he wanted to be honest about how he felt for her. Not because he wanted to convince her to stay, but because he wanted to be real about his feelings. Kat, more than anyone else he'd ever met, had taught him that it was important to be real about what he was feeling. If she was leaving now, then he wanted her to leave knowing exactly how he felt.

Then she could use that information however she wished, without any expectations from him.

The problem was he'd been looking for her all day and hadn't been able to find her. He hadn't seen her anywhere in the ER.

It was a slow day, and there hadn't been many calls coming in that morning, but when an EMT brought in a tourist with an ankle fracture Jack offered to take the patient up to Radiology for X-rays, hoping he might see Kat there. No luck.

She wasn't in the hematology lab, nor any of the operating suites. He began popping his head into individual exam rooms, but she was nowhere to be found.

He gave up searching and went back to the reception desk, where he found Selena and Marceline.

"Is Kat coming in today?" he asked.

"She'd better," Selena said. "We're planning a surprise goodbye party for her." Then she glanced at her watch with a worried frown. "She's thirty minutes late for her shift, though. That's not like her."

Jack had stopped absorbing information after the words "surprise goodbye party."

"Wait a minute," he said. "Isn't a goodbye party a little preemptive? We don't even know if she's definitely decided to leave yet."

Selena gave him a sympathetic look. "I'd like to cling to the hope that she'll stay here too," she said. "But Kat is a talented physician. I don't think she'll turn down a job offer like this just to keep working at our little hospital." She narrowed her eyes at Jack. "Unless, of course, she has some *other reason* to stay."

Jack decided he wasn't going to rise to the bait—especially as the other half of Selena's statement had started to sink in.

"What do you mean, she's thirty minutes late for her shift?" he said.

His concern started to rise. Thirty minutes was an

eternity where Kat was concerned; she usually preferred to arrive for her shift at least twenty minutes early, so she could enjoy a cup of coffee while she prepared herself for incoming patients. Of course more recently that time had been used for their supply closet trysts…but no one needed to know that.

"You know how Kat feels about being on time for things," he said. "She wouldn't be late without a reason. Has anyone heard from her? Is anyone looking for her?"

"Now you're the one being preemptive," Selena said. "I agree that it's strange for Kat to be late for anything, but it's a little early to start worrying. For now, let's keep an eye out and assume that whatever's holding Kat up isn't too much of an emergency."

Jack didn't like it, but he knew that Selena was right. Catastrophizing wasn't going to help. But he was still worried. Kat was punctual to a fault, and he knew she wouldn't be late unless something serious had come up.

He walked by the reception desk and passed Kimo, who was preparing trays of pineapple and dried coconut for the break room.

"Hey, Jack, weren't you looking for Kat earlier?" Kimo said. "They just brought her in—in an ambulance. I think you can still catch her down there, if you hurry."

An ambulance? Oh, God. The minute he'd heard she was late he'd known something bad had to have happened.

He ran at full speed to the ambulance docking bay, where he saw a few EMTs milling about by an ambulance with open doors.

Inside he saw Kat, unconscious on a gurney.

He shoved his way through and leapt into the back

of the ambulance. He started checking Kat's vitals. She appeared to be breathing—good. What had happened? Why were the EMTs acting as though nothing was wrong? Why wasn't anybody taking care of her?

"Kat?" he said. "Kat, can you hear me?"

He couldn't lose her now. His jaw set. He'd do whatever it took to fix his mistakes…assuming they could be fixed at all.

She lay in front of him, her eyes closed, her breathing shallow. Her red hair curled about her neck in ringlets and he realized that it was dripping wet—the same as it had been the day they'd first met. In fact, her whole body was soaked.

Had she met with another mishap in the ocean? If she had, he hadn't been there to leap to her rescue.

"Kat," he said again. "Please wake up."

His eyes stung and he swallowed back tears, thinking about their last conversation. Now something was wrong, and he hadn't been there, and it was his fault for not being willing to take a chance, to open his heart and give himself to someone who deserved love wholeheartedly.

A wave of shame washed over him as he remembered how effortlessly Kat had leapt off the north shore cliff with him, how trustingly she'd clung to his hand. Kat had taken a leap of faith, but he'd been so scared to take a leap into a relationship that he'd pushed her away from him. And as a result he hadn't been there when she needed him most.

He felt for a pulse. It was there, strong, and that was a relief to him. But why wouldn't she wake up?

"I should have been there," he said aloud. "Whatever happened, I should have been there."

And he would have been there if it hadn't been for his stupid pride, his stupid unwillingness to trust someone who trusted him. If he'd lost her forever, it was his fault.

But then, to his utter surprise, she began to move. He felt relief wash over him—she'd been lying so still he'd even worried about a spinal cord injury, but if she could move on her own it was nothing severe. This was confirmed as she arched her back and stretched, lifting her arms over her head languorously. Then she opened her eyes with slow, sleepy blinks, saw him at her side, and smiled.

"Hey, Jack," she said.

"What's wrong?" he said, trying to hide the terror in his voice. "Where are you hurt? Why are you all wet?"

He looked out through the back of the ambulance, his eyes stormy with anger. Why had the paramedics left Kat alone? Why weren't they helping?

"Relax… I'm fine," she said. "I'm learning to surf."

"You're learning to *surf*?" He couldn't hide his confusion. What did surfing have to do with anything?

"I still need a lot of practice. Maybe we can do that together, though? It'll be fun. Did you know that dogs and babies can surf?"

Dogs and…? What?

She wasn't making any sense. He checked her pupils to see if they were dilated. Could she have gotten a head injury?

Your fault, your fault, your fault, the voice in the back of his head intoned.

She put her arms around his neck. "Jack, I'm fine.

You know, you were right about my needing a thrill, but that was only half of it. I needed some serenity, too. And you know what? I found it! For the first time in my life I went to the beach and I was actually able to relax."

"That's great," he said distractedly. "But where have you been hurt?"

"I haven't been hurt," she said, less sleepily than before. "Well, I got knocked over by a rogue wave, and that was pretty frightening, but I just relaxed and let myself float back to the surface. I'm getting *a lot* better at relaxing, thanks to you. Well, thanks to you and thanks to all the practice I've been putting in, of course. And thanks to the surfing lessons. Do you want to learn? I could teach you. I feel like I should teach you something after all you've taught me."

He gazed at her, baffled. She could sit up, and she was mobile enough that she could put her arms around his neck. As Jack's fear subsided he began to take in that maybe Kat *hadn't* suffered any serious injury.

"You're really fine?" he said.

"All body parts intact." She smiled. "Not even a scrape or a bruise."

"Then why…?"

"Why am I being hauled into work in an ambulance? There actually was a medical emergency on the beach near my apartment this morning—it just didn't involve me. Well, not as the patient, anyway. There was a child on the beach having an asthma attack, and the family had left his inhaler at the hotel. I swear, we need to give every tourist on this island a firm lecture about leaving important medical devices at their hotels. What good is an inhaler if you don't bring it with you when you go exploring?"

He smoothed her hair. "Sounds like your typical medical emergency. But you still haven't answered the question I'm most interested in: why have you been brought to the hospital in an ambulance?"

"After helping the EMTs out with the child on the beach I hitched a ride with them to work. And I got up so early this morning that I thought I'd take a little nap in the back while they drove." She frowned at the concern in his face. "I must have been sleeping pretty soundly… Jack, you weren't…*worried* about me, were you?"

He was so exasperated with her. "*Worried?* That doesn't cover half of it. Do you have *any* idea how *scared* I was when I saw you lying there?"

She gazed at him soberly. "I'm sorry, Jack. I didn't mean to alarm you. It was careless of me not to think about how it might look to you, me lying here asleep on a gurney. In fact, I've been careless about a lot of things. And I need to tell you something."

"I have something to tell you, too," he said.

"Actually—" she started.

"No, let me go first," he said. "I know you've only been here a short time, but I don't need more time to understand everything I already know I feel about you. I don't ever want to stand in the way of your career. I know that's what makes you happy. So I would never, in a million years, ask anything of you that would be too much for you to give. But someone I trust has told me something I firmly believe: secrets only hurt. So, in the interests of being honest with you, and with my-self, I hope you'll let me explain how I feel about you."

She looked as if she was about to say something, but he laid a finger on her lips.

"Kat Murphy," he continued, "from the moment I lay eyes on you I thought you were one of the most obnoxious, bossy, self-assured women I've ever met."

"Wow," said Kat. "Tell me how you *really* feel."

"Hold on," he said. "I'm getting to the important part. Matt was right—I need to tell you. Getting to know you, letting myself get close to you, was one of the best decisions I've ever made. I don't regret any of our time together—not one single minute—and even though it was a short time, it's impacted my life more than any relationship I've ever had. I love you. And I'm saying that without any expectations, not because I want anything from you, but because you deserve to know how I feel and—"

"Jack, I'm staying," she said, as though she couldn't hold it in any longer, and a smile appeared on her face.

"What—? But no!" he said, dismayed. "Why on earth would you do that?"

"Oh, Jack," she said. "Isn't it obvious?"

"No, it isn't!"

She laughed. "No? Okay, I'll explain it, then. I'm in love."

"Kat, you *can't* give up an opportunity like this just for me," he sputtered.

No matter what Matt had said, Jack would *not* be the reason that Kat slowed down in her career. They could do long distance. They could Skype. He could visit Chicago. Hell, he'd *move* to Chicago if he had to.

"My, aren't we arrogant?" she said, but she was smiling gently. "I didn't mean with you. I meant with Hawaii! Although," she said, and the look on her face was tender, "it's not as though you aren't a *very* nice perk as well."

"A nice *perk*?" he said, taking her into his arms. "I suppose I'll have to settle for being a small footnote in your tempestuous love affair with the island."

She laughed, but then grew serious. "Jack. Let me be clear. I do love it here, but there's an even more important reason that I'm staying."

"And what might that be?"

"Isn't it obvious?" she asked again.

And as she leaned against his chest and put her hands around his neck his heart melted.

"I love you," she said. "I'm happy here, but I'm happiest of all when I'm with you. I don't need to be working at some prestigious hospital to be happy. I can do exactly the kind of work I love right here. In fact, I think I've done some of my *best* work here. Because I'm working right beside someone I love."

He kissed her then—deeply, passionately, trying to put all the things he hadn't been able to say until now into the kiss. When they finally came up for air she rested her head against his chest, and he twined a curl of her hair around his fingers.

"So you're really staying?" he asked, still trying to believe it.

It was so much to take in: that she was here and that she really loved him. Somehow, against all the odds, it seemed as though his dreams really were going to come true.

He'd have to call Matt later, tell him about it...

"I really am," she said. "When I thought about going back to Chicago Grace I didn't feel excited about it. I have to admit that the idea of showing Christopher that he was wrong was appealing. But none of it felt as though it'd be worth what I'd be giving up."

"And what would that be, exactly?"

She grew thoughtful. "A chance to get what I want, rather than what other people expect of me. A chance to be happy." She snuggled closer to him and looked into his eyes. "And a chance at love."

"So, after everything that's happened, you believe in love, do you?"

"Oh, Jack, I do. I really do."

He held her close to him, breathed in the smell of her hair and smiled. "I do too," he said.

He pulled her toward him and was about to kiss her again when she placed a hand on his chest to stop him.

"Wait a minute," she said. "What did you mean earlier, when you said, 'Matt was right'?"

"I guess I haven't had a chance to tell you yet," he said. "I called my brother and we had a long talk about...about everything. I wouldn't say that things are back to normal between the two of us. I don't think they ever can be. But...we're talking again."

"Wow..." Kat said, and he saw that once again her eyes were wet with tears. "That must have been some conversation."

He let out a long, slow breath. "It was. But it's really thanks to you that I was able to have it in the first place."

"Thanks to me? How so?"

"You were the first person besides Matt who I felt

I could actually be real with. It reminded me of what it felt like to have someone to rely on. It reminded me that that was something I'd missed."

She smiled shyly. "I think you might have reminded me of that too."

She leaned toward him, her mouth inches from his, and Jack had a sense of *déjà-vu*. He remembered another moment, months ago, when he and Kat had almost kissed in this very ambulance. What had stopped them? What on earth had they been waiting for? Looking at Kat now, he couldn't imagine ever hesitating to kiss her—not even for a second.

They leaned in to kiss, and then, occupied as they were, there was a lengthy silence.

Finally Jack murmured, "Just so you know…there's a surprise farewell party going on for you in the hospital."

"A farewell party? Don't tell me I've been fired again."

"Are you kidding? No, the staff will seize any chance they can get to throw a luau. I'm sure it'll immediately turn into a welcome back party the moment you go in there and share the good news. Should we go and tell everyone now?"

"Maybe not right now," said Kat. "I was actually thinking that this might be a good time for another impulsive decision…"

Kat let her fingers work their way down Jack's chest, opening the buttons on his paramedic's uniform.

"Are you sure about this?" he murmured, even as he began to unbutton her blouse. "You don't want to make a pro-con list first?"

"Hmm, let me think about that…" she said.

She pressed her mouth against his, tasting the salty sweetness of his lips. And as she let the kiss linger, she felt the deep feeling in her gut that was going to guide her from now on—the feeling deep in her body that told her she was home.

That settled it.

She pulled off Jack's shirt.

"Nah," she said. "No lists necessary. Let's be spontaneous."

* * * * *

COMING SOON!

MILLS & BOON

Coming next month

TEMPTED BY THE BROODING VET

Shelley Rivers Good grief, could the man make it any clearer that he regretted asking to kiss her? What other reason explained his disagreeable attitude since her arrival? Was he scared she might take it into her head to embrace him in front of the other staff members? Or perhaps try and seduce him in a consultation room when no one was looking?

She'd never attempted such behaviour in her life, and she didn't plan to start with him.

'With me?' she asked, just to be certain.

'I'm not sure how to act around you,' he admitted. 'But, seeing as we're going to be working together, maybe we should just forget that last night I asked to…'

'Kiss me?' she taunted, unable to stop herself from reminding him. A perverse imp filled her with mischief. 'And you held me snugly against your half naked body.'

Alex cleared his throat. 'Yes.'

'Fine,' she said brightly. 'Because until you mentioned it I hadn't considered it a big deal or wasted much thought over it.'

Pleased she'd managed to keep her voice casual and indifferent throughout the lie, she resumed cleaning the area. No reason for Alex to know she'd relived that moment over and over for most of the night. Mentally rerunning each stimulating second until she'd wanted to scream with frustration and track him down to demand he give her the proposed kiss.

He frowned at her reply. 'Really?'

She bit hard on her inner lip to prevent a smile. The man certainly didn't like hearing that she found his romantic moves unmemorable.

'If you want to forget what happened—or rather didn't—then just be yourself when we're in the same room. Otherwise people might start to notice and that would create talk.'

'Are you sure I should?' he asked, not sounding convinced.

Unable to stop herself, she laughed. Alex's self-consciousness was rather refreshing and endearing. Every time the man forgot his stiff reserve passion smouldered from him. It intrigued her how his personality had two such different sides.

'I swear my hesitation had nothing to do with you or your request,' she said. 'It was all me—I promise. So I'll help you on Saturday at the stud farm?'

'Thanks. I'd appreciate it.'

Continue reading
TEMPTED BY THE BROODING VET
Shelley Rivers

Available next month
www.millsandboon.co.uk

LET'S TALK
Romance

For exclusive extracts, competitions
and special offers, find us online:

- facebook.com/millsandboon
- @MillsandBoon
- @MillsandBoonUK

Get in touch on 01413 063232